A
BRIGHT
HEART

A BRIGHT HEART

Kate Chenli

UNION
SQUARE
& CO.

NEW YORK

UNION
SQUARE
& CO.

NEW YORK

UNION SQUARE & CO. and the distinctive Union Square & Co.
logo are trademarks of Sterling Publishing Co., Inc.

Union Square & Co., LLC, is a subsidiary of Sterling Publishing Co., Inc.

ISBN 978-1-4549-4992-3 (hardcover)
ISBN 978-1-4549-4993-0 (e-book)
ISBN 978-1-4549-4994-7 (paperback)

Library of Congress Cataloging-in-Publication Data

Names: Chenli, Kate, author.
Title: A bright heart / by Kate Chenli.
Description: New York : Union Square and Co., 2023. | Audience: Ages 14-17.
| Summary: When sixteen-year-old Migshin wakes up two years before her
murder, she seeks to prevent all the horrors she unwittingly set in
motion, but the timeline has changed, forcing her to use her intellect
and wit to ensure the wrong man does not once again become king.
Identifiers: LCCN 2022059130 (print) | LCCN 2022059131 (ebook) |
ISBN 9781454949923 (hardcover) | ISBN 9781454949947 (paperback) |
ISBN 9781454949930 (epub)
Subjects: CYAC: Courts and courtiers—Fiction. | Kings, queens, rulers,
etc.—Fiction. | Space and time—Fiction. | Murder—Fiction. |
Love—Fiction. | Fantasy. | BISAC: YOUNG ADULT FICTION / Fantasy /
Historical | YOUNG ADULT FICTION / Fantasy / Epic | LCGFT: Fantasy
fiction. | Novels.
Classification: LCC PZ7.1.C49753 Br 2023 (print) | LCC PZ7.1.C49753
(ebook) | DDC [Fic]—dc23
LC record available at https://lccn.loc.gov/2022059130
LC ebook record available at https://lccn.loc.gov/2022059131

For information about custom editions, special sales, and premium purchases,
please contact specialsales@unionsquareandco.com.

Printed in the United States of America

2 4 6 8 10 9 7 5 3 1

unionsquareandco.com

Interior design by Julie Robine
Cover illustration by Sija Hong

For Don, my constant inspiration
and pillar of strength

CHAPTER 1

My scream echoes off the moldy walls of the dungeon.

The interrogator leans in, his breath foul. "I ask you one last time. Do you confess to the treason committed against the crown?"

I barely lift my head from the cold, damp stone floor. A bolt of pain shoots through me, and the room spins. Still, I lock my gaze on the interrogator, willing myself not to waver. My throat feels lacerated with sand, but I manage to rasp one last "No."

I spit at him. My spittle of blood smears across his thin lips.

He backhands me so hard my head snaps to the side and my ears ring. He wipes the blood away with a sleeve, then snarls. "You'll get what you deserve, filthy traitor."

He turns and gestures to the jailers standing watch. The two burly men stride over and yank me to my bare feet. My broken ribs give a vicious jab, and I nearly faint.

They drag me out of the interrogation chamber, their mocking laugh pealing distortedly. The instant we are through the door, a blast of frosty air slams into me. The wind slices at my bare flesh like an icy scythe—the ferocious whippings have plastered the shredded remains of what once passed for clothes onto my broken skin. I shiver uncontrollably.

It's snowing, and a carriage with a single driver awaits in the courtyard. Through the swirling white mass, I glimpse the tall, imposing prison walls looming in the distance.

As soon as the jailers dump me onto the hard floor of the carriage, it starts moving. I curl into myself. Where is the driver taking me? The execution block?

The image of Royal Lady Bai's lifeless body hanging from a rafter in her cell pops into my head. "We're all going to die," she said just yesterday. "The Royal Ladies, the princes, and you. Ren has accused us all of treason." She stared at me with feverish eyes, all her dignity gone. "His edict declared that we conspired together."

No! She was wrong. Ren couldn't possibly believe I had anything to do with the attempt on his life. He always said he trusted me above everyone else.

But why did he allow the guards to arrest me without even giving me a chance to defend myself? It's been three days. Why hasn't he come to see me? Does he know what I've been through?

The anger that has been brewing inside me swells into a storm. *Why haven't you rescued me, Ren? How could you let them treat me like this after your vows of love? Could the fears that have plagued me for these last few months be true? That you've been using my mind and money to help you attain the crown?*

I suck in a sharp, stinging breath as my chest seems to split open. No, it's too dangerous a thought, too horrible. I mustn't lose hope. That's all I have now.

The carriage jerks to a halt. A quick exchange of words outside, then we are moving again. When the carriage stops once more, I hear a thud, followed by footfalls. Moments later, the driver appears and pulls me out. An agonized groan escapes my parched lips.

The ruffian drops me in the snow, turns, and walks away.

"Wait." I shudder. "Why did you . . . bring me here?"

But he only hurries away faster. Without a word or a backward glance, he jumps onto the front seat and drives off.

Am I to freeze to death? I swallow a rising flood of panic and look around. Colossal buildings of wooden pillars, red crossbeams, and yellow-glazed roof tiles are connected by twisting cobblestone paths, with evergreens and courtyards interspersed between.

I've been brought to the royal palace.

I crawl to the lowest step of a flight of tall, wide stairs. At the top stands the Grand Throne Room, where Ren holds court daily.

I hear crunching on snow. I turn to see two palace guards approach me. Like the jailers, they hoist me between themselves and haul me up the stairs. Even the relentless cold isn't enough to numb my agony as my lesions scrape against the icy stone.

The men abandon me at the top, then disappear the way they came.

I jolt at the sight of someone standing before the Grand Throne Room with its shining marble walls. His back to me, he wears a robe heavily stitched with five-clawed golden dragons—the sacred creature only a monarch can wear.

Ren. The love of my life. The man I helped become King of Dazhou. He's finally here.

Ren extends his arms fully and tilts his head back, as if flying high above and savoring the feeling that the entire kingdom lies beneath his feet. He maintains that posture for a few moments before turning around and walking toward me.

He's as handsome as ever, with golden-brown eyes, lush ebony hair, and the sort of profile loved by sculptors and painters. But gone is the warm, gentle smile he has always shone on me, and in its place is a ruthless mask.

My heart, which has been lifted by a sudden flutter of hope, sinks, wings broken.

I stretch my mangled hand, to touch this man who once promised to collect the stars for me. "Water . . . please."

He eases away. "The assassin confessed that you and my brothers commissioned his service." Each word is as sharp as a knife. I can't believe they come from Ren, but they do.

"I didn't. I blocked his sword . . . with my body . . . when he ran at you. You saw it." Every muscle spasms as I struggle to point to the wound where the assassin's blade pierced my shoulder. But none of the pain compares to what I feel inside.

"And we were to marry," I plead. "Why would I have you murdered?"

"Did you honestly think I'd marry a merchant's daughter? Once all the traitors are put down, I'll wed Aylin and crown her as my Queen. She's a regal noblewoman fit for the position. In fact, she's the one I've always wanted."

It's as though Ren had reached into my chest and wrenched out my beating heart. I suck in a breath to hold back tears. "You used me, you bastard." Such simple words, but they take all my strength to utter. "Did you ever love me?"

"For two years, I had to stare at your plain, mooning face while saying pathetic words of love, putting on a show of passion. It sickened me."

Inside, my world crumbles to dust. I suspected that Ren harbored more than friendly feelings for Aylin, but I always attributed this to my insecurity and petty jealousy for my beautiful highborn cousin.

"Aylin loves me," I say with vehemence. "She wouldn't do this to me." My cousin tended me as I lay in my sickbed after the assassin's attack. She didn't defend my innocence when the palace guards came to arrest me, but she must have been too frightened.

Ren scoffs. "Her wedding gown is being made as we speak."

Her wedding gown. I close my eyes, imagining bright-red fabric the color of my blood.

"You forced her into an agreement of marriage," I spit out.

"Believe it all you want, but you won't live to see the wedding. After all, you are a traitor to the throne."

I feel as if the ground were splitting and shifting beneath me. He wants me *dead*. Why? Although he doesn't love me, he could just make me one of the many Royal Ladies in his harem, then put me aside, leaving me to wither away in humiliation and isolation.

A hot rush of rage rises, blazing through my anguish. "You staged your own assassination, then framed me and your brothers. All I've ever done is love and help you. Why do you hate me so much?"

"They say without your riches and strategies, I'd never have become King," Ren hisses with quietly controlled anger. "They shall be punished for their insolence. My brothers thought they were better, smarter. But I stand here while they await death."

Royal Lady Bai's last words echo in my head. *We have all been fooled by that charlatan. Even his late father. He maintained his merciful reputation so well that everyone believed he was harmless, but look where it landed us.*

A masterful charlatan Ren is. No wonder there are no guards posted here—so he can taunt me without witnesses.

I bite on my lip until I taste blood. How I wish I hadn't been so desperate for love, for a family after Mother's passing, that I held on to him despite my suspicions about his true feelings for me.

In despair, my hand reaches for the stone pendant hanging around my neck. Father's family heirloom I've worn since childhood, given to me for his belief in my worth. It's of no value to anyone but me, so the jailers didn't rob me of it.

I've never prayed before. But as I clutch the pendant to draw strength from it, I send a fervent prayer to all the gods, to any divine power out there, that I be given a chance to do it all over again, to right all the wrongs inflicted by Ren.

"You're a monster," I growl, my voice seething with every drop of hatred that boils within. When he merely shrugs, my hatred flares white-hot, prompting me to goad him, "Royal Lady Bai told me Prince Jieh escaped."

Ren's smugness is gone in an instant. He grabs my chin and squeezes so hard I groan. His features contort. "I'll capture Jieh and crush him like I'm crushing you. *I* am the true King. He is dirt and no more."

For a moment it seems Ren is about to strangle me, but he smiles, releasing me. "You know I hate that scum more than anything. You said that on purpose, didn't you?" His smile grows more sinister. "As payback, allow me to divulge a little secret, wench. Your mother's drowning was *not* an accident, as your uncle made you believe. He had your cousin Bo kill her after she refused to hand over your father's business."

What's he saying? I shake all over. "No. No. You're lying." I've never liked Uncle Yi's insidious character, but he's not capable of murdering family. When Ren laughs in disdain, I realize he's finally telling the truth.

A wail rips from my throat. I don't know where I find the energy, but I leap up and throw myself at Ren. He jumps back, but not quickly enough. My fingernails dig bloody grooves into his cheeks. Too bad I don't gouge out his eyes.

He roars and slams a fist into my chest. I fly backward, my ribs cracking. *No, no, by my ancestors. I cannot die yet. Please!*

I tumble to the bottom of the stairs, landing near the feet of someone standing there. As I'm lying on my back, I see my cousin, the gorgeous Aylin, in an equally stunning white fox fur coat—ah, I know that coat. She looks at me as if I'm some diseased vermin.

With a final burst of will, I cry out, "Heaven above! Grant me another chance and I'll do anything to make it right."

Colorful light shoots up all around me, glowing as brightly as the sun. A wave of power washes over me and ripples out, far, far away.

So grand, so mighty, so—

A complete, endless darkness pulls me under.

CHAPTER 2

I bolt upright, screaming.

What happened? Where am I?

My scream cuts short.

For a moment, I linger in a void, mind and body.

Is this death?

Everything in me snaps into focus.

What does death look like?

My ragged breaths rasp in my ears as I scan my surroundings.

I'm sitting in a canopy bed covered in smooth, clean sheets and embroidered feather quilts. There's a large dresser, a wardrobe, a vanity desk, and an adjoining room for bathing. Coal smolders in a brazier a few feet from the end of the bed. Calligraphy scrolls and ink paintings of mountains, forests, and flowers hang on paneled walls that gleam with the dark mystery of well-polished mahogany. A gold-spined book, still open, lies on a nightstand.

A tremor wracks me from head to toe as my mind finally catches up with my eyes. This is the bedroom I lived in for two years before my death.

How did I end up here in the afterlife?

I look myself over and stretch my limbs. All my wounds and injuries are gone. Is this what happens to a spirit after it passes over? I press a palm to my breast and feel the rhythmic beating beneath my fingers. Does a specter even have a heart?

The title of the open book is scrawled in black ink: *History of the Continent.* It's one of my favorite topics, and—

The wooden door swings open. A girl dashes in, shouting, "Are you all right, Miss?"

"Mai?" I gasp as I recognize the girl with a round face and doe eyes.

Mai had been my handmaiden until Aylin caught her stealing—an offense often punished by having the thief's hand chopped off.

Guilt slashes through me. I trusted Aylin's word instead of my maid's plea of innocence. Despite my shame, I begged Aylin not to have Mai maimed. The last time I saw her, my uncle's steward was selling her to a servant trader.

Have Mai and I been reunited in this afterlife?

I open my mouth to apologize to her, but then she moves farther into the room with a lively bounce in her step. "Did you have a nightmare, Miss?" She turns and bows. "Mistress," she says, yielding her way.

A familiar figure hurries into view. All the air rushes out of me, and I clutch at my chest. Heaven above, what would I not have given to see her again?

For one infinite, glorious moment, I gape at Mother, blood thundering in my ears.

She stops next to me and caresses my cheeks with both hands, her brows furrowed. "I heard you scream. Are you all right, Shin'ar?"

At the name of endearment only used by my parents, a loud weeping sound escapes my lips. I throw my arms around Mother's waist, my tears flowing.

"Shin'ar, what happened? You are scaring me."

"I miss you, Ma," I say, my voice muffled by heaving sobs.

She smooths a hand down my back. "Silly girl. You just saw me last night."

But that's not true. I lost her half a year ago. I've never forgotten how I fell to my knees next to her bloated body, just fished out of the dark waters of a pond. She was so still, so cold as I held her swollen face. I wept and wept, until I passed out from grief and exhaustion.

Mother feels solid and warm now. Her touch is gentle and caring. Still hugging her—I don't want to ever let go—I lift my head. She looks radiant, beautiful, and hale.

We must have been sent to Paradise in the afterlife. But why are Mother and Mai acting like they still live in the past? I glance at the book again. I spent every night reading it over the first few months after Mother and I moved into Uncle Yi's home. How did it follow me into death?

Glancing at the mirror on the vanity desk, I catch a glimpse of myself. My ordinary face shows baby fat, the way I looked when I was a little younger.

The moments right before my death flash through my mind.

I prayed, begging for another life, a chance to do it all over again. In response, there was a burst of dazzling light; its power radiated throughout.

My pulse quickens as a strange, impossible idea occurs to me. "What day and year is it, Ma?"

She frowns, but replies, "It's Year 105, Month of Er, Day twenty-one, of the Jin dynasty." She looks me over again.

Year 105. My heart is pounding so fast I feel giddy. Did the gods really answer my prayers and turn my life back two years? Month of

Er, Day twenty-one. Exactly two weeks after we arrived at Jingshi, the capital. Only a month ago, Mother and I celebrated my sixteenth birthday, the day marking my rite of passage into adulthood.

"How are you feeling, Shin'ar?" Mother touches my forehead. "Should I summon a doctor?"

"No, I'm fine." Given how perceptive Mother is, though, she won't drop it if I don't give her a reasonable explanation for my strange behaviors earlier. "I dreamed of Baba. We were together as a family. It was so real I wished it were a different day and he were still with us. That's foolish . . . but I miss him, Ma." As soon as I say the words, I hear how true they ring. If only time had gone further back to when both my parents were alive.

Mother sighs. "I miss him, too."

We stay in each other's arms, sharing a quiet moment of mourning and tenderness.

I don't want to sadden Mother, so I release our embrace and smile at her. "We still have each other, Ma. I love you. I'll make you very, very happy."

"I love you, too, Shin'ar. And you've already made me very, very happy." She pokes gently at my chest, a familiar, comforting gesture that holds special significance for me: Mingshin, my name, means *a bright heart.*

Tears prick my eyes. Quickly I turn away. Only then do I notice the young woman standing next to Mai. It's Ning, Mother's loyal handmaiden, who "accidently" drowned along with her. After Ren's confession, I'm sure he and my cousin Bo murdered Ning as well.

But I won't lose any of you again. Definitely not to those monsters. A surge of torrid hatred sears through me to seethe in my core. I lower my head so no one sees my burning face or the veins pulsing in my neck.

Ren, Uncle Yi, Aylin, Bo. I'll bring the storm of vengeance upon you all. Feel its force as it sweeps down and destroys anyone who obstructs its path.

"Time to get up, my girl," Mother says. "I'll see you in a little while." She pats my cheek and departs.

Mai leaves to fill the washbasin. Standing before a full-length mirror, I strip off my sleeping gown. As I straighten, I startle at the reflection of my *sixteen*-year-old self.

Did the gods grant me a second chance at life? Now that I've had time to consider what I'm experiencing, doubts grow.

Legend has it that the gods left this human world ages ago and no longer concern themselves with human affairs—the main reason I'd never prayed to them for help before the twilight of my last moments. Why would they intervene on behalf of me, a girl without social standing and of no importance to anyone but my family?

My breath hitches as a notion strikes. If this miracle is not the product of gods, could it be magic?

I shake my head at the foolishness of my imagination. Only the people in Nan'Yü are capable of magic. Besides, I cannot fathom any kind of magic mighty enough to turn back time.

And that curtain of light humming with power in my last memory . . . did I actually see it, or was it a vision as I hovered on the verge of death? But its power felt so real, almost tangible.

I sigh. I must solve this mystery, but answers won't come easy.

I lift my five-colored pendant up to my eyes. In moments of despair, Father's gift gave me strength. It's a plain thing, but I cherish it more than all the gemstones in the world.

Father entrusted his family heirloom to me when I was only three years old. "You're worth this treasure, Shin'ar," he said. "Guard it well. One day, I'll tell you its history."

I stood taller and raised my chin, grinning up at him. Since then, I've never taken the pendant off except when I bathe.

But Father didn't get the chance to share its history with me before we lost him to illness.

I strangle a sob. *I miss you, Baba. Rest in peace; I promise you I'll protect Ma with all I have.*

When Mai returns, I wash my face and hands in the basin, then dry them with a fresh towel. She helps me into an emerald wool gown patterned with silver embroidery, and wraps a silk band around my waist. The early spring morning is still chilly, so she drapes a lilac velvet robe across my small frame.

At my request, Mai makes several thin braids and weaves them into a simple bun. I pick out a gold hairpin dangling with a few pearl beads for her to thread into my hair.

As I walk down the hall to the living room with Mai in tow, Ning approaches me with a smile. "Miss Aylin is here—"

Boom. A roar explodes in my head. Blood rushes to my face, and everything around me swirls in a swarm of reddish shapes. All I can see is Aylin standing over my broken body, her expression filled with loathing.

How dare she appear again in my life after her ultimate betrayal? How dare she?

"Miss!"

I'm startled out of my trance by urgent whispering. I turn, my vision still misted over with scarlet. But through it I detect Ning's worried face.

With a jolt, I catch myself. How many times did she call me before I heard her?

"Are you all right, Miss?" she asks with concern. Beside her, Mai is as taut as a bowstring.

The red mist dissipates. I nod weakly and lean on a wall, closing my eyes for a second. This is my new life. My death is still in the future, and Aylin's deceitfulness hasn't been revealed to me yet. How could she have fooled me so completely? For two years, she assured me I was loved like a sister. For two years, she acted like a trusted family member.

I want to storm into the room and tear the fake mask off Aylin's face. I want to shout about her betrayal for the whole world to hear. I want to strike her for harming Mai.

But my enemies must believe I still regard them as friends.

I inhale a long breath and stuff my rage and hatred back into the darkest part of my soul. Then, I paste a big smile on my face.

Two can play this game.

CHAPTER 3

As I enter the living room, Aylin stops her conversation with Mother and rises from the long couch.

Oh, my beautiful and sweet cousin, how she dazzles like a diamond, with her flawless skin, lustrous black hair, and a smile that steals all the sparkle from the gemstones she wears. Her face is a perfect oval, and her almond-shaped eyes are large and sensual. Cherry lips bloom beneath a delicate stem of a nose. A thin strip of silk sash is wrapped around her tiny waist, and a fitted pink gown accentuates her slender frame and soft curves.

How I was instantly charmed the first time I met her. A part of me envied her beauty, but a bigger part of me was joyful that such a lovely girl was my cousin and would become my friend.

Indeed, she not only became my best friend, but like a *sister*, who shared my happiness and sadness, whispered countless secrets with me beneath the same bedcover, and encouraged my wild nature.

Only to stab me in the back.

My chest tightens to the point of pain.

Aylin reaches me and pulls me into her arms. "Good morning," she says with her singsong voice.

I almost cringe, but instead I return her hug with equal enthusiasm. "Good morning."

Aylin loops her arm around mine and leads me back to the couch. She looks at Mother, whom she calls "Auntie," then at me. "Mingshin. Father sent me to deliver great news."

I perk up like Mother, although I already know what's coming.

"Oh Auntie, the Ministry of Justice dismissed your husband's half brothers' claims regarding the true ownership of his properties and business," Aylin says. "You need not worry anymore."

Mother brightens. "It wouldn't have happened without your father's help, Aylin."

My cousin beams. "The minister of justice is good friends with Baba. You understand he couldn't get directly involved. As the minister of personnel, he mustn't let his name be tarnished by acting on behalf of family, or his position would be compromised. But you are family, and he had to do everything he could to help." Aylin clasps her hands together. "I'm so happy that we succeeded in ridding you of these false claims of ownership."

I'll be damned if I let Uncle Yi take all the credit.

"The ministry should've dismissed their false claims from the very beginning," I say. "They declared that Baba's businesses belonged to the Lu family because he wouldn't have grown his wealth without their loan and support. That was a lie." Aylin wrings her hands and opens her mouth, but I don't give her the chance to interpose. "Baba started from scratch and never received any kind of help from his extended family. They only took an interest in him after he became successful. Now that he's gone, they want to steal his wealth."

Aylin blinks at me, apparently at a loss for words.

Am I acting too differently, showing too many teeth?

"It is not that simple," Mother says. "Everything you said is true, Shin'ar. But the Ministry of Justice could have conveniently chosen to overlook those facts." Aylin nods along eagerly. "In that case, your paternal uncles, as the male relatives, would've had stronger claims than we did despite your Baba's will, which passed everything to us."

Mother is right, but I can't help the bitter taste in my mouth.

The reason Mother and I moved to Uncle's Yi residence in Jingshi, the capital, was to defend our right of inheritance. Father accumulated vast wealth from his business endeavors. He was easily one of the richest men in the kingdom. Nonetheless, as a merchant, he was merely a step above peasants in social standing. So are his wife and daughter. It rankles me to admit that Uncle Yi's status has indeed helped us win the case against Father's extended family.

Like Mother, I used to be grateful to him. Although he was a bit too cunning in politics for my liking, I believed he helped us secure our wealth out of pride and the necessity to defend a family member. I know now his only motivation was to swindle our money away from us.

I return my attention to the ongoing conversation to hear Aylin say, "Oh, please stay as long as you like. We love having you both here with us."

"We shouldn't continue to bother you—" I begin.

"It's not a bother at all," Aylin says. "We enjoy your stay. Auntie, although we just recently met, I feel I've known you for a long time. Baba told us a lot about you. How much I looked like you. How much I reminded him of you as a child. He said you were feisty." Aylin giggles, then sighs. "He said he wished to know you more as his grown-up sister. Thank Heaven that our families are finally one and whole."

Mother tears up. I know in that instant we are not going to move back home. Mother was disowned by her parents after she eloped with my father, so she hasn't seen her family in nearly twenty years. To her, this newfound warmth is a great opportunity to rebuild her relationship with Uncle Yi, her brother and the only surviving link to her past.

Except that he has no interest in rebuilding their relationship. If his son, Bo, was involved in Mother's murder, the young man must have gotten the instruction from his father.

My anger reignites.

Aylin touches my hand. I snap my head at her, glaring.

She jumps a little. "Are you all right, Mingshin? Did I startle you?"

I grin, hoping she didn't catch the brief hatred that must have flared in my expression.

Aylin relaxes. "I enjoy our time together, Mingshin. I'm sure we'll become like true sisters."

As an only child, I've always wanted a sibling more than anything else. Is she preying on my deepest longings? But she sounds sincere and appears genuine, so much that I almost wonder if I imagined her being there in my dying moment. No, she *was* standing over me, and I perceived her contempt clearly.

Maybe she truly means her words in this moment. When did she start to betray me in my previous life? Or is she extremely good at disguising her dark soul?

My uncle thinks he can control us if we stay. Although I want to get us as far away from him as possible, we mustn't leave yet. If he feels we are distancing ourselves from him, he'll manipulate my father's extended family into reinstating their claims; without his support, we may not get a fair trial from the Ministry of Justice.

I must secure our right of inheritance through other means, with my own effort. I'll leave no part of my fate in another's hands.

"You're right," I say as cheerfully as I can muster. "We'll indeed become like sisters."

"I'm glad to hear that, Mingshin. Father will return from work early today, Auntie, and we'll celebrate. I'll see you both later."

Together, the three of us walk out of the living room. At the courtyard, Mother and I stop to see Aylin off. She joins her handmaiden, then turns and waves goodbye.

For a moment, it does strike me how much she and Mother look alike. The same almond eyes, oval-shaped face, and defined bone structure. Mother is no less beautiful than Aylin. While my cousin radiates with the vitality of youth, Mother manifests the mature refinement of a woman in the prime of life.

More importantly, Mother is beautiful inside and out. Aylin is like the flower of oleander—pleasing to the eye, but lethally poisonous.

Mother waves back to Aylin. I can't bring myself to do the same. My cousin will return to the manor of the residence, which isn't far from the guest building we stay in. I prefer our location, nestled in a quiet corner of their estate. Surrounded by silver fir plants and chrysanthemum flowers, the dwelling consists of a living room, a dining room, and two bedrooms.

As peaceful as our residence is, we aren't safe.

I turn to Mai. "Where are the Han twins?"

"They were told to stay in the servants' quarters unless summoned," Mai replies.

A smart strategy of my uncle's, to separate us from our guards.

"Please fetch them here for me," I say.

"Yes, Miss." Mai is on her way.

"Why do you need to see them now?" Mother asks.

"Since we are going to stay in Jingshi for an indefinite time, it's best to establish some new rules."

Mother nods and returns to our quarters, but I linger in the courtyard.

I know little about the Han twins' past—only that they became bodyguards to our family after Father saved them from the gallows. Ren's guards later replaced the pair in their duty—I was grateful for how considerate Ren was. Shortly before Mother "drowned," the Hans were discovered to be half Nan'Yüans and accused of dabbling in magic, forcing them to flee.

Half Nan'Yüan they may be, but I'm certain the magic part was a lie made up to get rid of them.

The Hans arrive, the brother leading and the sister chatting with Mai.

In his early twenties, Hui seems robust enough to walk through walls of stone. Fei is smaller, her body lined with trim muscles. But their physical appearance is only part of what makes them great bodyguards. Hui has this air about him, a stillness overlaying something dangerous; Fei always gives off the impression of granite, hard and tenacious— another reason I didn't feel close to them while surrounded by Ren's gentle demeanor and Aylin's cordial ambience.

The Hans would have made great allies if I'd learned to work with them. I won't repeat the mistake of estranging myself from those I should hold near and dear.

"Please come with me," I say.

Once inside, I ask Ning to close the door. While Mother and I are seated, the other four people form a half circle around us.

I smile at them. "Mai, Ning, you've been with my family for many years and have served faithfully. Hui, Fei, you've been with us for a shorter period, but are no less devoted. My mother and I consider you all family. You're the only people we trust."

Mother nods along with me.

"We are blessed to serve you, Mistress and Miss," Ning and Mai say, one after another.

"It's an honor to guard Master Lu's wife and daughter," Fei says, and Hui nods in agreement.

Master Lu is why the twins serve us. I'll earn their trust on my own.

"Thank you." I look hard at each one of them. "We're going to stay in my uncle's home for a while. We shall be very careful. I must warn you, no one in the capital is what they seem. *No one.*"

In the tense silence that ensues, the twins trade an uneasy look. The maids keep their heads bowed and their hands clasped in their laps. Ning is older and more prudent. Mai has a good heart, but is prone to gossip.

"Mai, you must guard your tongue while listening sharp," I order. "You will not be gossiping about me, about Mother, or about anyone else in the family, under any circumstances." My voice is firm, sturdy, ringing with command.

Mai blanches slightly. "Aye, Miss."

"But if you hear any useful gossip about my uncle and cousins, you'll pass it on to me immediately. Do you understand?"

Mai's eyes open wide in bewilderment, but she nods. I know how much she admires Aylin. Mother frowns, and my gut tightens, but she says nothing. Despite her doubt, she won't show her disagreement with me in front of our servants.

"A wise move, Miss," Hui says.

"Nobles always make me uncomfortable," Fei adds.

A weight lifts from my shoulders. At least, it seems I've gained some approval.

"Hui, Fei, I'd like you to sleep here from now on," I say. "We, as a family, should stay close."

The twins agree to my plan. For now, it doesn't matter whether it's because the servants' sleeping quarters are cramped and cold or they think they should stay near us. We decide that Hui will sleep on a cot in the living room while Fei will share the maids' bunk room with Mai.

I'm glad that Mother doesn't feel it necessary to discuss the new arrangement with my uncle. "They are my charges, not his," she states.

I ask Fei to stay behind after dismissing everyone.

"I have a request, if you don't mind," I tell her.

"Anything, Miss."

"I'd like you to train me in hand-to-hand combat."

She does a double take, then smiles. "You're petite, so strength won't work to your advantage. But I've seen you run and play outside. You're agile and bold." She ponders for a bit. "I shall teach you how to use speed rather than strength and train you with small weapons instead of a sword."

I grin, barely able to restrain myself from giving her a big hug. I lead her to the backyard. There's a small area shaded by large oak trees.

"I don't want my uncle or cousins to find out, so we'll need a secret training spot. What do you think of here?"

Fei nods. "This should be suitable for the purpose."

"When can we start?"

Her smile broadens at my enthusiasm. "First of all, we'll need to find you a weapon. It should fit you perfectly, like an extension of your arm."

"We'll go shopping tomorrow morning. This afternoon, you and Hui please get settled."

"A good plan."

I return inside to find Mother wiping a tear away. My stomach lurches. "Did I upset you, Ma, with what I said?" I say as I sit down next to her on the couch.

"No, not at all. You are right. The capital is a dangerous place. I should have thought of taking caution before you did." A steely thread runs in her voice. "I'm proud of you, Shin'ar. It seems that you've grown overnight. The confident way you spoke and handled yourself. The sensible and sound things you said. I saw your father in you."

"Oh, Ma," I whisper. *I failed you before.* "I'll be worthy of your pride."

She sets a hand on my shoulder. "You detest the nobles like your Baba did, but not all of them are bad. I was a noble lady once. Give it some time; you'll come to like your uncle and cousins. Bo is hardworking and respectful, and Aylin has grown into such a pleasant, well-mannered young lady."

Mother is a shrewd businesswoman, having often worked together with Father. But even she was duped by my uncle and cousins. The memory of her cold, bloated body returns with the force of an icy wave crashing into me, and I have difficulty breathing for a moment.

Looking at Mother's expectant eyes, I feel a sudden, insane urge to pour it all out: How Uncle Yi's family betrayed us, how I came back to this new life, intent on revenge.

But no. I give myself a firm mental shake. I'd only sound like a raving lunatic, a horrible child making up outlandish lies to sabotage Mother's relationship with her brother. I can't afford to lose her trust. Even if, by the slightest chance, she believes me, would she be able to hold her anger in? Assuming she agrees to play along, she may not act well enough. I can't risk arousing Uncle Yi's suspicion. One wrong step, and we would lose not only my father's business, but our lives.

Mother must see for herself the monsters they are.

"I'll get to know them *very* well, Ma," I promise.

CHAPTER 4

At four sharp, Aylin comes with her maid to call us to dinner. When she sees the Han twins, she crooks a brow.

"I'd like them to stay here with us," I say. "I hope Uncle won't mind."

Aylin's expression is as smooth as velvet while she sizes up the twins. "Of course not." She beams. "Anything you like, Mingshin."

Aylin and Mother chat as they lead the way. Our maids bring up the rear. My insides clench at the familiar sight of everything we pass. Hedges of evergreen line a cobblestoned lane, while occasional breaks in the foliage reveal glimpses of an artificial rock mountain with a small waterfall. On the opposite side, workers tend a colorful garden flourishing with peony flowers.

The estate has been passed down from generation to generation and has been well maintained, as is customary for the homes of government officials and their families. It undoubtedly holds many childhood memories for Mother. No wonder she can't bear the thought of leaving yet.

We soon reach the manor, an ornate dark-red-brick edifice with burgundy beams and a magenta-tiled roof. Liveried servants stand to either side of the tall wooden doors. They bow as we enter.

In the vestibule, tiles feature a repeating flower motif that grows along the walls to climb across the ceiling in brilliant pink and yellow blossoms. The vestibule opens into a great hall with a polished wood floor. Torches burn in brackets, and I smell wax and oil. A rich tapestry depicting a flower from each season hangs on one wall. Across from it stand a pair of six-foot porcelain vases hand-painted with scenes of mountains and streams.

Aylin leads us further along until we reach the dining room. At the center lies a large round table where my uncle and Cousin Bo are seated. They rise upon the sight of us.

I've prepared myself to keep my emotions in check. Still, a raw anger throbs through me like fire and simmers beneath my skin.

Uncle Yi is a man of medium height, with features similar to my mother and Aylin. He wears a blue full-body wool tunic under a navy knee-length robe. Both are simple in style, but an expensive cut. I've never liked his smile; it conjures up the image of a fox smiling at a rabbit. Only now do I understand that, in his greedy eyes, *Mother and I* are the prey.

Bo, at seventeen, is pale and gangly. He's dressed similarly to his father, except in forest green. There's an awkwardness to him that makes him appear vulnerable. How very misleading.

Uncle Yi tells us to take a seat. Mother expresses her gratitude.

"You're my little sister, Lili," Uncle Yi says. "Why the formality? I'm glad to be of help, anytime."

My stomach roils at his false sincerity, but Mother appears touched.

Uncle Yi gestures to the steward, a dry, sniffy little man, who then waves to the other servants. They flow out of the room and soon return with steaming trays of grilled lamb, roasted duck, slabs of venison, sweet potatoes, beans, and a large pot of winter melon soup.

As the steward pours rice wine into silver goblets, the maids fill our bowls and set them in front of us.

Uncle Yi lifts his goblet to offer a toast, and everyone else follows suit.

"Let's celebrate our success at keeping my brother-in-law's business in the hands of his one true family. May his legacy be carried forward. I believe in you, Lili."

"Thank you, brother," Mother says.

We take a sip of the wine, and dinner begins.

Aylin suddenly perks up like a proud peacock. "Prince Ren stopped by today."

The name hits me like a blow to the gut, and I nearly drop my chopsticks. Color drains from my face.

Fortunately, no one appears to take notice. Everyone's attention is focused on Aylin.

"He said he was looking for you, Baba, but surely he knew you were at work." Aylin looks pleased with herself. She's still young, only two months older than me. She cannot help showing off the attention she receives from a prince.

Uncle Yi scowls at her.

"I sent him away immediately," Aylin adds in a whisper.

Now that I've regained my composure, my suspicious instinct kicks in. Why does Uncle Yi seem displeased about Ren's visit? When did he pledge fealty to him in my prior life? I didn't pay much attention to politics until I fell in love with Ren. What does Uncle Yi think of him right now?

"Did Prince Ren come to seek your support for his mother, Uncle?" I ask. "Surely the opinions of someone as important as you matter much to the King."

Uncle Yi nods smugly. *Good.*

"If Prince Ren wants his mother to be the new Queen, does that mean he aspires to become the Crown Prince?" I ask.

Uncle Yi smirks. "All four princes do. And they have all sought out my counsel."

I'd sooner believe a fish can walk. But I pretend to be impressed. "All of them? But there can only be one Queen."

"It's not about the Queen," he says patiently. The dumber he thinks I am, the better.

Uncle Yi whispers to the steward, who then waves to the servants in a dismissive gesture. After they file out of the room, Uncle Yi turns to me. "A Queen's oldest son is normally the heir apparent. But our Queen recently passed away and left only a daughter behind. His Majesty has four adult sons from his Royal Ladies. He's decided to promote one of them to be his Queen, so her son will become the Crown Prince." Uncle Yi shakes his head. "But it only looks like that on the surface. It's actually a competition among the princes: Whichever one is deemed by the King to be the Crown Prince, his mother will be made the Queen."

I nod as if I have just come to understand. "Which prince do you support, Uncle? You know how people are. The lords and ladies will invite us to parties and ask questions. We don't want to make fools of ourselves. Or align ourselves with the wrong people and cause trouble for you as the minister of a high government office."

"Prince Jieh is the King's favorite." Again, Aylin can't help showing off her knowledge, which I used to find endearing, as I myself could also be a know-it-all at times. "Surely His Majesty will make Royal Lady Hwa the Queen so he can become the Crown Prince."

"Keep such foolish woman's views to yourself," Uncle Yi snaps at Aylin, who flinches. I'm glad to see Mother grimace at that. "A King doesn't rule with emotions. His Majesty is wise and farsighted. He wants an heir most worthy to rule."

"So Prince Ren has as much a chance as the others," I say, feigning innocence.

"It's not that simple," Uncle Yi says. "A long-winded competition like this will require strong support from each of the princes' maternal family; the more powerful the family, the more resources they have and the greater influence they can provide. Prince Ren's mother is only a governor's daughter, while the other three princes' mothers have far higher births."

That was why Ren needed my money. Uncle Yi is merely repeating the low opinion of him shared by the other nobles, which Ren will later exploit to make his brothers underestimate him and lower their guard around him.

My uncle has mapped out a Queen's future for his daughter; of course, he isn't keen on the idea of Aylin being close to Ren. After I was engaged to Ren, people whispered behind my back that I wasn't good enough for a prince. Uncle Yi encouraged me, stating his niece was good enough for any prince. Maybe it was mainly his pride talking, but it warmed me to him a bit.

Uncle Yi surveys us all. His expression and voice grow serious, as if he's making an official announcement. "Despite everything I've said, I must make it clear that I remain neutral on this entire subject. I shall devote my full support and loyalty to whomever His Majesty puts his faith in. As the members of my extended family, I request that you all follow my lead."

What a load of horse dung. He declares impartiality only because it's too early to predict which prince will emerge as the winner. After Ren took full control of my family business and the King began to think highly of him, Uncle Yi must have sensed the change in the direction the political wind was blowing and chosen his side. I'll ensure their alliance never comes to fruition.

"I also request you to keep this conversation private," Uncle Yi adds.

We nod.

Mother turns to Bo. "I hear that you enrolled in a private school to prepare yourself for the national officials' entry exam."

"Yes, Auntie," Bo says, brightening. "I hope to start a career in the government soon, like Baba."

"Wouldn't it be nice to know the exam subject beforehand?" I say.

Bo scratches his head slowly. "It would, but even if the supervising officials can be persuaded to take a bribe to give away the subject, the money they ask will be more than we can afford."

"Fool!" Uncle Yi barks and points a finger at Bo. "Whether you excel or fail, you must do so fairly. If I hear another word about cheating, I'll take a flogging to you myself."

Bo folds his hands before his chest and bows. "I am ashamed, Father. Thank you for your tireless teaching."

Mother pats Bo's back. Aylin sniffles with tears in her eyes. It's all I can do to not throw up right at the table.

In my last life, Bo made the top thirty qualifiers at the exam. Considering his lack of talent, I'm certain he and his father bribed the officials with the money they swindled from me.

After we return from dinner, Mother spends the evening drafting a letter to the steward of our home estate to inform him of our extended stay. He's trustworthy and has been with our family for twenty years. He'll be able to take care of household details and supervise the servants in our absence.

While Mother engrosses herself at a desk in a corner of the living room, with Ning grinding the inkstone for her, I ask Mai to dig my waychess set out of our luggage.

Yet, as she lays the elaborately carved board on the tea table in front of the couch, a pain lances through my heart at the familiar sight. I can almost see Father seated across from me, playing a game with me, teaching me to always strive for better.

I swallow the tight feeling in my throat. Then, I sit before the table and open the jars that contain black and white stones.

The main object of the game is to form your own territories with your pieces by occupying vacant areas of the board, while capturing enemy pieces by surrounding them. As I play, I imagine it's Ren's hand, instead of mine, placing the black pieces on the board. I'm familiar with his strategy—creep upon his opponents from the sides and pounce. But I steadily develop my base from the bottom up.

"Are you playing against yourself, Miss?" Mai pipes up.

"Yes," I say without stopping. The two sides have become quite tangled by this point.

"That's unusual."

"It helps me understand my enemy's point of view. To win, you must know both yourself and your enemy well."

"I . . . see," Mai says.

Mother pauses in her writing and glances up. "You are sounding more and more like your Baba."

She smiles at me, then abruptly turns away. The light from the oil lamps casts a golden glow upon her sad face. She's thinking of Father again.

I miss him, too. He was the smartest, kindest, and most faithful man I've ever known. Mother was unable to have more children after me, but Father didn't take any lesser wives despite being mocked and ridiculed by his peers for his lack of a male heir.

I have Mother's elegant nose and chin, but otherwise I take after Father in appearance, with deep-set eyes, coarse raven hair, and warm, summer skin. I'm neither homely nor pretty; I occupy an unremarkable spot in between. Father always emphasized it was my compassion and intelligence that made me special.

Because of his faith in me, I hoped to find the kind of love he and Mother had during their life together. I thought my dream came true when I met Ren. He seemed to genuinely appreciate my brain and always listened to my counsel on politics. Instead of mooning over my stunning, highborn cousin like most other men, he told me, "A woman's virtue is what makes her worthy in the gods' eyes, and her inner beauty is what warms my heart."

No wonder I fell for him despite my qualms about his hunger for power. He even promised to never take lesser consorts—Royal Ladies—so long as he had me as his Queen.

How he played with words. *So long as* he had me. Since I was never to be his Queen, he had no promise to keep.

I try to banish these horrible reminders, but Ren's vicious betrayal and cruel words slam into me. It feels as though a sword has run me through. Everything in me is torn to pieces, and there will be no mending my soul.

I draw a deep breath and catch my emotions in a firm grip. In this moment, I vow to never fall in love again; I will never give another man so much power over me.

I return to my waychess game. The two sides are about to collide in a brutal battle. The match is not over until one vanquishes the other or one side surrenders.

Except in real life, there's no surrender. If you lose, you die.

CHAPTER 5

"Should we disguise as men?" Fei asks at the dining table.

That would be the smart thing to do. But I'm tired of being told there are certain things I can't do simply because I'm a girl.

"Will they sell to two women?" I ask.

She shrugs. "Money is money."

That settles it, then. After a quick breakfast of hot soymilk, scrambled eggs, scallion pancakes, and berries, Fei and I head to a weapons store in the city's commercial district. She swears the store is the best of its kind in the capital.

For a while, we ride on well-paved streets in wealthy residential areas. Large estates sprawl across the horizon. Each has a pair of giant bronzed animal statues flanking the main gate, representing the goodwill wishes of the household—lions for protection, cranes for good luck, and turtles for longevity.

Once we reach the commercial district, the road widens into bustling avenues lined with perfect rows of trees and graceful buildings. Shops stand in close order, roof tiles glistening red and purple, with stalls and pens in the spaces between. Feathers of smoke drift upward from the chimneys of the taverns and inns; music and laughter float out from the common rooms as men jest and drink from mugs.

Officials, merchants, and peasants, in clothes of every shade and material, walk and ride and lead horses, oxen, and sheep. Large audiences cheer for street acrobats and jugglers; peddlers hawk their wares at the top of their lungs. The aroma of roasting garlic, onions, and pepper wafts over from food carts, making my mouth water.

Once, I was awed by the prosperity of the city. Just like I was impressed by the beauty of the nobles around me when I first arrived in Jingshi.

But during the two years of living here in my first life, I learned there's much more beneath the surface. As I look deeper, like before, I notice the disparity between classes and the clusters of shacks standing in inconspicuous corners; I smell the rot beneath the fine exterior.

The weapons store, a three-storied building, has an entrance supported by two polished black pillars engraved with crossed swords. Inside, the ceiling is more than ten feet high. Knives, daggers, and swords of various lengths and widths are displayed.

All the other customers are men, and they gawk at us. Some shake their heads, while others scowl.

Fei ignores them and walks on. But their open displeasure only makes me more defiant. I lift my chin and glower back. *Let them simmer; let them stew.*

I notice a young man, flanked by a pair of armed guards, watching us. There's no disapproval in his eyes, only a curious glint. Despite his thin frame, he carries himself with a brisk and effortless pride typical of someone important.

I frown inside. I can count on one hand the young men of prominent positions I recall from my past life, but I can't place him, despite his striking sense of familiarity.

My thoughts are interrupted by Fei's demanding voice. "My lady needs to see the finest, sharpest dagger you have here that fits her grip."

I approach the counter with swagger.

The man with the tallest hat—distinguishing him as the head clerk—dismisses his younger colleagues. He gives both of us a once-over, and whatever he sees seems to satisfy him. Next, he asks me to show him my weapon-wielding hand.

"I have something that meets your requirements perfectly," he says. "But it may cost you."

"I'll be the judge of that," I reply.

He disappears into the back of the store and brings out a sheathed dagger, clasping it like treasure.

It's about six inches long, with a brass-plated guard and contoured leather handle. I unsheathe it. Under the light, the blade gleams like silver frost on a frigid dawn. My breath catches.

The clerk sets a strand of hair against its sharp edge and blows. The hair splits in half instantly.

Fei's eyes light up. "See how it fits," she says.

Following her instructions, I stretch my arm out and give it a few flicks of my wrist. The dagger's weight feels like nothing and seems like a natural extension of my hand. "Perfect," Fei says.

"How much is it?" I ask the clerk.

"Fifty gold taels."

Even my uncle would not indulge himself in such a luxury. But to me, it's worth it. I reach into my sachet for money, but Fei stops me with a hand pressed to mine.

"You've just inflated the price," she tells the clerk. "Even a first-rate dagger like this shouldn't cost so much."

He barks a sharp laugh, his face reddening. "That's most absurd! What do women know about the value of any weapon?"

The men snicker loudly. Fei's jaw locks rigid.

Emboldened, the clerk puffs up his chest. "Trust an expert's word, milady," he says to me. "Fifty gold taels for this dagger, or no deal."

I turn away from him. "How much does something like this usually cost?" I ask Fei.

"Around thirty gold taels."

"Nonsense—" the clerk begins, but I cut him off.

"What does the Commercial Law state? *To ensure a prosperous commercial environment and promote healthy competition, no price inflation of more than five percent shall occur within a year.* I'm sure there's a record of the official price kept somewhere. So tell me again, how much is a reasonable price? Or should we find out if you are breaking the law?"

He goes pale as a shroud. "Forgive me, milady. There must be something wrong with my memory. Thirty gold taels it is."

After I pay him with three gold ingots, Fei tucks the dagger beneath her belt, next to a hidden short sword. As we walk away, the young man catches my gaze. He inclines his head at me with a smile.

I've definitely met him, but before I can remember where, we're out the door. Fei and I look at each other, then laugh in unison, bumping our elbows.

When we reach our carriage a block away, I suddenly chafe at the idea of having to return to the confines of my uncle's estate so soon. "I'd like to take a walk in the city. What do you think?" I ask Fei.

She smiles, her eyes crinkling at the corners. "A great idea."

I tell the driver to stay behind, then set out on a stroll with Fei.

Is it my imagination that the sun looks different somehow? It bleeds fire among the clouds, and the sky wears a golden-orange blush. Light glints off the colorful buildings and shiny windows. The savory-sweet fragrance of steaming rice, roasted nuts, and exotic spices fills the air. Children chase each other, their mouths wide open with laughter. Men hurry along as if dogs were nipping at their heels. Women chat like excited geese.

For the first time since the beginning of this new life, I feel blithe and lighthearted.

I really should go out more often.

We reach a busy intersection and are about to cross the street when we hear the rapid clatter of hooves, accompanied by a commanding shout, "Out! Out of the way!"

I spin to my left. A horse is galloping down the street. Pedestrians scurry away, screaming. Vendor stands are overturned. Fruits and vegetables fly everywhere, landing with a splat.

"My child!" screeches a woman near me.

A little girl stands right in the path of the horse, fear rooting her to the spot.

I race forward and push the child out of the way. In an instant, the horse is upon me. I lift an arm to shield myself, bracing for the inevitable.

It rears suddenly, its hooves kicking in the air. Fei grabs my arm and yanks me away just before the horse's legs land mere inches to my right. Something bright falls from the animal's side.

The girl bursts out crying. Her mother hurries over and leads her away.

"Are you all right?" Fei whispers urgently.

My heart thumps a drumbeat. The beast would have trampled me if the rider hadn't reined it in hard enough to give Fei the time to pull me out of harm's way.

At the thought, I glance up. To see a handsome young man staring down at me, his gaze acute and intent.

I nearly stumble back from shock. Who would've thought the first royal "acquaintance" I make in my new life would be this vain snob I disliked in my past one?

Prince Jieh, the most favored contender for the throne. At seventeen, he's already famous in the capital for his fine equestrian skills and unrivaled swordsmanship.

He gives me a quick nod. The gesture is meant to be appreciative, I suppose, but somehow he still manages to make it seem condescending, as though I should be grateful for the opportunity to prevent him from trampling a little girl.

The horse huffs and stomps and dances at the end of the reins. I remember the glitter of light as its hooves landed next to me.

I spy a silver dart lying beside my foot. I bend down and retrieve it by the feathered tip.

"This fell from your horse, my lord." I raise the dart for him to see.

He reaches down and snatches it from my hand. His features harden in a flash. With a feline grace, he leaps off his horse.

I spot a tiny trickle of blood from a small wound on the animal's flank. Prince Jieh notices it, too. His face tightens with fury, and I can almost see the cogs turning behind his eyes.

Likely it was a plot devised by one of his half brothers to cripple him.

King Reifeng encourages his sons to vie for the throne, but has made it explicit that he would not tolerate one inflicting harm upon another. Any son found or even suspected of such will be immediately disqualified. Still the princes try to eliminate their competition, but only when they can make it look like an accident or blame it on another person.

Someone shot that dart into Jieh's horse, making it go berserk. Whoever was behind this apparently hoped he would at least get injured.

More hoof-falls approach us fast. Prince Jieh's guards have finally caught up. They slow down and dismount. Jieh hands the dart to one of them, a bearded man built like a wall.

He examines it. "Should we go back to where your horse suddenly bolted, my lord, to see if we can find anyone?"

The prince shakes his head. "Whoever did this will have been long gone by now."

He thinks for a moment, then whispers something to his guards.

They call out, "If anyone is hurt, please come forward. His Lordship will cover your medical expenses." They don't say "His Highness." Obviously, he doesn't want his identity revealed.

The vendors and passersby shake their heads as they stoop to pick up the debris in the street.

The prince struts to another horse, ready to mount.

I hurry after him. "You can't leave yet, my lord."

He looks at me sharply.

I point around us. "Your horse has caused significant damage, even if no one was injured. Don't you think compensation is in order?"

He glares at me, his expression at once haughty and disbelieving.

"Do you know who you are speaking to?" the bearded guard snaps at me.

"I don't. But another person here might recognize you, my lord. If words reach the Censorate, it may not serve Your Lordship's reputation well." The Censors are the eyes and ears of the King and check administrators at each level to prevent corruption and malfeasance. The princes are not exempt from their scrutiny. Jieh is in the middle of a competition for the throne. He can't afford to have the Censorate bring scandalous claims about him to his father.

Jieh takes a step closer to me. Fei's hand is on her belt in an instant.

I give her a slight, firm shake of my head. She doesn't know who he is. Attacking a prince would forfeit her own life.

Head and shoulders taller, Jieh towers over me. I have to admit that he's breathtakingly handsome, with a face that looks like it had been sculpted by the gods themselves—chiseled cheekbones, a strong, straight nose, and a square jaw that has a hint of stubbornness about it. His eyes are a stunning shade of rich brown. Thick, coal-colored hair flows to his collarbone in waves, setting off the golden hue in his skin to perfection. He has broad shoulders, and the lines of his muscular body are evident even through his dark-blue and silver tunic.

Jieh peers down his nose at me, like I'm an ant he can easily crush. I return an equally steely gaze of my own.

"You wait here," he commands, then pivots toward his guards. "Take a tally of the damage. Each person shall be compensated with ten silver taels."

The guards hurry to obey his order.

"Thank you, my lord," the crowd cheers. "May Heaven bless you." Sure, he's being generous.

But I have no intention of waiting around. I glance about furtively. Just then, a hand touches my arm, startling me, but it's only the mother of the little girl I saved. "Come with me, milady," she whispers.

I beckon to Fei, and both of us follow her rapidly into an alley hidden behind a row of kiosks. She leads us through two more turns and back to a thoroughfare.

I thank her and ask her for directions back to the area where we left our coach. She obliges gladly. I grin when I imagine how furious Prince Jieh will be when he finds me gone.

Fei overtakes me with a few strides and stops abruptly, bringing me to a halt. Her gaze is keen and her voice harsh. "You shouldn't put yourself in danger like that, Miss. The horse could've killed you; that nobleman might've lost his patience and harmed you."

My first reaction is to retort: *I didn't do anything wrong.* But sensing her concerns, I soften. "I'm sorry that I worried you. But we're all right now. We got away."

She crosses her arms. "That nobleman may still look for you."

"He may, but he doesn't know me. How is he going to find me in a sea of people? The chance of him running into me again is very slim, too."

She sighs. "Let's hope you are right." Her expression remains taut as she adds, "Promise me you won't ever put yourself in danger like that again."

"I promise."

We continue walking in silence. I wonder if she's still mad at me. I'm about to reassure her when she says suddenly, "I liked how you smacked that pretty boy's pompous ass."

I laugh, and after a bit, she joins me.

When we get back, Mai sews a pocket inside the interior lining of my boot for me to conceal my new dagger. For the better part of the afternoon, Fei shows me how to yank it out with one pull and makes me practice and practice until I can manage it with reasonable speed and dexterity.

That night, as I settle into sleep, I reflect on how and why I was granted this second chance. I consider the possibility of divine intervention, or even magic of some sort. But could there be magic this powerful? I know a little about it—I've read the forbidden scriptures in Father's secret library. He brought several back from his trips to Nan'Yü and hid them well after the knowledge of magic was banned ten years ago. The texts are often hard to understand; I was only able to finish reading them due to my curiosity.

I wish I had access to them now. We didn't think to bring any with us; it would have been too dangerous anyway.

I try to recall more details about the strange shower of light near my end, hoping it will offer me a clue. But with my consciousness slipping away on the brink of death, all I can remember is the light was too bright and the power engulfing me too overwhelming.

Grant me another chance and I'll do anything to make it right. If it indeed was the gods' doing, I don't believe they would have decided to bestow such a generous gift on me for no reason. There's an old saying, "For every gift there is a price." If a price must be paid for this new life, what can it be?

CHAPTER 6

Mai rushes into the living room, panting. "Miss! Master Chung has arrived."

I bolt up from the couch.

Mai smiles. "Miss Aylin greeted him at the manor. Once I saw them, I raced back here as you told me to."

"Good work, Mai. Thank you."

Mother knits in her bedroom. It's better she doesn't know what I have in mind. I hurry to the front yard. The Han twins are practicing sword fighting with each other, so I wave to get Fei's attention. They finish one more round of sparring before stopping.

"Come with me," I tell Fei. "We have a mission to accomplish today."

Hui shrugs at the mystery of my request. Fei puts down her sword and follows me at a brisk pace that matches mine.

We pass an archery range. A dozen wooden shooting targets, each painted with nine circles, stand at fifty, one hundred, and two hundred yards respectively. Nearby, a falcon is kept in a birdcage that hangs from a tree branch. It pecks at a handler's gloved hand as he tries to feed it.

My stomach clenches. Bo bragged that he had captured the bird of prey during a hunt. But in fact, Ren gave it to him as an offer of friendship.

Fei hisses in disgust. "The falcon belongs to the sky."

"One day, I'll set it free," I promise.

We stride past a large greenhouse, its windows clouded with condensation. A bit farther on, I hear music being played on a guzheng.

After telling Fei to remain behind, I enter a small building and follow the melodious sound to an open door. Careful to hide myself, I peer inside.

Aylin is seated behind a desk with a guzheng laid upon it. Master Chung stands next to her, showing her a special strumming technique.

Uncle Yi hired this top court musician at a terribly high cost to instruct Aylin. Not only to improve her music skills. More importantly, as the Royal Ladies' favorite entertainer, Master Chung's opinions carry weight with them, and they have a say in their sons' choice when it comes to a marriage partner.

I was aware that Uncle Yi was grooming Aylin to become the next Queen. Nonetheless, I turned a blind eye to his ambition. I'd never cared for power, but Ren craved nothing more than the throne, so I did my best to help him. I believed his goal justified, because his half brothers were no sheep, either, and would hurt him if any of them became King. After Ren was crowned, Aylin congratulated me. "I'm so happy for you, my dearest Mingshin. You'll be Queen!"

I fidgeted. "I don't really want to be Queen. I don't know how to be . . ."

She replied with her usual sweet smile. "Oh, your intelligence and compassion will make you a great Queen. I'm sure of it."

She was probably already conspiring with Ren to get rid of me when she said those words.

Could that be when she first betrayed me? When I, as Ren's fiancée, suddenly became an obstacle to *her* becoming Queen? If so, she must have turned against me as soon as Ren was made the heir.

I shove the memory firmly back into the shadows. Putting on a dreamy look, I wander into the classroom.

The music stops. As both people turn to me in shock, I stutter, "I'm sorry for the intrusion. The music drew me here. It's so wonderful . . ." My words trail off under their scrutiny, but I stare keenly at the guzheng.

Chung glances between me and the instrument. "Do you play music, Miss?" he asks with a lilting accent common among people from the north.

"A little."

"Would you be so kind as to grace these old ears for a bit?"

Aylin reaches for me and grabs my hands. "Come, Mingshin. I'm sure you'll play beautifully." She turns to her teacher. "Forgive me, Master Chung. This is my cousin Mingshin, daughter of Mr. Lu, a very successful merchant."

I sit behind the guzheng. In the last week, I'd been practicing every night in my room until I was sure I'd regained some of my skills—it's fortunate we live in a remote corner of the estate.

I play a piece that depicts spritely girls dancing for a harvest. The notes flow out smoothly as my fingers move across the strings.

When I finish, I lift my head to see Chung staring out the window with a bored expression. My heart skids and sputters in a rush of panic. I may have performed well, but no better than Aylin with the same kind of music. To impress Master Chung, I must be ten times better than Aylin, or I need to be different, unique.

I don't care much for music that suggests flowers, the moon, or a serene river, but that's what is expected of women. With Father's permission and encouragement, I've learned what many call "men's music"—music that's strong, resounding, and passionate, with melodies that conjure up images of surging ocean tides, a blazing sun, and raging battles—it actually makes me think of women like Mother or Fei.

Perhaps a true artist like Chung would have a more open mind. Or like other men, he might be disgusted by my choice. It's a risk I must take.

"Thank you, Miss Lu—" Chung begins.

My fingers strum and pick the strings fast and powerfully. As I continue, I imagine myself as a restless ship sailing through the hard-driving winds of a tempest. When I pluck the last note, my heart is pounding and my hands are throbbing.

"Interesting," Chung says, a sparkle in his eyes.

I didn't execute the piece as well as I would've liked, but I lost two years of skills with my return to age sixteen. "With more practice, I can do better." I put as much eagerness in my voice and expression as I dare.

"You are a girl," Aylin whispers urgently. "What will people think when they hear you play like that?"

Again, she appears genuinely concerned. How long will it stay that way?

Chung watches me, as if intrigued by my reply.

"As long as my music touches people's souls and inspires their minds," I say.

Aylin blinks. Then, Chung says, "Would you like to join our class in the future, Miss Lu?"

Yes! I want to jump off my seat and whoop. If there's one thing Chung loves as much as music and money, it's the discovery of a new talent that makes him shine as a master teacher.

I'm about to accept his invitation, but as if I've just remembered something, I snap my head up to look at Aylin.

She drapes a dazzling smile across her lips. "How wonderful that we'll learn from Master Chung together, Mingshin."

Does she mean that? I'm sure she didn't betray me this early in my former life. At any rate, I knew she'd say yes because she wants Master Chung to see her as an unselfish person so he'll speak favorably of her character to the Royal Ladies.

When I return, I tell Mother how I happened upon Aylin's music class and became Chung's student. "He's probably never seen a girl playing men's music before," I say at the end.

"I've always known you are different from other girls. I've given up raising you as a lady," she teases. "Like your Baba said, *let her be free and wild.*"

I smile and throw my arms around her. "Thank you for letting me be what I want to be, Ma."

In our small backyard, Fei and I stand facing each other. In today's training, she'll teach me to thrust and stab at my opponent. For safety's sake, I keep the dagger sheathed, and Fei wears a leather vest for protection.

She waves me forward. I charge and slash at her over and over, but she easily dodges my dagger attacks.

I halt, huffing in frustration.

"You realize why you failed?" Fei asks.

"I'm not as strong as you are."

"I'll never be as strong as my brother, but when we spar, I connect or make him retreat at least half of the time."

"Well, I'm trying to accomplish that."

"Then stop fighting like a man. Their way suits them, but it isn't superior. Men underestimate us because we lack their physical strength. But if they are fire and earth, we are water and air. Watch me."

She moves like a dancer, graceful and fluid. Her eyes are focused, her rhythm is precise, and she never swings her blade more than is necessary.

I do my best to imitate her while she corrects my footwork and redirects the flow of my arms. After half an hour of practice, my moves still feel awkward, but I have become more and more confident in this element.

Seeing me out of breath, Fei suggests we take a break. I plop down under the shade of an oak. Fei laughs as if amused by my unlady-like landing as she sits next to me.

"Women bodyguards are very rare, Fei. What made you become such a good fighter?"

"In my experience, you either learn to fight or you die." Her eyes gleam hard like polished obsidian. "Why are *you* suddenly interested in learning to fight, Miss? You've always had a wild streak, but *this* is rather unusual even for you."

A moment passes while I ponder the question. "I had a long, ter-rible dream in which I failed my family and lost my life. I tried to become like those noble ladies and let myself be used in the name of love. I won't allow it to become reality, Fei. I'll stay true to my heart and fight to protect the people most important to me."

Fei nods. "Keep it that way, Miss. Tomorrow I shall teach you more on defense." She stands. "Now, back to work."

I leap up eagerly.

CHAPTER 7

Three mornings a week, I join Aylin in her music lessons. Uncle Yi congratulates me on earning Master Chung's appreciation, but I doubt he likes it at all.

Master Chung is impressed with my progress—I've been practicing day and night, until my fingers almost bleed. When I gush with admiration about a score he's composed, a masterful blend of soft and strong notes, he decides Aylin and I should play it in a duet two months from now, at the royal banquet to celebrate the King's birthday.

I share the news with Mother, who is as excited as I am. But later that day, Mai informs us that Aylin got so angry she shattered her teacups. Through the gossip with the maids, she learned my cousin had been yelling, "It's my moment! How dare she steal it? I won't allow it."

Mother frowns. "What was Aylin talking about?"

A cold stone settles in my gut and I snort. "She's mad at me, Ma, for sharing her center stage moment at the banquet."

Aylin has been eager for an opportunity to impress the royals. In my last life, Ren asked me to join him at the banquet—how I giggled and lost sleep over his request like a foolish, lovestruck girl. There, Aylin had played her piece wondrously, gaining adoration from the court.

Securing Master Chung's invitation is my only way to attend the banquet in this life. A duet would still give Aylin a chance to shine, but apparently, she hates to share, even with someone she claims to be a "near-sister." She wants to be the sole focus of admiration.

My cousin has revealed her true color fast.

A huge, dark, terrible truth twists inside me.

Aylin is a nobleman's daughter and beautiful. I'm a merchant's child and plain-looking. I never posed a threat to her, so she could be friends with me, often even in a genuine way. That was how I was lured into a sense of security, never doubting her. But once she felt I hurt her interests, she turned against me. In my prior life, it happened when Ren was made the heir. Now, it's as soon as she feels that I may steal her moment at the banquet.

Mother has paused her knitting, her expression thoughtful. When she resumes her work, she says, "I pay for Aylin's guzheng lessons."

"What? I didn't know that."

"Your uncle mentioned it in passing, saying how much Aylin loved music and how sad he was about being unable to afford Master Chung, so I offered to pay."

I feel a flame of fury. My uncle has always been good at manipulating people into giving him what he wants.

"You were too kind, Ma."

"You make it sound like being kind is a bad thing," she says.

"A kind heart makes you soft, weak, and vulnerable to your enemies." *Didn't I learn that lesson with the price of my life?*

"When a kind heart is directed at the right people, it's strength, not weakness."

I shrug. Even if Ma is right, my uncle and cousins don't deserve kindness.

Just like before, Uncle Yi has nurtured Aylin, his exquisite flower, to be presented for the first time to the court, to bloom right before their eyes at the royal banquet. I'll make sure she wilts.

In the days following Master Chung's decision, Aylin appears dejected. When I inquire about this, she replies that she isn't feeling well. When I offer to summon a doctor, she forces herself to brighten up.

Then one day she shows up to class in an unusually cheerful mood.

"Oh, I'm so excited at this opportunity for us to play together," she says. "I want our performance to be perfect. Please join me for tea this afternoon so we can plan everything out."

Alarm bells ring in my head, but I keep a pleasant smile on. "Of course."

What does she have in mind? I wouldn't put it past her to poison me with tea to keep me bedridden long enough to miss the practice and, therefore, the planned performance.

I join Aylin in the living room at the agreed time. She invites me to sit on the couch. Before us, on the tea table, lies her delicate set of porcelain teacups, painted with brilliantly plumaged birds.

The first day Mother and I arrived at her home, Aylin showed us her tea art skills. The tea is brewed in certain ways to display different patterns, such as a lotus flower growing out of the water or a fairy spreading its wings. They all taste different, some like spring flowers, some like summer fruits, and others like honey.

In my former life, it only intensified my admiration for Aylin that she had mastered the difficult tea art, the most fashionable trend among the noblewomen. Now I know better: Whatever skill increases her value in a political marriage, she puts in quite the effort to perfect it.

I pick up a teacup and peer down into it. "The butterfly is beautiful, Aylin." I raise the cup to my lips.

As I instructed her earlier, Mai sneezes loudly. I startle and drop my cup. It shatters on the floor between me and Aylin. Black tea splashes all over our dresses.

Aylin lets out a squeak and leaps up.

"Oh, I'm sorry." I fumble to help her.

Aylin forces a smile. "It's all right." She takes a deep breath. "Forgive me, Mingshin, but I must go and change. Perhaps another time." She leaves in a hurry.

Two days later, Aylin asks Mother and me to dine with her. Normally we eat separately, as Uncle Yi and Bo often meet with officials during dinner. Aylin, too, spends a lot of time visiting other noblewomen.

I can't think of an excuse to turn down her invitation. It's unlikely she'll poison us at the dinner, anyway, since we will share the food.

Halfway through our meals, Aylin asks, "Didn't you go out on the day after our celebration dinner, Mingshin?"

I nod, but every nerve in me tingles. That was the day Fei and I went out to buy my dagger and ran into Prince Jieh. Has he somehow tracked me down?

"When I was visiting a noble lady the other day, she told me her husband saw two women shopping at a weapons store." Aylin leans forward like she is sharing some conspiracy. "She thought it was scandalous. The physical description of the two women matched you and your female guard. Of course, I mentioned nothing of the sort to the lady. I presume you went there to look for a weapon for your guard, but you mustn't do so. If anyone finds out, it could ruin your reputation—it's unseemly for a refined woman to be seen in such places without a chaperone or escort." Her brows are knit together as though she were genuinely concerned. "But don't worry, I didn't tell anyone, not even Baba. I don't want him to be mad at you. Besides, I want you there with me at the royal banquet. We play together so well."

My insides curdle. I don't care about those who may judge me harshly for not being ladylike enough to suit them. But Aylin could use the opportunity to smear my name and have me removed from the royal banquet's invitation list, so why hasn't she?

Mother gives me a stern look before turning to my cousin. "Thank you for being protective of Shin'ar, Aylin. Speaking of the royal banquet, have you decided on your dress for the event?"

"No, Auntie." Aylin sighs. "It's hard to find something I like that is also affordable."

"Seek out the best seamstress in the capital and choose your favorite style. Don't concern yourself with the price. The dress is my pleasure."

"Oh no, how can I have you pay for it?"

"Accept it as a gift from me. For everything you are doing for Mingshin." Mother sets a hand on Aylin's. "Please. I insist."

Aylin clutches at her breast. "Oh, thank you, Auntie."

I can only imagine the outrageous price tag Mother will get. Under the table, my hands are balled into fists. But I only have myself to blame.

As soon as we return to our rooms, I kneel before Mother, my head hung low. "I'm sorry, Ma. I told everyone to be careful, but I overlooked my own advice. I've shamed you by not concerning myself with what others may think."

Mother holds my arms on either side and makes me rise. "I understand what you did, Shin'ar. Your father never restricted you from going anywhere as a girl. But as you said yourself, the capital is a strange, dangerous place, and the people here play by a different set of rules."

"I'll never make that mistake again, Ma. I promise."

Mother ruffles my hair. "I believe you."

"I don't understand, Ma. Aylin could use the incident to smear my reputation. Why hasn't she done it yet?"

"Because if she did, it would also taint your uncle's reputation since we are his guests, and in turn hers. Still, it would do you greater harm than it would her, so she played a petty game to get something nice in exchange for her silence."

Mother saw right through Aylin. Although I possess knowledge from my past life, I still have much to learn.

"Don't be mad at Aylin," Mother says. "Young women at your age are prone to jealousy. It doesn't mean she's a bad person. You'll both get over your petty competition one day. After all, we are family."

A frustrated sound claws up my throat. Mother still believes in the good Aylin. I inhale a breath. I must be patient.

I'm sure Aylin hasn't given up on stopping me from attending the royal banquet. Nor has Uncle Yi, a far more formidable opponent than my cousin. He wouldn't want me to steal his daughter's grand moment. My chest tightens. With me out in the open and him in the dark, I have difficulty gauging his moves against me. It may be too late before I see the danger coming.

CHAPTER 8

When Aylin invites me for fish feeding at the pond in the back of the estate, I warn Mai to watch out for her maid—I don't relish "accidently" falling into the water.

It's a beautiful summer afternoon. Standing upon the half-moon bridge that spans the length of the pond, we lean over the rail. While her maid holds a jar of fish flakes and pellets, Aylin drops a handful into the clear water. Fish of various colors gather, fighting for the food. We point, shout, and laugh.

A memory hits suddenly, with such a dizzying rush of clarity that I can't breathe for a moment. I recall being at this place precisely on this same day.

I was so excited I asked Aylin if I could play with the fish in the water. "Of course," she said. I took off my shoes and waded into the shallow water, my skirt held high. Aylin cheered me on. I paused and scooped up a few tiny fish, holding them out for her to see them swimming in my cupped palms.

"Oh, that's wonderful!" Aylin cried. "You're the best, my sister!"

I giggled and moved farther into the pond while Aylin dropped more flakes near me. I splashed water at her. Caught by surprise, she got a bit wet around her shoulders. But she just laughed and challenged me to do better.

Then I slipped on a rock. Choking on water and not knowing how to swim, I flailed my arms and legs, which only worsened the situation. Aylin screamed and ran for help with her maid.

I was saved.

Mai told me later that Bo had hesitated, but Ren had not for an instant. He plunged into the water, grabbed me, and pulled me to the shore, whispering comforting words all along.

When I was lucid enough, I found myself staring at the most beautiful man I'd ever seen: bright eyes; dark, rich hair; the perfect planes of his features.

He smiled in relief. If he was any other nobleman, he would have ridiculed or laughed at me, but Ren did neither. His eyes held sympathy and concern; his soft voice soothed me.

My heart stumbles a beat as a pleasant warmth floods me from head to toe.

A wave of nausea sweeps over me. How could I have, just now, experienced the same feeling I had the moment I fell for Ren? "I'm sorry, Aylin. I don't feel well. I'd like to return to my room."

Aylin's face quickly transforms into a look of concern. "Certainly. Shall I summon a doctor?"

"No need for the bother, thank you. It's most likely due to the change of season."

Aylin insists on walking me back to my room. As we round the rock mountain, I hear two men talking, their voices growing louder as they head our way.

"Thank you for lending us your herbalist, Your Highness. I can't express my gratitude enough." It's Bo speaking.

"My pleasure . . ."

I freeze, ice flowing through me. I'd recognize that second voice anywhere.

Ren.

The two men emerge. They spot us as well, but there's no break in their stride or conversation.

It seems fate has brought me to meet Ren on this same day. I'm not ready to face him, but there's no escape.

I can see him clearly. Now, his gorgeous eyes only appear as a disguise for a heart that holds darkness. His chiseled features look sharp, like serrated blades. Even the elegant lines of his body remind me of the sinuous way a snake slithers.

Ren frowns in confusion. I turn away. He must have caught the hatred in my glare. I corral the multitude of emotions stampeding through my chest, taming them. Aylin is too busy dazzling him with her beauty to pay me heed.

Mai ogles him, her mouth hanging open like a dumbfounded frog. I clear my throat.

She flushes a deep scarlet. "I'm sorry, Miss," she mumbles and lowers her head.

I settle on a look of indifference and force myself to face the men in front of us.

As they exchange pleasantries, Aylin dips into a curtsy. She smiles at Ren with court-trained grace, neither too intimate nor too distant.

Bo extends a hand. "May I introduce Mingshin, the daughter of the greatest businessman of the decade, my late uncle Lu Kang? Mingshin, please meet His Highness, Prince Ren."

Ren's eyes glitter. He knows the wealth my name represents. He's probably already calculating how much support he could buy and how many royal courtiers he could bribe with my money. Despite the monthly allowance he receives as a prince, he can't compete with his half brothers, whose maternal families are far richer.

From this moment on, I am Ren's target. But he won't hit the mark this time. Instead, I intend to ram the arrow of vengeance into his heart, break it open, and bleed all the hope out.

I curtsy, but the gesture feels stiff. "Honored to meet you, Your Highness."

Ren reaches for my hand to help me rise. Without thinking, I let him take it, just as I have many times before.

A memory strikes me like a slap across the cheek. "Aylin is the one I've always wanted," Ren said as I lay dying in the snow. "For two years I had to stare at your plain, mooning face . . . It sickened me."

I jerk my hand away from Ren as though bitten by a viper.

My cousins snap their heads toward me in shock. Anger pulls Ren's features into harsh lines, but he soon smooths his countenance over, as if I've done nothing offensive.

I try to calm my pulse—the throbbing feels like hammers against my temples. How very foolishly I have acted.

"I'm sorry, Your Highness, I'm not feeling well," I say in a rush, "I beg you to excuse me."

Without waiting for his reply, I whirl around and stride off.

After a bit, I notice Mai isn't following me. I glance back, just in time to see Ren pick up her kerchief off the ground and hand it to her with a genial smile. Mai curtsies, turns, and runs to me, her cheeks as red as tomatoes.

I sigh. Once, I was unable to resist his charm, either. I thought it must be Heaven's Fortune that he had been named just like his character—"Ren" means kind, merciful. What a cruel joke Heaven played on me.

Mai pads silently behind. Finally, the heat of wrath and hatred cools down and drains away, leaving my thoughts sharper, clearer.

How could I have forgotten myself back there and let that disgusting creature take my hand? And I mustn't lose control again.

My mind traces back to the wisp of conversation I overheard between Ren and Bo. From my past experience, I know what it was about.

Uncle Yi was lucky to obtain a millennium-old lingzhi, often nicknamed "fairy herb." It was placed in Bo's care and will be offered as a gift for the King's birthday. But it hasn't been doing well in the greenhouse, and Ren's herbalist helped save it.

Now, Uncle Yi is in Ren's debt. And debts always come due.

When Bo has a day off from school, he invites Ren to visit the estate. The two men decide to practice at the archery range. In the courtyard, Aylin asks if I'd like to come along and watch with her.

I keep my demeanor calm and act gracefully this time. "Oh, archery always bores me. I think I'll pass."

Ren smiles. "You remind me of a cousin, Miss . . . do you mind if I call you Mingshin?"

I give a small nod and he continues, "She doesn't like this type of sport either, but when she visited Jingshi last summer, I took her to the Spirit Hill, and she quite enjoyed the view there. Perhaps you'll grant me the honor of taking you there, too? How about tomorrow?"

Sure, right. I was with him for two years, and he'd never mentioned such a cousin.

"I thank you for your kind invitation, Your Highness, but I've made plans for the rest of the week." I smile at them all. "I pray you have a wonderful time."

Ren nods his acknowledgement, but I sense disappointment in his bearing as he leaves with my cousins.

Mai gawks after Ren's retreating back. I snap a finger before her.

She glances at me, then ducks her head. "I'm sorry, Miss. I've never met a nobleman like Prince Ren. He's so kind, so gentle." She blushes a shade deeper. "And he's very handsome, too."

"Remember what I told you, Mai? No one in the capital is what they seem." I sigh. "The more beautiful they are on the outside, the uglier they are inside."

"Not Miss Aylin."

She's one of the worst! I force my jaw to unclench. I can't blame Mai for thinking that way. I was in her position once. Given time, she'll see my cousin's true colors.

As we roam the grounds, a dragonfly flits overhead. Mai grows excited and tries to capture it. The wild part of me clamors to be free, so I join her in the chase. Hindered by my trailing dress, though, I soon fall behind.

As she rounds the rectangular corner of the hedge maze, I hear a crunch of feet on gravel, then a loud "ouch" and an angry yelp.

I rush forward. Mai's hand is clasped over her mouth. She has collided with a man who, judging by his fine clothes, must be noble.

When he sees me, he frowns, as if trying to remember something.

I suck in a cold breath. What's the chance I'd encounter Prince Jieh again, and so soon?

CHAPTER 9

Uncle Yi's steward hurries to Jieh's side. "My apologies, Your Highness." He spins to Mai, a hand raised.

I won't make it in time to stop him from slapping Mai. Just then, she drops to her knees, and the steward's hand swipes through the air.

Clever girl.

I put ice in my voice as I whirl to the steward. "Know your place. Don't you ever lay a hand on *my* maid. Am I understood?"

His face turns an ugly, blotchy red, but he mumbles, "Yes, Miss."

I look away to find both Jieh and his young companion studying me.

Uh oh. So much for not drawing attention to myself.

Jieh's gaze is intent, trapping me in the spot. Did he recognize me? But he doesn't appear angry. *Be calm. Don't panic. No one remembers an ordinary-looking girl like me.*

Of shorter and slimmer build, Jieh's friend has a gentle face, a long nose, and eyes rich and warm like freshly tilled earth. Yao, the son of Grand General Chen and Jieh's constant companion, possesses the official position of assistant to the Lord High Constable.

Although reluctant, the steward is obliged to introduce us to each other.

I ease into a perfect curtsy. "Your Highness. Your Lordship." What are they doing here, I wonder.

"You're Minister Sun's niece," Yao says, a friendly gleam in his eyes.

"Yes, my lord." Although Jieh is a well-known snob, Yao has always struck me as cordial and fun-loving. How the two get along so well is a mystery beyond me.

A smile lifts a corner of Jieh's lips, the look both menacing and enticing. He leans down to whisper in my ear, "Aren't you the woman who offered me her prudent advice about the Censorate?"

My gut wrenches sharply. I force out a laugh, but it sounds more like a giggle. Quickly, I say, "Is Your Highness here to see my cousin Bo?" I pause, as if just remembering something else. "Or Prince Ren?"

The way I emphasize Ren's name succeeds in shifting Jieh's attention. He exchanges a meaningful look with Yao.

"You know where Ren and Bo are," Jieh states. "You'll lead us there so as to spare the steward the trouble." He waves at the small man to dismiss him.

The steward glances at Mai and opens his mouth. But I won't give him the chance to get her punished by Jieh.

"Mai, apologize to His Highness," I say. "He has such a generous soul and surely will—"

Jieh cuts me off with a snap of command, "Lead the way."

I nod for Mai to leave. She rises, shuffles a few steps, and runs off.

"Please follow me to the archery range," I say while walking ahead.

"I can't wait to get my hands on a bow," Yao says, rubbing his palms together. "It's always me against you, Jieh. What a chance! Wouldn't it be fun to have a go at it with someone else?"

"You always lose to me, so it would be a nice change to see you win for once."

Yao makes a sound as though he's been offended, but I'll wager he's faking it.

Jieh takes a step closer to me. "I found who injured my horse . . . he's been taken care of."

Why is he telling me this? Which of his half brothers hired the man to shoot a dart at Jieh's horse? I'm sensible enough not to ask.

Jieh stares down at me out of the corner of his eye. "What's Ren doing here with your cousin?"

"If you and Lord Yao heed my advice, you may learn a secret of Prince Ren's that I believe concerns you."

"Oh, what's this *new* advice of yours?"

I ignore his patronizing tone. "We'll approach the archery range quietly so no one hears us. And we'll stop at a distance and watch."

He scowls. This pompous ass always favors a dramatic entrance, where he's showered with flattery.

"The secret will be worth it," I say.

He considers that for a moment, then nods at his friend. Yao nods back.

"You are wondering why I'm here at your uncle's estate," Jieh states.

I decide to push my luck a bit. "You're not seeking my uncle's support, are you?"

He snorts like he's insulted. No doubt, he believes everyone should rally behind his claim for the throne without him lobbying them in support of his quest.

"I misspoke, Your Highness. Please forgive me. As I understand it, the influence and prestige of your uncle, Lord Protector Hwa, is unmatchable." That isn't an exaggeration. Lord Protector is the only hereditary peerage in the Jin dynasty—the same rank as prime minister.

It was granted to Jieh's maternal ancestor, who made the biggest contribution to its first King, Gaodru, during his effort to overthrow the last dynasty. The current Lord Protector Hwa has numerous protégés across the kingdom. "Like him, many lords have wisely decided that you're destined for greatness."

"You certainly know much for a commoner," he says with a sneer. Then, in a lower voice, he adds, "And you are quite bold."

My heart kicks once against my ribs. There's something strange in his tone, almost like fascination, but surely I'm reading too much into his words.

As we approach the archery range from a wooded flank, I signal for the two men to stop among a copse of small trees and peer through the leafy branches.

Jieh frowns, and I cast him a cautionary stare. He exhales and turns to the archery range.

Bo is shooting. Ren stands near the stock of bows and arrows. To the left, the cage holding the falcon, Ren's token of friendship, sways from a tree branch. The handler stays close by.

To the far right, Aylin lounges in a chair. The way she chews the grapes, seductively yet gracefully, is a work of art, something I couldn't master in a thousand years.

She smiles when she catches Ren watching her. For a moment, even the air shimmers. He seems unable to look away.

I nearly double over; a punch to the belly would have been gentler than the hurt and humiliation I feel.

Bo whoops in delight, pulling my attention back to him. He has hit the bull's-eye on a one-hundred-yard target.

Aylin applauds. "Bravo, brother!"

Ren claps Bo on the shoulder. "Good work."

Bo laughs. Ren shoots next. He fires five arrows in a row, all slamming into the center of the target.

I turn to find a glint enter Jieh's eyes, a bright flash like sun off cold steel.

To lower his brothers' expectations of him, Ren often hides his talent and downplays his ability while in front of them. But he must prove he's strong and smart to those nobles whose support he seeks, including Uncle Yi. To demonstrate his skills, he doesn't hold back in front of Bo. This chance meeting with Jieh has given me the opportunity to expose his deceit.

I've achieved my purpose, and it's time for Jieh's dramatic entrance.

"That's spectacular," I cry out.

Everyone whirls in my direction. Ren pales at the sight of Jieh but quickly recovers.

Bo hurries forward to greet the newcomers. "What an honor, Your Highness. Welcome, Lord Yao."

Ren nods at Jieh, his smile ingratiating. Jieh ignores him as usual, as if this half brother didn't exist or was far beneath his notice. I feel an instant twinge of pity. Oh, that's silly. It must be the residue of my old feelings: How I used to hate Jieh for the supercilious way he treated Ren.

Ren would often share with me his resentment after such encounters with his brothers, or when the officials didn't take him seriously enough. Revealing his doubts meant far more to me than when he revealed his desires. If a man is willing to expose his vulnerabilities to you, it must mean he fully trusts you. Therefore, despite his flaws, I continued to love him.

One should always choose to listen to her head over her heart.

If Aylin has been sweet with Ren, now her smile is loaded with honey. "Prince Jieh, Lord Yao," she says with a voice that could melt butter, or a man's soul.

Yao appears enamored, but Jieh throws her a bored glance. I find myself instantly disliking him less. But surely he isn't blind? He has beautiful women fawning over him all the time, but a stunning one like Aylin would be impossible to neglect. More likely, he's feigning disinterest.

Aylin flushes a glorious ruby red, but she keeps her court-trained smile plastered on her face.

Jieh is already picking up a bow and five arrows. He can't help showing off, can he?

Jieh aims and shoots. The first arrow strikes the bull's-eye, and each of the following pierces the shaft of the previous arrow, all the way to the end, sound and precise.

We gape. A complete silence descends but for the vibrating hum of the remaining shaft.

Ren appears as calm and unmoved as a wall of clay, but I know him better than that. A muscle feathers at his chin, quick and subtle, then it's gone.

I look away just in time to see Aylin leaning into Jieh, her shoulder almost touching his arm.

"Oh, Your Highness, no wonder you became the champion of the tournament the last three years," she purrs. "I wish I'd been there to see you winning. I'm sure you'll defend your title again next year. I look forward to seeing it myself."

Jieh turns away from her with a grimace. I almost laugh. He's becoming less intolerable by the minute.

"Miss Lu, would you mind demonstrating your prowess in archery?" Jieh says.

What?

"Can you beat that?" Jieh points at the arrows still stuck in the target. "If you do, I'll disregard your previous insolence," he says only for my ears.

I stare at him, at the tight lines of his face. Heaven above, he's serious.

I haven't pulled a single bowstring in a while. What will he do to me if I decline his challenge?

Aylin claps her hands. "What an exciting idea! I'll cheer for you, Mingshin." Cheer for my failure, she means.

Ren flicks me a sympathetic look, then sighs, as if coming to a hard decision, and turns to his brother. I know exactly what he's going to do: He'll ask Jieh to let me go, and withstand his wrath for my sake. What a hero.

I don't need Ren's "rescue." Ever. And I won't give my cousins the satisfaction of seeing me made a fool of.

"What if I can make my arrow fly farther than yours?" I announce to Jieh and everyone.

He frowns, obviously wondering if I have some trick up my sleeve.

I raise a brow. "You're not afraid of losing to me, are you?"

He lifts his chin. "I accept your challenge." For my ears only, he adds, "No matter what trickery you pull off, I'll win."

"You first, Your Highness."

Under Jieh's instruction, Bo and Yao move a target to three hundred yards. Once more, he hits the bull's-eye. He needles me with a smirk.

I take one arrow and walk to the falcon's cage, feeling everyone's stare focused upon my back.

I borrow the handler's gloves. After pulling a ribbon free from my hair, I wrap it around the shaft of the arrow. Then I reach into the cage and secure the other end of the ribbon to the falcon's leg as it screeches and pecks at my gloves.

"What are you doing?" Bo squeals. He takes a step forward but halts immediately when Jieh blocks his path with an extended arm.

"As promised, here is your freedom," I whisper to the bird of prey.

As soon as I open the cage door, the falcon takes flight. Soon enough it becomes a speck in the sky.

"My arrow has flown at least ten times as far," I say. "Can you beat that, Prince Jieh?"

Bo's jaw drops and hangs slack. Ren appears thoughtful. Aylin's eyes have grown as big as her teacups.

Yao bursts out laughing. "This is wonderful, Jieh. Admit defeat."

Jieh's face is a kaleidoscope of emotion. Annoyance? Amusement? Disbelief?

"I'm a man of my word," he says regally and puts down the bow and arrows. "You win this challenge." His nose is up in the air again. "Next time, you won't be so lucky." He stalks off.

My heart skips over itself. *Next time?*

Yao winks at me before following his friend.

Bo runs to catch up with Jieh. "Are you here to see the lingzhi? I'm glad you accepted my invitation and found the time to come . . ." His voice fades into the distance.

Aylin comes to stand next to me. "You amazed me, cousin." There's an odd twinkle in her eyes that I don't like one bit. I meant to stay meek, but now she's seen me extend my claws. Unfortunately, this day has come sooner than I hoped.

"Thanks for cheering for me," I say, equally innocent.

"Anytime." She glides away with her usual grace.

I start to move off, but Ren intercepts me. My entire body stiffens.

"It's rare to find such wisdom in a young lady of your age, Mingshin," he says. "You have my respect, and I hope you'll give me a chance to know you better."

Wisdom? I outsmarted Jieh with a trick. Truth be told, if I were so wise, I would've been able to see through Ren and my cousins long before my murder.

I don't even bother glossing it over. "Your praise is too much for me, Your Highness, and I'm afraid I don't deserve it. As a commoner's daughter, I shall not overstep my station by befriending a prince."

Seething with rage, I curtsy and walk away, ignoring the anger radiating off him.

Two women wait for me at the edge of the archery range. Mai must have been worried about me and gone to fetch Fei. Their loyalty warms my heart.

That night I dream.

I stand inside a vast, magnificent building. White marble pillars support a soaring vaulted ceiling that boasts a map of the night sky. On the map I see carvings of the sun and the full moon, and a background spangled with silver stars. The floor is pure granite, stunningly engraved with an intricate pattern of a nine-rayed star, its beams blazing out in waves. Light permeates the stony walls, seeping through the heavy blocks as if they were made of smoked glass. But there are no windows, no candlelight to account for the brightness here.

A thrill flits down my spine. The structure itself glows, as if it has somehow managed to entrap streams of daylight.

The far wall is covered with gold-encrusted mosaics displaying nine colorful images. The top three show nature: fire, ocean, and soil. In the middle row are vivid portraits of a child waving a giant sword, a woman with her eyes wide open and her ears perked up, and a man with double faces. The bottom three are more abstract, with light and darkness swirling together, a golden ball surrounded by spiraling orbs, and a shimmering gateway leading to a different world.

Nine images and nine-rayed stars. The matching numbers must represent something significant. Like the nine layers of Hell. The nine gates of Heaven.

In the center of the room is something I can only describe as an altar. For one second, it looks eerily translucent, like jade illuminated from within, but in the next, it seems to be created out of pearls.

Yet, what draws my attention most is the crystal jar lying upon the altar. It appears too plain compared to everything around it, but I feel pulled toward it like a sunflower drawn toward the sun.

I thrust my hand into the jar and immediately feel something smooth and solid. The small object hums and throbs like it has a life of its own.

I pull my hand out and look down at my palm.

Every part of me goes still.

I am clutching my five-colored stone pendant.

My mind is a jumble, unable to think. I just stare at it, both perplexed and awed.

A cascade of light blasts from the stone, as bright as if a new sun were being born. Around me, the air explodes with crackles of energy.

I startle awake, panting. A glitter catches my eye. I look down, and all the breath rushes out of me.

My pendant shimmers with the soft light of the five colors embedded within it: blue, yellow, red, green, and purple. I grab it, but my hand instantly jerks away. The stone is scalding hot.

I examine my fingers, expecting blisters, but there isn't even a scorch mark on my skin.

The light slowly fades. A wire of angst tightens inside me, pinching my gut. I've had the pendant my entire life, but something like this has never happened before.

What could be the cause?

CHAPTER 10

"Are you sure you don't want more shadow, Miss?" Mai says. "Miss Aylin spent all morning primping. And Ru told me her dress cost a fortune."

Her dress, paid for with *our* money.

I examine myself in the full-length mirror.

Mai has powdered my face to make my skin as flawless as possible. She's also lined my eyes with kohl and painted my lips bright pink. A gold headdress, made of small flowers linked together, is threaded through my hair, while sparkling diamonds dangle from my ears. Silvery embroidery woven into elaborate designs resembling swans adorns the front of my aquamarine silk gown. The full, billowing skirt shimmers like rippling water whenever I move.

I shake my head at Mai. No matter how much makeup I wear and regardless of how fancy my dress is, Aylin will still be more beautiful. So why bother? Might as well be true to myself: simple yet elegant.

But I will outshine Aylin with my abilities and intellect.

My ears sing with a rush of blood. The day is finally here; I shall secure a future for myself, my mother, and our family business. To do that, I must win King Reifeng's favor.

My excitement is only tempered by occasional anxiety about my pendant. Did it show me the vision? How? *What* was that wondrous place? The building and everything inside it felt so real, like I could touch it all if I only reached out beyond the veil of the dream.

Does my pendant contain magic?

"Shin'ar."

I turn to see Mother walk in.

"You look beautiful," she says. I open my mouth to protest, but she continues, "You *are* beautiful. Don't let other people demean you or tell you otherwise. For true value lies in here." She points at my heart.

I doubt most people share her views, but I nod. "Yes, Ma. I'll make you proud." I sigh. "I wish you could come with me." Only those who received a royal invitation are allowed to attend the banquet.

"You can hold your own. Trust in yourself." Mother cups my face in her hands. "You have the fiery spirit of the sun and the bright heart of the moon. Remember that."

I meet Aylin in the vestibule of the manor. I am stunned, and I swear Mai's jaw flops to the floor.

Aylin looks like a Night Goddess.

Her shining silver gown embraces her tender curves with sinful perfection. It's embellished with a rainbow of colored thread, making it twinkle like a star-dusted sky. Her hair is piled up in a cloud bun, adorned with a tall, gem-studded headdress in the shape of a firebird taking flight. The exquisite makeup brings out her large eyes, sensual lips, and striking cheekbones even more.

"Oh Mingshin, isn't this gorgeous?" she coos and spins. The skirt twirls along with her. It seems as if the stars have been plucked from the sky to dance with her, for her.

A pang of jealousy strikes me. I set a hand upon my heart. The ache fades, and a calm pride fills me. I shall live up to Mother's words.

"Thank you, Mingshin, for gifting me this wonderful dress." Then she gasps. "Why do you wear such little makeup? Let me lend you my artist."

"Thank you, but there isn't time. Let's leave now."

A light of exhilaration sparks in Aylin's expression. "You're right." She waves at her handmaiden, Ru, who comes forward, clutching the wooden case with Aylin's guzheng.

My cousin glances at the case holding my guzheng, which Mai cradles. The light in her eyes dims for a split second, but when she looks at me again, they shine as brightly as before.

Bo appears. He's dressed in formfitting trousers and a blue, knee-length silk tunic; the silver embroidery on the edges is of the finest quality.

He seizes Aylin's hands. "Oh, my dear sister," he gushes. Then he turns and smiles at me. "You look lovely too, Mingshin."

"Thank you, Bo," I reply.

A few maids help Aylin into the coach, carefully arranging her gown so the fabric won't get wrinkled. I, on the other hand, dismiss their service. Mai and Ru climb in after us. Fei rides with the driver while Bo and two guards escort us on horseback.

Our coach rolls out of the main gate, down an avenue lined with a forest of evergreens on either side, and then swerves onto a wide boulevard. Ru fans Aylin so she won't perspire and ruin her makeup. Mai alternates between fanning me and herself, as I instructed her.

"You'll feel better once we are in the Receiving Hall," I tell the maids. "I've heard that in the winter, the royal family has chunks of ice brought from frozen mountain lakes and stored in nearby caves. In summer months, they have the ice retrieved for use on special occasions."

The maids nod in appreciation.

Aylin gazes out the window with a happy smile. "Ah, the city is beautiful."

Indeed. The capital is in a festive mood. Shops are painted in bright colors. The aroma of freshly baked sesame cookies and rice cakes floats through the air. Stages feature female dancers accompanied by men playing reed pipes and flutes. Everywhere I look, customers laugh, cheer, and clink mugs with their companions.

But my mind is elsewhere, tumbling, searching. What will Aylin do to prevent me from performing alongside her? Since she wrung the dress deal from Mother, she hasn't attempted anything harmful. But considering how important this event is to her, there's no way she'll let me share her moment of glory.

I'm sure Uncle Yi has set a plan in motion. With Fei, Mai, and me all keeping our eyes peeled, no trickery or ruse from my cousins could have escaped our notice, but we've had no access to Uncle Yi or his resources. I've tried to get Aylin to talk, hoping she'd let something slip about her father's plot, but she hasn't revealed anything.

I decide to give it one more try. "What if I can't play, Aylin? I'm so nervous."

"Oh, Mingshin, you're going to be fine. We'll be amazing together." She points. "Look at those acrobats! Aren't they wonderful?"

Just like before, she changes the subject fast. I'll get nothing out of her.

Slowly, the streets become wider and emptier, until the coach rolls along a tall stretch of redbrick wall. Inside, magnificent towers rise above the protective bulwark.

My pulse pounds in my ears. We've reached the royal palace.

The first time I visited here, I was filled with nervous excitement. Now, I feel like a warrior going to the battlefield with only one goal in mind: fight and win.

The main entrance is tall, stately copper double doors under a domed archway, flanked by a pair of giant bronze statues of winged qilin resting on marble terraces. Two dozen armed soldiers in chain-mail stand watch, their eyes roaming everywhere. The way they hold themselves, erect but loose, alert but relaxed, gives me the impression of coiled steel.

The palace guards check our invitations and make sure we carry no weapons, then wave us in. Our coach rides up a broad, paved path bordered by rows of elegant trees. Military boots thump on the concrete as soldiers in grey uniforms march past. To my left and right, manicured gardens of vibrant colors stretch into the distance. Farther away, the Grand Throne Room sits proudly atop a tall flight of wide stairs.

I suddenly cannot breathe, can hardly move a muscle. That is where I died, at the bottom of these stairs. That is where my love transformed into hatred, my hope shattered as Ren revealed his monstrous nature. Despite the hot sun, the cold of that day seeps through time to penetrate me, and I shiver.

"Are you all right?" Aylin asks. The way she looks at me, she must be thinking I, a green provincial girl, am awed by the palace.

Let her regard me that way. "Yes," I reply, but she pays me no more heed. She, too, is staring up at the Grand Throne Room, her eyes lit with an inner fire.

A derisive smile tugs at the corner of my mouth. She must be imagining herself sitting on the Queen's throne.

The memory of her standing over me before my death comes rolling back, its details sharpening. The contempt in her mien was unmistakable. Oh, and that beautiful fur coat she had on. When Ren killed the foxes and offered the furs to Aylin instead of me, I acted as if I accepted his explanation that the present was his expression of gratitude for her looking after me. But that was when I started to wonder if Ren harbored more than friendly feelings for Aylin. Later, she tried to give the coat to me, saying I was more worthy of it than she. I berated myself for my petty jealousy and begged her to keep it. She never wore it, and I appreciated her consideration for my feelings, until the day I died.

The coach halts. Aylin exits with the maids' assistance. We are in a giant courtyard, where dozens of carriages have gathered. A few groomsmen take the reins of the horses. While Fei and the guards remain behind, a palace maid comes forward and leads the rest of us away.

We follow her past a rolling lawn with an ornate pavilion in its center overlooking a lake. Then we stand before the Receiving Hall.

The maid addresses us. "You have the royal family's most warm welcome." She turns to our attendants. "Please follow me to the storage to drop off your instruments. It will be a while before the performance begins."

Our handmaidens walk away with her. At the wide-open doors of the Receiving Hall, Aylin draws a deep breath and puts on her best smile—she appears sweet yet dignified.

Floral bouquets line the entry hall on both sides, forming a path to usher us through a foyer and past yet another set of large doors. Once again, I'm struck by its sheer massiveness as we step into the room of polished wood and glossy windows, a honeycomb of light. The ceilings stretch in tall, airy arches dozens of feet above, supported by massive columns painted with sunflowers. Glass balls holding candles in their center hang from above. The floor is made of colored marble set in an intricate mosaic of shapes that form pictures of celestial beings flying among fluffy clouds.

Low tables, surrounded by ebony chairs, line the walls. They are covered with silk cloth and brim with appetizers served in silver dishes. Two huge silver thrones sit on a raised dais against the far wall. On either side, several gilded, cushioned chairs are laid out close to each other.

Noble men and women group together, an ocean of brilliant colors and expensive fabric. They turn in unison as Aylin glides past them. Young women's eyes shine with jealousy while older women put on an air of aloofness, to no avail. Men's eyes sparkle with lust.

No one notices me as I follow my cousins, not even the servants who attend to guests by serving iced drinks.

Bo leads us to a group of young nobles. The men eagerly ingratiate themselves with Aylin, who greets everyone with an aura equally innocent and lofty.

Bo introduces me to his friends. The only reaction they show is slight surprise at my name and the wealth associated with it. They devote their rapt attention to Aylin. A young man strolls over, his fervent gaze fastened on her. Everyone bows to him.

It's Prince Wen. Will he once again fall for Aylin's charm completely in this life?

Like his half brothers, he's fit and handsome. At sixteen, he has a round face, unkempt hair, eyes that gleam like polished chestnuts. He doesn't stand out in either character or achievements among the four princes vying for the throne, but he has one advantage: His mother is the sister of Grand Scholar Yu, arguably the most knowledgeable man in the kingdom and a close adviser to the King on all aspects of national affairs. But I doubt even he could successfully advise Wen on how he might improve his intelligence enough to be of value to the kingdom.

Bo introduces Aylin and me to Wen, but the prince spares no glance my way. I don't let the slight bother me. I wonder if my skin would sour and peel off if I had to keep a social smile glued to my face all the time.

More guests trickle in through the huge set of doors, but neither Jieh nor Ren is present.

Not a surprise. Jieh is always the last among his brothers to arrive at events like this. Just to show how important he is. And Ren doesn't wish to be seen fraternizing with anyone.

Mai and Ru report back to us shortly. Aylin gives Ru a questioning frown, and the maid simply nods. A meaningful look passes between the brother and sister. When Bo smiles, Aylin relaxes.

The exchange is so swift and subtle I would've missed it if I hadn't been watching them closely for deceit. As it is, warning bells go off in my head.

I edge out of Aylin's circle and rush to catch up with Mai, who is leaving with Ru to go to a side room reserved for the attendants.

We wait until Ru disappears into the crowd, then I pull Mai into a corner. "Tell me exactly what happened at the storage."

"Ru told the keeper that her guzheng is for Miss Sun Aylin and that mine is for Miss Lu Mingshin, then we left the instruments with him."

My anxiety grows, like bands of iron stretching across my back. "Do you remember the way to the storage?" I ask Mai.

She nods.

I glance back. Aylin and her new "friends" are engrossed in conversation. "Take me there."

The storage is nearby. Mai points to a small building as we're about thirty yards away. "Wait here," I tell her. I cannot let the keeper recognize her.

I continue walking. The keeper, a scalpel of a man with a flat nose, bows to me as I near.

"I forgot my makeup case in the pocket of my dancing clothes," I say. "I'll be eternally grateful if you're so kind as to let me have a look."

He frowns slightly. "The room is packed full of clothes. It'll take me forever to find it. What's it like?"

"I can find it more easily than you." I hand him a silver tael. "Please. I need my makeup case desperately. I'll die if Prince Wen won't look at me again tonight."

He slips the coin into his pocket with practiced ease and clicks his tongue in exaggerated sympathy. "I'm a compassionate man. It would be unfortunate if Your Ladyship's heart were to be broken tonight. Please be quick."

I recover my guzheng on a table. I take it out of the case and examine it carefully. It seems fine, intact. But when I pluck the strings, dry, scratchy notes tumble out.

My heart jumps with nerves. I spin the guzheng to the side, then I see it: All the strings have been frayed at the edge. They will break as soon as I start playing. Not only would I have no choice but to let Aylin finish our duet by herself, I'd also be disgraced in front of the entire court.

A flame fills my throat, and my fingers curl into claws.

CHAPTER 11

I turn at the sound of footfalls.

The keeper storms toward me. "You're not supposed to touch any instruments, milady. I must ask you to leave immediately."

I fix him with a granite stare. "My name is Lu Mingshin, and this is my guzheng."

His eyes open wide in recognition, followed by a flash of panic. This reaction is enough to confirm my suspicion that Bo bribed him to tamper with my guzheng.

He swallows and draws himself tall. "You lied to me," he barks. "You said you needed to retrieve your makeup case."

"My guzheng is broken. You, as keeper, shall be held responsible."

He cackles, a nervous tremble in his voice. "It must've been broken before your maid handed it to me."

Of course he would deny my accusations. I have no proof. *A malicious but clever move. I'll give you that, Uncle Yi.*

I have no choice, but to bow out of the performance. For now, I just need to make the keeper apprehensive enough so he'll hustle me out the door and forget about me lying to him. We both could be in trouble if the incident reaches royal ears.

"Who's in there?" a girl cries out suddenly.

The keeper's face turns grey. He rushes to the door. "Your Highness," he stutters.

Every muscle in my body locks up.

"Who's in there with you?" a regal female voice asks.

It's Princess Yunle, the deceased Queen's daughter!

The keeper gulps audibly.

"We heard you argue," says the first voice, which must be from one of Yunle's maids.

There's no point hiding. If I'm to be punished, I might as well face it with dignity. Clutching the guzheng, I stride forward and curtsy. "Your Highness." I meet Yunle's intense scrutiny, holding myself straight and proud.

I've always thought Yunle looks the perfect combination of art and edge and sanguine confidence, with eyes like onyx, a chin that narrows like an arrow's tip, and a willowy figure. But I've never heard men call Yunle pretty. They likely find her intimidating: She has a bold, intelligent gaze that causes most to find sudden interest in their shoes, and she always carries herself with brisk, effortless poise.

"Who are you?" Yunle asks.

"My name is Lu Mingshin. I'm supposed to perform tonight, Your Highness. I just found my instrument damaged." I display the tattered edges of the strings.

Her brow arches in interest. Of course, she grew up at the court and knows all about double-dealing and backstabbing. "Are you to perform solo tonight?"

"No. Master Chung was kind enough to invite me to play a duet alongside my cousin, Sun Aylin."

"You are Minister Sun's niece," she says. "The court loves Master Chung. We'd hate to see him disappointed, wouldn't we?" She nods to her maid. "Bring my guzheng here. I'll lend it to Miss Lu."

The maid runs off.

I bow from my waist. "You have my deepest gratitude, Your Highness."

Yunle turns to the man. "You will keep a watchful eye on my guzheng. I don't want a single scratch on it. Later, you'll hand it to Miss Lu's attendant. I trust you won't fail me in such a simple task?"

The keeper nods so vehemently I'm afraid his head may become unhinged from his neck.

"I hope your music is as bold as two women shopping for daggers," Yunle says with a twinkle in her eyes, then she's gone.

I gasp. The young man at the weapons store was the princess in disguise! No wonder she looked familiar. She seemed to approve of my actions back then. Is that why she helped me? But was her motive simple kindness? I know none at the court give out charity just for the purpose of generosity.

The keeper wipes sweat from his forehead with a sleeve as we wait for Yunle's maid to come back. Is he angrier at me for his failure or more scared of Bo's revenge later?

When the maid returns with the guzheng, the keeper carefully slips it into my instrument case.

I leave afterward. On our way back, I tell Mai what happened, leaving out my cousins' involvement. I want to open her eyes to the ugliness and darkness of the beautiful and radiant nobility, but knowing my cousins were behind it would make her too nervous and edgy around them.

"Did someone bribe the keeper to ruin your guzheng, Miss?" Fear strains Mai's voice. "A noblewoman who's jealous of your skill?"

"Likely. This is the lesson I want you to learn, Mai, that there's danger everywhere we step. Be careful and trust no one but ourselves."

"I understand, Miss. We're so lucky the princess agreed to lend you her guzheng."

More nobles have shown up at the Receiving Hall. I spot my uncle conversing with a group of his peers in a corner.

During social events like this, it's common for young men and women to express their attractions by improvising poems for each other. As a matter of fact, it's one of the few occasions in which that's allowed, so almost every single person takes advantage of the opportunity.

I'm sure Aylin has been swamped with admirers, so she didn't even notice I had gone, but Bo did.

"Where have you been?" he asks with a frown.

"Outside for some fresh air." I flash him a hurt look. "No one cares to write me a poem anyway."

He relaxes. "Oh Mingshin. I'm sure a gentleman will come along—"

At that very moment, an uproar at the entrance makes every head turn.

Prince Jieh has arrived, with Yao on his heels. While strutting with his usual superior air, Jieh seems a bit distracted. His eyes roam the entire hall. He must be blind not to notice all the women flocking to him, batting their lashes and waving their silk kerchiefs at him.

I search for my cousin. Aylin stands in the center of the hall and preens like a dazzling goddess, probably hoping Jieh's attention will land and stay locked on her.

I turn just in time for my gaze to collide with Jieh's. He's staring *directly at me*. His lips curve in a delighted smile, then he raises his chin haughtily and looks away.

What was *that* about?

Jieh glances at Aylin, and she immediately lifts her kerchief. But he turns away and waves at some noblemen. They swarm over him.

Aylin strides toward us, her lips tight, and snatches a goblet of wine along the way. She gulps down a few mouthfuls. I fight to hide the grin that threatens to pop out.

Bo lays a hand on his sister's shoulder. She nods, sucks in a breath, then smiles, dispelling the humiliating moment.

Prince Wen reappears, eyes alight with a sparkle. "Miss Aylin, I've been looking for you. I hope you'll listen to a poem I just wrote. For you."

"My pleasure, Your Highness."

They saunter away shoulder to shoulder.

"Mingshin, may I have the honor of offering you a poem this afternoon?"

The voice is warm, gentle, like a spring breeze, but I feel blood freeze in my veins. A fist clamped, I reach for the best smile I can muster under the circumstances, before turning to Ren and curtsying.

As I straighten, my heart trembles with a sudden bittersweet pang at the look on his face, like he only sees me, as if I'm the most beautiful woman in the world.

He holds out a rolled-up piece of bamboo paper. "Please?" he says.

As if entranced, I accept the paper. My hand brushes his, and a jolt goes through me. Hasn't this happened before? On this same day, in another life, Ren uttered these same words, made the same gestures, and gazed upon me in the same way. I was ecstatic.

I still remember his poem. It was gorgeously written and would have touched any girl's soul. I read his captivating verses again and again until every word was etched in my mind, until the paper frayed from the constant rolling and unrolling. Even after the ink faded, I kept it safely tucked away in my most precious treasure box.

But he must have had Aylin in mind when he created this marvelous lyric.

It's all I can do not to throw the bamboo paper right back at him.

I pretend to be perusing the poem, but I fix my gaze on a spot on the floor. When I'm certain that I'm calm enough, I raise my head. "Thank you for the poem. It's very nice."

A hint of disappointment flickers across his eyes at my lukewarm reception. But he composes himself fast and puts on an earnest look. "I wrote it for you in particular. Please keep it."

Not a chance. As soon as I'm out of his sight, the bamboo paper will go in the trash. But I nod and roll it up and put it in the silk sachet attached to my sash.

"I'm glad for this opportunity to speak with you, Mingshin. You don't like me for some reason. Have I done something to offend you? You must give me a chance to rectify this."

"Oh, I'm sorry if I have given you any reason to believe I've been offended, Your Highness. Besides, it would not be my place, as a merchant's daughter, to feel that way."

"Call me Ren, please."

"If you insist, Ren."

He smiles. "A minister's daughter or a merchant's daughter makes no difference to me. A woman's virtue is what makes her worthy in the gods' eyes, and her inner beauty is what warms my heart."

The same lie he told me before, word for word.

I want to laugh and scratch my nails across his perfectly handsome face. *Did you honestly think I'd marry a merchant's daughter? Once all the traitors are put down, I'll wed Aylin and crown her as my Queen. She's a regal noblewoman fit for the position,*" he said to me on my dying breath.

I fight the urge to retch. "It's refreshing to hear that from a royal, Ren," I say evenly.

He appears more relaxed. "I'm glad we have reached an understanding, Mingshin. I hope we'll become friends." He adds with a brighter smile, "Or more."

Oh, Heaven above, he *is* sickening.

My peripheral vision catches someone watching me. It's Prince Jieh. He scowls at us, ignoring the pretty girl practically hanging on him. She tugs at his arm, and he cuts her a glower. She flinches, but doesn't let go.

Nearby, Aylin listens raptly to another young man, who speaks with a blunt tone, his demeanor polite but cool. He's ruggedly handsome, with dark eyes, angular cheekbones, and a proud, hawkish nose.

Aylin would, of course, try to entice Kai. King Reifeng likes him for his decisiveness and efficiency. That makes this eighteen-year-old prince a strong contender for the throne, besides the fact that his uncle is the minister of treasury.

But like Jieh, he lost the competition to Ren. As a result, he was arrested for treason, and his mother, Royal Lady Bai, hanged herself in the cell next to mine.

A trumpet blares. Everyone quiets.

"On your knees for His Majesty King Reifeng and the Majestic Royal Lady Lan," a herald announces.

We kneel.

"Your Majesty, may you live ten thousand years! Your Majestic Ladyship, may you live a thousand years," we chorus.

"Rise and be seated," the herald declares.

The government officials take their assigned places near the front, while the rest of us scatter to find chairs. Aylin, Bo and I choose seats next to each other. A large space is left open in the center, offering everyone a clear view of the thrones.

King Reifeng was dashing, handsome, and physically fit in his youth, so it's baffling that he's been plagued by illness while only in his forties. Still, he remains a formidable figure, commanding obedience and respect. He wears a full-length ivory-colored tunic trimmed with diamonds and stitched with dragons.

Reifeng—meaning propitious and abundant—isn't his real name, but his reign title. A sovereign's birth name must never be said by anyone beneath him, so the tradition has always been that he adopts a reign title as soon as he ascends to the crown.

The Queen's throne to Reifeng's right is empty. Royal Lady Lan, Ren's mother, is seated in a chair next to it. Since the Queen passed away, the Royal Ladies have been taking turns accompanying King Reifeng to formal occasions such as this.

Lan is beautiful, with ivory skin, dainty features and a swan-like neck. She has on a bright purple gown with a belt crusted with opals cinched around her waist. Her headdress is in the shape of a phoenix, with strands of rubies and sapphires dangling from its seven pairs of wings—only a Queen can wear a phoenix with nine pairs.

Lan holds herself with dignity and grace, layered in a calm so deep nothing seems able to shatter it. She used to tell me that I was like a daughter to her and closer to her heart than her own son. Yet, while I was in prison, she never came to see me.

"Welcome, officials and citizens," King Reifeng booms.

"It's an honor," the nobles respond.

Reifeng begins his royal speech about what another prosperous year this has been for the kingdom, and how a better future will come along.

But I'm not listening. Princess Yunle settles next to Royal Lady Lan while the princes sit in the row of chairs on the King's left by the order of age: Kai, Jieh, Ren, and Wen. My attention, however, is captured by the young man seated immediately to the left of Reifeng. Many nobles are sneaking curious, uneasy glances at him.

My scalp tingles. I've never met this man before.

He has the kind of bold look that catches the eye and holds it: stormy brows, a strong nose, a high, aristocratic forehead. His long, dark hair is wrangled back from his face and tied in a ponytail. He exudes a casual pride and confidence that shows in every line of his body.

King Reifeng stands, and so does everyone else. He gestures toward the stranger. "I'd like to introduce our special guest for this celebration. Please welcome Elder Hanxin, a senior member of the Elders Council from Nan'Yü."

His hard-edged words are like stones dropped into a pond, causing a murmur to ripple through the congregation, mixed in with scattered gasps of alarm.

A flutter of nerves flicker through me. What's a member of the ruling body in Nan'Yü doing here? There are no diplomatic relations between our country and his. This Elder Hanxin never appeared in my prior life. Why is he here now? What's caused this deviation?

"Elder Hanxin conferred with me and expressed his interest in reviving diplomacy between his land and our kingdom," Reifeng continues. "As a sign of friendship, he asked for an official visit, and I have granted his request by allowing his entry into Dazhou. I'm glad his delegation came with the approval of Chancellor Lew'Bung, the leader of the Elders Council." The King doesn't sound glad at all. His voice is sharpened steel. "The delegation arrived in the capital yesterday and has since met with the ministry and my counselors." Reifeng beckons toward Prime Minister Ang and Lord Protector Hwa, who are standing at the front of the officials. The two old men bow in return. "The delegation brings regards from Chancellor Lew'Bung and his wishes for peace and friendship."

More murmurs, and I sense a subtle current of unrest growing beneath the calm surface. It's common knowledge that the citizens of Dazhou distrust the Nan'Yüans because of their affinity to magic. I suspect the feelings are mutual, considering Dazhou tried to invade its southern neighbor for centuries and only gave up a hundred years ago after many failed attempts.

What's Hanxin's true purpose for this visit? My stomach spasms and knots. Will his unexpected appearance disrupt my carefully laid-out plan for today?

The King sits down, and everyone follows his lead.

The herald steps forward and gives a dramatic flourish of his arm. "Let the celebration begin."

I shove away my angst. I must stay focused. Whatever surprise factor Hanxin brings into the game, I'll deal with it.

My goal hasn't changed.

CHAPTER 12

We perform in an order based on the herald's drawing of lots. The central space of the hall has been left open to serve as our stage.

The first performer is a young lady who sings a song lauding the greatness of the Jin dynasty. She has an angelic voice. A second noblewoman captivates us with a dance where she waves four colorful ribbons rhythmically through the air as she glides across the floor.

Our attendants reappear behind us. Mai removes the princess's guzheng from its case. Aylin peeks at it, so I grasp the guzheng in such a way that my arm covers the whole length of the strings.

"A duet by Miss Sun Aylin and Miss Lu Mingshin," the herald announces.

We stand and walk forward as the palace servants place a table and two chairs at the center of the stage. We curtsy to the throne, then sit and set our guzhengs on the table. Royal Lady Lan maintains her graceful smile and posture, but King Reifeng's head has begun to droop.

Aylin plucks the strings. Soft, soothing notes cascade through the quiet room.

A stream flows through a forest, in perfect harmony with the singing of an oriole flying among the green leaves. Sunlight shines on flowers, morning dew glistening like gemstones. Tree branches hang heavy with fruit. Beyond them and above, snatches of blue sky slowly darken to gray.

My fingers strum across all the strings, creating a sound like a boom.

A storm descends upon the forest. Lightning flashes and thunder rumbles. Sheets of rainwater pour down upon the trees. A wind roars and leaves rustle until the whole forest howls.

Aylin glances at me frantically, her fingers faltering.

My hands move fast and powerfully; I imagine myself as a tree standing tall and proud, withstanding the storm that threatens to beat me down and snap me in half.

Our duet is supposed to be a perfect combination of soft and hard scores. But I play much more vigorously than in our practice, and the resonance of my raging storm completely overwhelms the tranquility of Aylin's peaceful forest. She's struggling to make herself heard.

Tsen! With one final resounding note, I finish the piece.

A silence falls like a pall over the hall. The nobles exchange looks among themselves, apparently at a loss for how they should react to a woman performing such "masculine" music. Quite a few appear alarmed, even disgusted. Aylin's eyes glitter.

My insides clench like a fist. Have I made the wrong gamble?

Reifeng's booming voice cuts through the quiet. "Bravura. I'm impressed that a young woman plays strong music so well."

Like a dam breaking, compliments flood forth from the nobles.

"What a treat!"

"How wonderful."

Royal Lady Lan waves me forward. "You have delighted me."

I curtsy. "You are most kind, Your Majestic Ladyship."

She puts my hand in hers. "Aren't you Master Chung's student, Mingshin?" She glances at my teacher watching from a corner. "He must be proud."

Master Chung gives me a curt nod of approval. A tight part of me relaxes. I was afraid he'd be angry that I played so aggressively. I suppose he's happy as long as the King is happy.

"I hope to hear more of your playing." Lan lets go of my hand.

"It's my deepest honor." I curtsy again. She's just saying it to please Reifeng. I certainly have no interest in entertaining her.

As Aylin and I double back to our chairs, I dart a grateful look in the princess's direction. She returns a smile.

Both the King and Royal Lady Lan ignored Aylin completely. How much she must be hating me now, but she'll stay composed. There's no way she'd lose control in front of the entire court.

I notice Jieh observing me. I can't quite make out his expression from this distance. Ren's eyes follow me instead of Aylin. Has he found value in me aside from my money, now that I've caught the King's attention?

The thought pierces me like a scalding knife. As in my former life, all he cares about is my usefulness to him.

No, I'm stronger than that. I've done well so far, but I must remain sharp for whatever comes next.

As we return to our seats next to Bo, his jawline twitches, his face pinched in confusion.

"Congratulations, Mingshin," Aylin grits out as soon as we sit down. "I haven't known you to play that well during rehearsals."

"Thank you—Oh, are you angry? I'm sorry. Did I play too fast? I was so nervous. I've never played in front of so many people, not to mention all the nobles and the royals!"

"Enough!" Aylin pulls in a long breath and gathers herself. "I accept your apology."

She turns to Bo. Her back to me, I can't see the look she gives her brother, but he cringes.

A grin teases across my lips as I wonder what Uncle Yi must be thinking right now.

Bo keeps glancing at me, perplexed. I pretend not to notice and focus on the performance instead. He doesn't have enough brains to figure out what happened. Even if he speaks to the keeper, that man wouldn't dare to mention anything about the princess to him.

During the next two hours, my cousins sit rigidly in their chairs. Neither makes eye contact with me or speaks to me.

King Reifeng has slipped into a half slumber, but Elder Hanxin stays alert, his eyes raking across the room. An icy prickle creeps up my spine. He's studying everyone here, weighing us in his mind, but there's no sign on his face of what the scales tell him.

I'll watch out for this newly emerging presence in my game. Something significant must have changed in my current life to have altered his life course as well. He appears only several years older than me. For someone to be elected to be a member of the Elders Council in Nan'Yü at such a young age, he must be extraordinary in either magic or politics.

After the final performance, the herald steps forward again and asks the nobles to deliver their gifts and good wishes to the King.

Their birthday presents range from luxurious jewelry to expensive fabrics, from a gilded mirror to the sturdiest of leather boots, and more. But Uncle Yi's lingzhi beats them all. With its umbrella-sized, golden-colored blossom, there's no doubt the fairy herb is at least a millennium old.

"My family wishes eternal health and longevity to Your Majesty," he says.

Legend has it that a millennium-old lingzhi, a gift from the God of Harvest himself, promotes wellbeing, helps preserve a youthful appearance, and prolong one's lifespan. But fairy herbs are rare and difficult to find, as they only grow on steep precipices in areas with climates that are warm year-round. Many people fall to their death while attempting to procure these exotic plants. My uncle is indeed very lucky, or just very cunning.

For the first time the entire afternoon, Reifeng smiles with approval.

Princess Yunle's present for her father is a jade statuette of the God of Prosperity. The princes try to outdo each other: Jieh's flawless imperial sable furs, Kai's sword with sapphires embedded in the hilt and a silver-plated scabbard, and Wen's imported luxurious wines. They all draw words of admiration from the audience.

Undoubtedly, none of the guests except me could have predicted the gift from Ren: a handwritten replica of the Diamond Sutra, one of the few scriptures left behind by the gods and still in existence. It's written in an ancient language hard to emulate.

"You copied all three hundred pages yourself?" asks Reifeng, amazed. It's believed that when a godly scripture is hand-copied by someone, the gesture of faith will move Heaven and bring special blessings to those honored with such a gift.

Ren bows. "Yes, Father. I pray Heaven will grant my wishes that the Jin dynasty shall stand forever, guided by your wisdom."

The King laughs and puts a hand on Ren's shoulder. "My son has his heart in the right place."

Royal Lady Lan's eyes glisten.

Ren has won this round against his half brothers. Perhaps this is when his circle of confidantes begins to spread lies about his wonderful heart of gold.

Elder Hanxin stands and bows to the King. "On behalf of the people of Nan'Yü, I wish Your Majesty a long, happy life." He speaks in an accent distinct from ours, with long vowels. "The Elders Council has prepared three *liwu* for Your Majesty. *Liwu* is a special Nan'Yüan term *loosely* meaning 'present.' I say *loosely* because we believe nothing is given and everything must be earned."

His last comment rips a collective gasp from the nobles.

"How presumptuous he is!" hisses an old official.

"How dare he insult us by demanding we *earn* his gifts," another growls.

I scoff. What does this lot know about another country's customs? Their expertise lies in drinking, partying, and cavorting. Although I'm also surprised at Hanxin's boldness, I know he didn't lie. Nan'Yüans indeed give nothing for free. Even children have to earn their *liwu*.

Grand Scholar Yu whispers into the King's ear, perhaps counseling him on the Nan'Yüan tradition. I hope he's as knowledgeable as his reputation suggests.

Wen jumps up. "Who cares about your gifts? We have plenty!"

Like an owl striking, Hanxin whips his eyes to him. Wen glares back. Grand Scholar Yu scowls, clearly annoyed by his nephew's stupidity.

"Stay back," Reifeng warns, his voice as rock-hard as his features. Wen swallows and sits down.

"How do you recommend we earn these *liwu*, Respectable Elder?" Yunle asks, tranquil as a lake on a windless day.

"Simple enough. I will put forth three obstacles. If anyone here can overcome them on behalf of His Majesty, the *liwu* are earned. I've been told that everyone gathered here is the elite of Dazhou. I'm sure your guests will easily rise to meet each challenge."

It sounds like flattery but leaves no room for refusal. To not accept his terms would be tantamount to admitting Dazhouans have been cowed by the challenge.

Reifeng's gaze, as sharp as a hawk's, sweeps the entire hall. I'm sure everyone reads the significance in that look.

"I give my respect to the Nan'Yüan customs," the King says.

Hanxin inclines his head in acknowledgement.

A thrill shoots through my veins. While the Elder's unexpected appearance has disrupted my original plan, these challenges may offer me another chance to attain the King's goodwill.

CHAPTER 13

"I shall warn you, my lords and ladies," Hanxin says, "each *liwu* is worth a greater value than the previous one, so each obstacle will get progressively harder to overcome."

Everyone listens intently, aware they'd cultivate the King's favor if they win a *liwu*, because it concerns the honor of Dazhou. It's a rare opportunity for any of the four princes to stand out among their competitors.

Hanxin claps his hands three times.

Two Nan'Yüan men carry a wooden case past us and place it on the floor. One opens it, and the other extracts a tray covered in cloth. Both stand reverently as Elder Hanxin ambles over, his gait perfectly balanced and fluid despite his muscular build.

"I've heard seventeen is the lucky number in Dazhou. Therefore, my first *liwu* is seventeen East Sea pearls," Hanxin announces as he pulls off the cloth to reveal a row of quail egg–sized pearls. They're of top quality with smooth, lustrous and almost transparent surfaces.

"Half shall go to His Majesty. I don't think any of the princes would care for the pearls," Hanxin says, earning a chuckle from the audience. "One third shall go to the beautiful Royal Lady, and one ninth to the lovely princess." He turns to the rest. "Please bestow upon me the honor by dividing the pearls as instructed while keeping them whole."

The nobles put their heads together in discussion.

To keep one ninth whole, the total number of pearls would have to be a multiple of nine. But there are seventeen. So what's the trick?

My mind whirls as I watch my cousins go back and forth between themselves.

Think beyond the ordinary.

Ah, there it is!

I run through the scenario in my head a few times, to make sure I'm absolutely correct. My gut leaps when Bo seems about to stand, but he's only shifting in his chair.

Someone else may claim the prize if I delay any longer.

I stand. All eyes latch onto me as I stride forward and stop near the tray. I bow to Reifeng. "I'd like to try, if you'll allow me, Your Majesty."

"Are you confident, Miss Lu?" His voice carries a steely thread of command.

The consequences could be severe if I lose the Elder's first *liwu*. For a moment, I falter, but then I catch the outraged murmurs of "the audacity!" behind me.

I hold the iron in my spine. Let my audacity be my new mantle. "Yes, Your Majesty," I say.

He beckons me to proceed.

I remove an earring and place it next to the row of pearls. "Let's pretend this is another pearl. Now we have eighteen." I push nine pearls to the left. "This half to the King." Next, I nudge two over to the right. "One ninth to the princess." Leaving six in the middle. "And one third to the Royal Lady." Only my earring remains. I pick it up, step back, and put it on. "And mine is still mine."

King Reifeng pours out a rich, rolling laugh. "Elder Hanxin, are you satisfied with Miss Lu's solution?"

"The first *liwu* has been earned," Hanxin replies with a smile.

I breathe a sigh of relief.

A Nan'Yüan servant kneels and raises the tray above his head. The herald comes forward to accept the pearls.

"Well done, Miss Lu," the King says jovially. "Today seems like a day for you to shine."

"Thank you for the kind praise, Your Majesty."

Someone applauds as I trek back to my chair. From my vantage point, I see that it's Yao. A few others join him, and the applause spreads from there. Once again, my gaze catches Jieh's. His stare is so intense I have to glance away.

"Congratulations, Mingshin." The sugar coating Aylin's voice fails to mask her sour undertone.

"Thank you."

Aylin bites her lip, then leans in and whispers. "Everyone already loves you. I need the King to like me, too. Please give me the solution, if you know how to overcome the next obstacle."

I set a hand on hers. "Of course I will."

The two Nan'Yüan servants open the case again and take out something large draped in cloth.

"They call your kingdom a pioneer in waychess," Hanxin says. "We hear that everyone in Dazhou starts to learn the art as young as the age of three. Our second *liwu* is a waychess set fashioned wholly of lantian jade."

Sounds of amazement pass through the hall like a sudden breeze. Lantian is the purest jade in the world, but like all things precious, it's rare in supply and arduous to mine. It would take Dazhouans months to build such a large set entirely out of lantian jade, but with magic, it was likely a different matter for the Nan'Yüans.

Hanxin yanks off the cloth, revealing the waychess set. The pieces are arranged in such a way it appears that the match has already begun. About three-quarters of the board is occupied by black and white stones, each imagined player blocking the path of the other.

"I found this rather fascinating waychess puzzle in an ancient book," Hanxin says. "Please put down one piece to break the deadlock, while making sure you are still in position to win the battle in the end. Everyone is welcome to try against me, but there's a two-hour limit and then this challenge is over."

People surge to huddle around the board laid upon the wooden case, forming a shoulder to shoulder ring. The Elder must have predicted this situation, for Nan'Yüan servants immediately begin passing out drawings of the position on the board to those who are unable to get close.

Aylin elbows me. I make a stumped face. "Sorry, I'm no expert on waychess."

She gives a frustrated huff and turns to Bo. He shakes his head. Aylin finds her father in the crowd and hurries to him.

Finally, I have a good look at the riddle.

I've studied many waychess master games, but I've never seen anything like this. The whole layout looks too tangled for either side to gain an advantage. I attempt various solutions, but the furthest I can manage is ten steps before I reach a dead end.

Several men try their hand at the challenge, countered by Hanxin playing the other side. Everyone else watching shouts their opinion. I listen. No Dazhouans have succeeded, but their suggestions might give me inspiration. So far, I've heard nothing useful.

Ren approaches the board. *No, he can't win the second liwu!* I rush ahead and watch through a small gap in the crowd, my heart pounding in my throat. He tackles the game, cheered on by the others. Hanxin loses ground quickly, and I start to shake.

Then Ren finds himself locked in, unable to make another move.

The assembly lets out a disappointed sigh. My heart falls back into its rightful place as I wipe my wet palms on my dress.

"Ren played well," someone says next to me.

I turn to find Princess Yunle smiling at me.

I smile back. "It was a tough game, Your Highness," I say noncommittally.

She points. "You saw how Ren pushed himself into that corner there?"

I nod. As I stare and mull over his move, an idea sparks in my head. Quickly, I look down at the puzzle. My mind works fast, conjuring up each subsequent maneuver and every possible counterattack.

My pulse jumps wildly. With a finger, I make a circle around the bottom-right corner of my drawing. "Twelve sacrifices—that's the key," I whisper, barely able to keep my voice from shaking.

Yunle's face lights up. As her eyes explore the maze, I can almost hear the cogs of her brain whirring. "You solved the puzzle, Miss Lu," she breathes. "Go ahead."

"No, your words gave me the inspiration. You should claim the second *liwu*."

"Are you sure?"

"Yes." I give her a reassuring nod. "Go on. The clock is ticking."

"Thank you." Turning away, she bellows, "I'll try."

The nobles recede to give her space, forming a looser circle that allows me to peek between shoulders.

Yunle picks a black piece out of the jar and places it in the bottom-right corner of the board.

"What? You'll lose a dozen pieces immediately!" a man cries, and the others echo him.

Then some of the better players see it. "Wait!" They tell the others, and finally everyone catches on.

Twelve black pieces are sacrificed, but the deadlock is broken. No matter how the white pieces are played, the princess is ready to attack and, step-by-step, knock down her enemy's defenses.

"What do you think, Elder Hanxin?" Yunle asks.

"Your skill is remarkable, princess. The second *liwu* has been earned."

The nobles applaud more enthusiastically than they did for me. Royal Lady Lan embraces Yunle.

Aylin pokes me in the back. "What were you and the princess talking about?" she hisses. "Did you help her?"

Heaven above, has she been spying on me? "She came up with the solution herself." I spread my hands. "I was only expressing my admiration. If you don't believe me, you can ask her."

Aylin looks uncertain. Finally she stamps a foot before storming off.

But I know a seed of doubt has been planted in her mind. What will Uncle Yi make of it when she tells him of her suspicions?

I take a deep breath. Whatever is coming, I'll withstand it.

Hanxin resumes his command in the center of the hall. "Lords and ladies, my third *liwu* is a purebred Beorn stallion."

Gasps erupt through the hall. Everyone has heard of these legendary beasts: They're the biggest, strongest, fastest horses. It is believed that a Beorn stallion can run two hundred miles in a single day without fatigue and charge through enemy lines as if formidable soldiers were mere scarecrows.

But there're only thirty Beorn stallions thought to exist in the world. The secrets of their origin and ways of breeding have been jealously guarded for centuries by the Ziya tribe warriors in Nan'Yü. Occasionally a Beorn stallion is gifted to a foreign monarch. It's extremely difficult to tame a Beorn stallion, but once domesticated, the beast will obey its master for life, never taking orders from another.

"If you'll allow me to show you, Your Majesty," Hanxin says.

King Reifeng leads the way, and the throng of guests flows out of the Receiving Hall in avid pursuit.

An enormous wheeled cage with vertical bars sits in the middle of the courtyard, tended by twenty men. Inside the cage is the most magnificent creature I've ever laid eyes on, with a thick orange-golden mane, graceful and powerful neck, straight legs, and a black coat like polished silk. The stallion's body seems built from a combination of metal, flint, and fire—a solid monolith that towers eighteen hands off the floor. It tosses its head, neighs, and paws at the floorboards, eager to break free of its prison. The Nan'Yüan guards fidget, regarding it with unease.

"Its sweat really is red!" someone shouts. "I thought it was a myth."

Others join him, pointing and marveling.

"How do we earn this *liwu*, Elder Hanxin?" Reifeng asks.

Hanxin doesn't respond right away. He walks around the gargantuan cart with predatory confidence, unhurried, yet there's no mistaking his potential for swift violence.

A tall, brawny man stands a few feet away from Hanxin, his posture alert. Judging by the way his eyes constantly scrutinize the men near the Elder, he must be Hanxin's bodyguard. He has a hard face anchored by an ax-sharp nose, and looks like he'd be mean in a fight. He's the sort you want watching your back, not sneaking up behind you.

When Hanxin finally stops, he looks at Jieh. "I challenge the champion of your annual tournament, Prince Jieh, to a horse race. If he wins, the *liwu* is earned. Of course, we'll use our normal mounts for the contest. Symbolic items of His Majesty's choosing will await us at the end of the track, and whoever returns with his appointed item first shall be declared the winner. If you wish, guards may be deployed along the sideline of the track to ensure a fair match."

There is a single beat of silence, then a shockwave of frenzied whispers sweeps through the congregation.

A fair match. Does Hanxin mean his team won't use magic?

Jieh's eyes burst with light. Before he says anything, Hanxin adds, "To make the game more interesting, we will each ride with a woman. The victor must return with her holding the retrieved item."

A number of ladies blanch at his suggestion. Yunle raises a nicely arched brow.

"Challenge accepted," Jieh says, lifting his chin imperiously.

Wen snickers. Kai's expression is tight—could he be jealous that Jieh is getting another opportunity to prove himself? Ren whispers something to Jieh, making him smirk wider.

Ren is great at flattery, but the candy he hands you is often wrapped in poison.

"I'll ride with a Nan'Yüan woman," Hanxin says.

Reifeng nods to his favorite son. "You may pick anyone, Jieh."

The majority of the ladies withdraw. They're no fools. A defeat will make anyone look unfavorable in the King's eyes. Although inflicting serious bodily harm on each other is strictly forbidden in such competitions, obstruction is not only acceptable but expected, and just a few accidental scars could reduce a woman's value in an arranged political marriage.

Several noble ladies, though, including Aylin and the girl who was pawing at Jieh earlier, remain at the front of the gathering, trying to get Jieh's attention.

My chest clenches.

Ayin isn't afraid of danger when the potential outcome benefits her; I once loved this wild, bold side of hers that's also a part of me.

If Jieh is smart enough, he'll choose Yunle. The princess has been trained in archery and light swordsmanship. Unlike the other women, she would be helpful to Jieh rather than a hindrance. Besides, Hanxin wouldn't dare inflict a single scratch on Yunle.

Jieh bows. "Yes, Father." When he straightens, he says, "Lu Mingshin."

CHAPTER 14

My heart tumbles on a beat. My fingers feel like they're freezing. Then my breath rushes back in a painful heave.

Jieh uttered my name. I haven't heard wrong, for all eyes are focused on me.

I can already see how the race will end.

If Jieh and I win, all the glory will be his. But if we lose, I'll take the blame.

Elder Hanxin must be skilled enough to believe he'll prevail over Jieh in this dare. Why did the prince select me if he hoped to improve his chance of winning? I've been trained by Fei in hand-to-hand combat, but that won't be of much use while he and Hanxin are busy trying to strike each other down.

"Miss Lu," Reifeng says, his tone a deadly whip in its quiet intensity.

I hold onto my outward serenity like a drowning person clutches a floating board, as I stride toward him and bow.

"My son has confidence in you," he says.

Indeed. That pompous ass Jieh has a ridiculously ebullient grin on his face. How dare he drag me into this?

I swallow a quick gust of anger. My voice is even when I say, "It's an honor, Your Majesty."

"You have impressed me in more ways than one, Miss Lu. I trust you will help Prince Jieh in whatever way you can, and in doing so, you will strengthen my confidence in you as well."

"I shall do my best, Your Majesty."

"Get yourself ready."

"I'll help you," Princess Yunle says, tapping my arm.

As the horde starts toward the racetrack, I catch Aylin waving a hand, as if to wish me luck. But there's too bright a twinkle in her eyes.

She hopes I'll lose. When I'm blamed for the defeat at Hanxin's hands and for tainting the kingdom's honor, I'll be punished, perhaps even thrown in jail. I shudder at the thought of our family business falling into Uncle Yi's hands. And dear Ma! What will they do to her after her daughter is disgraced?

A flinty resolve flows through me. For Mother, I must help Jieh win. No matter the cost.

"If I may have my handmaiden with me, Your Highness," I ask Yunle. "She'll be dreadfully worried about being separated from me."

"Certainly." Yunle sends a palace guard to fetch Mai.

We walk together.

"Thank you for letting me claim the second *liwu* for my father," she says. "You are excellent at waychess. How did you get so good?"

"My father was a master player. He taught me well."

"That's wonderful. We should get together sometime to play."

I fold both hands at my breast. "That would be an honor, Your Highness. I look forward to it. And thank you again for lending me your guzheng."

Her smile comes in full, lighting up her features. "Well, it seems we helped each other." In a more solemn tone, she adds, "Use that amazing head of yours to win this race."

After leading me to a room near the track, Yunle instructs a few maids to equip me. Only a year older than me, the princess is half a head taller but just as thin, so her riding tunic, pants, and leather armor fit me. She also orders the servants to fetch her old riding boots. I'm not allowed to carry weapons, though.

When Mai arrives, she looks wracked with nerves.

"I'll be fine," I tell her.

She nods jerkily, then peers around, making sure nobody is watching. Moving closer, she deftly slips something into my hand. "Prince Ren asked me to give you this, Miss. He said the talisman is a family heirloom of his and would protect you from harm. He'll pray for your safety."

I look at the talisman that bears the image of a three-colored koi fish, a symbol of good luck. It's indeed a family heirloom, gifted to him by his maternal grandfather when Ren was born.

He has upped his effort to woo me.

I press down the seed of rage that sprouts in me. Mai shouldn't have accepted a gift from Ren without my permission. Despite my warnings, she trusts him, a prince who always treats her kindly. I won't reprimand her here in front of others, but I must send her a clear message.

While she watches, I toss the amulet onto the floor. She gasps, a hand flying to her mouth. I walk away from her without a word.

Yunle wishes me good luck before she leaves. Jieh arrives soon afterward, a sword strapped to the belt of his light armor. Despite myself, I catch my breath. He appears even taller and broader, and his arrogance seems to have transformed into reassuring confidence. His eyes are bright, as if a fire burned within. He looks the perfect picture of grace and power, his movements like coils of storm surf, fast and mighty.

No wonder so many noblewomen fawn over him.

"Entranced by my charm?" Jieh whispers to me with a coy smile. I roll my eyes.

"What did you say to Yunle that helped her solve the second puzzle?" So he also saw us. "She solved it herself."

"I doubt it. Yunle's waychess skill is mediocre at best. You helped her."

As his smile turns unbearably smug, I blurt, "Why did you choose me, Your Highness? You know this race calls for speed and brutal strength."

He laughs. "I have plenty of those for both of us—"

Whatever else he meant to say is interrupted by a guard announcing Reifeng's arrival. Hastily, I bob a curtsy.

The King grips Jieh's shoulders with both hands, squeezing them. "Win, my son."

"I will, Father. I'll make you proud."

Reifeng nods emphatically. "You always do. The Beorn stallion will be yours when you win."

Jieh drops to one knee. "Thank you, Father." His face glows like the spring sun rising, and his voice shakes.

I gape. The King is quite generous with his favorite son. If we triumph, Jieh's brothers will go mad with jealousy when he claims his reward.

After everyone leaves, Jieh asks me, "Are you ready?"

I'll hate him later. Right now I only have one goal in mind: victory. I can't allow any space for doubt or fear. I make my face stone, my heart a mountain.

As soon as we emerge into the sunlight, the onlookers erupt with thunderous applause. We step onto a platform where Reifeng and Lan are seated, along with Elder Hanxin and his companion, whom he introduces as Lafne. We bow to the King, then to each other, as is required by protocol.

Lafne has eyes like light-brown pebbles, and her skin is the color of honey. There's something strange about her, but I can't quite put my finger on it.

"You may mount your rides," Reifeng says.

We stride to the stallions waiting at the starting line. Jieh vaults onto his horse and extends a hand to me. I swing myself onto the saddle with practiced ease. He turns and raises a brow of approval.

I've never been so physically close to any other man besides Ren. But I don't hesitate as I circle my arms around Jieh's waist and pull myself forward. *Trust your partner.*

The crowd cheers for the prince, and my cheeks vibrate from the sheer volume of the roar. He waves to them. Hanxin and Lafne sit tall and proud, undisturbed in the least by the hoots of derision from the biased audience.

That's when I feel a tug in my chest. My eyes hone in on Lafne's hand. She stares ahead, but reaching under her sleeve, she peels something off the back of her wrist to reveal part of a vermillion tattoo etched into her skin. It seems to be pulsing with a dark, mysterious aura.

I've seen drawings like that before, in one of the forbidden scriptures about magic in Father's secret library.

My heart bangs against my ribs. Should I warn Jieh? Sharing my suspicion may get me into bigger trouble than losing the race.

Then I think of Ren's discarded talisman. He scores a win whenever Jieh loses.

"Your Highness," I whisper urgently. Jieh glances back at me. "The woman with Elder Hanxin is a sorceress."

Jieh's features sharpen, and his eyes run a quick scan of Lafne. "What kind?" he asks.

I let out a relieved puff of air. He doesn't question how I know. He gets straight to the point. It's also reassuring that he apparently knows something about sorcery, since he at least recognizes that there are differences.

As discreetly as possible, I peer at the *fuiin*—infused with magic—inscribed on Lafne's wrist. But with its other half covered by her sleeve, I can't make out its complete form.

Jieh shakes his head. "No matter. Hanxin swore an oath to my father that no members of his delegation would use magic during their stay, or they'd be expelled immediately."

But I'm not sure I can trust the Elder's words. If he doesn't intend to use magic, why bring a sorceress to the race? Besides, she obviously covered up her *fuiin* with something resembling skin to pass the guards' examination.

The referee shouts, holding a small flag aloft. "Ready?"

Jieh's blitheness dissipates, and true steel, honed by a decade of warrior training, shines through. "Let's show them what Dazhouans are made of. That Beorn stallion is mine."

"Go!" the referee bellows as he sweeps the flag down.

Our horses shoot forward. Lafne's sleeve recedes as she jerks back, giving me a glimpse of the full shape of her red *fuiin*. It looks like a perfectly shaped blood drop.

Ice floods the pit of my stomach.

Lafne is a blood sorceress who can tamper with minds.

But I've lost the chance to tell Jieh. I hold on tight as wind whips my face and a dense blur of trees flies past. For the first minute, the animals run neck and neck, kicking up a vortex of dust.

I watch Lafne intently. Will she command magic? If so, how will she initiate it?

To effect blood sorcery, blood must be taken. Then his mind shall be yours until the magic runs its course or the blood sorcery is broken. To break blood sorcery, blood has to be sacrificed.

I recall these words from one Nan'Yüan scripture. Unfortunately, it's all I know about blood sorcery. And I have no idea what it means.

Hanxin pulls his sword free and swings it at our stallion. It's met by Jieh's sword halfway. The violent clash almost throws me off. The two men exchange swift slashes with their dull-edged blades. I strengthen my grip on Jieh, feeling the jolt of the blows through my shoulders.

As Jieh sweeps his weapon down, Hanxin hurls his upwards to thwart the momentum, but Jieh prevails and Hanxin has to withdraw. The prince swings his sword at the Elder in rapid succession. Hanxin's ride neighs and rears.

Jieh spurs our mount onward. I look behind. Hanxin has regained control of his horse and renewed his pursuit. He remains about thirty yards behind us and seems unable to catch up despite visible effort. But my insides keep knotting up in anticipation of whatever Lafne has planned for us.

Two golden cups, guarded by four soldiers, sit upon a tabletop at the end of the track. I jump off and run to fetch the cup marked with Jieh's name.

We've only made it a dozen yards on our way back when Hanxin charges toward us from the other direction, flinging his sword at Jieh. The men hack and block in turn, metal clanging upon metal. For a few seconds, they're entangled, unable to move. When Lafne lifts her arm slightly, alarm flares in my gut. Before I can cry out a warning, a streak of light shoots out from between her fingers.

Jieh withdraws fast, but not fast enough. Something silver, so tiny I can't tell what it is, brushes the back of his hand, drawing blood.

In the same instant, Hanxin peels away, and his steed gallops off.

Jieh glares at Hanxin's retreating back, his face incandescent with fury. His hand is bleeding. How did the sorceress hurt him? And why only a scratch?

Jieh reins his horse around. "I'll wait for this rogue to come back, then I'll challenge him to a true warrior's fight. No more dirty tricks."

Has he lost his mind? "Our goal is to win the race. You can challenge the Elder afterwards. Let's just hurry back—"

"Do not tell me what to do, woman," he snaps.

What in the nine hells? How could he let vanity get the better of him? A sense of urgency winds my nerves tighter as I watch the sorceress retrieve their golden cup.

The sorceress! At the notion, I snatch Jieh's head with both hands and yank it toward me. I peer into his eyes. There's a crazed look beneath his glare.

I let go, my whole body shaking. Jieh is bewitched.

To effect blood sorcery, blood must be taken.

Lafne needed to take Jieh's blood for her sorcery to work.

Palace guards are positioned alongside the track. But how can any bystander tell Lafne is wielding magic when she's working inside someone's head? Hanxin has taken Jieh's arrogance into account as well. It's completely in character for Jieh to act like this when he feels offended.

Even if I report to Reifeng about the use of sorcery after our defeat, Hanxin can claim that I'm lying in order to invalidate the result. And I'll have to explain to the King how I knew anything about sorcery in the first place.

A cold wave of understanding hits me. *I* must lift the spell.

Even as thoughts flit through my mind, Hanxin and Lafne catch up to us.

Jieh puts out his sword, intercepting them. "I challenge you, Elder of Nan'Yü, to a true warrior's contest. No victor shall be determined until one of us is unseated from his mount."

Hanxin's answering smile is wicked, as if it were cut into his face with a knife.

The two men strike at each other vigorously. My ears ring, and my arms go numb in a wash of tingling, from elbows to fingertips. Soon enough, Jieh's attacks slacken, and his defense grows sloppy. He deflects each assault at a maddeningly slow speed, and in the middle of a swing, he suddenly pulls back, giving Hanxin a chance to press his advantage.

A scream builds in the back of my throat. I must do something. If we are unseated from our horse, it's the end for both of us.

To break blood sorcery, blood has to be sacrificed.

Must I bleed the sorceress to stop her magic?

I stuff the golden cup into our saddlebag and focus my attention on Lafne. Like me, she wears tall, sturdy boots and a leather vest that covers her torso. If my guess is right, just a scratch on her neck should do the trick.

The animals are jittery and keep moving. There's only one way to get near Lafne in order to injure her.

I swing my left leg off the horseback to the right, then leap, committing my entire life force behind the dive. Lafne whips her head around. As I crash into her, I claw at her neck, but fall short.

She shoves me off. Then we're both falling. As I collide with the ground, wind explodes out of me in a rush, and I feel as though my bones might crack.

Get up! I scramble to my feet and find Lafne doing the same. She trains her left hand on my leg, and her middle finger glints. I jump to my left. A twinkle of light streaks past a mere inch from my thigh.

Sweat runs clammy against my skin. I've caught a glimpse of the weapon she used to draw blood from Jieh. It's some sort of needle, shot from a mechanism she wears on her finger. The guards must have thought it was a ring and let her keep it. Now she's trying to bewitch me as well.

I hear a surprised grunt. Lafne and I whirl in unison. Jieh has just parried an overhand strike from Hanxin, his movement smooth and powerful.

A shiver of relief darts down my spine. I've distracted the sorceress, so her hold on Jieh has weakened. I turn back to Lafne. Her eyes narrow and her lips part. Before she can fortify her spell, I rush at her and throw my weight on her. She falls, and I pin her arms down.

I scratch at her neck, breaking skin. My heart sings in triumph at the sight of the blood, but then she hooks her legs around my shoulders and rolls, flipping me. Sand sprays around us. She winds up on top, but I hurl her off with a swift twist. As I leap up, she shoots another needle at me.

I whirl away, daring a quick peek at the duel between the two men. My stomach drops like a stone. Jieh is still in Lafne's thrall, waving his sword like a drunkard while Hanxin rains his attacks down upon him. It won't be long before the Elder finishes him off.

My thoughts spin by at a blinding speed. Bleeding the sorceress hasn't broken the sorcery. What should I do?

Lafne keeps unleashing needles at me, and I have to duck. The *fuiin* engraved across her wrist darts in and out of sight, bright and shining red like real blood.

An idea blazes into my head.

But for it to work, I must use myself as the bait.

I shudder. What if I'm wrong? I'll fall under her spell as well.

No risk, no gain.

I swerve to my left to dodge a needle, which puts me nearer to her. When she catapults another needle at me, I sidestep just enough for it to graze my arm. There's a prickly pain, and my sleeve turns red. Lafne smirks, a snarling rictus, then purses her lips as if to cast a spell. In that instant, with her defenses down, I sharpen my focus into one single point and rake my nails across the vermillion *fuin* on her wrist. Blood gushes forth.

She shrieks and lurches backward as though she's been kicked by an enormous brute. A bewildered expression comes over her face, then she sinks to the ground, appearing lost.

Jieh roars, a sound of pure rage. He hacks at Hanxin with such ferocity I wonder if he's gone berserk. Hanxin tries to duck and block the onslaught of blows, but he's faltering and failing fast. Even I see it coming as Jieh delivers his final strike, toppling Hanxin from his horse.

"Mingshin!" he bellows as he rides in my direction.

I blink at the sound of my first name coming from him as I extend a hand. He snatches it and pulls me up. I rise to the saddle and throw my leg over the steed's rump while yanking myself closer to Jieh.

"Are you all right?" he asks, twisting his head around as we gallop on.

"Only a scratch, like you." I'm not sure the same could be said of Lafne. "She used sorcery on you!" I shout at Jieh. "She tampered with your mind."

"I know," he shouts back.

I turn to find Hanxin helping the sorceress back onto his horse. I keep an eye on them as we speed toward the finish.

Deafening cheers greet us as soon as we come into view of the spectators. Jieh and I dismount. A groom runs over to take the reins from him. I pull the golden cup from our saddlebag as we walk to the raised dais.

We bow to the King. I present the cup to him. "I hope we haven't let you down, Your Majesty."

Reifeng glows with pride, seeming to shed a decade off his age.

Hanxin and Lafne return soon afterward. The woman seems disoriented, but the Elder appears gracious enough as he bows to Reifeng. "I concede, Your Majesty. Prince Jieh has earned the third *liwu*."

The King lifts our cup into the air. "I announce Prince Jieh's team as the winner of the race."

The mass roars their adoration. Jieh waves at them with equal enthusiasm. As he turns in a circle, his gaze lingers for a moment on Lafne.

My belly quivers. What if Jieh confronts Hanxin and reveals Lafne's use of magic to the King? I wouldn't put it past him given how much he detests being played for a fool. If so, my limited knowledge of sorcery will be exposed, condemning me to a painful death.

But Jieh looks away, so nonchalantly as if he'd forgotten the sorceress's existence.

My shoulders slacken and I breathe a little easier. For now, I'm safe. Still, I need to find a chance later to persuade him to keep my knowledge of sorcery a secret.

"I hereby reward my third *liwu* to the champion, Prince Jieh," the King says. "I hope you don't mind, Elder Hanxin."

"The *liwu* is yours to do with as you please, Your Majesty."

A murmur spreads among the bystanders, amazement and anxiety the two clearest notes in the changing swell of noise. By bestowing upon Jieh a legendary beast befitting a ruler, Reifeng has stirred the political pot.

Jieh strides to the wheeled cage holding the Beorn stallion. At his approach, the beast rears and kicks its front legs, a mighty movement that sends the floorboards creaking and the wheels skidding. Its caretakers jump, but Jieh stops just a pace away from the magnificent animal and stares into its eyes.

"One day you will be mine," he says loudly enough for everyone to hear. With that he glances at me, then back at the stallion.

My heart does a somersault. Is he thinking of "taming" me? *You'd better not. I won't be yours or anybody else's.*

"I think we've had enough excitement for the day," Reifeng says, and the nobles chuckle appreciatively. "Please join us for dinner, Respectable Elder."

We start walking. As Hanxin passes me by, he turns and catches my gaze. He doesn't appear angry or dejected at all. Instead, he's grinning, the grin of a hunter who has his prey cornered, his teeth flashing like perfectly sharpened fangs.

CHAPTER 15

I take a quick bath in the nobles' guest quarters. With great reluctance, I remove my pendant and set it aside.

When I finish bathing, I put it on first. Mai and the maid help me change back into my blue dress and redo my hair. All the while, Mai chirps like an excited bird about how amazing I was in the race. On the way to the dining hall, I try to catch Prince Jieh but fail to encounter him.

At the entrance, the maid leaves us. Mai and I have a moment alone. I look at her, and she blanches.

"I'm sorry, Miss. I shouldn't have accepted a gift for you from anyone without your permission. Please forgive me. I won't do it again."

"The capital is a treacherous place, Mai. I need all the help I can rely on. I have faith in you and hope to continue to do so. For that, you must heed my warnings not to trust the royals or nobles blindly."

She nods like a chicken pecking at food. That's good enough for now.

While she stays behind, I step into the vast dining hall, a marvelous room with a high-arched ceiling and floor tiled in a multicolored mosaic. Dozens of lamps line the gold-veined marble walls.

Most of the nobles have been seated at two long tables. On a dais, Reifeng and Lan chat airily at the head table, flanked by Elder Hanxin and the rest of the royals.

As soon as Ren sees me, he smiles and strides over. "I'm glad you are safe, Mingshin. I hope my talisman helped."

He looks so sincere that for a moment I almost feel sorry for having discarded his family heirloom. Then I remember the true person beneath his earnest mask.

I gasp, putting a hand to my chest. "Oh, I'm so sorry, Ren. I must've lost it in the struggle."

His eyes blaze, a spark of fire, and his lips tighten into a thin, colorless line.

Let's pour some oil on this fire. "I'd be happy to compensate you, Your Highness. It must've been expensive. Name your price," I plead.

His jaw looks ready to shatter given how taut it's clenched. *I dare you to lose your temper. I hope you do.*

He forces a smile, though it looks as if it might crack his face. "It was an accident, Mingshin. Please don't let money come between our friendship."

The me in my old life would have appreciated his forgiving soul. But now, I realize that if a man can hide his emotions so deeply, I should be frightened of him.

"I'm grateful, Ren."

He nods stiffly. "I shall talk to you later, Mingshin."

I'm offered a seat of honor next to Yunle, right across from Jieh, Hanxin, and Ren. I glance at the two princes on Yunle's other side. Kai has a grim set to his mouth, while Wen looks like he's swallowed rancid milk.

Servants wearing bright livery march in step like soldiers, bringing steaming plates of marbled beef, glazed slabs of venison, braised pork, fried fish, and crispy shrimp, each dish surrounded by rings of nuts, herbs, and peas. There are also numerous fruit cakes, pastries drizzled with honey, coconut rice balls, and buns with various stuffing ranging from pork to celery. Stewards and their many assistants serve endless streams of rice wine, grape wine, and amber wine. The pinnacle of the feast is the dish of fowls: a peacock cooked and presented in its own feathers, a great towering piece of fancy.

"I knew you'd win," Yunle says, raising a wine glass to me.

I return her gesture. "Thanks for your confidence in me, Your Highness."

"I've heard the report from the palace guards. The way you tackled that Lafne woman was amazing. How did you learn to fight like that?"

"I've been training with my female bodyguard. She can beat several men together in a sword fight."

"Was it the woman who accompanied you to the weapons store? She looked strong and fast."

I nod. "Were you looking for anything in particular at that store?"

"Not really. I was just curious. I begged my father often enough that he finally agreed to let me visit places like that. Under one condition, though. I must disguise myself as a man and keep my guards with me at all times. When you walked in like you owned the place, not bothering to dress like a man, I was impressed, even a bit jealous. After you taught the greedy clerk a lesson, I thought to myself, now there's a woman I'd like to meet." She laughs. "But you'd likely have thought it strange if I asked your name as a man."

I grin. "I'm glad we met again, Your Highness, and helped each other."

"Please, call me Yunle." She pauses. "You know, I've always wanted a friend like you."

My mouth falls open. I like Yunle; she's confident, assertive, and smart. But I must heed my own advice. *Do not trust the royals blindly.* For now, though, I can at least accept her goodwill. I clink my glass with hers. "To the beginning of our friendship, Yunle."

She laughs a hearty sound. "To our friendship."

We both take a sip.

Yunle drops her voice conspiratorially. "Jieh has been looking your way every ten seconds."

I almost choke on my wine. "How do you know? You don't have two pairs of eyes."

"Believe me."

I glance at Jieh. He's engaged in a lively conversation with Hanxin. I may have underestimated him. He must be mad at the Elder for cheating, but he puts up a convincing charade.

His gaze jumps to me, holding mine. A faint warmth blooms across my cheeks. Quickly, I turn away to hide my face behind my cup.

Yunle chuckles, and then it dawns on me. "No way," I blurt. "You must be imagining things." She can't possibly mean Jieh is romantically interested in me. The more I think about it, the more ridiculous it sounds. "Have you heard the story of Jiarmu in Foism, the dominant religion of Ude?"

"Shame on me. Although my mother was an Udess princess, I've only read some recent history about Foism. Pray tell."

"Jiarmu was a demigod famous for his unrivaled beauty and strength. He fell in love with himself and couldn't bear the company of others. In the end, he drove everyone away and died of loneliness." I raise a brow. "Doesn't that remind you of someone else who seems endlessly fascinated with himself?"

Yunle winks. "If Jieh reminds you of Jiarmu, you must think he's very handsome."

"He is, but there're many handsome men who are ugly inside. One just needs to look deeper."

I follow Ren's gaze to find it snared on Aylin. It's obvious that he adores her. *While he tries to woo me.* It feels like a dagger thrust into my gut, and I suck in a breath.

Why does it still hurt? I'm stronger than this.

I turn back to Yunle. "Believe me, I'm content to be without a man. What about you?"

She sighs. "Love doesn't matter to a princess anyway. Marry a foreign prince for some political alliance. That's the only purpose we serve."

Memory jolts me. In my former life, she indeed was married off to another kingdom. Although she was to be Queen, I very much doubt she lived a happy life with a total stranger, in a distant land with a vastly different culture.

I wasn't close to Yunle then, but now that I know her a little better, I'd hate to see her become a political sacrifice, to see that passionate, fierce spark in her dim and vanish. She deserves so much more.

"Sometimes I wonder why Father even bothers letting me participate in his Royal Council meetings," Yunle adds.

That surprises me. "His Majesty lets you attend?"

"After years of me peeking in and listening through doors or the cracks between rafters," she grins at my wide-open eyes, "he finally granted me permission to sit in at the Royal Council. But I'm not allowed to speak up. I just sit in a corner and listen. Perhaps he hopes my knowledge of state affairs will better serve Dazhou's interests once I become a foreign Queen." Her smile turns bitter. "My brothers can actively present their proposals and express their opinions whenever they like."

"That's unfair, but still better than being totally left out," I say.

"I suppose you're right. Let's drink to that."

We down our glasses.

Soon afterward, the King and Royal Lady Lan rise to leave. Elder Hanxin departs next. I finally have a chance to speak to Jieh. But as soon as Yunle stands, he pulls her aside and mutters something to her. Together, they vanish through the back of the hall.

I glance around. Most of the nobles are still deep in their cups.

Uncle Yi approaches my table. A smirk spreads over his features like oil on water. "You've brought honor to our family, Mingshin. I shall speak to His Majesty. You deserve a worthy reward for what you accomplished today."

White-hot anger boils up inside me. He's going to take all the credit for himself. He has the King's ear, and with the right words, he can make it sound as though my success was due to him and his family connection to me.

If only I could speak to the King before he does. But how can I possibly approach Reifeng without him summoning me first?

Even after Uncle Yi leaves, I sit tight, my jaw clenched and my cheeks burning.

Yunle reappears and waves me toward her. She grabs my hand, her face serious and her voice barely above a whisper. "Jieh asked me to let you know that he's telling Father Lafne used sorcery during the race."

My heart contracts and my blood turns to ice. Jieh is probably reporting to the King right now. Just a minute ago, I was hoping for an audience with Reifeng, but now all I want is to flee and hide.

"He told me that he recognized Lafne as a blood sorceress who can tamper with minds," Yunle continues. "And that he told you this before the race, but it was you who worked out how to foil her sorcery and break her spells."

Wait! Jieh *lied* to Yunle about who identified Lafne as a sorceress and the type of magic she commanded? I stagger with relief even as shock jells my tongue. Jieh will probably tell the King the same lie, or he already did. Why? Granted, possessing knowledge about sorcery may be considered an advantage for a future ruler, although for everyday citizens it's treated as a crime. But a King like Reifeng has zero tolerance for lies. Jieh could lose his chance for the crown if his father finds out the truth. Why would he take such a risk?

"Be careful. My father may summon you," Yunle says. After giving me a penetrating gaze, she turns to leave.

"Thank you, Yunle," I whisper.

She nods. As soon as she disappears, a steward approaches and conveys the King's command to speak to me.

I trail a guard out of the dining hall and across a courtyard. Night has fallen; a large moon hangs among a scattering of brilliant stars. We enter another building and walk along a carpeted hallway to King Reifeng's study. A band tightens around my ribcage with every step.

What will the King ask of me? Does he believe Jieh?

The hallway is eerily silent, its walls depicting hunting scenes carved into pure white stone. The guard leads me to a set of double doors watched over by a pair of armed men. They open the door for me.

I square my shoulders, shaking off the pressure building in my chest, and step in.

A dangling candelabra bathes the study in soft, creamy light. King Reifeng sits behind a dark mahogany desk polished to a mirror shine. His face is a mask, but I sense a fearsomely cold rage beneath its serene surface.

Jieh stands next to him. His posture is relaxed, but the tautness around his eyes suggests he's fully aware of the risk he's taking by lying to his father.

I kneel. "Your Majesty."

Reifeng gestures for me to rise. "I've heard my son's account of the race. Let's hear it from you, Miss Lu."

I force steadiness into my voice. "Right before the race, Prince Jieh told me that he believed the Nan'Yüan woman was a blood sorceress who could manipulate minds, because of the blood drop tattoo she had inscribed on her wrist. But he assured me Elder Hanxin had vowed that none in his delegation would use magic during their stay. I was relieved, until Prince Jieh started acting strangely." I relate the truth about the rest of the race.

A chill emanates from Reifeng. "Everything we speak of will remain in this room and be carried to your tombs," he says.

Both Jieh and I bow. "I swear it on my life, Sire."

Reifeng falls silent, his forehead creased in thought.

A bolt of sharp dread spikes through me. I will either be rewarded or eliminated to ensure the secret is never revealed. It's a thin line Reifeng straddles, and I must pull him to the side beneficial to me.

Jieh pipes up. "Miss Lu has found a way to help us defeat blood sorcery if we encounter it in the future, Father." He smiles my way. "I haven't forgotten the first puzzle she solved this afternoon, either."

I, too, must make the King see the value in me. "I'm glad to serve, Your Majesty, as a proud citizen of Dazhou. My soul and my mind are yours, and I'm confident you will find my service useful for more than just solving puzzles and helping to win horse races."

Reifeng gives a curt nod. "You certainly have an intuitive mind. I'm confident that I'll find good uses for it." He pauses. "I don't let contributions to the kingdom go unrewarded, Miss Lu. What prize do you claim?"

I try hard not to shake with excitement. "I only ask that my mother, Sun Lili, and I have full control of the Lu family business so that no others, whether they be extended family members or competitors, shall be able to lay false claim to it."

"Granted. It shall be made into a royal decree starting tomorrow."

My heart roars with triumphant joy. My father's relatives will never dare to lay claims to our family business or properties from this moment on. We no longer need Uncle Yi's influence to protect our inheritance.

I promised I would control my own fate. This is only the first step in a long journey, but I will get to my destination.

As I take my leave, I wonder what will happen to Hanxin and the rest of his delegation now that the King knows the Elder has broken his oath.

I'm just outside the building when a man's voice calls from behind, "Mingshin."

There again. First name only. I turn and curtsy. "Your Highness."

"I'll be participating in the upcoming Elite Hunt, an invitation-only event." Jieh looks down his nose at me. "I shall extend to you the honor of accompanying me."

I stop just short of rolling my eyes. I know of the Elite Hunt, which always starts on the first full moon of autumn. "What an honor, Your Highness, but I'm afraid it's too much for me to bear. I shall leave it to a lady more deserving."

I turn around to walk away, but he moves fast to intercept me. "This is the first time I've asked a woman . . ." He struggles for a moment, a storm cloud building on his face. "You don't know how many women would throw themselves at such an opportunity."

"In that case, why doesn't Your Highness extend the honor to one of those lovely ladies? Oh, may I make a recommendation—"

"Forget those stupid women!" He pivots on his heel and stalks off.

I take the long way back to the dining hall. If he'd asked nicely, I would've accepted his invitation despite my misgivings. After all, he protected me by lying to the King, and his gesture helped me secure my family business.

Suspicion wriggles up from the shadows of my mind. Has he found my family wealth useful to his cause as well, like Ren? But that doesn't make much sense. Ren needs my money; Jieh doesn't. What could he possibly gain from my affection? A union with either the prime minister's or the grand general's daughter would better suit his purpose.

Whatever his true intent is, I will discover it.

CHAPTER 16

Mai rushes toward me as soon as she sees me. "Miss Aylin has left!" she cries. "Prince Wen escorted her. I begged her to wait, but she said the King had ordered you to stay at the royal palace overnight." She hesitates for a moment before forging on. "Prince Ren said I should go home with Miss Aylin. But I . . . I didn't believe them. And my place is with you, Miss. I dare not leave you here alone."

I hold her arms and smile at her. "You've done the right thing, Mai." I let go. "The King just needed to speak to me."

"They lied to me, Miss." Mai sniffs, partly in indignation, partly in panic. "How . . . how are we going to get home?"

"Don't worry. We'll find a way."

She follows me into the dining hall. Only a handful of men still remain, Ren and Yao among them.

Ren looks shocked at the sight of me. "Your cousins thought my father intended to keep you here all night," he says. "Please let me take you home, Mingshin."

I have a feeling that he stayed behind for this. Bo probably left early to give him the opportunity, as a favor for the help he received from Ren in saving the lingzhi.

"Thank you, Your Highness, but I shall not bother you this late." Just the thought of being confined in a tiny space with this loathsome creature and breathing the same air makes me nauseated. I'd rather ride with a lizard.

Jieh emerges from the entrance to the dining hall.

"It's not a bother at all," Ren says. "I'll be glad to—"

Jieh reaches me and puts a possessive arm around my shoulders. "I'll escort Mingshin home."

He spears Ren with a challenging gaze. The few straggling nobles peek our way furtively. The veins pulse in Ren's temple, and red spots mar his cheeks.

I'm almost disappointed when he lets out a long breath and sweeps out of the room.

Jieh waves a guard over. "Inform the captain to prepare my coach."

The guard bows and hastens off.

Jieh gestures at Yao to follow, then steers me out of the dining hall. Mai shuffles after us. As soon as we are outside the building, I pull away. Jieh's arm stiffens, but he lets go.

"Thank you, Your Highness, for everything," I say as we continue walking.

That surprises him, for he almost trips over his own feet. He stares at me, a honeyed curve to his lips.

Yao catches up with us and claps Jieh on the shoulder. "Have you thought of a name for the Beorn stallion?"

"No. *My* Beorn stallion deserves a worthy name. It will take time."

"You want to wager how long it'll take you to domesticate that beast?" Yao asks.

Jieh keeps his back straight, calm dominance radiating from every inch of his body. "I'd give it three weeks."

Three weeks! How conceited is he to think he can tame a legendary beast in such a short amount of time? Some things never change.

Yao laughs. "I'll hold you to your word, Jieh."

When we reach the courtyard where the coaches gathered earlier, Fei is waiting alone, her lips pursed and her fists tight at her sides. She relaxes a little when she sees me.

Jieh decides that my maid and bodyguard will ride in Yao's carriage while I accompany him in his. Since we're stranded here, I've little choice but to accept this arrangement.

Jieh's coach is driven by two men with tree-trunk forearms, barrel chests, and broad shoulders. Inside, the leather seats are draped in silk blankets heavily fleeced with soft furs. It feels like I'm sitting upon clouds.

"You don't like Ren very much, do you?" Jieh asks as soon as he plants himself across from me.

My spine stiffens. "You misjudge me."

He doesn't press, but reclines, clasping his hands behind his head. "I sent people to look into Ren after you led me to the archery field the other day. It turns out your impressions about my gentle, unassuming half brother were accurate and he isn't as he presents himself. Quite the contrary, he's ambitious, cunning, and perhaps more insidious than Kai. While my other half brothers aim at me as their main target, dear Ren has been quietly gathering supporters. Mostly minor officials whose voices my father hasn't bothered to hear, but combined, they could be a formidable force."

Some of the tension flows out of me. At least in this life he won't underestimate Ren. "I'm glad you see him clearly for what he is."

"You need not worry. My eyes are open." He unclasps his hands and leans forward. "I never got to thank you for what you did in the race, Mingshin. I couldn't be happier that I picked you as my partner." He grins. "A seasoned warrior couldn't have done better than you."

I'm so shocked to hear admiration from *him*, I gawk.

"I'm just curious," he says. "How did you learn about magic?"

The blood drains from my face.

"Never mind," he says quickly, touching my arm. "Forget that I asked. It doesn't matter. I lied to my father anyway."

I regain a bit of color. "Why did you lie to the King?"

He throws me a look that says, *isn't it obvious?*

"You lied for *me*?" I murmur, incredulous.

"My father detests magic. If he hears that you know anything at all about sorcery, he won't take kindly to you. I'd hate to see you punished for helping me."

"You said you knew the sorceress tampered with your mind."

The first hint of irritation creeps into his expression and voice. "There were moments I felt like I was slipping in and out of a dream. I alternated between having command of my body and none at all. It was happening the whole time you were fighting the sorceress."

So I was right. He recovered partial control of his senses when Lafne's mind manipulation was weakened by my attack.

"But *you* beat her, Mingshin," he says, brightening up again. He moves closer and fixes me with an intense look. "Will you please accompany me to the Elite Hunt?"

Ren didn't invite me to either Elite Hunt during the two years we were together. He claimed he didn't wish to put me in harm's way, but I wondered what danger there could be, since most of the women would only be waiting at the campsite while the men were off hunting wild animals. I was disappointed—the adventurous side of me had anticipated his invitation and relished the prospect. In the end, I told him

I appreciated him caring about my well-being, although deep down I suspected his true reason was that he thought I would be of no use to him during the hunt; I could offer no counsel at a competition in which only physical strength mattered. Thinking back on it now, I realize my absence also left him free to pursue Aylin there.

Anger at Ren's treatment of me, but more at myself for allowing it, rears up in me like a snake. Quickly, I shove it down and return my attention to Jieh.

Although there's still a haughty slant to the tilt of his mouth, he appears eager, even nervous, as he waits for my reply.

"I'd be glad to join you," I say.

He beams, transforming his face from strikingly handsome into far too appealing in less than a heartbeat. A breathless little flutter goes through my chest.

He cups my chin, his eyes glowing. He smells like bright, sunny days. Heat radiates from my face as his fingers graze my cheek. My pulse ratchets up to a thunderous beat as he leans nearer, enough that we breathe in and out together.

He's going to kiss me; I feel it in every fiber of my being.

He's just using you! My mind shouts at me.

I gasp and draw back, so suddenly that my head bumps the wall behind me. I yelp.

Jieh grabs my arm. "Are you all right?"

"Y . . . yes," I stutter.

He releases my arm, and we lapse into an awkward silence. A dark seed of doubt takes root. Why did he invite me to join him on this hunt? Why did he try to kiss me?

I look at him. He's reverted back to his smug self, as if his fleeting moment of tenderness had never happened.

I will myself to become as hard as iron. "Let's be frank with each other, Prince Jieh. If there's anything you believe I can do to help you attain the throne, I'll gladly make a deal with you." Wen doesn't stand much of a chance. I hate Ren and distrust Kai. But there's at least a measure of goodwill between Jieh and me. "I'll help you all I can in your quest to become the next King so long as you promise to uphold the royal decree that maintains my mother's and my full control over my father's business." I swallow and sit up straighter. "I hope you'll accept my honest pledge and tell me what you want from me."

His eyes widen in disbelief, then burn so fiercely I fear they'll throw sparks. His shout is the bellow of a wrathful god. "Silly girl! There's nothing you can offer me. I already have everything I need. How dare you even suggest that!" He glances around wildly like a beast searching for something to tear apart.

Horror coils in my gut. He'll kick me and my companions out of the coaches, leaving us stranded on this dark street.

His glare pins me like a dart. "All I want is—forget it!" He stares out the window, ignoring me.

I sag in my seat. He's not going to throw us out.

We fall back into silence, but my mind howls with thought.

Why was he outraged at my proposal to help him become King, which would serve his own interests? "All I want is—" What did he mean to say?

A notion drops straight and bright into my head. Yunle believes he's romantically interested in me.

A thrill races through me like fire. I do find him attractive. He's handsome, smart, and genuine, or at least much too proud to wear a disguise.

But everyone around me thought Ren loved me as well.

That memory douses the fire like a bucket of ice water.

There's only one thing Ren holds dear: power. Jieh is no different. He wants to be the next King. For all these men who chase power relentlessly, love is a synonym for "silly games." They'll use you, wring you dry, and cast you aside once you're no longer of value to them.

Perhaps Jieh is just tired of beautiful but empty-headed women and now seeks some new thrill with a different type of girl.

Heaven above, I almost let him kiss me. He appeared so sincere I let my guard down. But that won't happen ever again.

When we arrive at our destination, Jieh helps me off the coach without a word. Fei and Mai come out of their coaches to join me.

The main gate, made of elaborately carved iron, is framed beneath a high wall. It's closed now, but the two lanterns hanging on either side give off enough illumination. Fei approaches the gate and knocks. It opens immediately. Mother and Uncle Yi rush out, followed by Hui, Ning, and a few servants holding lanterns.

"Shin'ar," Mother cries and hugs me. "Thank Heaven you are home."

I return her embrace, guilt needling my insides. She must've been terribly worried.

Uncle Yi bows to Jieh, greets Yao, and invites them both inside.

Jieh waves him off. "It's too late. We must leave now."

Mother curtsies to Jieh. "Thank you, Your Highness, for bringing my daughter home."

"My pleasure, Mistress Lu." He glances between me and Mother, then nods at Uncle Yi. "I shall see you tomorrow, Minister Sun," he says and is off with Yao.

Uncle Yi gives me a significant look—sure, I was escorted home by the hero of the day, while his daughter came back with a dolt of a prince—then he's all smiles again. "Come in, Mingshin. I'm glad you are home. Everyone told Bo and Aylin that the King would keep you in the palace all night, so they left on their own. I scolded them, and they were upset for leaving you behind; Aylin cried. Your Ma and I were just going to leave for the palace to fetch you."

"Thank you, Uncle. Please tell Bo and Aylin it's all right and that I don't blame them."

"You have a good heart, Mingshin. They'll be happy to know you came home safe. Sleep well."

How much longer will my uncle be able to keep that smile on? I can't wait for the day it's scrubbed off his face.

Once we reach our dwelling, I remove Ren's bamboo paper from my sachet. I tear it into shreds and dump them into the trash with more force than intended.

"What is it?" Mother asks.

"A stupid poem from a drunken nobleman," I say.

Mother wants to know everything that occurred at the banquet. We share her bed so I can relate the events to her.

"Are you sure it was your uncle's idea to have your guzheng damaged?" is her first question of the night.

"Yes. Who but Aylin had the motive? Uncle did it for her."

Mother is silent, her brow knitted.

I skip the poem exchange part and jump right to Hanxin's three *liwu* and obstacles. Pride shines in Mother's expression at my success, and terror widens her eyes when I mention that *Prince Jieh* identified the Nan'Yüan woman as a sorceress—I don't want to worry Mother with the fact that he's aware of my knowledge of magic.

"You have the fiery spirit of the sun and the bright heart of the moon," she says at the end. "You showed them, Shin'ar."

My throat tightens. Hearing her praise still does that to me. I won't fail her again.

"Was it necessary?" Mother says when I tell her about the reward I reaped. "The Ministry of Justice already dismissed your Baba's relatives' claims."

"The verdict from the Ministry of Justice isn't final. If I didn't obtain a royal edict, Baba's half brothers could still appeal their cases under different circumstances." *For example, Uncle Yi could instigate them to do so if he doesn't get what he wants from us.* But I can't voice that to Mother yet. I may have shown her a glimpse of my uncle's devious character, but she still doesn't believe he's evil. "We can't always rely on Uncle to solve problems for us. After the royal decree is announced, Baba's business will be forever out of the reach of his extended family."

"I trust your judgement on this," Mother tucks a loose hair behind my ear. "Something is troubling you."

"I've been thinking. Did Aylin really assume the King would keep me overnight at the palace without an explicit order? No. She was mad at me and abandoned us on purpose. If Prince Jieh didn't happen to be there, I would've been stranded with no way to come home."

I don't bother to mention Ren's offer. I exaggerate how dire my situation was, because I know Mother gives no room for negotiation where my safety is concerned. I hate to lie to her in any shape or form, but right now she needs a little push. The sooner I make her see the true colors of my uncle's family, the better.

As expected, a hot ember of anger flares in Mother's eyes.

"Ma, I think you should return home," I say.

"I should? What about you?"

I bite my lip. "I have unfinished business here."

She frowns, then gasps and snatches my hand. "Have you an interest in Prince Jieh? He's very handsome and has been nice to you, but—"

"Oh no, Ma!" I hear her kind of horror reflected in my own voice. "I must stay in Jingshi. This fight for the crown is affecting all of us.

Knowing which way the political winds are blowing is vitally important for our family business."

Ren must fail. I'll see to that.

I have another reason to remain in the capital. I need to find out what granted me this second chance and why. Since both my old life ended and my new one began in this city, the answer has to lie somewhere here as well.

Mother's gaze is firm, her chin set at the same stubborn angle as mine. "If you are determined to stay, I'll stay, too." She smiles. "It's time we buy a new residence for ourselves."

On the following day, Aylin and Bo congratulate me and Mother for permanently securing our family business. They also convey their father's blessing, but he's personally unable to join us for dinner due to a prearranged obligation.

I suppose even my uncle finds it too hard at the moment to keep up a cordial pretense after losing the leverage he had against us.

But he won't give up on his desire for our family wealth. What will be his new strategy? If he supports a prince that doesn't look favorably upon us, and if that prince becomes the next King, he could overturn Reifeng's edict and hand our family business over to Uncle Yi as a reward for his loyalty.

Whoever Minister Sun supports for the throne must fail. I'll make sure of it.

Despite my determination, a new kind of worry gnaws at me. Elder Hanxin's appearance in this life may mean I'll follow a very different path this time around; I must challenge my instincts and perceptions, as I can no longer predict what will happen in the near future.

CHAPTER 17

A week later, Yunle invites me to visit her in the princess's wing of the royal palace. Upon our arrival, Fei stays with our coach and Mai goes off to make small talk with the other attendants in the kitchen. I follow a maid to the tearoom, which is artfully arranged with polished wood furniture, a leather couch, and cushioned chairs. Silk brocade drapes frame a wall of windows that let in brilliant sunlight. The lacquered wood floor, scattered with plush woven rugs, gleams like polished copper.

Yunle introduces me to her ladies-in-waiting. We exchange pleasantries. They compliment me on my music, and I thank them.

Yunle dismisses them and asks me to sit across from her. "I'd like to play waychess with you. Promise me you won't hold back. I won't improve if you do."

I smile. "I shall oblige with pleasure."

A maid puts a waychess board on a tea table and leaves. As we play, I tell Yunle of our search for a new home—it was with some effort that I persuaded Mother not to share our plan to move out with Uncle Yi yet. "We've looked at a number of estates, but they aren't ideal."

Yunle muses for a bit. "I have a residence in mind. The seller is a kind man who owes me a small favor; I think the location will be to your liking. I shall steer you toward it if you're interested."

I clasp my hands together. "That would be wonderful."

We decide on a time to meet for a tour of the estate next week.

Treading lightly, I ask, "Elder Hanxin's delegation still stays in the envoy's manor house just outside the royal palace, doesn't it?"

"Apparently so," Yunle replies.

"After the incident at the horse race, I was hoping they'd be expelled from Dazhou."

Yunle gives me a sharp glance. "Well, given how involved you already are . . ." She lowers her voice, her dark eyes intent. "What I'm about to tell you, you must guard your tongue and not share with another soul."

I nod, my whole body strung tight.

"Father confronted Hanxin, but he denied any involvement, saying Lafne must've gone against his order. Jieh was there, along with only two other people, Grand General Chen and Commander Bai of the royal guards. Jieh said . . . Hanxin was furious and seemed genuinely astounded. Then the Elder summoned Lafne and slit her throat in front of everyone."

I nearly drop the game piece I'm holding, my breath quickening. Hanxin killed the sorceress just like that? Seconds pass before I find my voice again. "And your father believed Hanxin?"

"Maybe. But it doesn't matter anymore. From their conversations and the information the spies collected, Father believes Hanxin has some ulterior motive for coming to Jingshi, like he's looking for something very important to Nan'Yü. Father wants to keep him around to figure out what he's searching for."

I set my piece down, careful to keep my hand from shaking. Hanxin has another purpose for visiting Dazhou, just as I suspected.

And Yunle has told me more than I asked for, including things I'm not supposed to know. Does that mean she trusts me? But why would she, after only being my friend for such a short time? Ren also liked to discuss political matters with me, especially the kind only the royals were privy to, but he did it so I could help him devise strategies to gain the upper hand. Surely Yunle isn't like him. But what do I really know about her?

"How did you recognize Lafne as a sorceress?" Yunle asks.

My heart stops. How did she—

"The moment Jieh told me, I knew it was you, not him," Yunle says quickly. "I apologize for my bluntness. But rest assured I ask it out of mere curiosity." She grins as she puts a piece in the middle of the board. "I confess: I've sneaked into the forbidden section of the royal library to learn a bit about Nan'Yü and its magic."

Relief courses through me. If she wanted to report me, she would have done it by now. I believe she's sincerely curious.

Truth be told, I don't know what prompted me to look down at Lafne's hands except feeling that strange tug in my chest. "I glimpsed the blood drop–shaped tattoo on her wrist. It's called *fuiin* and supposedly imbued with magic. I read about it while studying Nan'Yüan culture."

"You did?" Her brows climb. "That's amazing. How did you learn about their culture?"

"My father taught me. Before the knowledge of magic was banned a decade ago, he had traveled often to Nan'Yü to trade." I spot a weakness in Yunle's game strategy. She's going to lose in a dozen steps if I play carefully.

I ask her something I've long been curious about, which even Father had no answer for. "Do you know what led the King to . . ."

"Move all the books on magic into the forbidden section of the royal library? Order citizens to either hand in such books or burn them, on pain of death?"

My belly coils up. *Father managed to hide his entire collection of scriptures in a secret place.* Is Yunle testing my reaction to her words?

But her eyes are fixed on the waychess board. I relax a little.

"It's complicated," she says after a brief pause, and I sense she knows more than she's likely to share.

Keeping my voice even, I say, "What's your opinion of Nan'Yü and its magic, Yunle, if you don't mind me asking?"

"Well, we're told to be wary of magic, that it's inherently sinful, but wasn't magic granted by the gods themselves? Besides, didn't Nan'Yüans and Dazhouans originate from the same ancestors? You must know more about the topic than I do."

During our history lessons, Father often taught me how to separate myth from fact. "Legend has it that Nan'Yü was founded by a people who helped the gods defeat ancient demons and drive them forever from our world. When the gods ascended to Heaven, they awarded these brave men and women divine magic. That group of people never left the land of their forefathers, which is said to be where the last battle against the demons was fought. Eons passed, and Nan'Yü prospered with a growing population. Many non-magic people were also born; after being treated as second-class citizens for decades, they rebelled, fighting for more rights, but failed. Eventually, the non-magic people left Nan'Yü and formed other countries around it. That's why we speak the same language, albeit with different dialects and accents depending on the region."

"That aligns with what I learned in secret," Yunle says, considering her next move. "Due to the violent history, I understand why the newer nations banned magic right from the start. There was peace for a long time after the founding of the new nations. Then meaningless wars broke out, for which Dazhou bears some responsibility."

The princess sounds more open-minded than most people. I nod my agreement. For centuries, the larger surrounding kingdoms, including Dazhou, tried to invade Nan'Yü with their mighty armies, but they gave up eventually after numerous failures. I've only read about magic at a superficial level, but I can imagine Fire and Strength magic would be capable of causing incredible damage to enemies on the battlefield. The Nan'Yüans could also maneuver their army more easily with Portal magic, which transports people over a long distance in mere seconds. "Nan'Yü finally learned from its mistake and evolved after a revolution, granting non-magic people equal rights. My father's theory," I confide, "was that Dazhou, Ude, and Xiland started the war to destroy magic, not only because magic caused their ancestors pain and suffering, but because people are usually afraid of things they don't understand."

"He sounds wise. The practice of magic has always been outlawed in Dazhou, but it's outright absurd to ban the knowledge of magic and punish citizens for that. What can Dazhouans do with it anyway? We all know only Nan'Yüans can do magic."

I never thought Yunle would be daring enough to criticize her own father. "I've heard that the family of Prince Zejun, the King's brother, fell victim to dark magic. Since His Majesty banned the knowledge of magic immediately after their deaths, the public believes he did it out of grief."

"I've heard that rumor, too." She looks away for a moment. When she turns back to me, she says, "I don't believe the magic in Nan'Yü has always been evil. I read that things changed around five generations ago."

"That's what I was taught, too. None of the other kingdoms knew why or what happened, but that only made them all the more suspicious and alert." Lafne's Blood sorcery was definitely dark and repugnant, but it still shocks me how she met her end.

I set my next piece down, and Yunle loses nine of hers at once.

She groans. "We should concentrate on our game."

She valiantly tries to prevent a defeat, but I win in the end. Afterward, I show her which moves she made that doomed her.

"I've learned a lot from you," she says. "Let's do more of this in the future."

"I look forward to it." And I mean it.

She laughs, a lively, joyful sound.

On our ride home, I decide not to take the normal, short route, but the one that will bring us past the envoy's manor house. It will probably be a waste of time, since I can't go in to see what Hanxin is up to in there or even watch the building from a distance without drawing attention to myself.

But as the coach passes the front of the manor at a pace slower than usual, I spot Hanxin's bodyguard speaking with a few delegation members just outside the entrance. Judging from their constant bowing and nodding, it seems they are all deferring to him.

Why would they show that kind of respect to a bodyguard?

The question follows me all the way home.

I don't know if it's all the talk about magic during the day, but when I go to sleep at night, I will my pendant to shine, to show me the grand building as it did before. Despite my yearning for answers, it remains a plain stone. Does it contain magic? If so, why would my father's family possess a magical artifact?

For now, I must keep it a secret.

CHAPTER 18

"It's really happening!" I exclaim to Mother as we ride in our coach. "We're going to have our own home in the capital."

Mother chuckles along with my laughter.

With the help of the princess, Mother and I spent half a day visiting a delightful property in the city. We both liked it and accepted the seller's price immediately.

Upon our return to Uncle Yi's estate, we enjoy a quick lunch. Minister Sun is at work, Bo is attending school, and somehow even Aylin isn't home. Mother wants to inform my uncle first before we move out, believing it would be rude to start packing without telling him in advance.

While I grind the inkstone, Mother sits behind the desk to write a letter to our steward back in our hometown.

Ning enters. "Lord Sun's steward asks to see you on an urgent matter, Mistress."

That man has never set foot in our quiet corner of the residence before.

"Oh," Mother says in surprise. She tells Ning to bring him in.

The steward bows to Mother in a perfunctory way. "Mistress Lu, there are constables waiting in the front yard of the estate. Lord Mayor Tan has issued an order calling for Han Hui to be brought in for questioning."

A cold tide of alarm seizes me. Ning and Mai stare at him in apprehension.

Mother stands. "What for?" she demands.

"For that, you'll have to ask the constables, Mistress Lu." The steward sounds composed, almost too composed.

"I intend to do exactly that," Mother says, her voice steel-edged. She turns to Ning. "Get Hui. We're going out to meet the constables."

The twins join Mother and me in the courtyard. Tension knots Fei's shoulders. Ever the pillar of calm, Hui doesn't show a hint of distress.

Ning and Mai volunteer to come along as well. All six of us follow the steward to the front yard. There, half a dozen constables in green uniforms wait, their fists clenched around the hilts of the short swords hanging from their belts. They fan out behind another man who, judging by his bearing, must be their leader. He dangles a pair of manacles from his hand.

A sharp pressure clamps my belly. This is an *arrest*.

Mother's back is ramrod straight as she halts a few feet from the head constable. We stop behind her.

"Good afternoon, Sir," Mother says.

The stony-faced man gives a curt nod. "We are here on official business, Mistress. A citizen has accused your servant, Han Hui, of beating him so severely that his leg was broken. Considering the violent nature of this crime, Lord Mayor Tan has ordered that we bring in the accused immediately for questioning."

"Who is this citizen, may I ask, good Sir?" Mother says.

"He holds a respectful position in the community." In other words, he's some sort of official. "Surely you understand why Lord

Mayor Tan has attached such an importance to the case, and ordered swift action."

Fei growls. Hui crosses his arms before his broad chest, eyes smoldering. Ning and Mai exchange terrified looks.

Mother turns around and asks Hui, "Is this accusation true?"

"No," comes his firm reply.

I believe Hui. He's great with a sword and his fists, but he's not violent by nature and would never go around picking fights with strangers. Especially since he's also wise enough to understand the consequences of attacking someone of a higher status.

Mother returns to the head constable. "I shall come along in case a witness is needed or a testimony of my servant's character is warranted." Her voice rings out smooth and clear.

I step forward to stand beside Mother, my chin lifted. "Me too."

The head constable's brow shoots up. He's probably never encountered anyone willing to defend their servant like this.

"Lord Mayor Tan shall call upon either of you if a witness or testimony is needed," he says. "Our order is to bring in only the suspect." His eyes narrow. "Step aside now, so we can make the arrest and be on our way."

This sounds awfully suspicious. Why does he insist we not come along? Does the mayor intend to send Hui directly to prison without questioning, or will they flog him to wrangle a confession out of him?

The steward comes forward. "Mistress Lu, I *implore* you to cooperate with the authorities and not cause any trouble for Lord Sun," he says, but there's nothing imploring about his tone.

I have to restrain myself from punching this weasel.

When neither Mother nor I move, the head constable's voice takes on a chill. "You must step back, or I'll have you all arrested for creating a disturbance."

"I'll go with you," Hui bellows. "Leave them alone."

"No!" I grab his arm. I remember how in my last life the twins were whisked off for allegedly dabbling in magic. If I let them take Hui this time, I may never see him again.

The head constable waves at his subordinates. "Take the suspect and hold everyone else back."

The constables surge ahead, swords flying out of their scabbards. My hand darts to my dagger. Fei pulls Mother behind her. Chaos is about to break loose when I hear a commanding shout, "What's going on here?"

In unison, we turn in the direction of the new voice. My heart thumps a wild beat. It's Jieh! Lord Yao stands a few steps behind him.

The steward and the constables all fall to their knees. "Your Highness."

We genuflect, too.

"You may rise," Jieh says. He approaches me in three fast strides. "Are you all right?" he asks, looking me over.

I nod. In spite of myself, a blush creeps across my face because of his full attention.

Finally his stance relaxes, as though in relief. He scowls at the head constable. "What's happening here?" he demands.

The man bows. "An official accused Mistress Lu's guard, Han Hui, of breaking his leg in a brutal attack. Lord Mayor Tan ordered us to arrest him immediately."

"Who's the accuser?"

"The third clerk at the Ministry of Treasury."

"What's this commotion about?"

"Mistress Lu and Miss Lu insist on coming along, but Lord Mayor Tan commanded us to bring Han Hui in alone. I must follow his directive exactly as ordered."

"Is that so?" Jieh sneers, fixing the other man with a piercing gaze. Sweat breaks out on the constable's forehead.

"I won't make it hard for you," Jieh says. "Take Han Hui. I'll come with you and have a word with Tan." He turns to me. "Stay here, Mingshin. Leave it to me. I'll take care of it. Hui will come home safe and sound. Trust me."

Maybe it's the effortless pride he exudes, or the reassuring confidence he easily projects, I don't really know, but in this moment, I believe wholeheartedly that he will sort this mess out. I nod.

"Has he been convicted?" Jieh asks the head constable as he moves forward to put the manacles around Hui's wrist.

The man's hands jerk away as if scorched. "Uh, no."

"Then there's no need to chain him," Jieh says. "Certainly the seven of you can handle one of him?"

The constables all leave, two of them grasping Hui by the arms. Jieh and Yao remount their horses and follow.

I set a hand on Fei's back. "Hui will be fine. I promise you."

Fei nods, her lips tight. I turn to see the steward behind us, his face as sour as old milk.

We spend the next three hours waiting anxiously in our living quarters. When the men return, I hear their laughter before they enter the front yard.

We rush out.

"Hui has been declared innocent," Jieh announces.

Fei's face softens into cherubic lines as she embraces her brother, who responds with a bear hug. Ning and Mai grasp each other's hands, beaming.

I curtsy to Jieh. "Thank you, Your Highness. I'm deeply grateful."

"I'm glad to be of help, Mingshin. Call me Jieh."

I look at Mother. She hesitates a moment before nodding.

"As you wish, Jieh." A pleasant shiver curls through me at the taste of his first name on my lips. But I shouldn't feel like this. I shouldn't.

Hui gives a quick bow. "Thank you, Your Highness, Lord Yao, for clearing my name. Thank you, Mistress, Miss, for believing in my innocence."

Yao punches Hui's arm playfully. "It's nothing, Hui. Ouch, you *are* strong! We should spar sometime."

Hui throws his head back in a roar of laughter. "I'd be honored to accept such a challenge, my lord."

We all grin.

Mother welcomes Jieh and Yao into the living room.

"How was it that you arrived here just as this ruckus started?" I ask Jieh. "My cousins weren't home to greet you."

"I wasn't here to visit with your family. I ran into Yunle, and she told me that you bought a new property in the city. I just wanted to stop by and congratulate you."

Yao winks at me. "As if he needed an excuse to come see you," he whispers.

Jieh shoots his friend a glare. Yao backs away as if cowed, pressing a finger to his lips.

Jieh came to see me? Heat floods my cheeks when I remember him trying to kiss me.

Mother invites Jieh and Yao to sit down and orders the maids to bring tea.

"What happened?" I ask the men.

"When we got to the City Hall of Justice, Jieh told Mayor Tan that he'd oversee the interrogation," Yao replies. "Tan was obviously concerned by Jieh's request, but he quickly realized his place and came to his senses." Yao imitates the way the mayor bowed and scraped before the prince, making strained expressions and bringing a smile to my face.

I can imagine Lord Tan's servile behavior. After being awarded the Beorn stallion, a prize worthy of a ruler, Jieh has become the clear front-runner in the competition for the throne.

"In the beginning, the clerk changed his story and said he may have identified the wrong person," Yao says, spreading his arms in an exaggerated way. "After some cajoling, intimidation, and persuasion, he finally confessed. He fell from a horse and broke his leg. Soon after the incident, he received a letter from an anonymous source claiming they had evidence that he stole one hundred gold taels from the national treasury. If he didn't want his crime reported, all he needed to do was accuse Hui of attacking him."

"So someone else was behind this false allegation against Hui," I say, aghast.

Jieh nods. "Apparently. But the clerk didn't know who it was."

"After his confession, Mayor Tan transferred the clerk and his embezzlement case to the Ministry of Justice and proclaimed Hui innocent," Yao finishes.

Mother frowns. "Why would they go to such lengths to harm a guard?"

I already have an idea about who and why, but I won't voice it in front of everyone present. "Whoever it was and whatever their motive, we'll find out," I say.

Everyone nods their agreement.

"It's getting late," Mother says. "Your Highness, Lord Yao, would you please honor us by joining us for dinner?"

Jieh grins. "Gladly, Mistress Lu."

During dinner, Jieh entertains us with stories about the Elite Hunts he's taken part in over the last three years. Even Hui listens intently, eyes lit like struck flint.

Although Jieh spends more time than necessary describing how mighty and dauntless he was, I don't find it off-putting. Instead, I admire him as a wonderful storyteller and take in every word he speaks, feeling every emotion he feels. My blood runs wild as he recounts a tale about riding through the forest, searching for wolves. I grasp the edge of the table as he relates how he tracked a bear with his father. I bask in the same pride that must have filled him after he captured a rare golden fox.

"The Elite Hunt sounds like fun. I look forward to participating in it," I say.

"You'll enjoy it. I'm glad you're still joining me." Jieh's smile brightens up his entire face, gorgeous and dazzling.

My heart does a stupid flip. He was afraid I wouldn't go with him after our little argument a few days ago?

I catch Mother watching me, her expression full of concern.

A wistful pang strikes a sweet, sad chord within me. Mother is right—Jieh and I can be friends, but nothing more.

After Jieh and Yao leave, I ask everyone to gather in the living room. Our guards and maids deserve to hear what I'm about to reveal.

"Ma, you wondered earlier why someone would try to harm Hui. I think I know."

In my prior life, Mother "drowned" soon after the twins disappeared. "We are their target," I say. "Hui just happened to be in the way. If they had succeeded in hurting Hui, they'd have gone after Fei next. They are trying to strip away our protection bit by bit, lay us bare, and make us vulnerable." This same strategy was employed against us in my previous life. Except in this life, the timeline has been moved up.

Everyone tenses up. Mother's gaze is razor-sharp. "You already have someone in mind," she says.

"Yes, Ma. Don't you find it strange that even Aylin isn't home today?" I meet her gaze squarely. "I think it was Uncle Yi who sent the clerk the letter."

I hear the loud intakes of breath all around me.

"This is a serious accusation against my brother, Mingshin," Mother says. My gut sinks. She rarely calls me by my proper name. If she doesn't believe me . . .

Then she adds, "But I know you don't make accusations lightly."

She pauses, perhaps pondering what I told her about the royal banquet. I'd thwarted Uncle Yi's plan to sabotage my performance. Aylin suspected I handed the solution to the waychess puzzle to the princess instead of her. They know I distrust them. It makes sense for Uncle Yi to take action against us already.

"And Hui is also family," Mother continues. "I'll hire the best investigator to discover the truth. Be careful, Mingshin. If you are wrong, you will dishonor me for defaming my brother." Her tone is stern, hard-edged.

Despite believing I'm right, my stomach clenches.

"If indeed it was Yi's doing, he'll no longer be a welcome brother," Mother says firmly.

The twins trade a glance. In that look, I know Mother and I have finally earned their loyalty on our own.

My uncle is a clever schemer, but one thing he'd never take into account is that Mother and I consider Hui and Fei our family and will do everything we can to defend them. That may make us lowly in his eyes, but I remember my conversation with Mother a while ago. She's right: when a kind heart is directed at the right people, it's a strength, not a weakness.

It takes us only a day to move into our new home, since we didn't bring much luggage to the capital. I didn't know Mother could be such a fine diplomat. She manages to make it sound like the main reason we are leaving is because we don't wish to bring any further trouble to Uncle Yi. I'm sure he's heard of the development with the clerk's case by now, but he sounds pleasant and understanding enough. He apologizes for not being here to support Mother and reprimands the steward for not fetching his help.

My cousins put on a good show in pretending they don't want us to leave. Aylin even cries. A fleeting pain twists in my chest. Once, her tears had been shed whenever I was in affliction, but now she's probably just sad to part with our money.

As we leave in our coach, Uncle Yi and my cousins wave goodbye. But I know the fight to preserve our family wealth, and our lives, is far from over.

I wonder what Uncle Yi's next move will be.

Jieh may have damaged his own cause by aiding us.

He may not need Uncle Yi as an ally in his quest for the throne, but he certainly doesn't need him as an enemy. Minister Sun is an excellent player at politics; he has certain influence with the King. I believe it was he who convinced Reifeng in his final days that Jieh would be too arrogant as a ruler to listen to his advisors, and taught Ren to play up his pretense so Reifeng eventually believed that Ren may be the only prince who would not hurt his half brothers upon attaining the crown—now I wonder if the King's fear of his sons harming each other may be connected to his own experience with a brother trying to assassinate him.

Given how close Jieh is to us, my uncle knows he won't be able to steal our family wealth if Jieh becomes King. As a result, he may throw his support behind one of the other princes. Whoever his choice is, the minister of personnel's pledged allegiance would certainly be a strong boost to that prince's circle of support.

But I'm a force to be reckoned with as well. I'll use all that I know to help Jieh succeed.

Because he's an ally and someone I can depend on.

Last night, when we were alone, I promised Mother again and again that I harbored no romantic feelings for Jieh. She has many valid reasons for wishing I not become a member of the royal family.

"He may like you now, but he'll have many consorts, especially if he becomes King. What will happen to you once he tires of you?"

I needed no reminder from her. A prince who faces many temptations would never be faithful to any woman.

Mother warned me against Ren in my last life as well. He persuaded her otherwise with his persistence, modesty, and the fact that he always listened to my counsel. But look where it landed us.

I've sworn to never fall in love again. This promise has given me strength and purpose in life. So why does it now make me feel like an essential need has been torn from me by the betrayals of my past, leaving an emptiness behind that frightens me?

CHAPTER 19

I stand inside a shining, magnificent edifice. I gasp when I realize I've been eager to come back to this place.

Am I in another dream?

I walk around, admiring the grandeur. I didn't truly grasp how large this place was the last time it appeared to me—the interior spans nearly a hundred yards in both length and width. The vaulted ceiling soars a hundred feet above the floor; I thought it was *carved* with the images of celestial objects, but now that I look closer, they appear *real*.

The sun is a golden disc suspended in the pink sky, incandescent in its unrestrained beauty. Time seems to barely pass when dusk gives way to night, the moon resplendent and cloaked in a silver robe, and countless stars burning strong and bright in their frosty light.

The stone walls glitter like pearlescent jewels. Stately pillars stand as tall as ancient trees, each engraved with the shape of a god or goddess offering a blessing from a lotus position. The nine pictures on the far wall stand out in stark detail, and the nine-rayed star image beneath my feet shimmers in alternating colors.

Again, I am pulled to the crystal jar like iron drawn to a magnet. I reach inside the jar and extract my pendant.

It shines in a brilliant swirl of five colors. I breathe a sound of wonder as it expands to the size of my head within a split second, while still feeling weightless as a feather.

Emotions swell within me. I feel like laughing and weeping at the same time.

A sheet of light in five colors shoots up from inside the pendant. It glows as brightly as the sun, but somehow the light doesn't blind me. A familiar kind of power envelopes me, washing over me, throbbing like the heartbeat of the world.

I long to stay in this moment forever, to be immersed in this power . . .

But above all, I thirst for answers. What is this grand place? Why was I brought here?

The need to know vibrates through me, singing to my heart, flooding my veins.

Tell me everything, I cry from the depths of my soul.

"Welcome to the Holy Temple," a female's regal voice booms.

I jump. There's nobody around! I jump again when I realize the voice has come from my *pendant*. It has an unusual accent I've never heard before.

I try to muster some scrap of calm, but my voice quivers when I ask, "What are you?"

"I am a spirit residing in the Divine Stone you hold."

I stare at my pendant. "Divine Stone?"

"Yes. It embodies Life and Death. Past and Future. The Magic there once was, and the Magic that will be."

My brain stutters. What does that mean? Life and Death. Past and Future . . .

"Did the Divine Stone grant me my second life?" I ask.

"The Stone needed you, Mingshin. But you were weak-minded and foolish. However, when you begged for another life, you showed the potential of becoming what the Stone needed you to be. You deserved a second chance. Along the way, you have continued to demonstrate a strong will and growing determination. It was time to call you to the spiritual realm of the Divine Stone."

My mind whirls with a dozen questions, each one vying for attention. I ask the question that bothers me most. "What does the Stone need me to be?"

"For now, you must protect the Stone from falling into the wrong hands. Or else disaster will strike."

"Why? What can the Stone do besides turn back time?"

"You have no magic to summon its power, but for those who do, it holds magic powerful enough to remake or unmake the world."

My stomach plummets as if I've jumped from a great height. "The Holy Temple, you said this place is," I stammer. "What do the nine pictures represent? And the nine-rayed star?"

"They both symbolize the nine forms of magic," the spirit replies.

Ah, foolish me! I've read about them all, so I should have figured it out already. I point at the three drawings depicting nature on the top row. "Do these represent Fire, Water, and Earth magic?" I ask.

"Yes," the spirit replies.

"The portraits of the child waving a sword, the woman with her ears perked up, and the man with double faces must symbolize Strength, Sense, and Disguise magic respectively." I still don't quite understand the three abstract images though.

When I hesitate, the spirit says, "Blood, Seer, and Portal."

I'd like to know more, but then the spirit adds in a more commanding tone, "You must leave this dream state now. Stay here any longer and your mind will be trapped in the spiritual realm forever."

With a silent gasp, I lurch back into reality. My eyes snap open. I'm lying on my side and clutching my pendant. Like before, it gleams faintly with five colors, hot as an ember. I release it at once.

A storm roils within me.

I am the keeper of a magical artifact that possesses the power to remake or unmake the world.

Did Father know what my pendant really was? If so, why didn't he mention anything? How did it come into my ancestor's possession?

One thing is for certain: I mustn't let anyone else know about the Divine Stone and the power it contains.

A thought jerks me upright.

I've read about the Holy Temple before, but probably only in passing, as I can't remember any details. But in which book?

The door opens, and Mai steps in. Quickly I stuff the pendant beneath my sleeping gown, although its light has already faded to nothing.

"You're up, Miss," she chirps. "Mistress has left for business."

I notice how bright it is inside my room. "What time is it?"

"Nine o'clock, Miss."

I slept in that late? My neck warms with embarrassment. I climb out of the four-poster canopy bed that could easily sleep five. Mai helps me dress.

Someone knocks. "It's Fei, Miss."

"You may enter," I say.

Fei pokes her head in. "You have visitors, Miss: Prince Ren and Elder Hanxin."

Mai makes a squeaky noise.

From Jieh, I know the princes are taking turns guarding and entertaining the Nan'Yüan Elder, but what are *these two* doing here? Ren hasn't made any advances since the humiliation at Jieh's hand after the royal banquet. But he isn't the kind to be put off by petty slights, and he doesn't give up once he's set himself a goal. If he's here trying to court me, why did he bring Hanxin along?

"Did they state the purpose of their visit?" I ask.

"They said they'd like to congratulate you on moving into your new home."

The perfect excuse, isn't it?

How I wish my friends were the only ones to grace our household. When Uncle Yi and my cousins brought gifts and joined my family for dinner, everyone put on a friendly façade, but the atmosphere was lukewarm at best. Mother already hired a person with a solid reputation to uncover the truth behind Hui's false accusation. I hope we'll hear back from him soon.

I enter the living room to find two men seated around a tea table. Ren is drinking tea, his posture as perfect as someone posing for a painting. A familiar twinge of pain goes through me, but it no longer feels as sharp and raw as it did before, more like a dull ache.

Hanxin reclines on the sofa, his fingers crossed behind his head like a lazy cat, but I can't overlook a sense of something dangerous lying in wait, something coiled tight beneath that calm stillness. I glance at his bodyguard hovering nearby, who carries himself like a warrior ready to explode into movement at a moment's notice.

Fei positions herself in a corner, a presence never intrusive but not easily ignored. Mai stands close behind me.

Both Ren and Hanxin rise.

I curtsy. "Your Highness. Respectable Elder. Welcome."

"You have a beautiful home, Mingshin," Ren says, taking in the water-and-mountain paintings, the ornate vases filled with hibiscus, and the lamps made of colored glass. "I hope one day I'll have the honor of being invited as a guest."

"We'd be flattered, Prince Ren." I straighten. "May I be of help?"

Ren looks at Hanxin.

"If you'll grant me a few minutes of private talk, Miss Lu?" the Elder says.

I'm too stunned to respond. Hanxin is the one who wishes to speak to me?

"I shall respect your privacy," Ren says, then turns to me. "If you don't mind having a servant give me a tour of your home, Mingshin?"

What's going on here? Why is Ren so obliging to Hanxin's demands?

I can hardly object to a prince's request, though.

"Mai, please bring Fu here and tell him to kindly show His Highness around our home. You may stay behind." Fu is one of the new servants we recently hired. He's reticent and cautious. Ren won't obtain anything valuable from him if he tries to probe for information.

Mai hurries away. The Elder glances at Fei.

"You may speak freely in my guard's presence," I say.

"Fine." Hanxin sits back down, and I settle across from him.

We enjoy tea for a few quiet moments. When Fu arrives, Ren leaves with him.

Hanxin's eyes bore into mine with sudden, rapacious focus. "You are remarkable, Miss Lu. You solved my first puzzle and handed the second solution to the princess. Then, you recognized Lafne as a sorceress, and defeated her magic to help win the horse race."

My instant reaction is to tell Hanxin that Yunle solved the waychess puzzle all by herself, and that it was Jieh who identified the sorceress. But under Hanxin's steadfast gaze, I realize my denial would serve no use. He *knows*.

How does he? Was he watching me at the banquet? Goose bumps pebble my skin when I remember his predatory interest right after the horse race.

In my periphery, I catch Fei tensing up like a coil of wire. I think of her being blamed for dabbling in sorcery. A notion comes sharp and swift.

What kind of magic does Hanxin wield? Not every Nan'Yüan is capable of magic, but only those who are can be elected to the Elders Council. And he looks no older than twenty-one. How could he be a distinguished sorcerer at his age? I furtively look at his wrists, but I don't see any *fuiin*.

What of his bodyguard? If he's allowed to be a witness to our conversation, he must be one of the Elder's most trusted allies. The delegation members show respect to him despite his social status. Could it be because he's a powerful sorcerer as well?

Hanxin already perceives me as a tigress rather than a sheep waiting to be shorn, so I take the offensive. "Lafne used magic. You ordered her to."

"No. I simply did not forbid it."

"So you feigned shock and anger when confronted?" I scoff.

"I *was* shocked and angry. She got caught; that was inexcusable."

He knows that I can't tell Reifeng any of what he just admitted without incriminating myself.

"You *killed* her," I snarl.

"Death is the appropriate punishment for her failure."

How can he be so matter-of fact about this, like a person's life means nothing to him? "Why are you here, Respectable Elder?"

"To congratulate you on your gorgeous home, Miss Lu. And to show my admiration for your intelligence and resilience."

Is this man for real? "I thank you for your generous praise." My voice is stiff and my posture stiffer.

If Hanxin notices my reaction, he doesn't seem to care. "Your father, Mr. Lu Kang, conducted successful trade in Nan'Yü. No doubt he taught you about the respectful way women are treated in our country."

Hanxin has obviously researched my background, so there's no point in denying what he's learned about my father. Besides, I am curious. "Your culture dictates monogamy, and wives are free to leave their husbands if they choose. Nan'Yüan women can work in the govern-ment and hold important posts. The position of the spiritual leader has always been reserved for a female, by the title of High Priestess, who oversees Magic." In Dazhou, women are often limited to household roles. I admire Mother as a fine businesswoman, but I'm aware that the majority of the society regards her undertaking with disdain.

"Precisely," Hanxin says. "A woman with your exceptional intel-ligence could achieve greatness in Nan'Yü. I'd hate to see it wasted in this kingdom."

Despite my wariness of magic, I envy the freedom women enjoy in Nan'Yü, but Hanxin doesn't need to know this. "Even a woman like me without magic?" I throw the question at him as a challenge, not expecting him to catch it.

But he replies smoothly. "You understand that Nan'Yü granted all citizens equal rights after the revolution, which was led by many outstanding women, no less. A keen mind is its own kind of magic, as history has taught us."

A bright shock sparks through me. He's absolutely right, but I didn't expect such ideas to come from *him*.

"You are welcome to explore Nan'Yüan culture for yourself any time, Miss Lu."

One of my biggest wishes is to travel the continent and experience various cultures, just like Father did. I stare at Hanxin. Did he just invite me to visit his country?

Ren reappears at the doorway, and I immediately stand.

"Your home is even more beautiful than I imagined, Mingshin," he says.

"Thank you, Your Highness, for your overly kind words."

Hanxin rises. "We shall speak again, Miss Lu. I hope you'll be more open with me next time. Now I must take leave." With that he sweeps out of the room, and his guard follows at once.

"Please escort our guests out, Fei."

Fei complies with my wishes.

As I watch them go, my mind churns. What did Hanxin attempt to gain from this little visit? He strikes me as the type of person who doesn't do anything without a purpose. And all this talk about how women are treated in Nan'Yü . . . It sounds like he's curious about me, perhaps even truly appreciates my intelligence. But how does that benefit *him*?

Then there's his puzzling association with Ren. What kind of role is the traitorous prince playing? It seems he's given up wooing me. On one hand, I'm glad he has abandoned his advances. On the other, it means much has changed from my former life. What does it portend if Ren is no longer interested in my money? One thing remains the same, though: Ren will do anything to become King. He had my money, Uncle Yi's scheming, and my help with strategies. But in this life, he has no resources. Does he have a new plan to attain the throne? Considering how manipulative and deceptive he is, it has to be something dangerous, possibly even something involving Hanxin. He granted Hanxin access to me in exchange for something, but what?

When Fei returns, her jaw is granite, lines of tension furrowing her brow. "What's that sly bastard driving at?" she hisses. "I'll kill him if he tries to harm you."

"I don't think that's his intent." But that doesn't make Hanxin any less of a threat. "I agree, though, that we need to be more careful around him."

A ripple of joy bubbles up in me when Jieh drops by in the afternoon. I assure myself that it's only because I appreciate a visit from someone I trust, especially after Ren's foul presence, despite its brevity.

As Jieh and I stroll through the garden, I tell him of the morning visit by Ren and Hanxin.

He stops in his tracks. "What could Hanxin want from you?" His forehead creases in thought. "You know my brothers and I are taking turns guarding the Elder. By the King's secret order, though, we're also watching him. My father hopes we'll find out what he's searching for in Jingshi."

I scowl. "But instead of watching Hanxin, Ren seems to be cozying up to him. What kind of game is he playing?" How do a snake and a fox get along, I wonder?

"Your concern merits further investigation. I'll look into this."

"Be careful."

I notice I have grabbed his arm without thinking. I let go, but he snatches my hand in his. "I don't know what Ren did to you that makes you hate him so, Mingshin, but I promise I'll protect you from him."

"I'm not afraid of him."

He smiles. "That's the spirit I admire in you."

My heart stutters a beat in response. Quickly I look away.

His tone turns serious. "I've had people spread the word about Ren's deceitful ways. Kai and Wen are now paying more attention to him. He won't be able to hide under his disguise for long."

I nod. "He'll be forced to pursue actions that reveal his true colors."

We saunter on in silence. I become acutely aware of the closeness between us. I smell the lavender soap and fresh cotton on him. When his arm brushes mine, my skin tingles.

He stops suddenly, pulling me to a halt. "I meant what I said earlier, Mingshin."

My heart jumps into a skittery dance.

He cups my face. "I admire your fierce and dauntless spirit. Truly. But I stand by my words. I will protect you."

His eyes hold an intensity that halts my breath. He leans down, and before I can move, before I can even think, he kisses me. I gasp against his mouth. The world turns; the moment stretches. I close my eyes and sway. He presses down, his warm lips moving against mine, soft and gentle. A thousand wings unfurl in me, sending a shiver of longing through me.

No. This is the line I must never cross.

The moment ends. I pull away, and our lips part. I cast my eyes to the ground, almost afraid to look at him.

His hand reaches hesitantly for my arm, then drops halfway. "Did I . . . offend you?" he whispers.

"No." I inhale a breath. "But . . . I think you should go."

An instant of pin-drop silence, then he says, "All right." A pause. "I'll see you on the morning of the Elite Hunt?"

I nod.

Even long after he leaves, I remain in the same spot, trying to unravel the tangled skeins of my thoughts and feelings.

I can find neither the beginning nor the end.

CHAPTER 20

During our weekly waychess match, I relate my unusual meeting with Hanxin to Yunle.

"It sounds like he's interested in you," she says. "Not in a romantic way. But in some strange, twisted way."

Romantic or not, I don't care for his attention. "I wish I knew what he wants from me."

"Be careful around him, my friend." Yunle leans closer over the board. "The official document states that Hanxin came here to start the process of building a diplomatic relationship between the two nations, supposedly at Chancellor Lew'Bung's request. We all know this isn't his true purpose. Father's spies failed to find out what he's looking for in Dazhou, but they did discover that it was actually the Nan'Yüan High Priestess who sent him here."

A bolt of nerves flashes through me. "Could that mean Hanxin's mission is related to magic?"

Yunle nods.

I've wondered if Hanxin wants to get close to me because he's seeking the Divine Stone. But he can't possibly know I have it. If he does, and if the Stone is indeed what he's looking for, he'd surely have seized it by force or magic by now, or at least tried to.

"Have you ever wondered what kind of magic Hanxin might wield?" I say as I consider my next waychess move. It's becoming harder and harder to beat Yunle. "And his bodyguard . . . I think he's more than that."

"Well, that's the interesting part," she says. "Hanxin was recommended to the Elders Council by the High Priestess herself. Due to her status in Nan'Yü, he was automatically elected. No one has seen him use magic or knows what kind he wields. Hanxin brought along his own bodyguard named Longzo; they are almost inseparable. The spies can't confirm if he's a sorcerer, and Hanxin's delegation members either don't know or have been sworn to secrecy."

A realization hits me like a rock in the gut. "If Hanxin and Longzo are connected to the High Priestess, they have to be sorcerers, or maybe even mages." That makes them all the more dangerous. Mages excel in multiple forms of magic instead of one; they are much rarer and mightier than sorcerers and don't even need a *fuiin* to work their magic. That could explain the absence of Hanxin's *fuiin*.

"Likely. All this business makes Father cranky these days, especially given he hates magic more than anyone in the kingdom."

I resist the urge to touch the Divine Stone hidden beneath my clothes. "Hanxin knows I possess certain knowledge of magic, but I don't think he'll tell His Majesty," I say.

"Ha!" Yunle exclaims as she sets a stone down.

I'll lose six of my pieces in two steps, and there's nothing I can do to save them. I groan.

Yunle giggles, then her face grows more serious. "About what you said earlier . . . Now that we've been friends for a while, I know I can trust you with this . . . you mentioned the rumor that my father banned the knowledge of magic out of grief after his brother, Prince Zejun, and

Zejun's family, fell victim to dark magic and died. While growing up in the harem, I heard a different story, just bits and pieces I later put together, but I believe it to be true."

My heart starts hammering.

Yunle's voice is a whisper now. "Zejun bought a Nan'Yuan sorcerer's help to kill his brother so he could become King. His plot failed, but my father was still injured by the magic. Not wanting to have the royal scandal exposed, he ordered Zejun's entire family executed in secret overnight."

I clap a hand over my mouth, my pulses going wild. Despite the cruelty of King Reifeng's reaction, it made him no different than any other monarch. The penalty for attempted regicide has always been the execution of the perpetrator's entire family, sometimes even of distant relatives. "His Majesty was injured by the magic," I murmur so low I can barely hear myself. "Is that why he's in such bad health even though he's only in his forties?"

Yunle nods gravely. "Forty-two, to be exact."

"Do any of the princes know the truth?"

"I'm not sure; we don't talk about it. Father never speaks of his brother's death, either."

"What a horrible incident. I'm so sorry, Yunle. I hope your father regains his health, and that the innocent souls of his brother's family find peace in the afterlife."

Yunle sighs. "So do I."

We finish the rest of the waychess game in silence.

"Your skills have improved a lot," I say. "When we began, I could easily win with thirty points over you. Now, I only win with around ten—and that's with a lot of effort!"

"It's all thanks to you generously sharing your knowledge and strategies. Many people would have guarded their secrets and special tactics."

"How can I call you a friend if I'm not willing to share something precious with you? And thank you for always being honest and straightforward with me."

"How can I call you a friend if I'm not so? I just hope you won't grow tired of listening to me talk about history and politics so much."

"Oh, never." I mostly listen—as a royal, she certainly has more freedom in expressing her views without fear of repercussions. I'm not sure whether she trusts me or just likes me as a listener. Either way, she often amazes me with her strategic knowledge and her ability to appreciate matters of state. It's indeed a pity that she shall be denied the opportunity to rule because of her gender.

"You would've made a great Chancellor if you'd been born in Nan'Yü," I blurt. Then I gasp. What did I just say? It must be Hanxin's bad influence. "Oh, I'm sorry . . ."

"No need to apologize. I consider it a compliment, unless it isn't?" Her eyes twinkle.

"Of course it is."

"Besides, you may very well be right." Yunle looks thoughtful. I wonder if she's ever harbored the ambition that she could be King if she'd been born a boy.

"I have a request, Yunle. May I visit the royal library? There are a few books I'd like to read."

"Sure!" she exclaims. "None of my ladies-in-waiting enjoy reading like I do. I may yet find a reading companion in you."

"I'm at your service anytime you need something."

She takes me to the royal library. It's massive, consisting of three oak-paneled sections. All the walls are covered with tall, book-lined shelves. A narrow balcony runs the full length of the chamber, revealing an even taller second level of bookcases. Everywhere I look, ladders with little wheels at the bottom hang down from the ceilings.

Great writing desks hold oil lamps, surrounded by comfortable-looking chairs.

While Yunle focuses on a volume about military strategies, I browse through the war history section with a particular book in mind. I finally recalled its title after racking my brain. There's a copy in Father's library back home, and I've read it a few times.

I eagerly snatch the book from the shelf when I find it, and sit down across from Yunle.

There, on page thirty-six, is the brief text I've been searching for:

The Holy Temple was where each generation of High Priestess and her group of priests used to reside. The temple vanished without a trace one hundred and eighty years ago, along with High Priestess Sudaji and all her priests; their bodies were never found. What a befitting punishment for Nan' Yü's blasphemous claim that it was the gods who assigned their priests the task of overseeing Magic at the Holy Temple.

The book was written before I was born. The acrid tone of the last sentence reminds me of a piece of text I read in a Nan'Yüan scripture. Although the mysterious disappearance of the Holy Temple baffled and saddened Nan'Yü, other nations cheered it as an act of the gods. To their dismay, though, Nan'Yüan magic did not die out, or even decline, as they'd hoped.

A few pages later, the book states that after the incident, a new High Priestess was selected from among the most powerful mages, and another grand residence was built, although this one was simply called the Temple of Magic.

Has the Holy Temple existed in the spiritual realm of the Divine Stone all this time? How and why? Still, I've never previously read about or heard of any reference to the Divine Stone. If everything the spirit said about it is true, wars would be waged to fight for its possession. Did my father and his father even know what my pendant really was or the power it contained?

Heaven above, I have so many questions.

In the past week, I've prayed and wished that I'd be taken back to the Holy Temple, but nothing has happened. It's as if my pendant had a mind of its own.

I must find a way to enter the spiritual realm myself.

CHAPTER 21

The day of the Elite Hunt dawns bright and clear. King Reifeng and the princes lead the long procession out of the city to the hunting fields, joined by Elder Hanxin and flanked by two dozen royal guards. The officials and their sons make up the middle part of the entourage, accompanied by the wardens in charge of the hounds. Ladies follow with their chaperones. While all the noblemen ride horses, most women rely on the comfort of their coaches. Servants and soldiers on foot bring up the rear.

Yunle and I are among the few women who prefer the view of the open sky to an enclosed space. We joke about her favoring my company over her father's and brothers'. Fei and a pair of Yunle's guards ride beside us.

Far ahead, Jieh rides his Beorn stallion, Sky Dancer—named after the largest constellation in the northern sky. The pair are quite the perfect fit: both are exceptionally handsome and imperious, their movements laced with power.

But what amazes me is that Jieh has domesticated this legendary beast in such a short time. Even the King couldn't hold back his delight when Jieh arrived sitting tall on his stallion. As his son dismounted and knelt, Reifeng pulled him up, clapped him on the shoulders, and hugged him with one arm, laughing like any father lavishing his approval on a child who makes him proud.

"My son, just like your name," Reifeng roared.

Just like your name: Jieh, meaning *outstanding.*

Wen's mouth twisted as if he'd just eaten a bitter lemon. Kai's face was set as hard as marble. Ren, however, offered his congratulations.

Later, Hanxin commended Jieh, and Yunle pulled me aside to join her.

It's midafternoon when we reach the encampment. A few tents have been pitched. Even as I dismount, I notice the yellow one in the center stitched with emblems of dragons. The largest of all, it looks more like a pavilion than a place to sleep.

"I'll have my tent set up near my father's," Yunle says.

I nod. "I'll see you later."

As soon as she leaves, a soldier directs me and Fei to follow him. We lead the horses to our spot on the outskirts of the growing cluster of tents: red, orange, purple, and blue, all nestled upon a sea of green quivering in the breeze. Some have flags displaying family names flying atop their center poles.

Fei unrolls the bundle tied to her mare, and I help her erect our tent. I've done it before, but it isn't easy with only two of us.

"Mingshin?"

Still wrestling with the stubborn tentpole, I look up to find Jieh standing a few feet away, with Yao by his side.

"This is not ladies' work," Yao says, smiling.

I roll my eyes. "I'm not a lady anyway."

Jieh scowls. I'm certain his guards set up his tent, like all the other nobles leaving such drudgery to their servants. I ignore him and continue with my struggle. It seems a war is being fought in his head, but eventually he gives a curt nod. "Stop prattling and come help," he tells Yao.

Frankly, I'm surprised he *deigns* to perform a workman's labor. I'd be lying to myself if I say I'm not touched by his gesture. Still, a voice persists in my head: *Keep him at a distance.* This morning, he escorted me to join the procession. My chat with him was brusque and perfunctory. If he detected my detachment, he didn't show it.

With the four of us working together, our tent is up in minutes.

"I must go see my father now," Jieh says. "He's summoned me and my brothers. As soon as we're finished, I'll return to help you get settled in."

After he and Yao leave, Fei and I wander toward a clearing. In the middle of it, a long table is lined with plates of fruits and pastry and surrounded by servants offering wine. A dozen old men lounge nearby, conversing; not many officials have joined the hunt, as it's considered a sport more suitable for young people. I don't see my uncle among them, so that's a blessing.

Small groups of men and women around my age gather to my left, a colorful party wobbling and chirping like excited geese. I spot Aylin. She speaks little, her face glazed with an empty social smile.

To my right, soldiers grapple with a pack of barking hounds. Farther, at the trailhead, a collection of young nobles is busy stringing their bows near a green forest on the verge of turning orange and yellow. Cousin Bo is among them, talking and laughing.

As I stand at the edge of the clearing, debating whether to stroll around the encampment, a maid approaches me. I glance around to see who she's looking for, but there is no one else other than Fei. She is definitely heading toward *me*. Fei regards her with narrowed eyes.

The newcomer stops an arm's length from me. "You must be Miss Lu."

I try to hide my surprise. "Yes, I am."

"You're the only woman here who doesn't wear makeup."

I'm not sure if that's meant to be a compliment or an insult.

She points behind her. "Royal Lady Hwa would like to speak to you."

My breath catches. Royal Lady Hwa is Jieh's mother. What does she want to speak to me about?

As I follow the maid, I feel the icy grip of a gaze. It's Aylin. Her face melts into a smile, and she waves at me when I look her way. I wave back.

Hwa's tent, of red, is slightly smaller than the King's. Two men stand guard at the entrance.

I recognize Jieh's dark-blue tent staked out nearby, with Sky Dancer grazing behind it. While all the other horses are tied to trees, the Beorn stallion isn't. It watches every passerby, tossing its great head as if challenging them to come closer. *Once a Beorn stallion is tamed, it's yours for life.*

The maid asks me to wait outside while she reports my arrival. I review what little I know about Royal Lady Hwa. I never had any interactions with her and only saw her from afar several times in my previous life. She became Reifeng's consort at sixteen. When she gave birth to Jieh a year later, the King was delirious with happiness even though Jieh was his second son. She was Reifeng's favorite for years, but eventually he lost interest in her, his eyes drawn to younger, newer women.

I wait and wait, but the maid never comes out to announce me. Fei frowns. I lean closer to the flap; the pair of guards scowl but make no movement.

There's no sound of conversation or any movement inside.

Hwa doesn't have other visitors at the moment. She's made me wait on purpose.

I smooth a hand over the front of my skirt. Is Hwa toying with me? If she thinks I'm intimidated by her act, she's dreadfully mistaken.

I haven't forgotten I am in the King's favor, and there's nothing she can do to me unless I commit a crime.

I bellow into the tent. "If Her Majestic Ladyship has no time to receive me right now, I shall come another time."

I turn to leave. At the same instant, the flap is lifted and the maid steps out. "I apologize for the delay, Miss Lu. Her Majestic Ladyship will see you now."

Fei follows me, but the maid intercepts her with an extended arm. "Miss Lu only."

Fei snarls, but I wave to indicate I'll be fine. It's not like Hwa will attempt to harm me, and by insisting on bringing my bodyguard, I'll signal weakness.

As soon as I enter, I notice how cozy it is inside. Soft carpet covers the floor. A fluffy bed lies to one side, lush with pillows, draperies, and tasseled trim. On the north side, a woman sits on a long couch.

Her gaze hones in on me.

I curtsy. "Your Majestic Ladyship. May you live a thousand years."

In her mid-thirties, Royal Lady Hwa is still stunning, with large, heavily lashed eyes, a fine upturned nose, and a sensual mouth. Her skin has the flawless sheen of a rose petal, and her hair is thick and shiny. An emerald silk dress clings to every soft curve, accentuating her narrow waist and the gentle rise of her breasts. But I'm more struck by her demeanor, her bearing: It's like Jieh's haughtiness was cast from her mold.

Seeing how imperious she is, I suddenly understand why she resisted the arrest from Ren's royal guards in my first life—for that she was executed on the spot.

Hwa doesn't tell me to rise, but I straighten anyway. She raises a perfectly shaped brow. Annoyed or surprised? I'm not sure.

"Jieh speaks of you often. I can see a reason or two why he thinks highly of you. You have bold eyes. Still, what a small, plain creature."

That's not the worst insult I've ever heard. Besides, I *am* small and plain. But Father always told me I have a generous soul and a brilliant mind. Yunle appreciates my intelligence, and Mother is proud of my fiery spirit. I listen to those who bring the best out of me, not to those who find fault with me.

"My son's attention must have given you the wrong idea," Hwa says. Her voice cuts icy and even. "Don't misunderstand it. You are but one of many who capture his adolescent fancy. Soon it will pass. Men seeking power are all like that."

"You mean like what His Majesty did to you?" It's a low blow, but I can't help it.

She glares at me.

It's amazing that she still looks beautiful in her fury. Then, as though somebody lit a candle behind my eyes, I suddenly see. Beauty alone cannot bring you true love. Men may lust for women like Hwa, like Aylin, more than they ever will for me, but that's not love. Father fell in love with Mother not only because of her beauty but because she is kind, smart, and fun to be with.

Hwa stands. By Heaven, is she tall, even taller than Yunle. She looks down her nose at me. "Jieh is destined for greatness. As you may well know, my son is His Majesty's favorite. Once he's made the Crown Prince, he'll marry an Udess or Xi princess, not some lowly merchant's daughter."

Something inside me splinters. I draw a fortifying breath and look at her. "Your Majestic Ladyship may rest assured that I have no ambitious thoughts about Prince Jieh."

"That would be wise, for you are not good enough to be made his Royal Lady, either."

"I aspire to be no one's *lesser* wife."

Her eyes seem to catch fire. She takes a step closer, towering over me. "Stay away from my son, or I'll destroy you."

I hate her patronizing way, but as I leave her tent, I wish I'd held my barbs back. Even though her words had confirmed my suspicion about Jieh: I am but one of many girls who capture his ephemeral fancy, and a commoner girl to boot.

Fei hurries after me. I walk so fast I don't realize I'm on a collision path with another person until I bump right into his chest, a wall of solid muscles.

"Ouch!" I cry as Jieh holds my shoulders and tilts my head back.

I suddenly have a desire to scratch that smirk off his handsome face. That's silly. Hwa is right about one thing: I should stay away from him.

"Are you all right?" he says.

I try to pull out of his grip, but he holds on tight. He looks at Fei, then in the direction of Hwa's tent. As understanding dawns on him, storm clouds gather in his eyes. "Did my mother say something to you?" he asks, a quiet thunder rolling in his voice.

"Why don't you go ask her yourself?"

He releases my shoulders but snatches my hand. He turns me around. "Come with me." He starts dragging me toward his mother's tent.

"Stop!" I pound at his arm and his back and tug at him, but he won't let go.

Hwa's maid gives a startled gasp as Jieh sweeps the tent flap aside and stalks in, yanking me behind him. The Royal Lady halts in the middle of pacing and whirls to him.

"What did you say to my friend Mingshin?" Jieh demands.

Hwa lifts her chin like a proud peacock. "I told her the truth."

"Truth? What truth?"

Hwa lets out an exasperated sigh. "She's far beneath you, Jieh. You deserve much better."

"You don't get to choose which girl I like, what friends I make."

My cheeks warm.

"I believe you owe Mingshin an apology," Jieh says.

Hwa's eyes fly wide. "An apology? Are you out of your mind?"

"No, Mother. I respect you, and you shall respect me as well."

They both stand their ground, stares and wills locked against each other. The mother and son look so much alike. From the high, perfectly aligned cheekbones to the fullness of their mouths. From the imposing stature to their domineering demeanor.

"I'm a Royal Lady, the King's consort," Hwa growls. "I won't apologize to a commoner. I did this for your own good, Jieh."

"Fine. I shall not speak to you again until you apologize to my friend."

As he spins around, lugging me behind him, I catch a hint of pure hatred on Hwa's face. The spark of a thought springs forth.

If I'm merely one of Jieh's transitory fancies and he'll soon be rid of me, as Hwa made clear, she should have nothing to worry about. So why did she bother trying to intimidate me into avoiding her son?

A giddy rush rolls through me. Hwa considers me a threat, something more than a fleeting fancy of Jieh's.

I force my mind away from this thought. I need to keep my head out of the clouds. "Jieh, you probably made things worse between your mother and me."

He grunts. "She can't treat you like that. I won't allow it."

I sigh. "Where are we going?" I ask as he continues pulling me along.

That elicits a smile from him. "Just wait and see. I'm sure you'll like it."

With Fei in tow, we trek past the encampment and the clearing, then through a small coppice. I hear Yao's uproarious laughter before we reach the other side. A dozen young lords lounge at the bank of a river; they bow to Jieh at the sight of him. The servants, their pant legs rolled up, stand in the middle of the river, catching fish with nets.

Jieh introduces me to the group. I recognize a couple of the men as his cousins—Lord Protector Hwa's sons. Jieh's attitude clearly commands that they all treat me with respect. So for that afternoon and well into the evening under the full moon, we drink, talk, and eat fish grilled over a fire. Even Fei lets down her guard and tries the fish. "It's delicious," she says, and asks for more.

Watching Jieh's happy smile and feeling my own heart beating along next to his, I'm afraid it's becoming harder and harder to keep him at a distance.

CHAPTER 22

When the first horn sounds early the next morning, I run out of my tent to meet Yao for the commencement ceremony. Since Jieh can't be with me, his best friend will.

A small group of people have gathered in the clearing by the time Yao and I arrive. Fortunately, we are able to secure a couple of spots near the front.

In the center of the clearing stands an object draped in red cloth, as tall and wide as a man. The four princes surround it like they are its loyal guardians, again positioning themselves by age: Kai, Jieh, Ren, and Wen. All of them wear leather jerkins and high riding boots. Each has his hand closed around the hilt of the sword strapped to his waist.

The princes hold themselves tall and proud. No one could overlook their differences. Jieh's expression is the haughtiest, and Ren's the gentlest—only I know there's nothing gentle about his nature. While Kai's demeanor reflects a soul of unbendable steel, Wen looks like he'd jump into action at the simplest provocation.

More people have turned up by now. "What's that thing guarded in the center?" I ask Yao.

He winks at me. "You'll see. Don't want to ruin the surprise for you."

When the horn blows once again, the assembly quiets and separates to form a path. We bow deeply as King Reifeng passes us, followed closely by Royal Lady Hwa and Royal Lady Yu, Wen's mother, side by side. The trio wear matching crimson cloaks. While the Royal Ladies' gowns are made of gorgeous satin, Reifeng is dressed for hunting: black boots, hosen, and a rich brown jacket.

Yunle and Hanxin strut past us. My friend looks fierce and sharp in her baldric-adorned maroon tunic, black leggings, and knee-high boots. A bow is hung from her shoulder and a quiver across her back. A blue-hooded cape complements her huntress attire, giving her overall appearance a feminine touch.

The King pauses a few feet from the cloaked object, the Royal Ladies right behind him. The princes turn in unison and bow to their father, then step back to stay at the front of the crowd.

Commander Bai of the royal guards appears beside the King. At a nod from Reifeng, he strides forward and removes the cloth to reveal a huge bow and a long arrow, both resting on a holder. Judging from the peeling patches along its grip and limbs, the bow has seen many years of use.

Upon the sight, something in my memory glimmers. Something concerning a conversation with Ren about what happened at the ceremony in my previous life.

"The bow was specially made for Gaodru, the first King of Jin dynasty," Yao whispers to me. "He was said to be a giant, over seven feet tall, with shoulders twice as wide as those of an average-sized man. Over a hundred years ago, he used that bow to shoot the arrow that pierced the heart of the last King of the former dynasty. The bow has become a symbol since then. At every Elite Hunt, the King fires the first arrow to bring good fortune."

In a flash, I remember.

Ren didn't invite me to the Elite Hunt, but he boasted later that Jieh's downfall began with a *bow* incident at the commencement ceremony. He wouldn't tell me exactly what took place, except that he had nothing to do with it and that it must have been the gods' hands that brought about Jieh's undoing.

Staring at this ancient bow, I have a gut feeling that it was somehow involved in the incident Ren spoke of.

Will history repeat? Not if I can help it. My heart pounds in swift, hot determination. No harm will come to Jieh or his chances, I'll ensure that.

Reifeng resumes walking. Suddenly he freezes, and his body spasms once before he staggers into the arms of the two Royal Ladies, who have acted fast to catch him.

The throng collectively gasps. The King is in poor health, but judging from the shock on the nobles' faces, nothing like this has happened in public before.

I recall what Yunle believes to be the true reason behind Reifeng's illness. What kind of magic harmed him? Fire, Strength, or something else?

The two royal physicians appear at the King's side. Reifeng presses a hand to his chest, brow furrowed. Commander Bai hovers nearby, tense and alert. Royal Lady Hwa whispers something into the King's ear.

He shakes his head. The congregation waits in silence. After a few moments, his face begins to relax. Neither the doctors nor the Royal Ladies seem terribly nervous. Perhaps this is a recurring scenario for them and they know it will pass.

Reifeng squints at the bow. There is no way he can shoot the enormous artifact in his present condition.

Sudden tension blankets the clearing.

"Tradition dictates that if a King is unable to open the hunt, a Crown Prince must take his place," Yao says under his breath.

My stomach gives a lurch at the underlying significance of his words.

Jieh appears keen to volunteer. Ren and Kai stay relatively calm, but the light shining in their eyes suggests they are also avid to seize this opportunity.

Wen keeps glancing between Jieh and the bow while his fingers tap tense beats on his thigh. That's odd. Given his character, it's more likely he would be jumping up and down in eagerness.

Royal Lady Hwa's eyes sparkle. If Jieh is chosen, it would mean the crown is within his grasp.

Royal Lady Yu, on the contrary, chews on her lip and watches Jieh anxiously.

Wen and his mother are acting strangely. It's like they both expect Jieh, no, *want* him, to open the hunt. Why?

All of a sudden, I realize what transpired at the last commencement ceremony.

Jieh must have been chosen to fire the arrow for the King, but he failed somehow.

I swallow to keep my heart from leaping past my teeth, and turn to Yao. "I need you to approach Jieh immediately and tell him that he must not offer to shoot the bow."

Yao's eyes open wide in alarm. "Why?"

"I don't have time to explain. Something terrible is going to happen if you don't hurry," I hiss. "Please, Yao, you must trust me on this. You know I care about him. Tell him to trust me like he did in the horse race."

He stares at me and gulps. "All right. Jieh values your cleverness, so . . ."

He pushes his way to Jieh. For the first time, I appreciate my small size, as I easily wriggle past the crowd to get to Ren.

I hesitate. I know I'm taking a huge risk. This is the man who killed me once already.

Anger flares, lighting my courage. There's no time to waste playing it safe.

I take the last step to reach Ren.

He nods at me. "Good morning, Mingshin." Even in a moment like this, he keeps his manners immaculate.

"Isn't this a great opportunity to demonstrate your fine archery skills to the court, Prince Ren? I think you've earned it."

He frowns slightly. "Aren't you Jieh's friend?"

I offer a mocking laugh. "With a mother like his?" I'm sure the whole camp has heard of Hwa's altercation with me by now, probably exaggerated tenfold.

Ren doesn't reply, but glances at his three brothers.

Yao stands a few paces behind Jieh. My pulse beats wildly. I hope Jieh has taken my words to heart.

Reifeng announces, "One of the princes shall receive the honor of shooting the first arrow for me."

"Hurry," I whisper.

That's all the push Ren needs. He steps forward. "My father King, if I may deserve the honor."

My pulse ratchets higher when Jieh seems to move forward. But instead of challenging Ren's request, he concedes with a nod. A wave of relief crashes through me.

Kai is already advancing, but he pauses, his eyes riveted on Jieh. Given Jieh's propensity to show off, it's no wonder Kai grows suspicious. He breathes deeply and stays put.

Both Royal Ladies glare at Ren's back, hot enough to burn a hole through him.

If Reifeng is disappointed that his two favored sons haven't come forward, he doesn't show it. "Go on, Ren."

The nobles appear astonished. They have to be wondering why the other princes didn't volunteer.

Ren must have sensed that something is wrong. A vein in his temple twitches and his jaw tightens. But it's too late to turn back now.

As he reaches the bow, I resume my original spot. Yao joins me seconds later.

Commander Bai returns with an eagle in a cage. Ren pulls the bowstring back, seeming to test it. But there's no time for that. As soon as Bai opens the cage, the eagle takes flight. Ren nocks an arrow, aims, and releases the string.

With a sharp crack, the bow snaps in half.

For a moment, no one speaks or moves. The clearing is as quiet and still as an underground sea. I feel like I'm watching events through another person's eyes, from another body. Ren grunts in pain and reels back; Yunle plucks an arrow from her quiver, lifts her bow, and shoots. The arrow whistles through the air and pierces the eagle from tail to breast. The bird flaps its wings once weakly, then falls.

The moment breaks. The assembly erupts into noise and motion. Ignoring his bleeding cheek, Ren kneels before the King. The wrecked bow lies at his feet—a symbol of a century of good fortune broken in his hand.

This calamity is what Ren meant by the gods' undoing.

But did it have anything to do with the gods? Commander Bai would likely do everything within his power to help Kai, his second cousin, attain the throne. But I don't think he would dare to do something as brash as tampering with the bow: He'd have damned himself to death if caught. Besides, Kai appeared genuinely avid to try.

It was most likely Royal Lady Yu's doing. She's aware of the King's health condition. I guess she hoped to take Jieh down. In my prior life, the plan succeeded.

But the Royal Lady couldn't have plotted this. I remember her as an empty-headed beauty. There are whispers at the court that her brother, Grand Scholar Yu, took all the brainpower of the family and left her none.

Could it be that the grand scholar masterminded the sabotage? The thought puts a chill in my throat. He would make a formidable foe for Jieh. I recall seeing him yesterday. I look around, but can't find the gray-haired man in the throng.

"I'm sorry, Father," Ren says, a slight tremor in his voice. "The bow . . ." No more words come to his rescue. For the first time, his glibness fails him.

Reifeng sighs wearily. "Dismissed."

Ren rises, his face ashy. As he withdraws, Wen smirks. Jieh and Kai at least have the decency or wits to keep a neutral expression.

I have a good idea as to what many nobles must be thinking: The gods did not look favorably upon Ren and it was their hands that held the other princes back.

A thread of triumph unspools in my core. *Let's see you reverse this kind of damage, Ren.*

Reifeng nods to Yunle. His daughter reacted fast enough to prevent the commencement ceremony from becoming a complete disaster.

The commander raises the dead bird above his head for all to see. The gathering cheers.

"The first arrow has been shot. The eagle is down. The Elite Hunt has begun," Reifeng declares. "Whoever captures the most game shall be the winner on this first day. Be brave and be strong."

Yao and I weave through the dispersing crowd. Ren's gaze slices across the clearing and catches mine for a second. His face is an icy mask displaying zero emotion.

Something slimy slithers in my belly. This is exactly what makes him dangerous: always so composed, so in control, even when he's plotting revenge.

Jieh catches up with us. He holds my arm and leans over me. "How did you know?" he whispers.

I tell him my suspicion about Wen, Wen's mother, and Grand Scholar Yu. I want Jieh to be cognizant of the danger they present.

Yao curses under his breath.

Jieh's features pull into hard, angry lines. "Well, this sort of treachery is nothing new."

"Be careful when you hunt," I tell him.

Jieh snorts. "There's nothing they can do to me at the hunt. In fact, they'd better pray I don't put an arrow through them."

"I'll be there protecting your prince in shining armor," Yao quips.

Jieh flashes him a withering glare while I roll my eyes.

"I saw you approach Ren," Jieh says. "Did you encourage him to volunteer?"

I nod. "Opening the hunt in place of the King was too tempting an opportunity for him to resist. Besides, he knew his archery skills had been exposed to the other princes and that there was no point in hiding them any longer. All he needed was a little push, and I was happy to oblige."

Jieh frowns. "He'll try to harm you."

Ren sure will, but . . . "Will he try at the hunt? It'll look too obvious."

"He won't harm you openly, but there are always accidents during hunts. Someone gets injured by a stray arrow, or mauled by an escaped beast. He could make it look like an accident." Jieh's expression hardens. "I should stay near to protect you."

"No, you should go hunting. Defeat Ren and make him lose more," I say fiercely. "I'm not helpless. I've been keeping up my self-defense lessons, and Fei is worth ten fighters any time."

"Didn't I say I admire your spirit?" Jieh relaxes a little. "All right. Promise me you'll watch out and keep your bodyguard with you at all times."

"I promise."

"We'll fetch our horses and weapons now. I'll come by before heading out."

Fei is brushing my mare when I return to my tent. Lying in bed, I cannot help the excitement coursing through me. I've hurt Ren's chances for the throne. I won't stop until he's completely finished.

When I venture out again, Jieh is back with Sky Dancer. He's fully armed with a bow, a baldric holding several knives and daggers, and a quiver attached to the saddle of the stallion. Yao, Jieh's cousins, and a few guards await on horseback close by.

I don't approach Jieh, for a girl in a silk velvet gown is with him, whispering urgently to him. A look of annoyance draws his brows together.

I recognize her as the pretty girl who was hanging on to him during the poem exchange at the royal banquet.

As soon as Jieh sees me, he smiles and strides toward me. The girl snatches his arm. Jieh yanks it out of her grip. She appears on the verge of tears, but Jieh doesn't even glance back.

He pauses before me. "Please be extremely careful. Wait for my victorious return."

"I look forward to it."

He leans forward and surprises me with a kiss on my cheek. A fire races through me at this simple gesture.

After he leaves, I notice the girl still standing in the same spot, glowering at me.

Great, I've just made another enemy.

"Mingshin."

I turn and smile at the sight of Yunle approaching on horseback. "You're going to hunt?"

"Yes. I'm going with my father and his court."

I must look surprised, because she adds, "Father will simply take a leisurely ride through the forest."

I see. The King's reputation suffers if he just sits around.

"Beat them all," I tell Yunle.

She grins. "Even Jieh?"

"Especially Jieh."

We laugh.

"With your blessings, my friend, I certainly will," she says.

"Enjoy."

She rides away, followed by her bodyguards. Far ahead, her half brothers are entering the forest. Yunle is imposing and dignified, and she has a strong body and a shrewd mind. She's no less fit to rule than any of them.

A blast of heat flares in me. They say women can't rule because they lack men's intelligence, reason, and logical ways of thinking. But in Nan'Yü, there have been quite a few female Chancellors in its history, and one of them is regarded by its people as the greatest leader of all time. Even Hanxin mentioned that many outstanding women led the revolution that resulted in non-magic citizens winning equal rights in our southern neighbor.

Nonetheless, Dazhou scorns such tradition and considers it backward to allow women to gain political power.

I've suspected this before, but now I know it to be true: *Our* way is the backward one.

CHAPTER 23

For the rest of the morning, I stay in my tent reading *History of the Continent*. For lunch, Fei and I eat some dried meat and raisins, then we decide to find some activities to keep ourselves entertained for the afternoon.

Once outside the tent, I see most of the women have gathered around the two Royal Ladies in the clearing, embroidering and chatting. Two dozen soldiers patrol the perimeter.

As I watch, Aylin says something that makes Yu beam with delight. Even Hwa gives her an approving nod.

In both this life and the last, Aylin has never relinquished a single opportunity to endear herself to the royals.

Fei and I walk toward the tree where our mares are tethered. She wheels about suddenly, prompting me to turn as well. She's training a dagger right at the heart of someone a few feet away.

It's the girl who harassed Jieh this morning. She stands perfectly still. "It's just me," she splutters, eyes wide with fear.

I nod to Fei, who lowers her dagger.

The girl looses a shuddering sigh, then plasters a smile on her face. "Miss Lu, please allow me to introduce myself. I'm Chih, daughter of Prime Minister Ang."

She looks about my age, so she must be one of Ang's many daughters from his lesser wives.

"May I help you, Miss Ang?" I say.

She crosses her fingers at her breasts. "Oh, Miss Lu, all those wonderful tales about you!" Her words spill out in a breathless rush. "I saw how you solved Elder Hanxin's riddle and helped defeat him in the horse race. I'd like to get to know you better and make friends with you. Actually, I have a few lady friends who feel the same way. If you'll please honor us by joining us this afternoon!"

I'm sure I won't find goodwill among her circle of friends. She's left her bodyguard behind, and her maid as well, probably because she doesn't want witnesses for whatever she's planning.

"Joining you?" I say, feigning innocence.

"Ah yes!" Chih exclaims. "They're waiting for us by the river. Please, Miss Lu. I promised them I would bring you along. They'll be ecstatic."

"Thank you for your invitation, but I have prior engagements."

I continue toward my mare.

Chih follows me. "Please, Miss Lu. My friends will be disappointed if I fail them."

Fei appears on the verge of pulling her dagger again to make Chih retreat. I shake my head firmly. The prime minister is not someone my family can afford to offend. Declining an invitation is one thing. Threatening his daughter with a knife? Quite another.

Chih pads after me, begging and offering me the prospect of friendship. Ignoring her, I pretend she is no more than a fly buzzing around my ears.

I'm about to untie my horse when I notice Royal Lady Hwa watching us from the cluster of women, her face a cool mask.

A low and subtle alarm begins to sound in my head. Did Hwa put Chih up to this? Considering how much Chih wants Jieh, she'd probably leap at any opportunity to ingratiate herself with his mother. If Hwa is behind this young woman's silly request, I want to find out what she has in store for me.

I turn to Chih. "You've convinced me. I'd like to meet your friends."

She stops speaking midway through, her mouth a big *O* of surprise. She snaps it closed and claps her hands. "That's fantastic. I'm glad you've decided to join us, Miss Lu." As she whirls away, I catch a hint of triumph in her eyes.

When Fei gives me a quizzical frown, I point my chin in the general direction of Hwa. "I'm afraid this meeting at the river may be more than a lovelorn maiden's plan for revenge. Watch my back."

"Always do."

We follow Chih across the encampment, through the clearing. I keep my guard up, my every sense concentrated. As we trek across the small trail lined with scattered trees, Chih's gait becomes less spritely and her back more rigid. Even her breathing sounds shallow.

On the other side of the copse, a few women sit on boulders at the riverbank, chatting. One catches sight of us and elbows another. Slowly, they all turn in our direction.

My mind is on everyone and everything at once. There are thick woods to my left, and an open area to my right. Fei's wary eyes sweep the whole region with practiced efficiency.

Chih waves both hands at her friends, giggling. "Hello, ladies. I've brought Miss Lu here."

"Welcome," they chorus.

My first reaction is to push away when Chih latches onto me like an octopus. But I freeze when I notice the other women fanning out and forming a half circle around me, leaving the riverside open.

So that's their plan: push me into the river, perhaps adding in some kicking, hairpulling, and a warning that I'd better know my place and stay away from Jieh.

But if Hwa is involved, there has to be something darker than scaring me off as a potential partner for her son. Danger prickles at the edge of my awareness.

"Come join us, Miss Lu." Chih pulls me toward her friends.

Fei strides forward, but I stop her with a hand. I can handle these girls myself. If they want to play mean, I can be meaner.

I glance around. Which girl's face should I shove into the dirt first?

"Down, Miss!" Fei bellows.

I crash into Chih, who yelps. We both fall, with me on top of her. Something whistles past where my heart was just seconds ago.

Fei plunges into the woods, as nimble as a leopard. She sweeps her sword through the air, cutting another soaring arrow in half. A shadow shifts near the wooded edge, but Fei leaps onto it. A man grunts. There's a thud, then nothing.

I stare at the arrow sticking out of the muddy ground, my heart racing. If Fei hadn't trained me to heed her warnings so well . . .

I turn in time to see Chih faint. The other young women have descended into chaos, screaming and running. I scramble up as soldiers arrive and surround us on the riverbank. After a swift survey of the situation, one of the men shouts to the others to bring a stretcher to carry Chih.

I rush into the woods to find Fei bending over an unconscious man. He's ordinary looking, dressed in plain, dark clothing like any of the guards or servants.

Several soldiers have followed me. The soil here is wetter and softer. Behind a thick bush, I spy two large footprints. Pointing at them, I ask, "How deep do you think these are?"

"About two inches," a soldier replies.

I stamp a foot, making a small dent in the mud. "This man has been hiding here for a while, long enough to leave two very deep footprints."

A murmur sweeps through the small group as they nod to each other. Then someone says, "He's been waiting for you. He knew you'd be here."

After the soldiers have bound the assassin, Fei and I follow them as they drag him back to the clearing. The women jump back like frightened rabbits as the soldiers pass the open area near them.

I search for Aylin and locate her. She appears as tensely wound as the string of a pi-pa—perhaps even tenser, as though she might snap at any moment. When her gaze catches mine, she pales, then quickly looks away.

The soldiers report to the Royal Ladies about what just happened at the river.

"A murder attempt?" Yu squeals. "At the Elite Hunt!"

"Do you recognize this man, Miss Lu?" Hwa asks calmly.

I shake my head. "I've never seen him before."

Hwa orders the soldiers to rouse the assassin by pouring cold water on him.

"Who are you?" she demands as soon as he comes to. "Who do you work for?"

The man stays silent.

Yu's smile is false as a paper mask as she turns to the other Royal Lady. "I hear that you had a rather heated argument with Miss Lu yesterday, Hwa."

"What are you suggesting?" Hwa's voice is knife-sharp, her expression like ice.

"Just an observation," Yu says airily. She turns to me. "The King will render you justice, Miss Lu, once he returns from the hunt." She then commands the soldiers to take the assassin away and keep him under watch.

Afterward the crowd disperses, the air thick with tension.

Once we are inside our tent, Fei asks me, "Do you think Hwa is behind this?"

"I don't know." I pace, fury burning the anxiety straight out of me. "There are four people at this camp who have good reasons for wanting me dead. Royal Lady Hwa, Ren, and my cousins. Ren had no motive to kill me until this morning; there wasn't enough time for him to arrange a murder. Hwa sounds like the obvious suspect. But this plan seems too risky for her. She has enough money and power to arrange better ways to destroy me. However, if my cousins were involved, how did the assassination play so well into the timing of Chih's prank?"

Fei's face is tight with resolve. "If your cousins are behind this, I'll deal with them."

The news of the assassination attempt quickly spreads to the rest of the hunting party. When Reifeng returns with his courtiers, a hearing is immediately called to order.

Everyone attends the inquiry. The royal family and Hanxin are the only ones seated, shielded by soldiers. The Elder's bodyguard,

Longzo, hovers near him like a vulture. Lord High Constable Wang and Commander Bai stand flanking the throne.

Reifeng's face is hard, his eyes glacial. It's an affront to him that a crime was committed during the Elite Hunt, especially with a foreign dignitary present.

Yunle and Jieh sit next to each other. By royal order, I stand behind the princess. They both express relief that I was unharmed.

"Your bodyguard . . . her name is Fei, right?" Yunle says. "She must be a keen observer. Most bodyguards wouldn't have noticed an arrow coming until it was too late."

I nod. "I'm very fortunate to have her as my protector."

"We'll find the person behind this attempt on your life," Jieh says. "I'll kill him with my own hands."

My chest pinches. What if it turns out to be his mother?

Lord High Constable Wang asks the assembly for silence.

A soldier rushes into the clearing and kneels before the King. "Your Majesty. The assassin is dead."

"What? How did this happen?" Bai barks. "Wasn't he under watch?"

"He was, milord. He'd been quiet all afternoon. Suddenly he screamed. We thought it was a trick at first, but then he started writhing and bleeding all over." The soldier's voice quivers as though he was reliving the gruesome scene. The hairs on my arms stand straight up. "He died in seconds."

"Poison," Wang says. "Should we send one of the royal physicians to examine him, Your Majesty?"

Reifeng nods. "Go, Doctor Tsai."

We wait in tense silence for a few minutes before the physician returns. "I found a trace of a substance in his mouth," he says. "It looks and smells the same as a type of poison I've seen once before; besides, it produces the same kind of death as the soldier described. This poison has a delayed effect. Twelve hours after a person consumes it, they die swiftly and painfully."

"What's the name of the poison?" Wang asks.

"I don't know. I've only seen it used once. To the best of my knowledge, no one has yet been able to trace this kind of poison back to its source or place of origin."

Wang dismisses Doctor Tsai, then turns to the soldier. "Did the murderer provide any useful information? Did he let anything slip?"

"Before he died, he said something . . ." Here the soldier hesitates. Sweat beads his upper lip.

"Spill it," Reifeng orders.

The soldier glances at Hwa once, then drops his head lower. "He said, 'what a vicious woman you are, Royal Lady Hwa. I did what you asked, and this is how you repay me. I'll haunt you in my death.'"

All heads snap toward Hwa. My stomach dips and twists.

Jieh bolts up, all lines and angles, sharp with rage. "This is nonsense—"

Yunle stops him with a tug on his sleeve. Jaw clenched, he plops back down.

The soldier looks like he'd rather be anywhere but here. "We all heard it, Your Majesty. I dare not hide it from you—"

Reifeng waves a hand to dismiss him, and looks at Hwa.

The Royal Lady stands, her lips bloodless and her knuckles white. "This is a lie. I've never met that scum in my life."

"Why did he name *you* and no one else?" Yu's smirk makes her sound almost shrill. She pauses as if in contemplation. "Is it because of this widely known discord between you and Miss Lu?"

Hwa looks ready to spit fire at her.

I step out of my spot and bow to the King. "May I speak, Your Majesty?"

"As the intended victim, you have more rights than anyone here," Reifeng says.

"Thank you." I tell him about my discovery in the woods.

Reifeng summons the relevant soldiers to corroborate my account.

"So the assassin had been lying in wait for a while," Wang says at the end. "He already knew Miss Ang would lead you to the river. Does that mean she was involved?"

"Not necessarily," I reply. "Someone else may have given her the idea to lure me there."

"And Miss Ang will be able to tell us who that person is," Wang states. He nods at Bai, who waves to a couple of guards.

Chih has melted into a puddle by the time she's brought before the King. It's a mercy her father took ill and couldn't join the hunt. The prime minister wouldn't tolerate such disgrace from his daughter.

"I had nothing to do with the murder attempt," Chih squeaks.

"Nobody says you did, Miss Ang," I coo. "You just need to explain everything truthfully to His Majesty."

She shivers as her eyes meet Reifeng's. "It was a prank. I was supposed to lure Miss Lu to the river, then we would push her into the water and warn her to stay away from Prince Jieh."

Jieh stares at Chih as if he's never seen her before.

"Why would you do that to me?" I ask.

"Because . . ." She lowers her head and sniffs. "Because . . . I love him."

The nobles snicker.

"You are stating your prank meant no serious harm, and it's just a coincidence that it occurred at the same time as a murder attempt," I say.

"Yes!"

"Who came up with the idea of the prank? Was it Royal Lady Hwa? Did she tell you to lead me to the river?"

"No! Of course not! It was just us girls talking about it." Chih scans the assembly frantically. Her face glows as if she's suddenly seen a way out. She points. Everyone follows the direction of her finger. Aylin is trying to withdraw from the gathering.

"Miss Sun prodded me. She said I'm prettier and a noblewoman and that Prince Jieh would notice me more if Miss Lu stopped seducing him. She suggested we teach her a lesson."

"Miss Sun," Reifeng commands.

Bo looks rigid and chalky pale as Aylin hurries to kneel before the King. "I confess I said such things, Your Majesty, but I know nothing about the murder attempt," she pleads. She whirls to Chih. "Why are you blaming me alone, Miss Ang? All the other ladies agreed that you should teach Miss Lu a lesson. And I wasn't the one who came up with the idea of the river."

"Who did?" Wang demands.

Chih thinks hard, her face scrunched up. "I . . . I don't remember. Everyone was suggesting different things."

Wang summons all the women who awaited me at the river. Each one declares her own innocence and denies that the prank was her idea.

"It doesn't have to be the same person who made the proposition," Yunle interjects, shutting everyone up. "As long as somebody *knew* the prank would happen at the river, she could have instructed the assassin to wait there. Don't you agree, Miss Sun? After all, you *planted* the idea of a prank in Miss Ang's head." Yunle pauses. "I've heard the Lu family wealth is vast."

"I don't know what you're implying, Your Highness, but please don't shame me without a shred of evidence," Aylin says—is the shaking in her voice from anger or fear? "I instigated a prank; that's all." She bites her lip. "I fancy Prince Jieh myself and can't stand my cousin being the one he's enamored with."

For the first time, I see a crack in the mask of Ren's expression. Does he love Aylin? Maybe he just feels insulted that he's her lesser choice. Considered inferior to Jieh in every way, he's driven himself hard to win the crown so that he can trample everyone who's ever looked down upon him.

Or perhaps he does love her. After all, they are both cut from the same cloth.

The picture becomes clearer to me now.

Chih and her bored friends had no motives to want me dead. She also stated that Royal Lady Hwa wasn't involved.

I don't know where Uncle Yi found the assassin or how he made him comply, but he has a gift for intimidating and using people. He obviously had means to obtain a mysterious poison even a royal physician couldn't identify—Doctor Tsai looked almost ashamed to admit this fact.

Not only did Minister Sun intend to have me killed, he also wanted to destroy Jieh's chance for the throne. Only a Queen's son can be made the heir, and Hwa, if convicted of my murder, could never have become Queen.

I put nothing past my uncle because he's resorted to deadly measures before. If I died, his family would certainly try to control my mother by manipulating her grief.

I absorb my wrath and let it feed me, transforming it into something bigger, stronger. I sure as hell will make these bastards pay for their crimes, past and present.

Nonetheless, I cannot prove their murderous intent to the King.

Wen snorts an irate sound. "It seems that Jieh not only has good hands for killing beasts but also for playing beautiful ladies."

Several noblemen laugh. When Reifeng's stern gaze sweeps over them, their laughter dies instantly. His penetrating eyes settle on Wen, who blanches and swallows.

This crude-tongued fool thinks he can be King one day.

I turn to Reifeng and speak loud enough for everyone to hear. "Miss Ang's account of the events clearly shows that Royal Lady Hwa had nothing to do with the attempt on my life, Your Majesty. She and I had a small argument, but people argue every day. It's ridiculous to suggest she'd want to kill me because of that. It seems that someone with evil intent tried to both kill me and use my murder to frame her."

Reifeng nods. "I declare Royal Lady Hwa innocent." Now that the victim has spoken, he accepts my words readily enough. He wouldn't want his favorite son's mother to be charged as a criminal, either.

"But my King, the assassin said Hwa—" Royal Lady Yu begins. Reifeng shoots her an icy glare. She flinches and clamps her mouth shut.

I wouldn't be surprised if both mother and son die of stupidity someday.

Without further evidence to determine who sent the assassin, Reifeng nevertheless promises that justice will be served. I accept his decision, although I know nothing will likely come of this.

After the inquiry ends, the kills from the hunt are counted. Jieh is named winner, and Kai ranks second. I feel a surge of pride for Yunle that she ties with Hanxin for third place. Ren is only one kill short of tying for third-best hunter. Wen fell far behind, as expected.

I eat at the same table as Yao, who expresses his delight that I was unharmed. The dinner begins in a subdued manner, but soon enough, drink loosens tongues and the mood. Jieh, however, barely imbibes and appears thoughtful throughout the meal.

I catch Hanxin watching me. As my gaze collides with his, he raises a cup to me and grins, as if to congratulate me on my lucky escape from death.

I return the gesture despite the needles climbing the length of my spine. Why does he take this creepy interest in me?

Midway through the meal, gossip has circulated regarding why Ren didn't make the top three in the hunt: He could've shot a doe, but when he saw a fawn nearby, he plucked his bowstrings to prompt the doe to run away.

I laugh until tears come. Yao gapes at me as if I've gone mad. No doubt people will believe the story and praise Ren's merciful heart. He's such a skilled charlatan that he probably invented the tale himself. Just like in my last life, he fools everyone. But not me.

After the feast, Royal Lady Hwa sends her maid to fetch me to her tent.

"It was your cousins, wasn't it?" she says without a preamble.

"Your Majestic Ladyship has read my mind."

"They covet your family wealth."

I nod. "And they could've dealt a severe blow to Prince Jieh's chance for the throne if they succeeded in framing his mother for murder."

"Which prince do they support?"

"From what I've gathered, my uncle remains neutral at this point, but Prince Ren has been trying to gain his support for months."

Her brows give a twitch of surprise. Then she smiles, sharp as glass. "If Minister Sun is as smart as I think he is, he would never pledge his allegiance to a prince with meager resources. Regardless, he'll regret the day he made me his enemy."

"I would not underestimate Prince Ren on account of his *meager* resources."

"I wouldn't have, but after his debacle at the commencement ceremony? He's done for." She scoffs. "And that story about the doe at the hunt. How touching."

At her words, a chill slices through me. Ren hasn't given up and never will. He's still maintaining his heart-of-gold image. As a matter of fact, after what happened at the commencement ceremony, his opponents will likely lower their guard further, just like Hwa seems to be doing. But a poisonous snake, even after its tail is cut off, can still bite. Ren's enemies won't expect his counterattack until it's too late.

I must watch him closely and warn Jieh.

Hwa thrusts her imperious chin forward. "I'm in your debt. You do possess a great head and seem to genuinely care for my son. If you help him become King, I shall reserve a Royal Lady's spot for you, despite your lack of noble lineage."

As if I'd be willing to share my future husband with other women.

I'm shocked to find Jieh waiting outside. Before I say anything, he sweeps me into a tight embrace. I fold into him, reveling in his strength and warmth.

For a moment, it feels as if nothing exists beyond where we're standing, beyond us, like we're drifting across a mirror-still sea with no land in sight.

"My whole body seized up when I heard someone tried to harm you," he whispers. "I don't know what I was thinking . . . If anything happened to you . . ."

"I'm all right. That's what matters."

He chuckles and presses into those last few inches of distance between us. One arm still around my waist, his other caresses my cheek. Heat flares over my skin.

He leans down. At the first touch of his lips, everything changes, or I change. A shudder of desire ripples through me, curling low in my belly. I close my eyes and run my hands over his muscular chest and shoulders, trailing my fingers up to the soft ringlets just above his collar.

His mouth presses against mine, over and over, one kiss melting into the next. I drink in his scent of musk and leather and tighten my grip on his hair, drawing him closer still. He moans softly before parting my lips with his tongue.

A rush of pure *want* steals my breath; at the same time, a thought crashes into my mind: *What am I doing?*

I snap back so quickly he gasps. I inhale deeply to regain control. He extends a hand toward my cheek, bewilderment knitting his brows. "Mingshin—"

I shrink away. "Please . . . don't."

The hurt on his face is unbearable. I harden my heart. I tell myself to tug it back, that he cannot have it.

He offers to escort me back to my tent. Fei has just now reappeared, although I don't remember her disappearing.

Jieh and I say nothing as we walk, sharing the stillness of the night.

But I know this peace won't last. Just like the turmoil raging inside me.

I mustn't let my feelings continue spiraling down this path. I'll only end up getting hurt all over again. I know my place. A royal prince would never truly, fully devote himself to a plain, commoner girl. If I cannot have all of a man's love, I'd rather not have any.

"Be careful of Ren," I call after Jieh as he leaves. "He's not going to give up."

He doesn't look back.

I steel myself. I must shut Jieh out, no matter how difficult it is.

My head tells me that's the right thing to do. But my heart yawns hollow with the emptiness left by this decision, even as I stand outside my tent and watch him fade into the darkness, my skin still burning from his touch and my lips throbbing from his kiss.

CHAPTER 24

The Elite Hunt continues into the next day. Jieh didn't say goodbye to me when he left to hunt this morning. He's a proud man, and I doubt he's ever been rejected by a woman in his life.

I should feel relieved if he decides to keep some distance between us. It would be best for both of us. But all day I've been moving around like a wooden puppet. A great void has opened up inside me, expanding and threatening to swallow me whole.

I try to focus on the people I need to keep an eye on. But Ren and Bo have also gone on the hunt. Aylin sticks with her group of confidantes, while Chih does the same. Whenever the two women pass each other, showers of angry sparks seem to go off.

Those two won't be plotting together anytime soon. Jokes about their fighting over Jieh have been circulating throughout the camp. No doubt their fathers will find their public humiliation less amusing. My reputation-obsessed uncle will have an especially difficult time answering to his superior, Prime Minister Ang, regarding Aylin's instigation of Chih's prank. That thought brings me a small measure of satisfaction.

Inside our tent, Fei promises to be even more vigilant around my cousins. "I miss Hui," she says. "If he were here, he'd have given your cousins the beating they deserve." She smiles at the look on my face. "Yes, he's very protective of those he cares about, even at the risk of his own life. When we were little, we got beaten often while begging, but he always used his body to shield me."

This is the first time I've heard Fei talk about her childhood. A lead weight drops in my stomach. I hadn't known . . .

"Later we joined a circus. Hui almost lost his life when he stopped a tiger's attack on me. He got three deep wounds on his shoulders and back that took a long time to heal and left large scars." Fei's face hardens, eyes glittering like black stones. "After that, I was determined to become as strong as my brother."

The lead in my stomach burns. My throat strains from holding back tears. I stand and hug Fei; she wraps her arms around me.

"He's very brave," I whisper. "So are you. I'm very happy to know both of you as my protectors and adopted members of our family."

The hunters return in the late afternoon. Jieh and Kai each captured a silver fox alive, but more interestingly, Elder Hanxin felled a kui and obtained its single antler. The exotic beast is the size of a bull, but more ferocious in nature and with a glossy, dark-green hide three times tougher to penetrate. Its horn-shaped antler is impossible to break and is said to have numerous medicinal benefits, including one related to manhood.

When everyone clamors to see the kui's body, Hanxin challenges them with a laugh. "Go find it yourselves! I've had enough fun for the day."

Surprisingly, Ren only sacked a few rabbits. As I watch him, I feel a strange leap in my gut, like there's something unsettling about him, almost sinister.

I brush off the feeling. It's probably just my growing repulsion at knowing what he truly is. Despite his betrayal, there had been a soft part in me reserved for him: I still felt some hurt, some anger, whenever I thought about how he used me, or when I saw him cuddling up to Aylin. That part seems to have gone.

Reifeng retires early from the feast, joined by the two Royal Ladies. In their absence, people choose to sit wherever they like. Yunle invites me to her table. She pours some wine and turns to my bodyguard. "This is for you, Fei. I haven't thanked you yet for saving my best friend's life."

Fei bows, then lifts the jade cup and downs it. She steps forward and, with my permission, fills another jade cup. With both hands, she presents the wine to Yunle. "Your Highness, please accept my admiration for you as a skilled hunter."

Yunle laughs. "Gladly." She takes the wine and downs it.

A wide grin cuts across my face. Fei bows again and assumes her original position. I catch her sneaking another glance at Yunle.

A loud guffaw bursts from nearby. I turn to find Yao sitting a few benches over from us, with Jieh and several other young lords. I watch them eating, drinking, and laughing. Jieh's had plenty of time to look in our direction, but he appears to be ignoring me.

My smile falls and my joy sours.

Yunle glances at Jieh, then at me. "What's going on between you two?"

"Oh, nothing."

She narrows her eyes. "I'm neither blind nor stupid, you know."

Embarrassed, I lower my head.

She sighs. "He adores you, and I've never seen him like this. I don't know why you are so guarded with your feelings, Mingshin, but you don't have to be."

She may as well have punched me in the belly. What can I say? That I may not be able to mend my heart if it gets broken again?

I've lost my appetite, so I stand and bid Yunle goodnight.

"Whatever you are afraid of, I'm here to listen," she says. "Or you can talk it out with Jieh. It may not be as hopeless as you think."

My tongue suddenly feels thick in my mouth. All I manage is a nod.

Once Fei and I get back to our tent, I plop down on a cushion. I should get ready for bed, but I don't want to move, don't feel like doing anything. I stare into the air.

It may not be as hopeless as you think.

Lately, I've been feeling a thread of yearning tug relentlessly at my core. Could Yunle be right? But that's a dangerous path to take—

Fei leaps suddenly to the tent flap, jolting me out of my thoughts. "Who's there?" she hisses, sword at the ready.

I rise, every muscle in my body tight.

"Miss Lu, if you'll allow me a few minutes?" comes Hanxin's deep, rich voice.

Fei and I exchange a wary look.

"I'm afraid it's not a good time, Respectable Elder," I say. "I'm ready to retire for the night."

"I won't be long. What I need to talk to you about is very important." There's a pause, then, "I cannot leave until we speak."

I groan inwardly. If someone sees him outside my tent, it could get me in trouble. I sigh and nod at Fei, who lifts the flap to reveal the Elder.

He strides in, followed closely by his bodyguard, Longzo.

"I've hoped to meet you again since our last conversation, Miss Lu. But it's been hard. Fortunately, it was Prince Wen's turn to watch me tonight. After a few good drinks and some flattery, he completely let his guard down. I regret that I was unable to speak to you last night. Please allow me to express my relief and happiness that you escaped harm and stayed safe."

He didn't take all this trouble just to say a few nice words to me. I'm curious about his purpose here, but the risk of being spotted alone with him isn't worth it. "Thank you, Respectable Elder. If there's nothing else, I bid you a good evening."

Hanxin glances around as if he hadn't heard me. His gaze settles on the book I left open on a pillow. *"History of the Continent.* How interesting. Are you learning more about Nan'Yü? You must have given some thought to our last conversation."

"I'm interested in learning about all cultures on the continent."

"But most of those cultures do not respect intelligent, brave women like you as much as we do in Nan'Yü. You'd achieve heights there unimaginable for a Dazhouan woman. I believe you'd enjoy living in my country."

His eyes are bright and keen. I've never seen him like this. Once again, I'm reminded of how young he is, only a few years older than me.

I'd love to travel the entire continent one day like Father did, but I'm not sure about living in a foreign country. Why did Hanxin even suggest that? "What do you want from me, Respectable Elder?" I ask.

He smiles. "Are you familiar with the Nan'Yüan traditions surrounding the marriage proposal, Miss Lu?"

"All I know is that a man or a woman normally presents a precious gift to whomever they are interested in and politely asks for permission to marry."

Hanxin reaches beneath his tunic, and Fei lifts her sword instantly, but he doesn't pull out a weapon. Instead, he draws out the kui's antler he acquired during the hunt, and presents it to me.

"I ask you to marry me, Miss Lu."

What? My mind reels, and the floor drops out from beneath me. Fei gasps.

"We'll thrive together as husband and wife, Miss Lu," Hanxin says. "I'll be faithful. You will have equal decision-making power in every domestic matter and state affair. This, I swear by the gods who granted my ancestors their power."

I open my mouth and shut it a few times. At last, I find my tongue. "Why do you want to marry me? We barely know each other and certainly don't love each other."

"Love cannot last forever, but respect can. I admire your intelligence, courage, and strong will."

I take a step back. "I'm flattered, but I cannot accept."

"Why?"

"Because I won't even consider the possibility without knowing the true reason behind this marriage proposal."

He studies me with his full-bore stare. I keep my gaze steady, my posture firm.

"What else can I do to convince you to change your mind?" he says.

"Nothing. Good night, Elder."

His smile spreads, teeth glinting like knifepoints. "I respect your decision, Miss Lu. We shall speak of this another time, and maybe by then you will be more receptive. Perhaps your reticence is due to the late hour." He inclines his head at me, then sweeps away. Longzo follows him like a faithful shadow.

It takes a few moments for me to shake off the lingering shock of Hanxin's outrageous suggestion.

"What does he want?" Fei growls. "Is he out of his mind?"

"Whatever he wants, you can be sure it's more than what he says."

I notice that Hanxin left the kui's antler on my bed. I tell Fei to hurry and return it to him.

She comes back soon, the precious piece still in hand. "I didn't see the Elder or his guard anywhere. It's like they just disappeared," she huffs.

I scowl. How could they have gotten away so fast?

"I don't think it wise to go to their tent and risk being seen."

"I agree. Let's hide his gift so no one sees it." I understand Nan'Yüan culture enough to know we can't throw a proposal gift away; Hanxin may request it back, and the kui's antler is too valuable. "We'll return it when we get a chance."

Fei nods. "What are you going to do about the Elder? I don't think he'll give up easily."

I fear she's right. Hanxin seems like the type of man who always gets what he wants no matter how many obstacles stand in his path.

"My sword can protect you against ten normal men." Fei doesn't sound scared, just worried. "But with magic in his arsenal—"

"We need to be more careful, is all. He won't use magic during the hunt. He can't afford to be caught again."

As I stare at the antler, however, it's Jieh who pops into my head. His passionate gaze, his warm kisses, even his arrogant smiles . . .

How can I feel both a fluttering in my chest and a jab in my gut in the same breath? I bite my lip as I wrench my thoughts away from Jieh.

CHAPTER 25

The next morning, we learn that King Reifeng has fallen ill, so he and the Royal Ladies will return to the palace. The majority of the royal court and guards will leave with them. As for Hanxin, the King has ordered he accompany him. After the Elder's peculiar marriage proposal, I'm especially pleased by his departure.

In the end, only the princes, the young lords, a dozen women, their guards, and a handful of soldiers remain at the encampment. Doctor Tsai was ordered to stay behind in case a hunter is injured.

Jieh rides past me on his way to the forest without saying a word. A sharp pain twists in my chest. But I shouldn't feel hurt. I shove every thought about Jieh into a vault in my head and mentally lean hard to shut the door.

As I turn around to go back to my tent, a sudden prickle runs down my spine.

I'm being watched. By something swirling with darkness.

I glance around, my breaths tight.

"What's wrong?" Fei asks at my alarmed look, a hand on the hilt of her sword.

The men have gone out hunting again. Even the women are scattered. None of the patrols are looking at me.

"Nothing," I say and resume walking.

The sensation of being watched doesn't ease. I shake my head and clear my mind, sure it's my imagination, but the feeling stays, so strong that goosebumps sprout all over my skin.

Could it be Hanxin? I can't think of anyone else this interested in me.

But Hanxin has left. Could his magic be this far-reaching? Perhaps it's Longzo. After all, he's only a servant. If Hanxin sent him back, it's possible no one has noticed.

Throughout the day, the creepy feeling comes and goes. If this continues, I fear I'll go mad. I consider telling Fei, but what can I say? It's something too strange to share even with someone as close to me as my bodyguard.

In the evening, the men remaining in the hunt light several bonfires and congregate to tell stories, sing songs, and roast game. I no longer feel a presence spying on me. If it's Longzo, he's probably afraid of detection given that there are so many people around now.

Yunle, Fei, and I sit together with two other women and a group of royal soldiers. Jieh revels and drinks with his friends around another fire. He never looks my way.

I grit my teeth, determined not to let my hurt show.

Yunle glances between Jieh and me, her brows pinched. But thankfully she says nothing. Instead, she hands me a stick of roasted meat. "Have some boar. It may have been my kill."

I accept it. Soon enough, we are all feasting and laughing, ladies' manners forgotten. Yunle squeezes Fei's upper arm, and Fei colors a deep rose. Which is amazing, for I've never seen my bodyguard blush in either of my lives.

Our party lasts past midnight. Slowly people disperse, retiring for the night. As Fei and I walk to our tent, I hear the princes assign patrol duties to the remaining soldiers.

In minutes, Fei's light snoring reaches me from the other end of the bed.

I fish my pendant out from beneath my sleeping gown and pull the blanket further up to my neck. Tonight I'm committed to finding out more about the Divine Stone so I can determine whether Hanxin has been searching for it.

What did the spirit say? "When you begged for another life, you showed the potential of becoming what the Stone needed you to be. . . ."

I may have begged for another life, but I also *demanded* one.

Along the way, I have continued to demonstrate *a strong will and growing determination*, according to the spirit.

Perhaps that's the key!

Take me to you, I command. *I have many more questions and I want answers.*

I repeat the demand over and over in my mind, pouring all my will into it, as I drift off to sleep.

I open my eyes to find myself in the Holy Temple. I snatch the Divine Stone from the jar eagerly. Again, it balloons to the size of my head in a blink, glowing with five colors. The nine-rayed star flares golden and hums with power, a vibration I feel in the soles of my feet.

Are you here? I ask the spirit.

The air ripples and shivers. I almost jump out of my skull when a woman shimmers into view before me.

She is—my breath hitches—*grand.* I wouldn't call her beautiful; the word sounds inadequate to describe her. She isn't tall, but her presence somehow fills the entire space. It's impossible to determine her age, for time no longer seems to affect her. She holds herself with impeccable grace, in a bright-yellow dress that seems woven from sunlight itself—the most exquisite creation I've ever seen.

She peers down at herself. "I've gained form," she whispers, her voice full of wonder. "How? It hasn't happened for two centuries."

I recognize her voice. "You're the spirit residing in the Stone," I exclaim.

She looks at me. The confusion clears from her eyes, and she appears and sounds regal again. "I am High Priestess Sudaji. I died two hundred years ago, and my soul has been trapped in the Divine Stone ever since."

That's why I couldn't place her accent. Then I remember her name.

"High Priestess Sudaji! You vanished along with your priests and the Holy Temple two centuries ago, and your . . ." I stop. It sounds terrible to mention that their bodies were never found.

Sadness overlays her face like frost.

"I'm sorry to hear you've been trapped in here for so long," I say. "It must've been very lonely."

She nods, then smiles. "It was, but not so much as I watched you grow from a baby into a kind, passionate young woman."

"You've been watching me all my life?" I gasp, horrified.

"I don't mean to sound intrusive, Mingshin, but seeing as you keep the Divine Stone with you all the time, it's hard *not* to watch you at least some of the time. Occasionally I wished I could send you advice through the Stone. But given the weakness of your will in your previous life, you wouldn't have been able to enter the spiritual realm even if I had summoned you. And even if you somehow could, I wouldn't have trusted you with the secret of the Divine Stone."

Her last words hit like a hammer blow. "You must've been disappointed with how I turned out in my first life."

"I won't deny that, but we've all been young and we've all made mistakes. You and I both trusted the wrong kind of people. I'm proud to see that, with your second chance at life, you've been growing strong in both mind and body."

My hurt flees in a rush, replaced by happiness.

"My mistake, however, was far larger and had a much bigger impact," she adds.

Curiosity burns in me, but I don't press her, for I can tell it's still causing her pain.

"I shall teach you the history, Mingshin," she says. "It's important for you to know. Let me start from the very beginning. When the gods ascended to Heaven, Goddess Nüwa left the Divine Stone to the ancestors of the Nan'Yüans and built the Holy Temple to preserve it."

"Goddess Nüwa, mother of mankind?" Awe fills my voice.

"Yes. The Stone is meant to be used to protect mankind from large-scale catastrophes. The High Priestess and her group of priests can call upon godly powers by channeling through the Stone. This must be done with perfect control, or there can be dire consequences. People may not be aware of it, but throughout history, the priests have used the Divine Stone several times to prevent mankind from being wiped out. They've always combined their powers, with the High Priestess as the leader."

I don't move or speak—I don't even breathe loudly.

"During my time, there was a very talented priest, Zisou, whose power soon surpassed mine. He grew greedy and aspired to take the Divine Stone. He secretly gathered followers among the priests by promising a share of the Stone's power for their personal use. When I discovered the plot, Zisou and his minions slaughtered the other priests, then tried to seize the Stone. Out of desperation, I channeled destructive power through the Stone. It was too much for me to handle alone. Although it vaporized Zisou and his minions, it killed me as well. The Holy Temple shielded my soul from being shredded, but as a result, both the temple and my soul were trapped in the spiritual realm of the Stone."

Sudaji stares down at her hands. A flare of anguish blooms across her face, so real and endless that I feel it in my gut. "*My* actions caused these horrendous consequences."

"You did the only thing you could under the circumstances," I say. "If you hadn't channeled the power, Zisou would have taken the Divine Stone. Worse things would have happened."

She sighs. "Knowing this doesn't ease my guilt."

I wish I could give her a moment of peace, but my questions are urgent. "How is it that there isn't any record of the Divine Stone, if it's been used for the good of mankind?" I ask.

She drops her hands and turns to me, once again the portrait of dignity. "The Divine Stone was a closely guarded secret at the Holy Temple. One must pass rigorous spiritual and magical tests to become a priest. Then, new priests were taught how to channel through the Stone. I'm afraid any knowledge of it has died along with me."

"So the public was told a lie. The priests in the temple weren't merely assigned the task of overseeing Magic there."

"Yes. Can you imagine the outcome if the public learned about the Divine Stone?'

Absolutely. Wars would be waged, blood would be spilled, and millions of lives would be lost as people fought over its possession.

"Does this mean that no one nowadays knows of the Divine Stone?" I ask.

"I believe so. Everyone who knew died in Zisou's revolt." Her voice trembles slightly here, but otherwise it's sturdy. "My loyal priests would never have betrayed to an outsider the secret they swore to guard with their lives. Zisou considered knowledge power; he and his clique would never have shared such precious knowledge with anyone, either."

Somehow this doesn't make me feel any better. If I'm the only person aware of the existence of the Divine Stone, the burden of protecting the secret alone would be heavy enough to crush me.

"Time was reset to give you a second chance at life," Sudaji says. "The most powerful seers can detect the altered flow of time if they look closely enough. They may not know what exactly caused that, but they'd deduce it was a magical tool with power unmatched by any other. People would want it for themselves. Fortunately, they'd never guess it's owned by you, a girl without magic."

"They might," I blurt. "A Nan'Yüan Elder was sent here by the High Priestess. He's taken enormous interest in me, and I have no idea why. He just asked me to marry him. Since then, I've had this horrible feeling that I'm being watched."

Sudaji's shoulders tense, eyes sharp like the edge of a blade. "Has he seen your pendant? Has anyone other than your parents?"

I shake my head firmly.

"You can no longer visit here, Mingshin." Her expression is strained and her voice tight. Could she be pained by this decision? "They may not know yet that you possess the Stone, but if they are watching you, every time you enter its spiritual realm you are making its presence clearer to them."

A shiver rips through me. "You don't think they are good people."

"After Zisou's betrayal, I don't trust anyone. Except you, because the Stone chose you. You should do the same, Mingshin. Protect the Stone from falling into the wrong hands. Leave now, if you don't wish to expose its existence to your enemies or risk being trapped here forever."

Then she's gone.

I'm lying in bed again, enveloped in darkness. All is quiet except Fei's light snoring. I hold tight to the blanket as the Divine Stone glimmers beneath it.

Emotions, roaring and nauseating, roil through me.

Hanxin may be pursuing me for the Divine Stone after all. But I cannot turn to anyone for help. Fortunately he doesn't know what the Stone looks like. Is that why he asks to marry me, to gain my trust, so I'll reveal the secret to him?

But why doesn't he just use Blood magic on me? Even if he doesn't possess it, he could easily order another Blood sorcerer to do so.

My head is pounding with confusion when a sudden, invisible force hits me like a cannonball filled with ice pellets. It only lasts seconds, but I'm left gasping.

Fei is awake in an instant. "Are you all right, Miss?" she asks in alarm.

"I . . . I don't know." I cannot put it into words, the small voice of warning sounding in the back of my head. "We should take a look outside."

I rise and put on a light dress over my nightshirt, then wrap myself in a cloak. Fei dons her leather jerkin, pants, and sword.

The full moon casts its generous light upon us. Several fires are still burning. I can make out the silhouettes of soldiers patrolling the perimeter.

Fei whirls to her right and strides to the north side of our tent. Uncertain, I follow. After a few steps, she turns to me and puts a finger to her mouth. I nod and tiptoe after her.

She comes to a halt and points. I squint, following her fingertip. Then I spy them.

Two men are squatting in the shadows. Using a thin reed, they appear to be blowing something into our tent through a tiny hole.

Fei dashes forward and knocks one man out by smacking him on the head with the hilt of her sword. The other sucks in a sharp breath, then falls backward.

When he doesn't move for a bit, Fei bends down and checks on him. "He's fainted," she whispers with a scowl.

I peer inside the tent through the hole. It's filled with some kind of dark-green smoke.

"He may have accidentally breathed in whatever he was blowing into the tent after we surprised him," I say.

"Could they have been sent by your uncle to murder us in our sleep?" Fei asks.

I shake my head. "No. He isn't foolish enough to try something like this so soon after his blunder at the river."

"You are right." Fei muses for a moment. "Could Hanxin be behind this?"

"Maybe." A fresh wave of anxiety throbs under my skin. If they were Hanxin's men, has he decided to drop his sham and abduct me instead?

Fei freezes, her face concentrating as if she's listening for something else. I dare not make a sound.

She leaps up and flits back the way we came. I hurry after her. She whips her head left and right, her expression stern. Abruptly, she breaks off running to the soldier posted in the innermost circle, who stands near a large gong. "Sound the alarm! Danger's coming!" she bellows.

I stand petrified, not understanding. But given her commanding tone, the man raises a mallet to strike the gong. Just then, a silver light streaks out of the darkness, accompanied by a sharp whistle that pierces the air. An arrow whams into the guard's chest. He wavers on his feet, then crumbles into a heap.

I bite down a scream as Fei yanks me to the ground along with her. We watch helplessly as the patrols drop one by one as more arrows rain down.

Fei's shouts have awakened some soldiers, and they come running out. But most of them are impaled almost immediately, and the rest are forced to shield themselves against a second barrage of arrows. Just when I think it can't get worse, dots of light burst out of the darkness; fire arrows soar toward the tents and ignite several at once.

My pulse races and my ribs feel tight. The people inside will be burned alive. Jieh, Yunle, and Yao are still asleep. As are all the other innocent men and women!

Given how much wine they consumed, I must make a bigger noise to rouse them.

Breathing courage into my lungs, I get on all fours and scramble away from Fei. I try not to wince as I pass behind and over the bodies of fallen soldiers. A shudder ripples through me as I spot the mallet almost within reach. Just then, a hiss splits the air behind me. I speed ahead, and an arrow thunks into the ground near my feet.

Keeping my panic in check, I vault forward and grab the mallet. Then I leap up and strike the gong again and again despite the deafening sound it produces.

The whole camp comes alive.

I let a small sigh of relief escape. It isn't even all the way out of my mouth when the earth rumbles like rolling thunder. Startled, I drop the mallet. A stampede of horses charges into the clearing carrying masked men dressed in black; the riders slash their swords ferociously at everyone in their path.

I barely dodge a horse bolting my way. Pandemonium reigns as the marauders swing their swords indiscriminately, cutting down tent ropes and men and women alike. More masked aggressors arrive on foot, similarly clothed. They rush into the encampment from all sides.

I try to get to Fei, but it's impossible with all the people and animals pressed between us. As I watch, she spins just in time to slam aside an assailant's sword. The momentum throws him off his steed. As the horse continues to run, the man gathers himself quickly and engages Fei in hand-to-hand combat.

I pull my dagger out of my boot and crawl low to conceal myself behind a small tree. Fires burn everywhere. Many bodies lie on the ground, some unmoving and others writhing in pain. A few people are aflame, shrieking in agony.

Ribbons of dread choke me. We are vastly outnumbered, with only a small contingent still standing to fight. Six raiders attack Kai and his two guards. Wen pulls Aylin behind him, struggling to reach safety. Fei fights her way toward me. Yunle is herding a group of screaming women away. The air fills with the ringing of steel on steel and the metallic stench of blood.

But Jieh is nowhere to be seen.

My heart twists upon itself.

Surely, he is fine. He's the most skilled swordsman of them all.

I spot a woman scurrying before a gelding. It's Chih. She falls and scrambles on all fours, desperate to get away.

I groan, but dash out of my hiding spot. I stab the rider in the leg with my dagger; its blade easily slides into muscle and draws blood. The man howls in pain and lurches off his horse.

I dart away. A few masked men spot me and rush after me. In the chaos, I don't know where I am racing to, only that I need to get somewhere that's not burning.

I stop at the edge of a rocky gorge. Beneath me, the river winds through the landscape like a long, shiny snake. Judging from the sound of the current, the water flows faster in this section of the river, and I have no idea how deep it is.

I turn, trying to find another way out of the madness around me, but I'm soon surrounded on three sides. I lift my dagger in front of me, ready to slash at anyone who gets too close.

But their weapons have a longer reach: dirks, scimitars, tall knives . . .

I swallow, sweat breaking out all over my skin. I hear hoof-beats approach, but I dare not take my eyes off the six men who have me cornered.

A neigh splits the air and a monstrous shape descends from the sky. A streak of light slices through the darkness. Screams ring out and blood sprays.

The man nearest me curses and jumps forward. I spin around and thrust my dagger forward with all my strength. It plunges between his ribs, and he collapses. I yank the blade out, fighting back the nausea sweeping over me.

"Mingshin!"

I turn to find Jieh on Sky Dancer. Two of my assailants have fled, but the others are lying on the ground, their bodies covered in blood.

Relief washes over me, fierce and bright.

In the same instant, I hear a vicious hiss in the air. Jieh vaults off Sky Dancer and embraces me, his strong arms wrapped around my waist. Then we're both rolling. Arrows slam into the ground around us.

A horse charges our way, followed by a group of men on foot. The masked rider brandishes his sword in the air. "That's Prince Jieh! Ten thousand gold taels on his head!"

Sky Dancer attacks from the side and knocks him off his steed. At the same time, Jieh springs up with the speed and grace of a pouncing tiger.

"Stay behind me!" he orders.

I obey, my back to the river. That's when I notice the dark patch spreading along his side. I gasp. He must have been wounded while using his body to shield me.

The masked intruders press forward and are soon upon Jieh. As his sword blocks their weapons, clanging sounds ring through the glade. He wields his saber so quickly and forcefully that the wind howls with every swing. Nearby, Sky Dancer fends off another rider to keep him away from his master.

Jieh runs his blade through a man while kicking another to the ground. He parries an overhand strike, then swings his sword in a great two-handed arc that slays the other. Two enemies down, but more keep coming. The dismounted rider joins the scuffle. He's much better than his companions. His steel dances too fast for my eyes to follow.

The loss of blood must be tiring Jieh. He's still deflecting their assaults, but we're being pushed farther and farther back. I desperately want to help. A few times I scoot out from behind him to stab at our enemy, only to withdraw when I realize I'm more likely a distraction.

Jieh knocks the dismounted rider's sword out of his grip and uses his free hand to punch another man in the throat. But his steps begin to falter and his breath is getting heavy. If only this nightmare would end so I could attend to his wound.

Someone strikes our enemies from the left side. As two men drop to the ground, the newcomer reaches us.

I'm stunned to see it's Kai. After exchanging a quick nod, the brothers fight side by side.

Sudden shouts break out from the campsite. "Retreat! Retreat!"

Our adversaries flee. Jieh remains where he is, a protective arm over me. Kai leaps at one straggler and pierces him in the heart. As he pulls his sword out, I take a step back to avoid being elbowed by him.

Suddenly I lose my footing and slip into a void. I let out a short cry, and Jieh twists to grab my hand. The next second, he grunts and pitches forward.

We free fall into the river.

CHAPTER 26

The cold steals my breath the instant I hit the water. A chill quickly spreads through my body, slicing to my bones with an icy blade.

I struggle to the surface, only to find myself being swept downstream. I kick my legs furiously to keep afloat while swinging my head from side to side, but Jieh is nowhere to be seen. Panic freezes my voice, until I finally force out a squeaky sound, "Jieh!"

No one answers me. My heart pounds, a scream building inside my head.

No. I must stay calm. First I need to get to shore—the one farthest from the cliff's edge—then I'll search for Jieh.

I fumble to untie my cloak, because its weight is dragging me down. Then I swim, committing my entire strength to each arduous stroke. It seems to take forever for my skills to return to me, and the frigid temperature of the water further saps my strength, but eventually I reach a boulder and hoist myself up. I am shivering and exhausted, but resolve propels me to move on.

"Jieh!" I dare not call out too loudly as I hike along the bank, searching the shadows for any moving object. But all is quiet and still.

Despair begins to sink its razor-sharp teeth into my chest, making my voice shake.

Then I spot a glimmer of light rippling across the water. I hurry forward. It's Jieh bobbing on the surface, his tunic snagged on a tree branch extending into the river. His hand still grips his sword, which sparkles. I plunge into the water, hissing at the shock of the cold. When I reach him, I check his breathing. He's weak but alive, and it seems his bleeding has stopped. Tears well up in my eyes.

I put my dagger back in my boot, then pull him through the water. His tall and muscular body and his wet clothing makes him extra heavy. When I finally drag him ashore, I want to sink to the ground with exhaustion. But there is no time to waste. With both hands on his chest, I press down again and again.

He coughs, river water spewing out of his mouth.

I fall on my bottom, dizzy with relief.

He opens his eyes. "Mingshin," he says weakly. "You're safe."

My safety is the first thing that comes to his mind? I feel a tiny crack in that cage I've built around my heart. "We must take care of your wound soon," I say. "And we need to find shelter. Can you walk?"

He nods. Propping himself up on one arm, he puts out a hand and brushes the wet hair away from my face. "Silly girl. I don't die easily."

I realize I've been crying. I turn and wipe my tears away.

He looks around. "I recognize this place," he says. "Once, on a hunting trip, I found a cave nearby."

"Good. Let's go there."

He sheaths his sword and stands. Immediately he leans on one foot, his brow flexing in pain. "I twisted my ankle." He doesn't say more, but I know it must have been when he arched his body trying to catch me.

I grab his arm and put it around my shoulders.

He doesn't move. A head and neck taller than me, he's probably afraid I won't be able to hold his weight.

"We need to go now," I say.

As we stagger further downstream, his slow pace makes it clear he's only putting a tiny portion of his weight on me. The thought somehow infuses me with enough warmth to fend off the numbing chill.

The cave is close, the one fortunate thing that has happened all night. It's surrounded by a ring of trees, next to an overgrown trail, its opening partially hidden. Jieh tells me to gather a few pine cones off the forest floor. After shoving the thick foliage aside to reveal the entrance, he throws the cones into the cave.

When no animals stir, Jieh lumbers forward. I follow him. The darkness is so complete it feels like a weightless veil covering my eyes.

"I have some signal fire sticks," he says. "Give me a moment to break the wax protecting them."

"Ah, these are useful," I exclaim.

He chuckles. Seconds later, light illuminates the cave, blinding me momentarily.

Jieh clutches a signal fire stick. He wavers on his feet, and I leap ahead to help him sit. He's even colder than I am. "I need to take off your clothes," I say. This is no time for modesty.

He unbuckles his sword and spreads his arms. I take off his jerkin, then gingerly peel the tunic off him. I catch a glimpse of his sculpted torso, the hard ridges of his abdomen. Heat creeps up my face but dissipates as soon as my eyes flicker to his wound.

I examine it. The arrow pierced his side, but fortunately it doesn't seem as though there's any internal damage, and the bleeding has stopped. The possibility of infection worries me, but we'll have to wait out the night before we can find our way back and have the wound checked by the royal physicians.

"I wish I had my cloak," I say.

"Use my clothes."

I tear a large swathe of his tunic off, then wrap it around his midriff, applying just enough pressure to prevent future bleeding.

He looks at me with renewed curiosity. "You've done this before?"

"Yes." I'd dressed Ren's wounds a few times in my former life.

He seems to want to ask for more details, but thankfully he doesn't pry further. "You must be a good swimmer," he says instead.

I nod. I learned to swim shortly after Ren saved me from drowning in the pond at Uncle Yi's estate.

I remove Jieh's boots and examine his ankle. It looks red and swollen.

"It's nothing serious," Jieh says. "A little rest and I'll be fine."

I hope he'll be able to walk tomorrow morning.

He notices me staring at the glowing fire stick planted in the rocky ground. "I'm sure you know how these work?"

"Yes. A normal fire stick only illuminates, but a signal fire stick can do more. If you shake it gently, it lights like a candle; if shaken violently, it shoots a stream of flame into the sky. They are usually limited to military use."

He doesn't seem surprised at my knowledge, instead smiling in satisfaction. "My father made a special order of this for each of his children. He commanded we carry them during the hunt in case we needed to signal for rescue. But I saw no use for the gift until now."

"Too bad we can't use them to send a signal now. It may draw our attackers back to us." I stand. "I'll go collect some wood. We need fire to dry our clothes."

The one thing that's not in shortage in the forest is wood. I quickly go about my task, gathering up fallen branches. When I return, I ignite the kindling with the fire stick, then sit across from Jieh and take off my boots. I lift my feet so the bottom of my raiment can face the fire. Oh gods, it feels good.

"You're going to dry your clothes while wearing them?" Jieh says, incredulous.

A blush rises in my cheeks.

Jieh chortles. "Let's sit back-to-back, I won't peek. I promise on my honor," he adds solemnly.

Since he's so proud, his honor must mean a lot to him. I sure hope so.

We prop some branches up. With my back to him, I take off my dress and hang it on our makeshift drying rack. Then I settle next to the fire with my nightshirt on and my pendant—the Divine Stone— tucked safely underneath it.

"Thank you for saving my life," he says, as he sits down with his back to me.

I shake my head. "You wouldn't have fallen into the river in the first place if you hadn't tried to catch me. You wouldn't have been wounded and separated from Sky Dancer if you hadn't blocked the arrows meant for me." I pause to take a deep breath. "Why?" I whisper. "Why did you do those things for me?"

He's silent and still for a moment. "I didn't really think. I just . . . did. I'd do it all over again . . . for you."

For you. At these two words, a knot of emotions tangles around my heart. It feels like half of me wants to yield while the other wants to hold out.

Jieh speaks again. I've never heard such a gentle voice from him before. "Do you remember the first time we met, Mingshin? The way you spoke to me, looked at me, I thought, wow, so fierce for such a small creature. It surprised me that I felt happy to have run into you at your uncle's home. I thought I'd never see you again . . ." He chuckles, and I imagine a soft smile forming on his face.

"Then you tricked me and won the archery contest. An ingenious move. When my father told me I could pick any woman to be my companion for the race, I didn't give anyone else a thought. And there you amazed me once again. You may not be a warrior of the sword, but you're one of the mind. Since then, everything in my life has changed. You're the first thing I think of when I wake up, and the last when I go to bed. I like how a corner of your mouth tilts up when you show disdain for fools, and how your eyes twinkle when you have a clever idea, and how content I feel just to see you smile."

My whole body tingles.

"I know you have feelings for me, the way you kissed me." He pauses. "Why are you always pushing me away?" It's spoken with a sigh, like a breath of wind whispering through leaves, but it strikes me to the core.

I want to pour it all out to him. I fight the urge. Fight him. Fight myself.

"I know it's not that you don't want me, Mingshin. Something in you is holding you back. A secret. I won't ask you about it. I just hope that one day I'll earn your trust, or at least enough that you'll choose to open your heart up to me."

Jieh's hand reaches out and finds mine. I let him take it. Somehow, the act calms me. A wash of serene peace settles over me.

Driven by some unknown force, we turn toward each other until our legs touch. My breathing becomes ragged as his eyes find mine in the flickering light—hungry, unyielding. He pulls me closer to him. I feel the warmth of his breath as an impact that spreads deliciously down my neck, dancing along every fiber of my body.

He smooths the tangled tendrils of hair back from my face. The contact sends pleasant shivers through me. Then he's caressing my cheek, his thumb stroking my lip. I start to pull away before I catch fire. But he holds my face in his hands. There's nowhere to run to. And there's nowhere I *want* to run.

He presses his gentle lips to mine. The pit of my stomach drops away as I open my mouth to his. His tongue sweeps in, caressing mine. I moan at the taste of him. My whole world narrows to the softness of his lips, the eager tangling of our tongues, and the tight, warm ache in my belly.

His hands roam over my back, sending flames of desire through me. He kisses my hair, breathes against the hollow of my throat, and nibbles my ear. Every molecule inside me explodes with light.

He seizes my lips again. A deeper, longer kiss that sizzles through me. I am nothing but pure sensation and energy. Heat floods me from my lips to my toes, and I melt into him.

My breasts touch his solid chest. Through the thin fabric of my nightshirt, I feel him tense.

Senses snap back into my brain. We are half naked, and this could lead to something we might both regret later if I let it continue.

I break our kiss and set a hand upon his shoulder, giving him a gentle push.

He closes his eyes. Shame blankets his face before he opens them again. "I'm sorry, Mingshin. It won't happen again, I swear."

We revert to sitting back-to-back.

"Get some sleep, Mingshin. I'll keep watch."

"No. You need the rest more than I do. *I* will keep watch."

"You're such a stubborn woman!"

We fall into silence, as it's obvious neither of us will give in.

After a few moments, I hear his breathing slow. With his injuries, exhaustion must've overtaken him. I gently lay him down on the floor. He doesn't even stir.

He looks so peaceful in his sleep. On the contrary, my body buzzes and my mind churns.

Jieh's kiss was passionate, and his desire for me ravenous and raw. Ren's kiss was always perfunctory. Like the way you'd kiss a family member. Once, he saw me getting ready for a bath. He immediately averted his eyes, apologized, and walked away.

At the time, I lauded his restraint and thought he was a gentleman, but a small part of me was disappointed. I didn't understand why I felt that way.

Now I do. I was disappointed that he didn't find me attractive enough to at least linger for a moment.

But why does Jieh, a devilishly handsome prince who can get almost any young woman in the kingdom, fancy me?

I stop myself. He already told me, didn't he?

I lie down next to him and put my hand on his chest. Watching his gorgeous face, I feel I could stay here in this moment forever.

CHAPTER 27

Chirping birds awaken me, and I bolt upright. I promised to keep watch! How did I fall asleep?

Relief turns my muscles to mush when I see Jieh lying on the cave floor where he slept, his head propped up on one arm and his eyes bright on me.

My cheeks flare red. "When . . . when did you wake up?" How long has he been watching me like this?

"Just a bit before you stirred." He sits up. The light embraces his striking profile. I stare, fascinated, at his golden, sun-kissed skin, the hard muscles on his chest . . .

"You're drooling," he says.

What? I sweep the back of my hand over my mouth. There's no drool.

Jieh laughs. I shoot him a glare, but then I am laughing, too. I can't help it: It *was* funny. I'm also amazed. The arrogant ass Jieh, who always sticks his nose in the air, can playfully tease? Who'd have thought?

He winks at me, then turns away. I realize I'm still only in my nightshirt. Lowering my head to hide a blush, I quickly put on my dress. He shuffles his pants on as well.

The fire has dwindled to a smoldering pile of ash. Sunlight trickles through gaps in the foliage, painting dots across my body.

"I wonder what happened to everyone else at the camp," Jieh says gravely.

The anxiety I've tamped down surges up again. Are Yunle and Fei safe? I hope that Fei saw Jieh with me and had the wisdom to seek sanctuary for herself rather than come after me.

"How's your ankle?" I ask Jieh.

He stands and puts weight on his left side. He blanks his expression quickly, but I've caught his momentary wince.

I sigh. As much as I want to find out what befell my friends, we can't go back yet. "We must wait until your ankle gets better before we travel."

"Sky Dancer will find us. Then we can ride back."

"He will?"

Jieh's eyes shine with pride. "He's the smartest of his kind. We've formed a special bond."

I don't know much about Beorn stallions beyond their legendary reputation, but I trust Jieh's confidence in Sky Dancer's abilities.

"We need food." I stand. "I'll go look."

He frowns deeply. I'm sure he hates feeling useless.

I peek out of the foliage first to make sure there's no danger lurking nearby. Judging by the position of the sun in the sky, we've slept away most of the morning.

I don't wander far before I come upon a bush covered in red berries. I'm not sure if they are edible. But Jieh is an experienced hunter and would likely know. I fold up the bottom of my dress like an apron and fill it with the berries before returning.

Jieh smiles. "Good work, Mingshin. We can eat these. They're safe."

As we sit across from each other munching on handfuls of berries, I ask, "Who do you think the masked men from last night were?"

"I have no idea."

"They shouted for your head." A chill ripples up my arms. "Could one of your brothers have plotted this?" I recall seeing Kai beset by invaders at the camp and Wen struggling to escape with Aylin in tow. The chill runs the rest of the way through me. "I never caught sight of Ren."

"I didn't see him, either. But I was trying to get to you and wasn't really looking."

Could Ren have gone into hiding because he planned the attack?

A muscle in my stomach pulls with a sickening twist when I remember the two men who blew smoke into my tent. I relate the event to Jieh. "Elder Hanxin might have sent them."

He scowls. "Why would he do that?"

I blush. "He asked me to marry him the night before—"

Jieh's back shoots up straighter than a trident. "He did *what*?" He looks like he'd strike Hanxin down if the Elder were standing in front of him right at this moment. Then his countenance turns anxious. "What did you say to his proposal?"

"I refused, of course. I don't love him." My blush deepens when his face brightens. "Besides, he never even pretended he loved me or had feelings for me. I suspect he has some ulterior motive, which I can't even begin to fathom."

"We'll find out his true purpose, Mingshin. Either way, I'm glad you turned him down." Happiness spills across his face in a broad grin.

A tiny flutter starts in my belly. Quickly, I look away before it can grow. "If the two men were indeed sent by Hanxin, he could be involved in the attack. The timing . . . it's almost like they knew what was going to happen and tried to get me away before the attack started." I'd suspected Hanxin was working with Ren in a mutually beneficial relationship, and now I fear I may have been right all along.

"If Hanxin was involved in the incident at your tent, you can be sure he'll answer for any attempt to harm you."

There's something I can't tell Jieh, or anyone else. Those masked men could have murdered us in our sleep if I hadn't sensed a warning. I can't explain how it happened, but I have an uncanny feeling that it has something to do with my connection to the Divine Stone. I shudder to think about the consequences if I hadn't acted upon the warning.

"So you were awake when the assault started," Jieh says.

I recount to him how Fei perceived the danger and how I hit the gong to wake the others.

"Wow, Mingshin. You were very brave." He speaks with so much admiration that I glow inside.

"So were you. You saved me."

Jieh claps his hands and leans forward, every line stiff. "When I . . . tried to catch you before you fell into the river, someone pushed me from behind."

I gasp. So that's why he toppled forward. Noticing the tension threading through his muscles, I suddenly understand. "Was it Prince Kai?"

"I didn't see him, but he was the only person I remember standing behind me."

"Whoever it was, the rogue used the opportunity to try and murder you. Everybody would have assumed you were killed by those marauders." I reach out and grab Jieh's hand. "The man behind the injured horse when I met you that first time . . ."

"It was Wen."

Although I'm well aware that the other princes want Jieh dead, it still horrifies me to learn of their actual deeds. I admit the next question isn't fair to him, but I have to know. "Your brothers have tried to murder you. Have you ever . . . done anything similar to them?"

A hard edge goes through his gaze. "No, Mingshin. And I never will."

"Why?"

"My father loves me, and I'll never hurt him by harming my brothers." Pride stiffens his jaw. "Everyone says I'm my father's favorite. It's because he knows I'm stronger and smarter than my brothers. One day I'll make them realize I'm better suited to be King, and they'll submit to my rule without jealousy or treachery."

He's arrogant to the point of naïvety. "Your brothers won't stop trying to hurt you until you are out of their way. You must never turn your back on them or relax your guard." I also feel a sliver of relief. I wouldn't want to be his friend if he turned out to be a monster like Ren.

Goose bumps spring up along my skin. In my previous life, Ren told me Jieh had attempted to kill him more than once. But he was a calculating liar and often painted himself as a victim.

If only I had tried to look past Jieh's imperious surface to learn his true character, I might've awakened myself sooner to Ren's deceit and manipulation.

"If any of them tries to hurt *you*, Mingshin, I *will* break my promise," Jieh adds.

The sincerity of his words reverberates through me.

"We haven't talked about this yet," he says. "Did your uncle and cousins send the assassin to kill you during that prank at the river?"

I heave out a breath and nod.

Jieh's furious look could've set wet grass on fire.

"My cousins may not have survived the attack. Even if they did, please don't do anything rash," I say hurriedly. He isn't a hothead like Wen, and he'll listen to reason. "Minister Sun is trusted by the King. You won't achieve anything but disgrace in your father's eyes if you try to bring the matter up with him. And I don't want you to drag yourself down to their level. Aylin's so-called prank at the river already makes her look suspicious. If they strike again, even a fool would be able to link her prank and another murder attempt. They won't take that risk." My whole face is a plea. "Promise me you won't try to kill my uncle or cousins or harm them physically."

He stares at me, reluctance showing in the muscles tightening along his chin. Then like iron suddenly cooled, his face hardens. "I promise. I also promise to protect you, Mingshin. No one can hurt you."

My heart leaps at his words. Quickly I say, "We should change your bandage."

I replace the wrapping on his wound with another piece of his tunic. There aren't any signs of infection yet. Still, he'll need a doctor before long to be sure.

Like last night, he never flinches or makes a sound. He appears energetic again and ready to swing a sword.

"I've never seen a man tougher than you," I say as a fact, not flattery. "How did you become so?"

"My mother had me train hard. She'd make me swim in a river in the winter and duel with my tutors for hours on sweltering summer days. Even after I was injured, she'd have me go on and on until I almost collapsed." I must look horrified, for he gives me a dismissive smile. "I felt resentful at the time, but I'm thankful now. It helped me develop the strength to cope with physical hardship."

"But what she did to you sounds cruel. You were only a child."

"She had her reasons. When she was my father's favorite, the court fawned over her and catered to her every need. She made enemies, including the Queen and the other Royal Ladies. You know how she is. Proud. Assertive. Sharp-tongued."

Overbearing, crafty, I add to my own mental list.

"Maybe more so when she was younger," he says. "After she fell out of my father's favor, they ridiculed her and were hostile toward her. As my father's favorite child, I was hated by the Queen, who lost her only son at birth. My uncle, Lord Protector Hwa, used his influence to deflect some of the harm for us, and took me to live at his estate every once in a while. If not for his help, my mother's protection, and my father's constant attention, I might have died in the harem."

My hand flies to my mouth. My chest squeezes, although I know Jieh survived his ordeal.

Despite their privilege, I've never felt envious of the royals. They enjoy copious luxury, and the King's favorite consorts can wield enormous power, but to me the harem seems like a prison.

"Mother wanted me to be strong enough to protect myself. My father showered me with affection; still, I wanted to excel at everything, for I knew his love for me could slip away just as easily as it did for my mother if I didn't keep up. She believes I will only be completely safe if I possess the highest power, and I agree. I also want to prove to my father that I'll be a great ruler that makes him proud."

This is the first time Jieh has shown vulnerability. I wonder how many people have seen this side of him.

I put my hands on his shoulders and lay my face on his back. He sets a hand on mine, his strength enveloping me.

We sit in silence like that for a long time, sharing the quiet of understanding.

In the late afternoon, Jieh periodically leaves the cave to call out for Sky Dancer. We eat more berries, but they barely stave off our hunger. We laugh at each other whenever our stomachs growl. He wants to go hunting, but he's in no shape for that.

To distract ourselves, we tell each other a bit more about our childhoods. Jieh is fascinated and wants to know more about my father's business trips, how he always brought home presents and stories. As I relate the tales, my heart yearns to one day see the world just like Father did.

Jieh's childhood mostly consisted of being schooled in swordsmanship, politics, and leadership.

"How did you and Yao become friends?" I ask, burning with curiosity.

"I was nine when I accompanied my father on a trip to the south to inspect the army stationed there. Yao's father was the general in charge of the southern army back then. When I was at their home, I saw how Yao's two elder brothers beat him in the practice field, mocking him and poking him with their wooden swords. He was trying hard to hold his tears in. They were much bigger than him, so it hardly seemed fair to me. I barreled into the courtyard and demanded they back off." Pride blooms in his eyes. "They didn't know I was a prince, so they challenged me. I beat them off good. Yao gaped at me in wonder, and I told him I would teach him how to become stronger. His father had planned to have him trained as a page anyway. Father accepted this request, so Yao came to the capital with the King's retinue. We've been best friends ever since. Later, he got a position assisting the lord high constable."

"Ah, so you have a heroic streak in you," I say.

"What? You don't think I'm a hero?" he teases back.

"You were a hero yesterday."

He shakes his head, crestfallen. "I didn't feel much like one—"

I set a hand on his arm. "You were my hero. You've done everything you could for me. I'll be forever grateful and hold the deepest respect for you."

He lays his hand over mine, brightening up. "You don't know how much your words mean to me, Mingshin."

For an endless moment, the air seems to crackle between us, alive in a way that makes my skin tingle.

Then he's kissing me again, slowly at first. The pleasure is instant—a flood of heat, a fiery rush. It's a good thing his arms are wrapped around me, because I feel like I have no bones in my body. His kiss deepens, and I lose myself in the hypnotizing press of give and take, the intoxicating feeling of joining my mouth with his.

In the evening, I ignite a fire with another signal fire stick. This time, I notice the drawing on its exterior: a firebird breathing flames.

I ask Jieh about it.

"Remember how I told you my father made a special order of the firesticks for me and my siblings? Each one of us got to choose what kind of pattern our sticks would create upon being shot into the sky. That drawing is what I devised and gave to the artisan and smithy who made the sticks."

"It's quite spectacular."

He grins at my compliment.

My belly pangs with hunger. It must be worse for Jieh, but he doesn't show it. We don't speak much more due to our waning energy. It's hard to fall asleep with an aching stomach, but we lie down and do our best.

It must be after midnight when he jumps up suddenly, his expression concentrated.

My insides flip. Has he heard something?

Then he's half limping, half running out of the cave, shoving aside the foliage covering the entrance. "It's Sky Dancer," he bellows.

With a soaring heart, I rush after him.

Under the moonlight, Jieh hugs Sky Dancer's neck, his face glowing. The stallion capers in equal excitement.

"We should leave now," Jieh says. "Our parents must be terribly worried."

I feel a sharp spasm in my gut. Has Mother heard of the news of the assault at the hunt? She'd be overwrought with distress and fright.

We extinguish the fire in the cave. Jieh dons his jerkin, and I stuff the signal fire stick in my boot. We agree not to use it since we are not sure if our attackers are still searching for us. Ten thousand gold taels, the reward money for Jieh's head, will afford anyone a luxurious life.

Outside, Jieh mounts Sky Dancer and pulls me up to sit behind him. "To the campsite, my boy," he commands.

Sky Dancer snorts and starts moving.

"He understands you," I breathe. "The bond between you two is amazing."

Jieh laughs and spurs the stallion into a trot.

CHAPTER 28

We ride through the night. We must go downstream first to get to a part shallow enough for Sky Dancer to safely wade across, then we have to circle back, which unfortunately means the distance we need to cover is far longer than our drift in the river. I almost nod off a couple of times, but Jieh pats my hand to keep me awake.

We are near the campsite when dawn breaks. We decide to stop for a rest after a sleepless night. Sky Dancer needs to graze, too.

"I'll catch a fish for us," I tell Jieh, feeling dizzy with hunger.

"Have you done that before?" he asks, amused.

"No. But I want to try."

His smile broadens. "I'll join you."

"Your ankle—"

"I can walk a bit."

We stroll along the bank, searching the river for signs of fish. But we don't see any.

Jieh stiffens suddenly, as dark and alert as a storm cloud. I scan about nervously. I haven't seen or heard anything. He looks back the way we came. We've wandered too far away from Sky Dancer.

Then the thunder of hoofbeats rings out. Jieh grabs my hand, and we run a few steps before dropping to the ground to hide behind a large bush.

A cluster of horses charges our way, then halts. My breath feels tight. Could it be our assailants still pursuing us?

Feet land on compact dirt, metal jangles, and boots crunch as they move down the slope toward the riverbank.

I'm struck first by the same strange, unsettling feeling I got from Ren that day when he returned with only a few rabbits. Then I hear his voice. "Look at the hoofprints. Tell me what you see."

The others may be Ren's personal guards.

"These markings are larger than a normal stallion's hoofprints, and fresh," a man replies. "There's none past this point. The Beorn stallion is likely grazing somewhere nearby."

"No doubt Jieh is near," Ren says.

"This is a great opportunity, Your Highness," another man says, his voice quivering with excitement. "There are six of us. Prince Jieh may be alone and injured . . ."

Dread grips my stomach at the suggestion conveyed by his words. Jieh has gone perfectly still, the alarm in his eyes as clear as a length of exposed steel.

"We are to bring my brother home, as my father ordered," Ren says blankly.

"But he may have already been killed by the marauders, his body dumped who-knows-where," the first man says, a conspiratorial note in his voice.

Ren snorts a cold laugh that makes my bones shiver. I've heard this laugh once before, as he smirked at me crawling in the snow on the verge of death.

"Spread out and search for Prince Jieh," Ren orders. "Call out to the rest of us immediately if you find him alone. I expect efficiency from all of you. No mess."

Jieh's face is flinty cold. My heart thumps madly. Ren's search is nothing more than a pretense. I'd bet my life that he intends to murder his brother and lay the blame on the masked men. No one would suspect him.

The guards scatter, with a couple heading our way. They're going to find us behind this bush and kill us.

Jieh mouths to me to stay in place and be quiet. Then he strides out of the bush and into plain view. From the confident way he walks, you'd think his ankle was perfectly fine. "Are you looking for me, Ren?" he says as casually as if they just happened to run into each other.

I part the branches and peek around an edge. The searchers freeze in shock, and Ren sweeps the area with his cutting gaze. His left arm is in a sling, but his sword arm seems to be working just fine. The offensive, otherworldly feeling radiating from him envelops me, strong enough to raise goose bumps on my skin.

Earlier I thought it was just my growing repulsion to him. Now I'm not so sure. Something is definitely wrong with him.

"I see you've come to finish what those raiders started," Jieh says, drawing Ren's attention away from my crouched position behind the bush.

"You misunderstand me, brother. Father was in a dither when he realized you were missing." Despite his efforts, resentment bleeds into Ren's voice. "Being a good son, I volunteered to join the search parties despite my own injury. You, the coward, could've at least stayed and fought with us."

"I need no lecture on cowardice from one who hides behind a thousand masks." Only Jieh is capable of making his voice drip with so much disdain.

A muscle jumps in Ren's cheek. He waves a hand, and his guards fan out in a circle. Jieh pulls his saber from its scabbard with a clang. The others do likewise. Sky Dancer charges from behind a thicket, coming to his master's defense, but two men lift their swords to block the steed's way.

At his best, Jieh would be able to hold his own against five well-trained swordsmen, but he's wounded, hungry and sleep-deprived, and his ankle hasn't fully healed yet. Even Sky Dancer's help may not be enough.

With a nod from Ren, the guards swoop in upon Jieh.

I grind my teeth as Jieh steps farther away from the bush. I refuse to let him die while trying to protect me from discovery.

If King Reifeng sent out search parties for Jieh, the assault at the encampment must've been contained and the situation under control. I pull the fire stick out of my boot and give it a furious shake. When it sparks, I point it skyward. A stream of yellow flame shoots out, and the image of a firebird breathing fire explodes into the sky, lingering for a moment before it dissipates.

While everyone pauses, taken by surprise, I step out of my hiding spot. "I thought it would be nice to let His Majesty know Prince Jieh is still alive by sending his unique signal," I say.

Ren's eyes taper to slits. "Miss Lu." He spits my name out like poison. No longer on a first-name basis as he insisted?

"Good to see you, too, Your Highness. Oh . . . I thought you wouldn't even hurt a doe, let alone . . . a brother?"

Ren's nostrils flare; he clenches his hands into fists and opens them again several times as though he wishes to strangle me with them.

Jieh steps in front of me, shielding me. The brothers glare at each other. Ren's guards trade glances among themselves, awaiting a further command. Seconds pass in silence. I can almost hear the gears in Ren's head turning furiously.

"Come on, brother." Jieh waves his sword as if challenging his foe to step forward and engage him. "It's an opportunity that only comes once in a lifetime. You can't afford to miss it."

I frown. Why is he goading Ren?

Then I spot a burst of colors in the distance moving through a veil of trees. Is it another search party? Facing the river, Ren doesn't see them. My word alone isn't enough to successfully accuse him of attempted murder before Reifeng, but if someone else witnesses him attacking Jieh, it would be a different matter.

Ren doesn't rise to the bait, though. He beckons to his guards, who put away their swords. Turning to Jieh, he grins mockingly. "It's a once-in-a-lifetime opportunity for me to be your *savior*, Jieh."

Jieh leaps ahead and seems about to run his sword through Ren. I grab him from behind. He looks at me. A mask of calm settles over his features, and he halts to sheath his sword.

A group on horseback emerges from the forest. Relief floods through me, and I let out a whoop. It's Yunle, Yao, and Fei leading a band of soldiers.

I wave both arms at them. The princess dismounts while her eyes scan the scene. I doubt anything escapes her scrutiny.

The newcomers rush down the slope.

Yunle embraces me. "Thank Heaven we found you." She lets go, stands back, and gives me a once-over, her features softening. "You don't look too bad, my friend."

"Not bad at all," I say with a smile.

I turn to Fei, my face bursting with the same happiness I see in hers. We embrace each other with the intensity of lifelong friends.

Yao hugs Jieh, clapping him on the back and roaring with laughter. Jieh winces.

"You were injured," Yao says in alarm. "Let me look."

Jieh waves his concern away. "It's nothing. Mingshin did a great job taking care of it."

Yunle shoots him a stern frown. "I appreciate Mingshin's work, but you should see a physician as soon as possible."

Jieh opens his mouth, perhaps to retort, so I cut in quickly. "Thank you all for looking for us. Did you see our signal?"

"Yes," Yunle replies. "That's how we found you."

I raise my head to find Ren observing us with narrowed eyes. Is there a trace of bitter jealousy I detect in his look? But then he notices me watching and blanks his face.

Yao gives us food, and we gorge ourselves on it.

"I never knew dried meat could taste so good," Jieh says, and we all laugh.

Jieh and I mount Sky Dancer. Yunle grins at me, at us. Even Yao winks. I burn from the inside out.

"I'll ride ahead to inform Father so he won't worry," Ren says and departs with his guards.

"Probably to make sure he receives all the credit for his *gallant* rescue," Yunle says dryly.

I've always been amazed at how perceptive the princess is. Still, it seems that she knows her half brother's character better than I thought.

We take a leisurely pace so as not to aggravate Jieh's wound. Along the way back to the capital, Yunle fills us in.

She managed to lead many of the women away during the assault, but most of the soldiers and guards who had remained behind for the rest of the hunt were either killed or injured. Wen had his legs trampled by horses and a runaway wagon.

"Doctor Tsai had to amputate his legs to save his life," Yunle says with a note of pity.

I have never liked Wen, and I'm still angry about his attempt to harm Jieh. On the other hand, I can't help but feel sorry for him. He's only sixteen, my age.

"The marauders shouted for Jieh's head. Do you think the princes were their prime targets?" I ask Yunle. Jieh tenses against me.

Her brows bunch like thunderheads. "I have my suspicions. If so, it's not surprising they didn't bother with the women. It seems that Jieh took the brunt of the attack. Kai escaped with only a few minor cuts."

A hot, angry rush surges in me. I consider telling her my suspicion about Kai pushing Jieh into the river. I decide against it. I don't want to pull her into the conflict. If Jieh chooses to share it with Yao, that's his decision.

"Ren killed the bandits' leader. Afterwards, they panicked and called a retreat, but we routed them and captured a few," Yunle says. "And another heroic tale has been spreading. If Ren hadn't risked his own life to shove away a mad horse that was about to step on Wen's neck, he would have been killed."

My mouth falls open. Ren emerged from the incident a hero? I don't believe it. Rage blazes through me, scorching my shock to ashes. What manipulative tactic did Ren employ to achieve this latest deception?

I squelch my fury before it engulfs me. "I didn't see Ren for half the battle. Then, at the perfect time, he showed up and killed the leader, pulling off an act of heroism in front of everyone."

Yunle arches a brow, but after a moment she continues with her recounting.

As soon as the attack was contained, Yao volunteered to lead a team in search of Jieh. Yunle was worried for me, but fortunately Fei had seen Jieh follow me into the forest. The princess offered to join Yao's search party. At the same time, the King ordered all captives to be sent to the death prison for interrogation.

"They won't stay tight-lipped there for long," Yunle states. I shiver.

"Mingshin helped save us," Jieh says. He describes to them how I roused the camp by sounding the alarm gong.

"That's fabulous, my friend," Yunle exclaims, "You should've told us sooner."

Yao raises a fist, punching the air. "Hail to Miss Lu."

"Thank you, Lord Yao," I say.

"Call me Yao, if you please."

"Then please call me Mingshin, Yao."

As my bodyguard and the princess ride side by side, Yunle playfully reaches over and nudges Fei. "You're lucky, Mingshin, to have such a loyal, brave guard," she says, her grin big and bright.

Fei glows with a kind of inner light. I've always known her to be fierce, but in this moment she also looks beautiful.

As soon as we reach the royal palace, we're herded into the Audience Chamber.

Fei stays outside while Yunle leads the rest of us in. I realize my hand is in Jieh's grip. I pull, but he doesn't let go. I don't try again lest it draw more attention.

King Reifeng sits on a throne set against the far wall. Lord High Constable Wang and Commander Bai stand flanking him. Royal Lady Hwa and Ren are inside the room as well.

Hwa rushes toward her son and embraces him. Jieh releases my hand to hug her.

"I knew you'd be safe. I knew you'd come back," Hwa asserts.

"Yes, Mother."

The King rises. "Come here, my boy!"

Jieh strides forward. It's a tangle of arms and laughter between father and son. The earnest way Ren smiles, you'd think it was an imposter who tried to kill us by the river.

"You were injured," Reifeng says to Jieh. "Show me."

Jieh shakes his head. "It's nothing serious. Have we discovered the identities of our attackers, Father?"

Heavy tension descends upon the chamber, thick as a winter blanket. Reifeng's eyes go from blazing quicksilver to frosty granite. The others are careful not to show emotion.

Reifeng resumes his seat and signals to Bai, who snaps to attention.

The commander looks at no one in particular as he announces, "The masked marauders were gathered from numerous mercenary groups across the kingdom. They confessed that Prince Kai orchestrated the attack with the help of a Nan'Yüan man. Prince Kai promised the mercenary leaders official positions upon the deaths of all the other princes, and paid the groups much gold for their service. Prince Kai has been arrested and imprisoned. We suspect the Nan'Yüan man in question is Elder Hanxin. He's gone missing, along with his closest bodyguard. His retinue has been detained."

Every drop of blood in my body goes cold and hot, awake and dead. My friends appear no less astounded than I feel. Ren wears an expression of pity.

"*Kai* orchestrated the attack?" Jieh says finally. "Why did he do it?"

No. It couldn't have been Kai. It doesn't make any sense.

Yunle shakes off her shock with visible effort. "How was Elder Hanxin involved?"

"We suspect magic was used," Bai replies.

"How?" Jieh asks.

"Later," Reifeng says. "Now, go to the physicians' ward and have your wound tended to." His tone clearly indicates it's an order.

Yao begs the King's permission to accompany Jieh, and Hwa asks to leave as well.

Reifeng grants their requests. Then he glances at me. "You stay here," he commands.

Jieh turns to his father, but I reassure him with my eyes. With reluctance he leaves, followed by Yao and Hwa.

At the King's request, I tell him what happened at the onslaught and afterwards. But I say nothing about the warning that alerted me. Instead I tell him I couldn't fall asleep because of the murder attempt made on me just two days before. I also omit the part where we caught the two men blowing smoke into my tent. I don't mention Ren's attempt to murder us or the possibility that Kai pushed Jieh into the river. If Jieh decides to tell his father, that's his choice.

"You sounded the alarm?" Reifeng asks me at the end, skeptical.

"I can vouch for that, Father," Yunle says. "I spoke to someone who witnessed her raising the alarm."

I keep my neutral expression firmly in place so my gratitude won't show. Yunle just lied for me, after joining the search team to rescue me. She has shown herself to be a true friend, and I regret my previous doubts about her intentions.

"Well done, Miss Lu." There's a little more kindness in Reifeng's voice now. When he looks at Ren again, he smiles with radiant approval.

A prickle of angst climbs up my spine. Ren's "heroism" against the enemy and his "protectiveness" of Wen have apparently worked in his favor. The latter probably holds even more importance to Reifeng because of his own brother's betrayal.

I doubt the King would believe Ren tried to kill us at the river. It's best that Jieh not mention it, or the King might think he's trying to frame Ren.

A guard shuffles in. "I'm sorry to disturb you, Your Majesty, but Royal Lady Yu begs for your audience."

Reifeng scowls. "Let her in."

Royal Lady Yu looks as though she's aged a decade overnight. Her eyes are two hollowed, blackened wells, and her hair is a tangled bird's nest.

She kneels before Reifeng and doesn't rise when he motions her to. "I've served you faithfully and devotedly all these years, my King. I only ask for justice for my son Wen."

Reifeng sighs wearily. "Kai is in jail, awaiting further investigation. Wen is my son as well. Justice shall be served, I promise you."

"I'm not talking about Kai, but the person who pushed Wen off the horse they rode on together just before he got trampled."

Yunle and I trade an appalled look; even Ren inhales a sharp breath.

Reifeng leans forward. "Who pushed Wen off his horse?"

Yu glances at me, then away.

Reifeng nods in my direction, a gesture of dismissal. I curtsy. As I reach the door, Yunle catches up with me. "Wait for me at the physicians' ward."

I nod. Fei greets me outside. As we walk away, I share what happened in the Audience Chamber.

"Several young lords died, and many more were injured," Fei says. "Their families have demanded justice. If Prince Kai is the culprit, even the King won't be able to protect him." She lowers her voice to a whisper. "I still have the kui's antler; I hid it well, but should we get rid of it as soon as possible?"

I know she kept the antler because we hoped to return it to Hanxin. But the situation has changed; the Elder is no longer a royal guest but a murder suspect. All connections to him must be severed immediately. "Yes. But let's wait until we can do it safely."

Jieh is resting in a richly decorated room in the physicians' ward. Yao stays with him, but neither Hwa nor the doctors are present.

"My mother left after my wound was cleaned, disinfected, and freshly bandaged," Jieh says.

I tell him and Yao about Royal Lady Yu's appearance.

Jieh's forehead wrinkles into a sober frown. "My mother said there would be a good show. I wonder if she was referring to Royal Lady Yu." He shakes his head. "What's the matter, Mingshin?"

"I've been thinking, why would Kai pay the mercenaries to kill us? He was in a good position to become the heir; there was no need for him to jeopardize his standing with an attack like this. He had no reason to take such a huge risk. But Ren had the motive after his bow incident at the commencement ceremony. If the other three princes were killed, he'd be the only candidate left. That didn't happen, but he's still managed to work his way back into the King's grace through so-called "heroic acts." He's the only one who's benefitted from the attack."

"You think *Ren* orchestrated the attack?" Jieh appears thoughtful. "But even if he got the motive after his debacle at the ceremony, there wasn't enough time for him to plan everything."

"Well, maybe he *had* plotted it for a while. With Hanxin's help." If the Elder was involved in the assault, it's highly possible that he sent the two men to abduct me from my tent.

"Ren is manipulative and vicious," Jieh says. "But I had people investigate Hanxin's association with him after their joint visit to your home, and they found no possible collaboration between the two."

Yao nods. He likely used his position as assistant to the Lord High Constable to gather information during the investigation.

"Trust me, Ren can be very discreet," I say. "Besides, why would Hanxin plot with *Kai*?"

Jieh lets out a long breath. "I'll go to the prison and speak to Kai tomorrow. Then I'll have a better sense of whether he's guilty or not."

"A large group of mercenaries gathered from across the kingdom," I say. "How did they travel all the way to the capital undetected, unchecked? Magic may be involved."

Comprehension dawns on Jieh's face. "Hanxin may have transported the mercenaries with Portal magic."

I remember how fast Hanxin and Longzo disappeared after they left my tent.

Jieh turns to Yao. "Please do not mention our conversation to anyone."

"You know me," Yao replies.

The door opens and Yunle barges in. "You'll never believe this! Wen is going to marry Sun Aylin," she announces.

"What?" we cry out simultaneously.

"How did that happen?" I ask, my mind still reeling.

"Royal Lady Yu claimed Aylin pushed Wen off the horse. Aylin denied it vehemently and begged Wen to speak the truth. But Wen corroborated his mother's accusation. Father told the guards to lock Aylin away. Wen then made the unusual request to marry her."

All our mouths have fallen open far enough to stuff an egg into each.

"Royal Lady Yu yelled that he was out of his mind, but Wen was adamant."

"Didn't anybody think it strange?" Jieh asks.

"Yes. Lord High Constable Wang questioned why Wen would want to marry a woman he just claimed had caused him such a horrible injury. Wen responded that it would be a fitting punishment for Aylin to have to service a legless man and obey his will and whim as his wife for the rest of her life."

So this is how Wen views the role of a wife? And why would marrying someone with a physical disability automatically be considered a punishment? So many aspects of this marriage are just terribly warped.

I wonder where Grand Scholar Yu was while all this craziness was going on. He would have put a stop to Wen's nonsense right there.

"Do *you* think Miss Sun is guilty?" Jieh asks Yunle.

"I don't know. She looked astonished when Father questioned her. Besides, why ask Wen to tell the truth if the truth would only condemn her?"

"Father agreed to Wen's request?"

"Yes. At the moment, I think Father would give Wen the moon if he asked for it." Reifeng has been ignoring Wen for sixteen years. Finally, he took notice of him, only after he lost his legs. "Prison or marriage to Wen, Father told Aylin. She agreed to marriage, but she was devastated."

Aylin craves to be Queen with her entire soul, but with his legs gone, it's unlikely Wen will become the royal heir.

"Father orders you to stay put for the evening," Yunle tells Jieh.

"I must escort Mingshin home," Jieh says, frowning.

"I'll do it," Yao says. "I'll see her safely home."

Jieh opens his mouth, but I talk over him. "I'm sure my safety is in good hands with Yao."

"Very well," Yunle says. "Wait for me at the gate. I'm going to arrange a coach for you."

Hwa enters as soon as the princess leaves. "I'm sure Yunle has told you about the show." She smirks.

"Were you behind this?" Jieh asks.

Hwa's smirk turns deadly cold. "I told you Minister Sun would regret the day he made me his enemy."

Jieh stares at his mother, incredulous.

The royal palace really is a nest of vipers.

CHAPTER 29

As we near home, Fei speaks up with a sudden bite to her voice. "I have no sympathy for your cousin, but these royal and noble women . . . they are vicious and mean."

"Yunle is a royal," I point out.

Her features soften slightly. "Yes, but the princess is different."

When we arrive at the gate of my residence, I invite Yao inside for tea.

"Thank you for your hospitality, but I haven't been home for several days," he says. "There are matters I must attend to immediately." He smiles. "Besides, I can't wait to wash all this travel dust off me."

I smile back. "I understand. Thank you for seeing me home."

"It's the least I can do after you saved my best friend's life."

"If not for me, Jieh wouldn't have fallen into the river in the first place."

He hesitates before saying, "If I may . . ."

"Anything, Yao."

"I've been friends with Jieh for many years, but I've never seen him around a woman the way he is around you . . ." He draws a deep breath, his grip tight on the reins. "Jieh cares much about you."

My pulse quickens.

"He gives his whole heart to those he loves. Please treat him well."

"Of course. You know I consider him a great friend."

"It's more than friendship he wants, but I'm sure you understand." He reins his horse around. "Good evening, Mingshin."

My insides roil as I watch him ride away. *Treat him well.* It almost sounds like Yao fears that *I* might hurt *Jieh*.

"Shin'ar!"

I whirl around to find Mother rushing toward me, followed by Hui, Ning, and Mai.

Mother and I fly into each other's arms and squeeze so tightly we can scarcely breathe for the sweet pain of it. She keeps murmuring my name against my hair. "You are finally home. Heaven above, you are well."

Warmth collects in my throat, thickening my words. "I'm sorry I worried you so, Ma."

"You're home, which is all that matters." She grasps my shoulders while looking me up and down. "Were you harmed in any way?"

I shake my head. "I'm perfectly fine, Ma."

The twins hug each other. Ning and Mai come forward to greet us, relief evident on their faces.

I link an arm with Mother's as we head back inside.

"We were so worried when we heard about the attack at the Elite Hunt," she says. "A royal guard came by earlier and told us you had returned. We waited and waited."

"I wish I could have come home sooner, Ma."

She pats my hand. "I understand you must answer to the King's summoning first."

Mother already had a feast prepared, and I eat to my heart's content. Afterward, she dismisses everyone and leads me into the study.

"Now tell me everything that happened," she says as soon as we sit down across from each other.

I oblige, leaving out my feelings for Jieh and the times we kissed. Mother listens intently, her every expression mirroring how I felt in each moment through my tale. At the end, she cups my cheeks in her hands. "My daughter, who has the fiery spirit of the sun and the bright heart of the moon." The words are spoken with such fierce pride that a thrill races through my blood.

But I haven't told her the whole story. I don't know how she would react if she learned about me and Jieh growing closer. I'm almost afraid to know. Would she be angry or disappointed in me?

Mother's face hardens. "You believe it was your uncle who sent the assassin after you at the river," she states.

"Yes, Ma," I say, suddenly nervous that she may not share my suspicion.

Mother gives a tight nod. "I believe you. I've already heard back from the people I hired to discover the person behind the false allegation against Hui. You were right, Shin'ar. It was your uncle." Her eyes say it all: flashes of rage and crashing waves of sorrow tossing and turning within.

My heart breaks a little. I grasp her hands. "I'm sorry, Ma. It must be hard to know your brother intended us harm."

"He's no longer my brother. He tried to murder my daughter," she growls. A part of her pain is still there—and probably always will be—but most of it has been replaced by a determination like nothing I've ever seen in her before. "He wants to steal our wealth? I'll destroy him before I let him hurt my family."

Later, when I return to my room, Fei shows me where she hid the kui's antler. We'll need to quickly find a place to dump it where no one will find it.

As I settle down to sleep, questions hammer in my head. What could Hanxin possibly hope to gain by helping Ren attack the hunt? But if he wasn't guilty, why did he run away?

The next morning, Yunle invites me to the princess' wing of the palace.

Jieh is also present. He embraces me, and I feel the tension winding his muscles taut beneath his tunic. The hairs on my arms stand up. Did something bad happen?

"How's your wound?" I ask him.

"It's improved much after a day and night of rest."

Yunle waves me to settle on the couch next to her. "I've sent my maids away for a couple of hours."

Three cups of tea sit steaming on the ebony table. I lift my cup and take a sip to ease my anxiety. "What's this little gathering for?"

Haltingly, as if struggling for breath, Yunle sets down her teacup and sighs. "The mercenary captives all dropped dead simultaneously last night."

I gasp. "How did that happen? Were they poisoned . . . ?"

"No. The doctors concluded that they weren't poisoned, and although they were tortured for information, they didn't die from their injuries either," Jieh says as he drums his fingers on the arm of the cushioned chair across from us.

"Your suspicion has proven true, Mingshin," Yunle says. "The mercenaries confessed that they were transferred to the campsite through magic portals. Hanxin's detained retinue finally cracked and admitted his closest bodyguard, Longzo, is capable of such magic. So it's reasonable to presume that the Nan'Yüan man who aided the mercenaries was Longzo."

A tight sickness clamps my belly. The strong force that hit me right before the assault . . . did I actually detect the use of Portal magic? Just like the tug on my chest when my attention was pulled to the *fuiin* inked on Lafne's wrist, and the harrowing feeling of being watched . . .

With an effort, I shake free of my thoughts. "Did Hanxin flee through a portal?" I ask.

"That's a possibility," Yunle says.

"If Portal magic was used to transport those mercenaries, it could also be another type of magic that simultaneously killed them."

Yunle nods darkly.

"I've spoken to Kai," Jieh says. "He insists on his innocence. He claims he had no interactions with Hanxin outside of his duty to watch him and that he's never met any of the mercenaries."

"Don't you find the timing of the captives' deaths convenient?" I say. "They all dropped dead after claiming Kai bought their service. Why not before?"

"Speaking of timing, Father and most of his royal soldiers left on the morning of the attack because he didn't feel well," Yunle says. "The royal physicians looked into his food and drink and found the residue of a fever-inducing herb in the tea he drank that morning. Kai had gone into Father's tent earlier."

"Who else did?" I ask.

"Grand Scholar Yu, Lord High Constable Wang, and a few servants. My other brothers and I only went to see Father after he started feeling poorly."

"Ren could've paid a servant to add the herb to the King's tea."

Yunle doesn't look convinced. "These servants are loyal to Father. No amount of money offered by Ren could've made them risk their lives like that."

"The mercenaries were also paid with lots of gold," Jieh puts in. "Ren doesn't have that kind of money, but Kai does."

They don't believe my accusations against Ren. I feel like screaming in frustration.

"The officials and other families are demanding justice for the young men who died and for those who were severely injured in the assault," Yunle says to me. "Father has to give them that. Unless you have strong evidence proving that someone else orchestrated the attack, Kai will take the blame." Yunle's piercing gaze snaps onto Jieh. "Did you find out if he pushed you into the river?"

So Jieh has told his sister about his suspicion. "I tested Kai. He denied it, but his reaction told me that he did it."

I trust Jieh's judgement. I have little sympathy for Kai, but I cannot let Ren get away with his crimes. I may not be able to prove it to the others yet, but my gut feeling tells me that he was the mastermind behind this whole tragic chain of events. The very fact that he suddenly stopped making advances on me leads me to believe he has found new benefactors and developed a more efficient plan to eliminate his competition.

At this point, there's only one person who can prove Ren's guilt.

"If we find Hanxin, we'll discover the truth," I say.

"Ren and I have been assigned the task of catching Hanxin," Jieh says. "We were informed of a sighting outside Jingshi, so we'll be gone for a few days."

"What about your wound?"

"It's nothing. I've had worse."

As proud as he is, Jieh doesn't like being fussed over, so I accept his answer despite my concern. "Don't let Ren get to Hanxin first. He may kill the Elder to cover up his complicity."

"I shall take every precaution to ensure Hanxin is captured alive so he can answer for his crimes." Jieh's voice rings out like iron on stone. His whole demeanor softens when he leans toward me. "I'm more worried about your safety. I won't be around to protect you from your uncle and cousins."

"I'll be safe at home, much safer than you. But you'll be out there traveling with Ren, and he's already tried to kill you."

Jieh snorts a contemptuous sound. "That coward wouldn't dare raise a finger against me now that I'm well."

"He'll backstab you the first chance he gets," I say, equally annoyed and anxious that Jieh isn't taking the threat of Ren's presence more seriously.

"You both need to be careful, all right?" Yunle interjects. Her eyes are dark and intense, lending weight to the words. She doesn't look away until we both swear to be vigilant.

Jieh rises. "I'm expected to convene with Ren this afternoon. I must leave to get ready."

We bid Yunle goodbye.

Jieh escorts me home on Sky Dancer. On our way, when a sudden foul, disquieting feeling pommels me, I lift the flap of the coach to find Ren riding in our direction. He gives Jieh a curt nod as they near each other, but Jieh ignores him as always.

Ren glances at me, and that repugnant feeling swells, enough that I almost throw up.

What's happening with him?

I've gained a strange sensing ability in this life, but even without that, I'm sure this did not occur in my prior one. It's completely new and different; something has changed with Ren in this timeline. But what is it?

In the courtyard, Jieh helps me exit the coach, then turns to Fei. "Protect Mingshin well. I don't want a single hair of hers missing when I return."

Fei faces him with unflinching resolve. "She'll be fine, exactly as you left her, Your Highness."

Jieh motions to his personal guards. Four men step forward. "I'm leaving my most trusted guards with you. Each of them is worth ten men in a fight. You won't go anywhere without their company."

Here's the arrogant ass part of him talking again. Irritation flares, but it evaporates as soon as I recognize the deep concern in his eyes.

"Please take it slow so you can recover from your wound," I say. "Bring plenty of guards with you. There will be lots of opportunities for danger."

Jieh nods absentmindedly. I feel a worrying shudder in my chest when I think of the awful, sinister aura around Ren.

I grab Jieh's hand and lead him away until we are out of the others' earshot.

I steel my nerves, for what I am about to tell him won't be easy. "You once asked me if I was keeping a secret. I am. I can't share the whole story with you yet because it would sound insane, but I promise it's true. This much I can say: I was once very close to Ren. He's the most manipulative, vile, cunning liar I've ever met. This lesson came at a steep price. I'm still recovering from it, and I don't want you to have to pay a similar price for underestimating him."

He stares at me. For a moment I'm afraid he'll laugh at me for how ridiculous I sound, or demand that I tell him more.

Then, he sweeps me into an embrace, burying his head in my hair. His voice is gentle and earnest. "Thank you for your trust in sharing this with me, Mingshin. I promise I'll always watch out for Ren."

I melt into him. The warmth of his body surrounds me, filling the little space between us, filling my mind. "I'll miss you, Mingshin." He lets go and kisses me on the forehead. "Try not to miss me too much, all right?" he adds with a smirk.

I feel my eyes involuntarily rolling skyward, but I pull them back.

He departs with the rest of his guards. As the gate closes behind them, he brings Sky Dancer around and waves to me. I raise a hand and return the gesture. He turns again, rounds a bend in the narrow road, and vanishes from sight.

But I continue staring, feeling an emptiness opening inside me, as if Jieh has taken a part of me with him.

CHAPTER 30

Fei and Mai have fallen asleep in the maids' room adjacent to mine. Clutching the pendant in my closed palms, I let myself sink into sleep as I repeatedly demand entry into the spiritual realm of the Divine Stone.

The air ripples and the Holy Temple emerges as grand as ever. Sudaji stands before the altar, a perfect combination of grace and steel. Her face is hard and grim. "Didn't I warn you that you'd be shining a beacon for your enemies seeking the Divine Stone every time you come here?"

"My enemies are far away, and I haven't had the feeling of being watched since I last spoke to you," I say. "I thought it would be safe to take a chance. Please, I have to see you. I have so many questions, and they are eating away at me." The sudden tightening of my chest makes me realize I've also missed seeing her.

Sudaji closes her eyes, her expression concentrated. When she looks at me again, she appears more relaxed. "I sense no mages or sorcerers nearby," she says. Did she just use her Sense magic?

Then she frowns. "The last time you were here, you said you felt you were being watched. How so?"

"It's strange. I can sense certain magic—magic that's being used for dark purposes, specifically. I think it started when I first came here."

She frowns more deeply. "Similarly, I've only recently gained this form you now see before you. These two phenomena may be connected." Her face brightens suddenly as she grasps my arms. "Perhaps you've finally started to acquire magic, Mingshin, although I don't understand how it could be possible."

I gape at her. "Acquire magic? What do you mean?"

She looks into my eyes, searching, probing, as if debating whether to reveal the truth. I hold her gaze and set my jaw. After a pause, she says, "It's Heaven's rule that every human soul must go through reincarnation, even those trapped by a strong force. So, after nearly two centuries, I was eventually reincarnated as you, Mingshin. However, the part of me that possesses magic was somehow left behind, in the form of a spirit. Therefore you don't have magic, although by rights you should."

"What? But don't you need to possess at least one-fourth Nan'Yüan blood for that? I have none."

She puts her arms down. "Are you sure? How much do you know about your parents' heritage?"

Father was an illegitimate child—the reason his family looked down upon him and shunned him until he became rich. His father never disclosed who his mother was.

"Did my Baba have magic? Was that why he traveled to Nan'Yü so often . . . to look for his mother?"

"The magic skipped him. I cannot answer your second question, as I had no access to the world until you were born with the Divine Stone, and even after that I could only see things happening around you."

My reply is a breathless squeak. "I was *born* with the Stone?"

She's quiet for a moment. "You didn't know," she whispers.

"My pendant isn't a family heirloom," I add, as though in a dream.

"No. The Stone was gone from the world, along with the Holy Temple, and it only reappeared with your birth."

I feel a blow deep in my bones. Father lied to me? Did Mother as well?

Sudaji sets a hand on my shoulder and squeezes it gently. But I find little comfort in her gesture.

"If I die again, will the Divine Stone revive me?" I ask.

"It did not revive you. *I* channeled through the Stone to reset Time. And two years was the most I could manage. I disobeyed the order of nature once; such a violation shouldn't happen again, or there could be dire consequences. I'm sorry, Mingshin, but if you die, you'll be reincarnated as someone else, someone who's also meant to possess the Stone."

I gulp, struggling a bit with her blunt honesty. "Still . . . I cannot thank you enough for giving me this second chance."

She holds both of my hands in hers. "I'm proud to see how you've utilized this chance to fulfill your purpose, Mingshin." Her expression hardens into granite. "One day, it will be your sacred duty to free the Holy Temple from the spiritual realm and restore the Divine Stone's glory."

The revelation is another shock to pile onto the already teetering stack. "How do I do that?"

"You must find the way yourself." She tenses suddenly, her face scrunched. "You said your enemies were far away."

I nod, but uncertainty grips me at the sharpness of her tone.

"I sense something close," she murmurs. "A power seeking the Stone. A might as great as the mountain itself, and as ferocious as thunder."

I glance around frantically.

She whirls toward me. "You must go! Stay away. Don't come back unless it's absolutely necessary."

I catch a whiff of a rotten and fetid presence just before she shoves me.

Then I am falling. Falling. And falling, a scream locked in my throat, almost choking me.

I should be waking up.

All around me, there is . . . nothingness. An emptiness. A void. But still I feel its presence. A dark and menacing power. Ghostlike yet pressing upon me.

My pulse races; its heavy, wild beats ring in my ears.

And I keep falling.

Must. Wake. Up.

I lift both arms above my head. Inside, I harden, willing my soul to be dry earth and my blood to be molten rock. Then I fight on, stretching for the surface of consciousness.

I break into the real world gasping for air. My hands clutch the bedsheet, my body soaked in sweat. The soft gleam of the Stone lights the room enough to show it's my bedroom.

With a sigh, I release the sheet and let my pounding heart calm.

What happened back there? It seems that someone was seeking out the Stone and did something horrible to me, almost trapping me in the spiritual realm—I'm not sure who or how, as I know so little about magic.

"I sense something close. A might as great as the mountain itself and as ferocious as thunder."

Hanxin has fled the city, so he isn't close. And I cannot imagine him being this powerful at his age; it's unheard of. That means I have another enemy, a mage much stronger and more frightening than Hanxin.

The next morning, as soon as I finish breakfast, I go to the study. Leaving Jieh's four guards outside, I enter. Mother lifts her eyes from a ledger on the desk to look at me.

"I need to speak to you alone, Ma, if you have a moment," I say.

"Of course." She sends Ning and the shop manager away, then comes to the couch to sit across from me. "What's the matter, Shin'ar?"

I pull the Divine Stone from beneath my dress and lift it in my palm. I make my voice as firm as a fist. "This pendant is not an heirloom from Baba's family, is it?"

Her expression tenses. "What makes you say that?"

"Please, Ma."

She turns away and sighs. "No, it's not."

Although I expected this, hearing the confirmation from her still hits me like a brick. "Why did you and Baba lie to me?"

"Because we didn't know how else to tell you . . ." Mother draws a deep breath and looks me in the eye. "The day before you were born, a goddess appeared in my dream—at least I thought it was a goddess, because she looked magnificent and her yellow dress was bright enough to rival the sun."

I know instantly that it was High Priestess Sudaji.

"She ordered me to only have your Baba with me when I gave birth," Mother continues. "No midwives, no maidservants. Otherwise it would put my child in great danger. Your Baba had the same strange dream. We decided to listen, although without a midwife present, he was very worried about my safety. During childbirth, I suffered excruciating pain, and your Baba nearly summoned the midwife despite the warning. But then you came into this world. And we knew why we had been warned." Mother points at my pendant. "In your tiny hand, you clutched this stone. It was glowing in five colors. I touched it. It was extremely hot, but didn't seem to hurt you at all. We didn't know what would've happened if a servant or a midwife had seen you born like this. They might even have thought you were an abomination. Your Baba and I were so glad we heeded the warning. Considering it was a gift from a goddess, we decided that the Stone had to stay with you at all times. But we never knew what it was really for."

I stare at my pendant. *I was born with the Divine Stone because I am Sudaji's reincarnation. And I should have magic.*

Mother sounds on the verge of tears. "I'm sorry we lied to you—"

I give her a quick hug. "It's all right, Ma. I understand why. It would be too much . . . for anyone to take." I pause a moment, to brace myself. "Do you know Baba's family? Did he ever tell you who his mother was?"

"Your Baba was kicked out of his family when he was only a teen, soon after his father died. After he made his fortune, they tried to force him to return and share his wealth. He rejected all their attempts. As far as I know, his father never revealed his mother's identity to him." Mother fixes me with a concerned look. "Has something happened to provoke these questions? Have you discovered the meaning of your pendant?"

I dare not tell her that powerful enemies may come after me for the Stone. If Mother knows the truth, she'll be terribly worried. It's my burden to shoulder alone.

I manage a weak smile. "The pendant was shining in five colors one night, so I was curious. I'm sure my having been born with it is a special blessing from Heaven."

A blessing indeed. I must free the Holy Temple from the spiritual realm and restore the Divine Stone's glory so it can be used to protect mankind from future disasters. I have no idea how to do that. I cannot risk another trip inside the Stone, not after my narrow escape.

CHAPTER 31

In the following days, I stay on high alert, feeling for any dark magic coming my way. But nothing happens. Whoever is seeking the Divine Stone hasn't discovered its connection to me. The dreadful knot of worry that has been tightening inside me begins to uncoil.

During my weekly date with Yunle, she informs me that the wedding planning for Prince Wen and Aylin is moving forward. "But the ceremony will wait until after Kai's trial concludes," she says, then frowns. "Wen is becoming more and more cantankerous. I ran into Sun Aylin a few times when I went to see him. I hear she visits him often to cheer him up. I doubt that works, as her presence always leaves me feeling cranky and depressed."

Maybe Aylin has realized that her future depends on Wen's mood. Has Uncle Yi accepted the fact that his daughter will never be Queen? There's nothing he can do to change the King's mind about Aylin's engagement to Wen. If he tries, he may very well jeopardize his own position.

But a cornered beast is all the more dangerous.

On our coach journey home, Fei seems especially vigilant as she oversees Jieh's guards riding alongside us.

The four sentries tag along wherever I go. They post themselves at the door of the dining room while I eat, and outside my bath while I bathe; at night, they take turns standing watch in twos, guarding my bedroom door. It's made finding an opportunity to dispose of the kui's antler almost impossible. Mother raised a brow after asking who they were, but thankfully she accepted my brief explanation without pressing for more details.

After passing the main gate of our home, the coach rolls through an open green space that stretches out beside a paved trail. Fifty yards in, the manor rises from the trees surrounding it like something carved from an enchanted forest, with its dark wooden walls and golden beams.

In the foyer, Mai helps remove my cloak. "Prince Jieh is here to see you, Miss," she says.

A pleasant shiver runs through me. I try to hide my excitement by using a casual tone to ask where Jieh is.

"He's waiting for you in the garden," Mai replies.

"Don't dally, Miss." Fei winks at me. "Hurry along."

Heat surges to my cheeks. I twirl away and stride out of the manor. But I suspect they saw my blush anyway. Fei's cheery laughter and Mai's teasing giggles pursue me.

As I skirt around the manor to get to the garden, I notice my quickened pace and the spring in my step. My face flares hotter.

Jieh waits next to a rosebush in the garden. He turns his head at my approach, and our eyes meet. How long we stand near, motionless, gazing at each other, I cannot say. He's so incredibly handsome in this moment—the sun sparkling off him forms a dazzling aura.

Jieh reaches me. Without a word, he wraps his arms around me, pulling me close to him, so close that as I shut my eyes and breathe him in, I cannot tell where he ends and I begin. "Mingshin," he whispers, like a feathery caress down my neck. My knees feel weak.

When he brings his gaze back to me, I can see the want in every part of him and feel it in the depths of me. His lips come down on mine, gentle, passionate, the sweetest taste I've ever imagined, my desire coming alight. I open my mouth under his. Every inch of me burns as his hot tongue rolls over mine.

His palms slide down my back. In one graceful, powerful movement, he sweeps me off my feet. I twine my arms around his neck, achingly aware of every point of contact. His warm lips moving over mine. His solid chest flush against me. His strong hands across my back. He deepens the kiss, intense, hungry. My fingers curl into his hair, and my tongue tangles more urgently with his. I cannot stop. My body ignites.

We consume each other with our fire until we are out of air. He breaks away from the kiss but doesn't pull back. Holding my waist, he sets me gently on my feet in the soft grass of the garden.

Hand in hand, we saunter past the bushes lining the garden path. His four guards keep a respectable distance.

"How's your wound?" I ask.

"Fully healed."

"Tell me what happened during your mission."

"We captured Longzo, although Hanxin once again escaped our grasp. We discovered that it takes great concentration and a lot of energy to work Portal magic, so we took precautions to prevent Longzo from using his power. Without his help, Hanxin should be easier to catch, but first we need to find him."

"How did Ren behave?"

"Well, he was acting strange. One day he asked to look at my wound in the presence of others, saying it demonstrated my bravery.

Then the next day he challenged me to a duel. I rebuffed both his requests and had Yao watch my back."

I scowl. "That *is* odd. If he wanted to hurt you, why would he ask to see your wound in the presence of others? And he would definitely lose to you in a duel, so why challenge you to one?" So many of Ren's recent actions defy logic.

Then I smile. Jieh listened to me; he took my warning seriously. I imagine he would have loved to beat Ren in a duel in front of the soldiers, but he held back his pride.

"Have you interrogated Longzo?" I ask.

"The lord high constable has taken charge of that. Freed of duty, I came here at once." Jieh stops and looks at me with a deep longing. "I've missed you, Mingshin. I thought about you all the time."

"I've missed you, too," I whisper.

Jieh's thumbs glide over my cheeks in a tender caress. "I'm in love with you, Mingshin."

A dizzying rush of heat sizzles through me. Did I hear him right?

His arms encircle me, drawing me close; his mouth molds to mine in another kiss that knocks the world out from under me.

He's in love with me.

I feel like I'm floating on air as I turn his words over and over in my mind. I so want to believe him.

But he's a prince, and he'll be King. Once upon a time, in another life, a prince I loved and helped become King told me that no self-respecting sovereign would make a commoner his Queen.

A horrible weight tugs at my core, dragging me down. I wrench away from Jieh.

He frowns, confusion written all over him.

He's not Ren. I know he has true feelings for me. But considering the vast difference in our social statuses, there's only one way we could be together, and I won't accept that for anything—I won't demean myself.

I contort my expression into a frosty look. "I will *not* be *one* of your Royal Ladies or concubines." My voice sounds harsh even to my ears.

He gasps. "What? No, Mingshin! I love you. You are the only woman who's ever made me feel this way. I care not that you're a merchant's daughter. Not now. Not ever. I want you to be my wife, my Queen."

His words coil around my heart. But they are so similar to the ones another prince spoke to me. "You are determined to become King." I bite my lip. "But I don't want to be Queen."

He appears shocked. "Every woman wants to be Queen."

"If that's what you believe, Jieh, you obviously don't know me as well as you think you do."

"Why do you not want to be Queen?"

I turn away. The crisp spice of pinesap infuses the cool air, blending with the musty perfume of dry leaves. Afar, the sky dissolves into a smear of tangerine. "You know the biggest wish in my life, Jieh? It's to one day travel the whole kingdom, to learn about different cultures and enjoy the wonders of the continent. I'd be suffocated by life at the royal court. I don't want to be surrounded by sycophants who always want something from me. I don't want to control other peoples' lives—they should be able to control their own. I'm not good at smoothing things over with people, or acting with the grace and poise noble ladies learn to wield, or sharing my husband with other women."

There's a tense moment of silence, then he says, "You can always be yourself, Mingshin. That's part of the reason why I love you. If you enjoy traveling, I'm sure we can make it happen as King and Queen."

That's wishful thinking on his part.

"I want no Royal Ladies or concubines. Only you."

"As the King, your first responsibility is to have an heir. A male heir." To ensure that, a monarch must have lesser consorts—Royal Ladies—in addition to his Queen. To produce as many male children as possible. "What if I can't give you a boy, Jieh? What will you do?"

"We can talk about it when we cross that bridge. But all these things aside, what about being with me?" Jieh grabs my arm and spins me around so that I'm facing him again. "Do you love me, Mingshin?"

The word "yes" surges to my tongue, and I start to lean into him. But memories swirl up, stealing my voice and immobilizing my body.

Ren professed his love with the most beautiful poem.

Ren proposed to me with stars shining in his eyes.

Ren told me that Aylin's wedding gown was being made while I lay dying in the snow.

The word turns to sand in my mouth. There is still a bruise on my heart, purple and swollen, painful to the touch. I can only watch Jieh helplessly and utter nothing.

"I see." His chest rises in a deep, measured breath. A mask of stone slams down over his face, void of feeling. "Goodbye, Mingshin." He whirls around and strides away.

I stand frozen for a moment, then race after him. "Jieh, stop! Please!"

He doesn't glance back or break his stride. He rounds a corner and, seconds later, I hear Sky Dancer neigh and gallop into the gray of dusk.

"Jieh, wait!" I scream, but he's gone.

I stop, suddenly queasy. *Goodbye, Mingshin.* Coming out of his mouth, the words sounded final. The ground tilts below me. I have to lean against a wall to keep myself steady.

Have I lost him forever?

Some figures move to my left. The guards Jieh assigned to protect me. They appear at a loss as to what to do.

"You should go back to your prince." I force a bitter smile. "He doesn't want you to stay here anymore."

They trade glances among themselves, then one of them says, "His Highness has given us specific orders. We'll continue to guard you until he rescinds those orders."

"Fine!" I storm into the manor and slam the door in their faces.

I raise a hand for Fei and Mai to leave me. I go directly to my bedroom and climb into my bed. I don't want to think, because whenever I do, my mind circles back to Jieh's hurt expression and his last words.

This is for the best, I tell myself. I shouldn't have grown emotionally attached to any of the princes. Once Jieh becomes King, I'll leave this place and live the kind of life I've always craved. But why does it feel like a knife is twisting and cutting deeply into my soul?

Suddenly I realize that I've shared the deepest desires of my heart with Jieh, something I never did with Ren.

Jieh will come back to me, right? He said he loves me.

Two voices war within me, and I fear I'll be ripped apart from within. Eventually, restless sleep finds me.

Days pass while I wait. Jieh does not return.

CHAPTER 32

"I lost," I admit.

Yunle sweeps the waychess pieces into jars. "This is my first win against you, but somehow I don't feel triumphant." She gives me a quizzical stare. "You are distracted and distraught."

I hate to sound like I'm whining, but she's my best friend and I don't want to hide my feelings from her—I've told myself to trust her. "The other day, Jieh said he loved me."

Yunle's eyes go wide. "Tell me more."

I relate the incident to her in greater detail. "He hasn't come to see me since then . . ." I bite my lip, my voice trailing off.

"What a man child," she exclaims. "Don't worry, he'll come around. Besides, he's probably been busy with other things."

"Ah yes. Other things." I'm glad for the change of subject. "How did the interrogation of Longzo turn out?"

"Longzo denied any of Hanxin's or his involvement in the attack at the hunt. He claims that his master had nothing to gain from such aggression and that someone else must have invoked Portal magic."

"Did he mention anything about Kai or Ren?" I ask, a nervous flutter in my belly.

"He claims that Hanxin has never collaborated with any of the princes. He wouldn't disclose where Hanxin is, not even under torture."

I know it's unavoidable, but the word "torture" still pierces me like a thorn.

"Lord High Constable Wang oversaw the interrogation. Jieh believes too much torture would lead to a false confession. Ren begged Father to give Longzo a respite because torture is cruel, and he volunteered to speak to Longzo in the hope of worming the truth out of him."

That disgusting piece of scum is flaunting his heart of gold again. He had no qualms about inflicting torture on me for three days.

"Ren has been talking to Longzo, and it seems he's making progress," Yunle says.

"Who knows what he's really been doing with Longzo? Perhaps he's making sure the guard's words can't incriminate him in any way."

"At Ren's request, Lord High Constable Wang was present whenever he spoke to Longzo. Jieh joined them most of the time, too. If Ren plays any kind of trick, they'll know."

"I still suspect Ren masterminded the attack."

When Yunle doesn't reply, frustration builds up inside me like water boiling in a kettle. Why can't anyone else see how evil and manipulative Ren is?

"Someone should check his left arm. I bet he faked his injury," I lash out.

"His sling has already been removed, but his left hand is still wrapped in bandages from a wound he suffered during the assault." Yunle touches my shoulder and says gently, "You are stressed, Mingshin. Once Hanxin is captured, the truth will be revealed. Because of his low status, Longzo may not dare to accuse any of the princes, but Hanxin would have no such reservations."

My frustration deflates. She's right. I need to be more patient.

It isn't until later, when I'm on my way home, that I remember Longzo's claim that his master had nothing to gain from such aggression. I have wondered about how Hanxin could possibly benefit from helping Ren but haven't been able to find an answer. What if Longzo told the truth and Hanxin wasn't involved? But if he's innocent, why is he hiding? Reifeng wouldn't want a war with our southern neighbor, so he can't have Hanxin tortured and must present strong evidence to the Nan'Yüan Elders Council before Hanxin can be punished accordingly.

What is the Elder afraid of that keeps him away?

My thoughts are interrupted by hoofbeats pounding nearby. I lift the small window flap of my coach to see a group of young men riding into the palace.

My heart races. It's Jieh on Sky Dancer, followed by Yao and a few lords on horseback.

I beam and wave at Jieh. Catching sight of my gesture, he turns in my direction. He raises a brow at the sight of me, then his face blanks. Quickly, he rides off.

The blood drains from my face so fast I get dizzy.

"Are you all right, Miss?" Mai asks, concern lining her eyes.

"Yes," I croak; inside I feel anything but. A great hole opens up in me, and oh, it hurts. It's like a dagger plunged into me.

I have no one to blame but myself. I told myself not to give anyone else the power to hurt me, but I yielded to my desire to be loved.

It's past time to lock that cage around my heart again and throw away the key.

"Your coach is ready," Fei tells me. In the crook of her arm, she's holding something wrapped in layers of cloth.

We are going to ride out of the city to bury the kui's antler deep in a forest. I should have done it sooner, but I was prevented by the constant vigilance of Jieh's guards, then distracted by my hurt over Jieh.

I put on my cloak. We are barely out of my bedroom when Mai dashes in, her eyes two big O's of fear. "Prince Jieh and Prince Ren are here. A royal edict announcer is with them. You have been ordered to take the edict immediately."

My stomach twists into a knot. Nine times out of ten, a royal edict announcer is bad news. But why is he accompanied by two princes?

"Hide it well," I mouth to Fei. She nods, understanding I mean the kui's antler.

I rush to the vestibule with Mai in tow. Everyone else in the household is already present. Mother reaches me and grasps my arm. "Shin'ar," she whispers, her face pale.

The palace official appears nonchalant. Jieh stands near the entrance, hands clasped behind his back. His mouth is set in a grim line, his face a hard mask. Ren's expression is as serene as a lake on a winter morning, but I detect a subtle smirk.

The knot in my stomach burns. But worse, that same abominable atmosphere around Ren seems to have grown even stronger now, almost suffocating me. Something very strange, very wrong, is happening with him.

"Take the royal edict now, Lu Mingshin," the official declares.

Although the edict is directed at me, my entire household kneels.

"By the blessing of Heaven, I, King Reifeng, give the order to have the citizen, Lu Mingshin, arrested immediately for her involvement in a plot of regicide."

I'm so shocked I even forget to be scared for a second. A plot of regicide?

As I pass Jieh, his face turned away from me, I beseech, my voice constricted into a sob, "My family has nothing to do with this. If you've ever loved me, please protect them. I beg you."

Surrounded by the burly guards, I'm dragged out the door before I can hear if Jieh responds at all.

CHAPTER 33

It's been three days since I was thrown into the death prison.

Nightmares have plagued my sleep in which I am tortured and taunted by strangers. Their faces are hideous and ruthless, their breath fetid. I keep telling them I'm innocent, but they won't relent. Whenever the torture becomes too much to bear, I wake up gasping, drenched in sweat.

Right now, I lean listlessly into a corner of the dark, cold, dingy cell. I am only given a cup of water each day, and no food. Oddly, I haven't been interrogated yet. It's almost as if the King has forgotten about my existence.

My belly aches with hunger, but it's nothing compared to the worry gnawing at me.

Will Reifeng punish Mother? He had his own brother's whole family executed for attempted regicide. I hope with my entire being that Jieh will shield my family from the King's wrath by making him see reason.

A flash of bitter heat pulses through me. Jieh hasn't visited me in prison. Could he really believe I'd be involved in a plot to murder his father to fulfill some prophecy with Hanxin? Maybe he doesn't, but as soon as I stood in his way of becoming King, he abandoned me. Could I have misjudged him? Is he no different from other men?

But if he has any love left for me, he may at least protect my family, right?

I touch my pendant beneath my filthy dress. For all its mighty power, I can't use it to save myself. I sigh and curl further into myself. If I die again, Sudaji won't reset Time again, and the Stone will be born with someone else. I strangle a sob. I don't want my life to end on an execution block, but I see no way out unless Longzo changes his story.

What really happened between him and Ren? Longzo wouldn't reveal his master's location even under torture, so why did he betray Hanxin's mission to Ren *after* their talk?

A flicker of motion catches the corner of my eye. I lift my head and see a man approach the iron bars of my cell, his eyes cold and hard like a shark's.

My stomach turns over, swirling with sickness. In my former life, this warden was assigned to be my last interrogator.

They've finally come to drag me to the torture chamber and force a false confession out of me. Just the thought makes my body shake and my muscles cramp.

"Warm regards from Prince Ren, you filthy little traitor," he smirks. "Your miserable life will be over soon."

"What . . . what do you mean?" I rasp.

He cackles. "The White Cloth will be here for you come morning."

A roar fills my ears. I'm meant to use the White Cloth to hang myself in my cell.

The man turns and strides away. I scramble to the bars on all fours. Is he working for Ren? He has no reason to lie about my upcoming doom. My lungs writhe and pull, begging for air. I can't die based on another false allegation. I must get away. But how?

There's nothing I can use to break out of this prison. Even my hairpins were confiscated by the wardens. I bang on the bars with what little strength I have left. "I'm innocent," I call out again and again in a pitiful voice.

In the distance, the wardens' barking reprimand and raucous laughter are the only reply.

Did I escape death from Ren only to die by his hands once again? I bury my head in my lap. Despair tightens its icy grip on me.

Exhausted, I fall asleep. And I dream. It's dark and I can barely see. I turn around and around, searching for a way out.

Something large slithers out of this pit of blackness, a monster with razor-sharp fangs. It smells rotten, like a corpse, and its eyes glow like embers. The monster leaps at me, but I'm too frozen with fear to move. As it bites and tears at my flesh, its face transforms into Ren's mocking grin, cold and cruel.

Fury explodes in me, so hot it courses through me like a raging fire. I rake a hand across Ren's cheek and punch at his ferocious jaw, but he holds on and drags me deeper down into the endless shadows.

I struggle, committing my entire being to defeating this demon.

Sudden light pours down upon us. As if burned by it, Ren releases me. A hand appears from above and reaches for me.

I run toward the light, the hand guiding me. It seems far away, but I keep going and going. Eventually I'm bathed in light, my heart at peace. The hand snatches mine and pulls me up and up until my eyes are level with a man's warm gaze.

I'm shaken awake.

"Miss!" It takes my sluggish mind a few moments to register the repeated, urgent whisper. A face swims into focus. I let out a cry of delight, but Fei clamps a hand over my mouth.

"Shh!" Then, "Can you walk?"

With a burst of energy that shocks me, I rise on my wobbly legs.

"There isn't much time, Miss. Please stay quiet and follow us." She's dressed like a man, her hair bundled under a hat.

We hurry out through the open cell door, but I sway, stars erupting in my vision. Fei catches me with both arms. That's when I notice someone else with her. It's Jieh holding a torch. *Am I still dreaming, or is this real?*

"Go!" he urges us. He stays a step ahead, his posture alert. More like he's patrolling ahead of us, ready to strike down any threats.

I notice the prison has gone deathly quiet except for the moans of a man a few cells back. I don't hear the wardens playing cards, threatening prisoners, or even them inspecting the jail.

"You are freeing me," I say and try to keep pace with them, half supported by Fei.

"Yes," Jieh replies. "Father intends to grant you the White Cloth tomorrow morning." He glances back at me, his jaw clenched and his eyes like flint. "I can't let him do that."

So the warden told the truth. Without a trial, King Reifeng has already condemned me.

The significance of what Jieh is doing floods over me. He's betraying his father. For a moment, my emotions are unsure where to settle. All this time, I've been thinking he abandoned me. But to have him make such an enormous sacrifice . . .

My throat grows thick, and I swallow. Right now, I need to concentrate.

"If I run away, my family will be punished," I say.

"Don't worry. Your mother dismissed all the servants. Ning and Mai begged to stay. Yunle and I have arranged for your mother, Hui, and the two maids to go into hiding."

So the princess helped, too. Gratitude boils up within me like a hot spring. I've never known such friendship before.

"Your Mother wanted to come, too. Hui persuaded her otherwise."

I whisper a silent "thank you" to Hui. I can always rely on his steadfastness, a stone pillar in the midst of a storm.

"Did you drug the wardens?" I ask.

Jieh gives a terse nod. "I sent four carts of palace wine, a way to thank them for their hard work."

"No one wanted to miss out on the expensive wine, obviously," Fei says.

"Do you . . . do you believe Longzo's words, about me?" I ask Jieh.

He fixes me with a fierce look, a tempest of emotions churning in his eyes. "Of course not!" he declares vehemently. "I know you'd never betray Dazhou or commit treason. I'm sorry that I had to stand by and let them arrest you. To witness your distress and fear and do nothing . . ." His voice chokes up, and I glimpse the anguished lines of his face as he abruptly turns away. "I'm sorry that I had to let you think I didn't care for you," he adds in a broken whisper.

My nose burns, and I sniffle. I realize that the last three days have been as much of a torture for him as they have been for me, perhaps even more so, as he had to play along with his father's orders so that no one would suspect he'd break me out.

"I understand," is all I manage to say.

"Father has ears only for Ren these days." Jieh shakes his head as if in disbelief. "Yunle and I were able to keep you from being tortured, but Father agreed when Ren recommended an immediate execution for you."

Ren is eager to get rid of me, isn't he? I cannot let him win. I won't. Resolve galvanizes me, transforming my anger and dread into fuel.

"We need to get to Longzo," I tell Jieh. "Only he knows where Hanxin is."

"He hasn't been coherent lately. He keeps telling us Hanxin is in a bubble. I'm not sure how useful he'll be."

I blink. A bubble? "Still, he's the only one who knows Hanxin's whereabouts. We must discover the truth from the Elder. We can't be fugitives forever, Jieh. Ren may well become the next King and we can't let that happen."

Jieh sighs. "You're right. Stay here. I'll get Longzo." He turns down another hall.

Fei and I wait in tense silence, each passing second feeling like an eternity. Every tiny sound makes me want to jump. Finally—it's probably only a minute or two—Jieh reappears, a shape slung over his shoulder like a sack of potatoes.

We hasten on again. When we round a corner, there are men slumped on the floor and against the walls—the drugged wardens. Some seem to be stirring already. Quickening our steps, we climb a flight of stairs and pass a room where more bodies lie in awkward positions, then we are out the door.

It's the dead of night and I'm glad for the cover of darkness. Jieh blows a low whistle. Sky Dancer trots into view, followed by a draft horse pulling a carriage. The hooded driver draws a head covering back to reveal herself.

Warmth suffuses my chest, and I fight to blink away my tears.

Yunle leaps off the carriage and we hug. She then helps me aboard while Fei takes the spot of the driver. Jieh dumps Longzo onto the floor of the coach before mounting Sky Dancer.

Yunle hands me a flask and a wedge of food wrapped in bamboo leaves. I drink greedily and wolf down a bun.

As we ride through the entrance, none of the keepers dare to question a prince. Only when we are about half a mile away do we relax slightly and speak. I tell Yunle that we must find Hanxin first.

"I agree," she says and glances at Longzo's prone form.

I bend forward and shake him. He jerks awake, growls, and flails his arms. I scoot backward. Yunle catches his hand just before it connects with my face.

His eyes focus on me, and he calms at once. "Miss Lu, tell my master I didn't mean to betray him. Prince Ren used Blood magic on me. He forced words out of me."

Yunle and I exchange a frown. Longzo sounds genuinely pained, but what hogwash is he babbling? Ren has no Nan'Yüan heritage at all. Maybe Jieh is right; Longzo has lost his senses and may not be able to help us.

Yunle rounds on him. "Are you saying the prophecy is true? That Hanxin has come to Dazhou to slay my father?"

"The dragon spoken of in the prophecy isn't your father, princess," he says weakly. "My master will explain everything, Miss Lu."

"Where is Hanxin?" I ask.

"I created a bubble to keep him safe. I can't tell you where he is, for I know not. But you have a way to communicate with him. The kui's antler he gave you is enchanted. Speak his name to the antler and my master will see and hear you."

I sigh. "The kui's antler was taken from me as evidence."

Yunle bends down and pulls out something from beneath her seat. "I stole it back!"

My mouth drops open. Indeed, in her hand is the antler. "How did you know to . . ."

"It was Fei. She suspected the kui's antler was important and that we might need it later. Isn't she amazing?"

I laugh. "You both are."

I offer Longzo the flask and a bun. He accepts and gobbles down the food.

Hanxin believes I'm the girl in the prophecy, so he won't hurt me. We have no other choice, anyway. "Let's find a safe place and contact Hanxin," I tell Yunle.

"I agree."

I open the front flap and tell Jieh and Fei what Lonzo told us. They urge the horses on faster, out to the forest where we planned to bury the kui's antler.

"You don't believe I'd try to murder your father," I say to Yunle.

"Of course not! It was foolish to think so. We'll open my father's eyes and make him see."

I wish it were that simple. Even if we prove my innocence, I doubt the King will completely forgive Jieh and Yunle. Historically, no monarchs have tolerated any kind of challenge to their power, even when they have come from their own children. I may never be able to repay my friends for their sacrifice. Jieh's involvement on my behalf may well cost him his bid for the throne.

My heart wrenches at the thought.

As if reading my mind, Yunle says, "Jieh and I can't let you die, Mingshin. We knew the risk we were taking when we rescued you, so don't you worry about us." She shrugs. "Who knows? I may finally be free of this prison called the royal palace and get to see the world."

I smile despite unshed tears. "Just don't forget to take me with you."

She laughs. "How can I not, my dearest friend?"

The city gate isn't far from the death prison. Again, no guards question why a prince needs to leave the city in the dead of night with a carriage in tow.

When we reach the edge of the forest, Jieh and Fei take one of the lanterns from the coach and venture into the tree line to make sure it's safe to enter. The rest of us wait.

"How did you enchant the kui's antler?" I ask Longzo. "And how did you avoid detection while imbuing it with magic?"

"It was already enchanted in Nan'Yü. My master didn't kill a kui at the Elite Hunt. He told the lie so no one would be suspicious of the antler's sudden appearance"

Of course. What were the chances Hanxin would've encountered such a rare beast?

When Jieh and Fei return, we ride deeper into the forest. We stop at a certain spot, and everyone crowds into the coach. Jieh settles beside me, one arm around my waist.

Yunle and Fei sit close, heads bent together and exchanging small smiles. A sweetness sparks in my belly. It seems that, despite the vast difference in their social statuses, they have developed a friendship. Then I notice the slight flush of their cheeks, the tender way they brush each other's hands, and the unspoken words held in their gazes upon each other. I remember Fei's first-ever blush when Yunle touched her arm.

A fierce rush of joy floods me and I grin.

Longzo clears his throat, and we all snap to attention. He tells me what I'm supposed to do with the antler. This is probably the first time my friends have witnessed magic. Despite their nervousness, there's no hesitation in their expressions.

We all understand this must be done.

CHAPTER 34

I shut my eyes and ride out a wave of anxiety. Holding the antler close, I utter "Hanxin" three times. A low hum runs through the antler, and its surface becomes transparent like a mirror. Then a face stares back at me.

"Miss Lu," Hanxin exclaims.

Startled, I almost drop the antler. "Respectable Elder," I say.

"Call me Hanxin. Who told you how to communicate with me?"

Longzo puts his head next to mine. "Master. I'm free, for now."

Hanxin beams with relief. "How did you break free?"

"Sorry to interrupt, Hanxin," I say. "But we have many questions for you and our time is short."

"*We?* Who else is with you?"

"Jieh, Yunle, and Fei." I move the antler farther away so Hanxin can see the others. His expression darkens, so I quickly add, "They helped free Longzo and me. We are all fugitives." Reifeng has probably learned by now that I escaped with the help of his two children. "Please, Hanxin, I know of the High Priestess's prophecy. I need to make sense of what's going on." I tell him what happened from the moment I was arrested until the present.

"Prince Ren used Blood magic on me, Master," Longzo hisses. "He compelled me to reveal our mission." Gods above, here's Longzo's crazy talk again.

Hanxin's eyes gleam hard as he asks, "Are you sure it was him?"

Longzo nods firmly.

Any trace of levity vanishes from Hanxin's face. A sick feeling winds its way through me as I remember the smothering aura Ren gave off. Something far beyond my understanding is going on.

Hanxin takes us all in. "Let's clarify a few things about the past events, prince, princess. None of my delegation was involved in the attack at the hunt."

"Why did you flee if you are innocent?" Jieh asks.

"Because I was attacked myself. A mage named Xiangyu, who calls himself the Night Dragon, sent his lackeys after me."

Realization hits me like a bucket of ice. "He's the dragon mentioned in the High Priestess's prophecy."

"That's correct. Xiangyu is likely the most powerful mage in Nan'Yü, capable of multiple forms of magic."

My friends and I trade an astonished look. I'm supposed to slay the most powerful mage?

"I can sense danger coming my way," Hanxin says. "However, there's a limit to my power: I can't foresee the shape or form the threat will take. Soon after I left the hunt with Reifeng, I felt the danger coming. I sent two men to fetch you to safety, Miss Lu, but obviously they failed. I had to run for my own life and only managed to escape at the last second."

So Hanxin is at least capable of Sense magic.

"I can tell you with confidence that Ren collaborated with Xiangyu to plot the attack at the hunt," Hanxin continues. "After Miss Lu sabotaged Ren's chance for the throne at the commencement ceremony, I believe he finally decided to move forward with the plans he'd made."

I hear gasps of disbelief around me, then Yunle asks, "How do you know it was Ren, not Kai?"

"Ren enlisted my help to eliminate his competition. I turned him down, for I had no interest in what he offered." Hanxin sneers. "It's apparent that Blood magic was at work on the mercenaries, so you can be sure that whatever your captives told you was a lie."

Jieh fixes the Elder with a marble stare. "How can we be sure *you* are telling the truth?"

Hanxin glares at him. "If you don't believe me, stop asking questions. I swear to the gods who granted my ancestors their power that I have told you nothing but the truth. And I do this for Miss Lu, no one else."

A silence meets his declaration. Then I say, "I believe you." It's a gut feeling, and his words make sense. If defeating the Night Dragon is paramount to him, he's smart enough to understand he can only get my help by winning my trust, and truth is the first step to getting there.

Hanxin nods in appreciation.

"How do you know Xiangyu was working with Ren?" I ask.

"I can tell whether a person possesses magic and what kind it is, if they are near. Ren had apparently been planning the attack for a while, with the help of magic, so a mage should have been around during the hunt, but I detected none. I found it baffling until Longzo confirmed that Ren had used Blood magic on him." Hanxin's jaw tightens. "I believe he borrowed magic from Xiangyu, as borrowed powers are the only kind I cannot detect."

"*Borrowed* magic?" we gasp in unison. I've never heard of such a thing.

"Yes. It's the darkest form of sorcery." The way Hanxin says it sends a shiver down my back. "Xiangyu is the only mage capable of lending his magic to others. Depending on how much one borrows and how long it lasts, one can lose anywhere between five years and twenty years of their life to him."

My chest contracts with a sharp spasm, squeezing the air from my lungs. Ren's greed for power has no boundaries. I think of the unsettling, ominous atmosphere he's given off lately. The first time I sensed it was the day after he broke the bow at the opening ceremony. He only captured a few rabbits because he hadn't spent most of the day hunting but working with this Night Dragon.

Why can I sense borrowed magic when even Hanxin can't?

"How long has Xiangyu been practicing this kind of dark magic?" Jieh asks, his face drawn tight. It seems he's decided to take Hanxin at his word.

"At least a decade, I think."

Something like recognition flashes across Jieh's eyes, then it's gone.

"Xiangyu has Chancellor Lew'Bung completely under his control. But ruling Nan'Yü won't be enough for him," Hanxin says. "He wants to have the next Dazhouan King under his thumb, too. Ren's desperation and blind ambition drove him right into what Xiangyu has planned for him."

Ren *is* desperate. I'm sure he had no interaction with Xiangyu in my last life. There was no need: He had full control of my money, the help of Uncle Yi's scheming, and my strategic mind.

Yunle's eyes show just a hint of fire. "I should've listened to you, Mingshin. I never thought Ren capable of such a monstrous alliance with a foreign enemy."

Jieh slams a fist on a wall of the coach. "That knave will not succeed." He lifts his chin. "Dazhou will never bend under the Night Dragon, no matter how mighty his magic is."

"In that case, I hope you'll triumph as the new King," Hanxin says.

There's still another puzzle haunting me. "What makes you think I'm the girl you've been searching for to fulfill the prophecy?" I ask Hanxin.

"I'd like to speak to you alone regarding that matter."

I open my mouth to protest, but he stops me with a raised hand. His expression is dead serious. "It concerns the fate of my country, and I'll only share such information with you. I must also ask you to swear that any private conversation between you and me will remain ours and ours alone. Otherwise I won't divulge anything further. Protecting my country is my top priority."

I glance uncertainly at my friends. If I agree to Hanxin's terms, it would feel like I'm hiding something from them.

Jieh smiles. "It's all right, Mingshin. I don't have to know everything. I just need to know enough for us to be safe."

"Well said, Jieh." Yunle gives me a comforting pat on the shoulder before scooting out of the coach.

The others follow her. I suppose Longzo will make sure they all stay far enough away.

I take a deep breath, then another, before facing Hanxin again. "I swear to Heaven and my ancestors that I won't disclose our private conversation to another soul."

"Thank you, Miss Lu. Here's High Priestess Lüzhi's full prophecy: Go to Jingshi and find this girl. She defied death and defeated you thrice. Join your hands with her, and you shall slay the Dragon together." He grins. "You defeated me by winning three *liwu* from me. After you survived the assassination attempt, I became certain that you are the girl. But prophecies are often difficult to decipher, and even seers don't grasp their meaning until they manifest themselves. Now that I think about it, you also defied death by surviving the attack at the camp."

But I know in my bones that I defied death by getting my second chance at life.

"I must warn you." Hanxin's tone grows grave. "Xiangyu is even more dangerous than I let on earlier."

"How so?"

"As intelligent as you are, you must know that the Holy Temple vanished two centuries ago without a trace. No one knows what happened or why."

I do my best to keep my expression neutral.

"Without the Holy Temple to ward off evil energy, slowly the magic turned dark. Thirty years ago, Xiangyu did the unthinkable. You see, demons are fallen gods, so their powers are practically the same. Although they were defeated and sealed away, they kept their powers." Hanxin's voice smolders with anger. "By offering human sacrifices to these demons, Xiangyu invented a way to reach them and access even greater magic. He started calling himself the Night Dragon and has gained many followers, luring them with promises of power."

My stomach churns with nausea. The mercenaries all dropped dead simultaneously. I bet they were the human sacrifices Ren made to borrow magic. His aura had grown darker when Jieh and I ran into him at the palace after our meeting with Yunle.

"But isn't this kind of evil magic forbidden in Nan'Yü?" I ask.

"All of this Xiangyu did in secret. Only High Priestess Lüzhi, a few priests and I are aware of his evil deeds. We conducted a dangerous investigation to learn the truth. Unfortunately, he's fully trusted by Chancellor Lew'Bung and the Elders Council, so we cannot accuse him."

I wonder how I can possibly go up against such a formidable enemy. And without magic, to boot.

"Each generation of High Priestess and her priests have devoted themselves to finding the Holy Temple since its disappearance," Hanxin says. "None have succeeded. But we finally we have a clue. A few months ago, High Priestess Lüzhi detected a disturbance in the flow of Time. After more study, she found that Time had been reset by a very powerful magical artifact, which she believes is connected to the Holy Temple. That was also when Her Holiness read the prophecy, which only exists in this timeline."

All the blood rushes from my head. Sudaji was right.

Hanxin must misinterpret my reaction. "It's much to take in, but please trust Her Holiness's judgement."

I manage a weak nod and indicate for him to go on.

"Unfortunately, Xiangyu also found out about the magical artifact. Imagine him getting his hands on a tool that can reset Time: It would be a catastrophe for the world."

This is why Hanxin doesn't want to share the conversation with my friends. He's afraid they'd pursue the magic tool or bring the information to Reifeng, the ruler of a rival kingdom. But Hanxin has no idea that one must possess magic to channel through the Stone, to call upon godly powers. Powers that go far beyond the ability to reset Time.

Xiangyu, the Night Dragon, almost trapped me in the spiritual realm of the Divine Stone forever. His power smelled rotten and corrupt, akin to the presence I felt watching me at the hunt.

Dread surges through me in a paralyzing wave. Has Xiangyu discovered my connection to the Stone? But if he has, he would have come after me, right?

I will a little strength into my veins.

Xiangyu doesn't know I possess the Divine Stone yet. And he mustn't find out. No one can know. Despite Hanxin's disclosures, I don't fully trust a man who cares more about the end than the means.

"Since the prophecy concerns me, a Dazhouan woman, surely it can be interpreted our way, too," I tell Hanxin. "By joining hands, it could simply mean working together as allies."

He muses. "You may be right. I accept you as my ally." He frowns. "Her Holiness only shared the full prophecy with me, and partially with Longzo. But Xiangyu is a seer as well and may have extracted the prophecy himself. Now that many people have learned of my marriage proposal to you, he'll know you're the girl spoken of in the prophecy. He'll try to harm you. Let's leave for Nan'Yü immediately and seek Her Holiness's aide."

Fear sweeps in afresh, but I push it back and fold it away for another time. "I can't yet. I must get rid of Ren and make sure my family and friends are safe. Then we can talk about how we are going to defeat the Night Dragon."

"Yunle and I talked about it," Jieh says as he and the princess return to the coach. "Father hasn't seemed quite himself in the last few days. He's sought Ren's counsel on everything and refused to listen to anyone else. Now that we've thought about it . . . if Ren truly borrowed magic from Xiangyu and used it on Longzo . . ."

My breath hitches. "You think Ren may have used it on the King, too."

"Yes. If so, he could make Father do anything he wants."

A realization blasts through me like a cold wind. "Ren was acting strange when you two led the mission to search for Hanxin. Asking to look at your wound, challenging you to a duel . . . I think he was trying to get your blood, because he needed it to use the magic on *you*. And the bandage wrapping his hand . . . it's to cover his *fuiin*."

Fei swears under her breath.

Jieh looks sick. "Thank Heaven I heeded your warning about him," he manages to say. His face hardens. "Yunle and I also discussed just now how Father was once hurt by magic. She said she already told you. What no one else knew was, Father only allowed me near his sick bed after he was injured. He kept mumbling in semi consciousness, 'Zejun used Fire magic on me. How could he do sorcery?' At the time, I thought he must be delirious, but earlier Hanxin confirmed Xiangyu has been practicing his dark magic for at least a decade . . ."

I gasp. "Prince Zejun borrowed Fire magic from Xiangyu!"

Jieh nods.

"Not knowing how Zejun possessed Fire magic, Father must have decided even the knowledge of magic was too dangerous and banned it in the kingdom," Yunle growls, her hands clamped into fists. "If Ren is using his borrowed magic on Father, it would wound him doubly. First, his brother, then his son. We must go back to stop Ren immediately. Once Father makes Ren the heir, who knows what he'll do to Father, to Kai, to us? Will he give Dazhou away to the Night Dragon?"

"If Ren is controlling the King with Blood magic, you can be sure there are already fugitive posters of us all over the city," Fei says.

Yunle nods. "We should find out about that first."

"I'll ride to the city gate and take a peek," Jieh says. "On Sky Dancer by myself, I can make it back in an hour."

It seems that my life lately has consisted of a lot of anxious waiting. But Jieh returns in time as promised. Worry lines crisscross his brow. "Yunle, Mingshin, and I are wanted as fugitives. Posters with drawings of us are all over the city walls promising rewards for our capture, with money being offered for even sightings. The guards are checking every single person coming in and out of the gate."

"So we can't get into the city the normal way," Yunle says.

At that, we turn to Longzo.

"I can get you past the city wall," he says.

"That'll be good enough," Yunle replies.

"I'll need some sleep to replenish my energy."

While Longzo slumbers in the coach, we keep watch.

"Are you thinking of getting inside the palace by taking one of the secret passageways?" Jieh asks Yunle. "Because Ren will expect us coming and have the passageways guarded."

"True, but I know of one he doesn't. It leads to a bedroom in the Queen's wing."

"I've never heard of that one."

"I found it by accident." Yunle scowls. "We'll need to be very careful. If Ren has Father spellbound, the whole palace will be under his order. We could be arrested and thrown into jail as soon as we are spotted."

Jieh crosses his arms. "That means we may never have a chance to even get near enough to break Ren's mind spell on Father."

"Since we're accused of betraying the King, Ren can sentence us to death without arousing any suspicion," I add. I think of how fast Ren moved on the Royal Ladies and his brothers after he was crowned in my former life. He had them arrested for treason and executed within days. "Believe me, he'll show none of us mercy."

"I just wish we'd listened to you sooner about Ren," Yunle tells me. "We may have been able to prevent this disaster."

"I've learned from my own mistakes," I say. "He wears his disguise well. Even your father was fooled by his 'heroic' acts at the hunt."

"You shouldn't come with us," Jieh says. "You are still charged with plotting regicide. You could be executed on the spot."

"We are all in this now. It's as dangerous for you as it is for me. You've never faced an enemy who can work with magic. At least I've defeated a Blood sorceress. I won't stay behind while you risk your lives. You need me, and you must believe in me."

"You have excellent instincts and we'll need them," Yunle says firmly.

Jieh's eyes sparkle. "I believe in you, Mingshin, always."

We all agree we need to be extra cautious. But we don't have a plan yet on how to search for Ren without inside help while avoiding detection. We'll have to improvise when we are within the walls and find out how tight the security is.

After the discussion, we decide to take a much-needed rest. I wish I could see Mother before we embark on our mission, but we don't have time.

Yunle and Fei move away with their arms linked.

Jieh and I are left alone. "You risked everything for me," I tell him, my voice grating out raw.

His arm slides around me, and he pulls me close to him as though nothing could ever come between us again. "I'd go to hell and back for you, Mingshin."

"Even if we stop Ren, your father may not forgive you for betraying him. I know how much becoming King means to you. You may never . . . It was my fault—"

"You've done nothing wrong," he says vehemently. "It was my choice. If I can't protect the woman I love, what good does becoming King do for me?" He cups my face in his hand. "You are the most resourceful, intelligent, fearless woman I've ever met. You are also the most intriguing and challenging." A laugh slips out of me at that. "And the most beautiful."

"Beautiful?" That's a first.

"You *are* the most beautiful woman to me."

So much joy swells in me that I must shine with it. I recall the dream I had in the death prison in which I fought the monster Ren and ran to the light. The man I met at the end was Jieh. I saw him clearly. But even before I reached the light, I knew it was him. My heart trusted him even when my head doubted him. I was just afraid to admit my true feelings to myself.

I circle my arms around his waist and nuzzle my face against his solid chest. "I love you, Jieh," I whisper.

His gasp of happiness is the sweetest sound I've heard.

Love may not last forever, but it's worth taking the risk. Because it is the light, the most promising hope.

CHAPTER 35

Sky Dancer and the coach will both stay behind, watched by Longzo. Meanwhile he'll try to bring Hanxin out of his bubble—it floats on a plane of existence independent of our world.

About a mile away from the city gate, Longzo creates a portal for us to pass through. It's rectangular and as tall as a man, with golden light shimmering around it.

I've touched a fish's underbelly before; I remember the cold, smooth-yet-slimy feeling. That's exactly how I feel all over my skin, as I step through the portal.

On the other side, we find ourselves in a narrow alley near the entrance of the secret passageway.

Fei leads the way, as her face is the only one not shown on the fugitive posters. The rest of us trail behind in single file, our heads lowered. The area is sparsely populated, and the pedestrians pay us little heed. Still, we dare not hasten for fear of drawing attention.

Fei suddenly hisses, "Hide!" and ducks into an alley. We quickly follow suit and watch as a small group of patrolling soldiers passes by. When one of them looks in our direction, we shrink farther into the shadows. My heart beats so hard I'm sure he hears it hammering. But then he turns away.

To be safe, we wait a little more until Fei gives us the all-clear signal. In a few more minutes, we arrive at our destination.

The trapdoor is buried in the cellar of an abandoned house. We take rickety stairs down, then follow a damp, twisting hallway, Jieh and Fei each holding a torch.

We climb up another flight of stairs at the end. Yunle removes a floorboard and leads us into an enormous wardrobe. We push aside rows of luxurious gowns to reach the door. Yunle tumbles out first, but halts abruptly.

I peek around her, and my heart sinks to my toes.

Commander Bai sits in a chair. A dozen soldiers are spread out across the room. At the sight of us, their hands fly to the hilts of their swords.

Bai stands, his expression nothing but stone. "My apologies, Your Highnesses. His Majesty has ordered me to guard this entry and arrest each of you on sight."

He lifts an arm to wave his soldiers forward.

"Do you want to prove Prince Kai's innocence, Commander? Because we can," I say.

At the mention of his second cousin, Bai's hand stills.

I have a very narrow window of time to persuade him. "What if the order you received isn't from His Majesty, Commander?" I ask.

Catching on, Jieh immediately says, "Don't you find that my father has been acting strange lately, Bai? He's ignored my counsel and yours, and even Grand Scholar Yu's. Yet he has taken every piece of advice Ren has offered him. That behavior is more than unusual."

"It's not my position to question His Majesty's—"

Yunle cuts in. "What if my father isn't acting of his own free will? What if someone is using magic on him?"

Bai narrows his eyes. "This is preposterous—"

We are losing him. "Prince Kai is innocent and you know it." I can see him waver very slightly. "It was Ren who masterminded the attack at the hunt." It would sound too outlandish to claim that Ren borrowed magic, so I declare instead, "Ren had the help of a mage. Take us to Ren and we can prove it, and Kai's name shall be cleared."

"My father's life is in danger, bound under a Blood magic spell," Jieh says. "You've sworn an oath to protect his life with your own. It falls upon you now to save him."

"How can I be sure you are right?" Bai demands.

"Think about it, Bai. Father's only had ears for Ren in the last few days. And do you honestly believe he would have me and Yunle hunted like animals? You've served him twenty years. You know he'd send spies to find us first. This is not like him."

Bai glances at the soldiers, who all appear flustered.

Yunle looks at them each in turn, holding their gaze for a moment before moving to the next. "All of you," she says, her voice fierce, commanding, and full of emotion. "You swore to protect my father with your own lives. Do you doubt, even for a moment, that Jieh and I wouldn't do the same? We're not asking you to give away your lives. We're simply asking you to let us get to Ren so we can save my father from him."

The soldiers trade uncertain looks among themselves, then they all turn to Bai. They appear swayed by Yunle's words, but they need their superior to make the final decision.

"If Ren becomes King, the first man he'll dismiss from his service is you, Commander," Jieh says. "Or he'll do worse. You gave your oath to my father, and you know how much he detests magic. You'll be rewarded for freeing him from this spell."

Bai's face hardens. "You swear to Heaven and your ancestors that you're speaking the truth and taking this action to protect His Majesty?"

"We so swear," Jieh and Yunle say sternly, to him and to the soldiers.

Bai gives a curt nod. "I'll take you to Prince Ren. But if you prove false, I'll lay my life down to take yours." He turns to the other men. "Stand down, soldiers. I'll take full responsibility for this."

Fei's sigh of relief stirs the hair on my nape. But the iron fist clenching around my chest doesn't loosen—our work here is far from over.

"Prince Ren is in the Grand Throne Room with a few guards," Bai says as we stride down an empty hallway. "Please follow my lead, Your Highnesses, and stay quiet."

We come upon no one in the Queen's wing—it's been unoccupied since she passed away.

Once we are outside the edifice, Bai increases his pace. "Hurry. The next patrol will come around in five minutes; we don't want to be spotted and questioned."

We remain in the shadows as much as possible. Soon enough, we arrive at the bottom of the stairs leading to the Grand Throne Room entrance.

At the sight, time stops. I'm suspended between breaths, looking back at the moment of my death frozen right here. I feel the anguish of Ren's betrayal anew. I again see myself bleeding my last seconds of life away.

But I refuse to let history repeat. Everything I do today has to be to stop Ren, preferably forever. Like a cobra, he'll raise his venomous hood and strike again if given a second chance.

"Mingshin." Jieh's gentle voice breaks the moment.

I swallow back a tremor of nerves. "I'm ready."

We climb the tall flight of stairs. My self-defense lessons with Fei have toned my body so I don't even feel winded when we reach the top.

There are no guards stationed outside the double doors. But I have no time to consider the oddity of missing sentries, because that awful feeling hits me once again, that smothering, foul atmosphere surrounding Ren these days. It's stronger than ever before, almost gagging me.

How much magic did Ren borrow and how many years of his life did he give away in this exchange with the Night Dragon?

We rush in, then skid to a halt.

There are only four people inside. King Reifeng sits slumped upon one of the high-backed thrones on the raised dais, apparently unconscious; only the slight rise and fall of his chest suggests he's still alive. Ren sits upon the other throne, a ruthless smirk on his face. Just as smug and vile as he was the day he killed me. The veins in my neck pulse, and my face burns, a surge of heat bringing my blood to a boil.

Surprisingly, Kai stands near Ren's side along with my cousin Bo. What are they doing here? Kai doesn't react at all to our presence, his face expressionless. Bo's jaw twitches.

Yunle and Jieh share a concerned look at the condition of the King.

"Get off the throne," Jieh snaps at Ren. "You don't belong there."

"You borrowed magic from a mage," I say. "Show us your bare hands." He wears gauntlets, but I can feel the blood drop–shaped *fuiin* pulsing on his left wrist, throbbing with a life of its own.

Bai's sword clangs out of its scabbard. "Is this true, Prince Ren?" he demands. The sight of the unconscious King, Kai's presence, and Ren sitting on the throne without the right to be there has obviously persuaded Bai that our allegations about the use of forbidden magic have merit.

"You have become quite a nuisance, Lu Mingshin," Ren snarls at the same time Yunle shouts, "Bai is bewitched!"

Everything happens so fast. Bai's sword dances. Yunle collapses to the floor, and Fei's saber blocks a downward cut from Bai that was meant for me. The commander's eyes are crazed.

Jieh's sword whisks out of its scabbard. "What in the nine hells?"

Fei and Bai exchange blows. I swallow, but my mouth is so dry it hurts.

Ren probably took Bai's blood earlier, but has only just now cast a spell on him. Maybe it was harder to control him from a distance. As far as I know, all magic has limits. If Yunle hadn't warned us, or Fei hadn't reacted fast enough, Bai would've beheaded me.

I rush to the princess's side. There's a goose egg–sized lump swelling on the back of her head. Bai must've knocked her out with the hilt of his sword.

Jieh points his rapier at Ren. "You shall die, traitor."

Kai growls, a beastly sound. A feral light enters his eyes.

A jab twists my gut. Ren has brought him here purposefully—

Kai charges at Jieh, his entire weight behind his dive, sword slashing through the air.

"Watch out!" I cry. "He's spellbound—"

Jieh blocks Kai's steel before twisting to the side and parrying with a hack. But Kai keeps coming like a mad bull. Their weapons collide in a shower of sparks.

The two men clash and deflect as they whirl back and forth across the room, so swift that their movements are visible only by the streaks of light they make.

"I don't want to kill you," Jieh bellows. "Wake up, Kai."

But Kai rumbles and attacks with more ferocity.

"Too bad our father isn't conscious to watch his two favorite sons kill each other," Ren says, voice dripping with venom.

I put two fingers to Yunle's nose. She's still breathing. Tears of relief well up, but they're immediately banished by terror.

Fei is defending herself admirably against Bai, while Jieh is hard-pressed in his battle because of his effort to avoid killing his half brother. Jieh inflicts a superficial wound, but Kai is undeterred. He fights like a mindless creature without an ounce of regard for his own life, thus making him ten times more deadly.

I look back at Ren. His eyes shine with relish.

A spark of rage like I've never known ignites in me; the fury sears through me. In this moment, I see Ren more clearly than I ever did before.

He could've just left me in that dungeon and let the wardens torture me to death, but no, he had to taunt me. To demonstrate he was in absolute control of my life, just like now, when he's in control of his brothers' fate. His warped sense of power brings him unbridled joy.

It sickens me to remember I once loved him.

I pull my dagger out of my boot. Considering how sharp its blade is, it should be able to cut through Ren's gauntlet and break the skin of his wrist, thus destroying the *fuiin*. I just need to get close enough to inflict the damage without falling prey to his evil magic.

I look at my cousin. Will he be an obstacle? Is he also enchanted by Ren?

Ren seems enraptured by the conflict surrounding him. I move toward him, keeping Bo in my peripheral vision. Just then, Ren's acid glare hones in on me. I freeze.

"Kill her," he orders Bo, his voice like ice.

My cousin pales, but he advances toward me, holding a short sword. A tiny muscle ticks under his eye as he stops near me.

"You are committing treason, Bo," I hiss.

Bo's throat moves. He shows real emotion, which is enough to convince me that Ren has let him keep his own wits.

"Don't forget your oath, Bo," Ren drawls. "Fail me and you can join her in the netherworld. Kill her and you'll be the son of the new prime minister."

Bo's eyes glow with fervor. He rushes at me, sword swinging wildly. I will strength into my limbs. He's had archery lessons, but he hasn't been trained in hand-to-hand combat. Neither he nor Ren knows I have been well trained by Fei.

I duck to the side, and Bo's sword whips through the air. As he turns to me, he looks surprised, then his slashings become more frantic. I slip beneath his guard and put distance between us before I lunge in again. My strikes aim true and fast, never letting him catch his breath. Seeing an opening, I spin around and slice my dagger across his arm.

He shrieks and drops his weapon. Seeing the blood gushing out of his arm, he screams even louder. It stops abruptly when Ren punches him, rendering him senseless.

"What a useless fool," Ren grumbles.

Focused on my fight with Bo, I never saw Ren approach. I raise my dagger and assume an attack position. Ren flips Bo's short sword into his hand with a foot, then he charges at me, blows coming fast. It's all I can do to block. He drops low and springs upward, his palm crashing into my chest. I land on my back with a breathless gasp.

As he leans down, I swing furiously at his approaching hand. But my dagger hangs suspended in the air, my wrist in Ren's firm grip. He strengthens his hold, and my bones feel like they'll splinter. My weapon clangs to the floor. With his other hand, Ren slaps me so hard stars burst into my vision and a metal taste fills my mouth.

"I would enjoy killing you right here, right now, but I have a better idea for your punishment. I want you to watch your lover die," Ren snarls.

"Mingshin!" Jieh bellows, his voice strained with worry.

I wipe the blood off my mouth and raise my head. Jieh and Kai are fighting near the doors. I cry out a warning, but horror chokes my voice down to a husky whisper.

Distracted, Jieh doesn't see the threshold behind him. He trips over it, falling backward. Kai's sword sweeps down, aiming for his heart. Jieh twists his torso out of the way, but Kai's blade pierces his thigh.

I scream.

Kai yanks his sword out, blood dripping from it, and lifts it for another blow. Jieh cuts him above the hip. Kai yelps in pain and staggers back.

Jieh drags himself upright and limps out of the room, with Kai in pursuit.

As soon as Ren releases me, I scramble up and race to the doors. Jieh is putting up a gallant fight, but he can barely stand on his bleeding leg.

I jump over the threshold to help him, but Ren snatches my arm, pinning me against his side. He raises a finger to caress my cheek like a lover.

"Who do you think will die first?" he muses, almost like he's eager to hear my answer.

I want to rake my fingers across his face, to gouge out his eyes. Or better yet, scrape the *fuiin* off his wrist.

Oh, such futile thoughts! His *fuiin* is well covered under his gauntlet. My mind flashes back to the moment right before my death. How helpless I was, just like now.

No! I refuse to die by his hands again.

While my mind whirls, Jieh barrels into Kai's defense, and shoves him down a flight of stairs. Kai doesn't reappear.

Jieh's shirt is now crimson from a wound on his shoulder as well. My panicked breath comes faster; my stomach churns like a water mill.

Ren draws his own saber. "One down like an animal. Let's see how long the other lasts."

He breaks away so fast I fail to catch him. He swoops upon Jieh, hacking left and right. Jieh stumbles back against Ren's vicious onslaught.

"Where is your pride, Jieh? You, the tournament champion, barely able to hold up your sword? That beastly horse of yours . . . I'll think of the best way to kill it slowly."

Ren is venting his rage after years of being looked down upon by his half brothers.

A blaze of defiance sizzles up my spine.

I won't let him harm anyone. I'll never be helpless again.

My strong will and growing determination . . . The Divine Stone chose me . . . That has to count for something.

Jieh topples. Ren raises his weapon to deliver a fatal strike.

"You pathetic scum, Ren!" I bellow. "You couldn't fight your brothers fairly because you knew you'd lose. I despise you with my entire being."

Ren freezes.

"Do you remember our first meeting?" I ask before he can decide to cut Jieh down. "How I humiliated you? Right. You deserved that."

Jieh rises to a kneeling position and grapples with Ren's legs. My chest constricts as his mouth shapes the word "run" at me.

I won't. "You're less than dung stuck to the bottom of my shoe, Ren. No matter what you do, you'll always be the most worthless of your brothers. Even Aylin could see that. You lust for her, but she only holds you in contempt."

Ren kicks Jieh away and points his sword at me. "You shall regret those words, you common bitch. I will make you do things so wicked you'll be ashamed to face your ancestors after death; I will make you suffer until you pray for death, but won't be able to die until I command you to. And it begins now."

I turn and run, but Ren catches up quickly. The blade grazes my arm. Blood seeps from a flesh wound; Ren's lips move as if to cast a spell.

I must believe. In this instant, I latch onto a single image: I run to the light to find Jieh.

But in the next breath, I feel a mighty tugging in my head telling me to surrender. A darkness seeps into my brain, and I have difficulty concentrating.

Fight it. Fight it. I run to the light to find Jieh.

The image slips in and out.

"Take this dagger and stab that man in the heart," Ren commands, pointing at a bloody mass at my feet.

Darkness and light war within me, each struggling to possess me. I see myself wavering with the dagger. Something is calling out for me to reach the light, to find Jieh—who is he? But it's so much easier to give in to the darkness, to this command echoing in my head.

I lift the dagger to swing down at the wounded man. Why isn't he resisting? Why is he staring up at me like he cares for me?

I think I know him . . .

Somehow it feels crucial to remember him.

I try to break through the darkness of my mind, but a pain cleaves my head and I screech. *Just obey the command!* I begin to bring the dagger down.

"I will always love you, Mingshin," the man says. The love shining in his look and voice could set fire to the sea.

A memory flashes through my mind like a bolt of lightning.

I've seen his eyes before, eyes filled with adoration. I've heard him say passionately, "You are the most resourceful, intelligent, fearless woman I've ever met."

I strive, I toil, but I reach the light to find Jieh.

Love floods through me, expelling Ren's darkness. The truth of my self-worth suffuses my spirit, bringing with it a new level of confidence.

My mind snaps back.

But I stay where I am, clutching my head. "Oh, it hurts," I groan. "What do you command me to do?"

Ren gets nearer. "Kill the man, now!"

I poise the dagger at Jieh's neck, breaking skin. On the blade's surface I see the reflection of Ren hovering closer, a triumphant smile emerging.

I whip around. With marvelous precision and swiftness and the rage of two lifetimes, I plunge the dagger into Ren's filthy heart, burying it to the hilt.

His eyes open wide. For a moment, we stare at each other, the visions of the past and present intermingling. He sees what truly happened. He killed me once, and now I've repaid him in full. A new kind of power, which has nothing to do with magic, permeates me. The light inside me flares into a shimmer strong enough to melt stone, vaporize iron, and make the air burst into flame.

"You are a vengeful force . . ." he whispers.

"Yes, I am. And I am more. I won, and you lost."

Utter fear replaces the disbelief on his face. He gurgles, blood frothing at his lips. I shove him, and he falls backward.

His head hits the step with a dull thud, then his body plummets to the bottom of the bloody stairs.

CHAPTER 36

I dash to Jieh, tearing sleeves off my dress. He's barely conscious.

"Stay with me," I say with a snap of command in my voice. "I love you. You cannot die on me now. I won't allow you to break my heart."

He smiles, a warm, honeyed curve of his lips. "I won't die. How can I after you finally said you love me?"

I wrap his wounds tight, applying pressure to stop the bleeding. A man's angry, harsh cry cuts into the air, then breaks off. I want to rush into the Grand Throne Room to find out what happened, but I cannot leave Jieh here by himself.

Fei bursts out of the room. After a quick scan of the scene, she hurries to my side. "Commander Bai seemed very confused for a few seconds. I used the chance to knock him out."

With Ren dead, Bai must have regained his senses. He had to be confounded about what was going on.

"Ren is dead, but Jieh is severely injured," I tell her. "Please do what you can to rouse Yunle and ask her to summon the royal physicians immediately."

Fei nods and hastens back into the room.

I hold Jieh in my arms. "You are the strongest man I know. You've sworn to protect me from harm. You must keep your word."

"I will."

But he sounds so weak. When he raises a hand to brush at my cheek, I realize I've been weeping.

"Haven't I told you I don't die easily?" he whispers.

"Stay with me, my love," I repeat again and again, pushing my soul into every word.

I catch sight of Kai stirring. As he lifts his bewildered face toward us, I wish he were dead. Jieh wouldn't have suffered this serious injury but for his decision to spare Kai's life.

Shouts rise from the bottom of the stairs. The patrols have seen Ren's body. Just then, Yunle and Fei come out of the room, supporting a stumbling King between them. The princess issues a quick series of orders to the patrols. When they hesitate, Reifeng snaps at them to obey immediately.

As we wait for the physicians to arrive, I relate what took place from the moment Commander Bai knocked Yunle unconscious. A glimmer of pain flashes across Reifeng's face when I mention Hanxin's warning about Ren's use of borrowed Blood magic.

In the end, I tell them that Jieh bravely fought long enough to give me time to kill Ren.

Jieh shifts at this part, but my eyes beg him to stay quiet. I hope he knows how important a role he played in helping me defeat Ren.

"How did you know Commander Bai was bewitched?" I ask Yunle.

"If Bai had been in his right mind, he would've trained his sword at Ren's heart as soon as he saw his treasonous behavior."

I have Yunle's shrewd perceptiveness to thank again. "You and Fei saved my life," I say.

Her eyes twinkle. "And you and Jieh saved the kingdom."

After the physicians and their assistants arrive, Yunle organizes them into different groups and puts them to work. While the physicians attend to Reifeng, several assistants lay Jieh on a stretcher. I follow. He doesn't let go of my hand even when he passes out.

I hold on to his just as tightly.

The following day, the King visits Jieh, who has regained consciousness. I remain near the bed while father and son converse. There are more weary creases at the corners of Reifeng's eyes and a further slope to his shoulders, but his presence is still domineering. He tells Jieh how proud he is of him and orders his wounded son to rest until he's fully recovered.

After the King departs, Yunle announces that my family will be united with me soon. Fei and I hug each other at the news, my throat choked with a relief so great that it borders on ecstasy.

Jieh asks about Kai.

"Since he's been declared innocent, he's been released from prison. He may come to see you in due time."

Jieh and I exchange a look. I read the same question in his eyes: Does that mean Kai is allowed back in the competition for the throne?

"Rest well and recover fast," Yunle says. "Everything else can be left for later."

We nod. She's right. *Let's worry about everything else later. As long as we have each other, we can tackle any problem.*

"What about my cousin Bo?" I ask. "Was he punished?"

"Father summoned Minister Sun. Your uncle insisted Bo had been put under a mind spell. He told Father that your judgment couldn't be completely reliable because of the chaos of the fight."

I hiss a sound of anger. That cunning bastard. "What does the King think?"

"I don't know. Bo suffered a head injury; at least for now, he cannot give testimony." Yunle stands. "Can I borrow Fei for a moment?"

"You can, for as long as you want," I reply.

Yunle grasps Fei's hand and they walk away, beaming and whispering to each other. Soon they disappear around the corner of the door. I smile to myself as I wonder if they've shared a kiss.

A maid enters with Jieh's medicine, a stewed herbal mixture blended with honey. I spoon-feed him. By the sublime look on his face, I can tell he's enjoying it.

"Thank you for taking care of me," he says.

"It's the least I can do for you."

"Why did you tell them that you were only able to kill Ren because of my brave fight? I failed to do anything. I couldn't protect you."

"You did. I told myself I'd fight Ren's spell, but I could feel my control slipping away. It was your love that helped pull me back to my senses."

His smile is like sunlight. "I love you, Mingshin, more than anything. I thought of conquering you when we first met, but in the end, I'm the one who's been conquered. You are my future. Be with me. Share this lifetime with me."

Lifetime. My thoughts turn to liquid, the warmth of the word flooding through me. It makes me want to laugh and sing and shake the world with my voice.

I inhale, willing my heart to settle. "I'll support you, and do all I can to help you become the next King. I probably won't like life at the royal court, but I'll try my best to fit in." Even as I say it, I'm not sure it's a decision I can live with.

"When I sit on the throne, I want you by my side. Only you. No one else. Ever. You once asked me what I would do if you could not give me a son. It makes no difference. I still won't take another woman as other men have done before me. I'll pass the throne to one of my nephews if necessary. This I swear to Heaven."

His sincerity leaves me feeling dazed, as though . . . I've been waiting forever for him.

His hand is the hand I want to hold. His voice is the sound I want to hear, and his smile isn't just something I want to see; I want to be the reason for it.

I push away my anxiety about our future, about a life at the court. Like Jieh said, we'll cross that bridge when we get there.

I lean into his gentle embrace. I feel lost within his arms and found anew; once broken but now made whole again. We're like two halves who have become one. We own this single moment, this sphere of breath, this heartbeat shared like a secret.

It's a tearful reunion with Mother, Hui, Ning, and Mai two days later. Words are not squandered as we embrace to express our mirth and relief.

Hanxin and Longzo were summoned back to the royal palace. I haven't had a chance to find out what the Elder discussed with Reifeng in private.

Jieh has had numerous visitors, including his mother, Yao, his cousins, and his uncle, Lord Protector Hwa. The Royal Lady completely ignores me. Kai's visit is brief; he leaves after exchanging a few polite words with his brother. He appears a little fidgety after weeks of imprisonment, but I suspect it's only temporary. I haven't forgotten that he pushed Jieh into the river.

Jieh is finally allowed by royal physicians to get out of bed. Reifeng waits another couple of days before summoning him to his study. An hour later, my presence is also requested.

My nerves wind tighter with each step I take toward the King's study. I helped subvert Ren's plot, but both Reifeng's daughter and favorite son defied their father because of me.

The King is seated behind his mahogany desk. Yunle stands to one side, and Jieh to the other.

I kneel, and Reifeng motions for me to rise.

"With your own hands, you slew a traitor and saved Dazhou, Miss Lu. Perhaps my son wasn't a fool to chase after you."

Is he being sarcastic? I don't know, so I say nothing.

"What reward do you claim for your selfless act of heroism, Miss Lu?" he continues.

I let out a relieved breath, the tension coiling around me loosening. The King may not be renowned for clemency, but he's always been known for fairness. I infuse my spine with mettle as I say, "It's my duty as a citizen of Dazhou to serve its needs. If I may ask a reward . . . I understand that Princess Yunle is allowed to listen at the Royal Council. If Your Majesty could also permit her to speak up, to express her opinions, I'm sure her intelligence and insight would serve the country well."

Reifeng's gaze sharpens, taking me in, probing and piercing. Have I overstepped? My stomach turns, but I force myself to stand tall, head held high.

Yunle seems to be holding her breath. Even Jieh stares expectantly at their father.

Reifeng smiles suddenly. "You can ask anything for yourself, but instead you've asked a reward for Yunle. She's fortunate to have you as a friend, just as you are blessed to have her as your confidant. Yes, my daughter has a brilliant mind. I approve your request."

Yunle gasps in delight. I bow to the King. "Thank you, Your Majesty."

Yunle curtsies. "Thank you, Father." She flashes me a smile full of gratitude.

I smile back.

"I shall grant you the title and status of a princessa," Reifeng continues.

I can barely keep my gaping mouth from hitting the floor. Princessa is a title usually granted to a non-heir prince's daughter. Because I asked nothing for myself, the King has given me more than I could have imagined.

"And I see why my son has deemed you worthy of his affection," Reifeng says. "I approve of you two being together."

My heart trips over its next beat. Have I heard him right?

Jieh's hand reaches for mine. He looks incandescent with ecstasy. My chest swells so fast and full, it's a small miracle that I don't float off the floor and up to the ceiling.

Yunle's eyes also shine with joy for me, for us.

"Thank you, Father," Jieh says with a shaking voice.

I fumble a curtsy. "Thank you, Your Majesty."

Reifeng's face hardens. *Never defy me again, Jieh.* Those words are not spoken out loud. There's no need. They ring like a hammer on iron.

Jieh bows.

"Join us for dinner tonight, Mingshin," Reifeng says.

He just called me by my first name! Just like he would a daughter-by-marriage.

I flush uncontrollably, heat painting me from head to toe.

King Reifeng makes a royal announcement in which he declares that Ren—whose title has been stripped posthumously—committed treason and wrongfully accused Kai. Jieh, Yunle, and I defended our kingdom against the traitor. Fei contributed, too, and is awarded generously with gold.

Mother is elated. In nervous anticipation, I ask her what she thinks about me and Jieh.

"You have my blessing, Shin'ar. I believe he truly loves you. I couldn't be happier for you."

The back of my throat pinches. I throw my arms around her. "Thank you, Ma, for your support and for believing in me."

"Enjoy your dinner tonight, my dear." She picks out a gorgeous lavender gown for me.

At the palace gate, my carriage is stopped when someone requests to speak to me. I lift the window flap to find Uncle Yi.

I want to hear what he has to say. I tell Mai to stay put and step out. Fei watches from horseback, alert.

"Mingshin, you seem to be doing well," he drawls with an air of superiority.

I never care about social status, but since my uncle likes to use that as a weapon, I can surely fire it back at him. "You don't get to talk to me like that. I am a princessa. Show your respect."

He makes a mock bow. "For a commoner like you to climb so high on the social ladder, I commend you for your ruthless ambition."

Ruthless? So be it. "His Majesty believes I saved the kingdom. I don't climb. I fly."

"We'll see how high you fly stepping on those who helped you."

I sharpen my voice to daggers. "*Helped* me? You mean by trying to murder me and steal my family wealth?"

His eyes narrow to midnight slits. "I can't imagine where you'd get such a ridiculous notion. Is that why you harmed Bo?"

"I didn't harm him. You and Ren did. Bo wouldn't have ended up in his current condition if you hadn't sent him into a monster's lair to demonstrate your misplaced loyalty." I walk away, then look over my shoulder at him. "Congratulations on Aylin's betrothal to Prince Wen."

His smirk returns, spreading like a stain. "Aylin is destined to be Queen."

He says that with so much confidence icy bumps ripple up my arms. "We shall speak again soon." And with that he departs.

I try not to let that short conversation bother me. There's nothing he can do to make Wen the heir.

Yunle and her maids help me prepare for the royal dinner tonight. When they're done, my friend has me stand in front of a full-length mirror.

I actually look . . . beautiful.

My gown is cut in a way that highlights every inch of my delicate curves. The neckline and hem are covered in hundreds of tiny sapphires arranged to look like flowers. My cloak is a luxurious fall of pure sable pelt that drapes from shoulder to floor, with just enough fur puddling at my feet.

My hair is fashioned into a cloud bun and held in place by two golden half-moon-shaped combs; strings of pearls tinkle from my hairpin, which is inlaid with jeweled peonies. One of Yunle's maids has painted my lips vermillion red, dusted my cheeks with shimmery powder, and lined my lids in kohl to make my brown eyes stand out more than usual.

Nonetheless, I know it's neither my makeup nor gown that makes me prettier but my newfound confidence and the happiness that emerges from the bottom of my heart.

When Jieh arrives at the princess's wing to take me to dinner, he's changed into dark fitted trousers and a sweeping, wine-colored coat trimmed with threads of gold. But he could stand there in a potato sack and he would still look every inch a prince.

Jieh lets out a gasp as he takes my hands. "You look so beautiful, Mingshin."

My insides dip, going cavernous and light. "You are very handsome, too." I don't think I'll ever tire of looking at his gorgeous face that seems chiseled by the gods—each angle and plane designed to complement the other, from the high cheekbones to the angular jaw.

"Come on you two lovebirds," Yunle calls.

Heat scalds my cheeks. Jieh's face, too, turns beet red. Seeing that somehow makes tenderness swell in my breast.

With my hand hooked in Jieh's arm, we leave.

The dining room is filled with orb-like golden oil lamps suspended from the ceiling by impossibly delicate chains. A massive blackwood round table sits at the center, the chairs high-backed and adorned with silk cushions.

A few royals are already present. Kai chats with his mother, Royal Lady Bai. It seems that he has returned to his old self; everything about him radiates confidence and self-assurance, and no doubt he still considers himself a contender for the throne.

While Royal Lady Hwa hugs her son, Hanxin struts over and pulls me aside.

"I told your King about the Night Dragon, but nothing from our private conversation," he whispers to me. "He lost his composure for a moment when I told him that Xiangyu started lending his magic about a decade ago."

I wonder if Reifeng has drawn the same conclusion as we did, that his brother borrowed Fire magic from the Night Dragon.

"Your King wants me to find out if Xiangyu is still in Dazhou, and if so, where," Hanxin continues. "Prince Kai has just now been assigned to assist me."

I feel a twitch in my gut. Has Kai been assigned such an important task because the King deems Jieh physically incapable of it at the moment, or because Jieh has lost his trust?

Hanxin's gaze cuts through me. "I hear your uncle, Minister Sun, is one of the most stalwart supporters of Prince Kai taking on the task."

Of course Uncle Yi would give his support to our competition. Although it's expected, sudden apprehension fills me at how much things have changed and how fast they are moving.

Commander Bai strides in. "By His Majesty's order, the dinner has been cancelled. Please return to your rooms. Your Highnesses, His Majesty requests your presence at once."

An instant tension grips the room. Jieh, Yunle, and Kai leave in a hurry. The rest of us exchange nervous looks before we obey the King's order, too.

I pace in the tearoom in the princess's wing. Something terrible must have happened.

When Yunle and Jieh return, they both appear visibly shaken.

"Wen is dead," Yunle says. "He drowned in a pond."

I let out a choked cry of shock.

"Lord High Constable Wang reported it directly to Father," Yunle says. "According to him, Wen most likely committed suicide by throwing himself off the bridge."

"Suicide? Why?" I ask.

"His physician says he'd become more and more despondent since losing his legs; he isolated himself and lost his temper quite often for no reason."

"Despondent? But he's going to marry the woman he's always wanted . . ."

Yunle scoffs. "Aylin fainted, out of grief apparently, upon hearing the news."

Jieh hasn't said a word, but his anguish is palpable.

"How is the King faring?" I ask carefully.

At my question, pain darts across Jieh's features, clear as glass and sharp as flint.

Yunle's tight expression cracks. "Father is inconsolable."

A lump hardens in my throat. No father deserves to suffer the loss of two sons, especially in such a short time.

But did Wen really kill himself?

Mother drowned in my previous life by Ren and Uncle Yi's design.

"Aylin is destined to be Queen," Uncle Yi said.

Minister Sun is one of the most stalwart supporters of Prince Kai taking on the task, Hanxin informed me.

A chill shivers through me.

While I was busy finding out the truth about the attack at the hunt, my uncle has been plotting. Like a predator, he enjoys hunting in the dark. I just never thought he had the guts to murder a prince.

Jieh escorts me home.

I tell him my suspicion that Uncle Yi had Wen murdered and may have acted as some kind of advisor to Kai. In exchange, Kai has probably promised to make Aylin his Queen when he becomes King.

Jieh's expression darkens to a storm. "Kai had better not be involved in Wen's death."

"We'll find out the truth." I hold his hand. "We've defeated Ren, a traitor and false sorcerer. No matter how crafty my uncle is and how vicious Kai is, we'll defeat them. Together."

A frown tugs at his brow. "They'll make you a target. It's too dangerous for you—"

"I'm not afraid." I keep my eyes hard as steel and fill my voice with fire. "We are a team, Jieh. We face everything together. We have and we will, forever."

Jieh's clear-cut features grow firm; respect gleams true and fierce in his eyes. "I've been blessed by Heaven to have you, Mingshin. We are a team; we are inseparable. Not only will we beat Kai, we'll defend our kingdom and defeat the Night Dragon together."

His arms go around me, circling me completely, and his mouth claims mine. We kiss deep and slow, a kiss I feel from the very tips of my toes to the core of my being. A kiss that tells me: *You are brave. You are beautiful. You are mine.* And most importantly: *We are one.*

Love has changed me, changed us. It makes us stronger.

I have the fiery spirit of the sun and the bright heart of the moon. I finally believe.

Acknowledgments

As solitary as the act of writing is, it takes a small army of wonderful people to turn a manuscript into a book. I owe them so many thanks that mere words won't be enough. Still, I'll give it a try.

My fervent thanks, first and always, to my husband, Don: You are my north star, my best friend, and safe harbor. Thank you for your dedication and encouragement, for the way you understand my stories, and how you always push me to be a better storyteller.

My eternal gratitude to Richard Lin, my awesome critique partner and best author friend. Not only have you worked tirelessly to help me make this book a reality, but you also provided me with unwavering support.

Tamar Rydzinski, thank you for being such a rock star of an agent, for answering millions of questions from me, for having my back no matter what. My deepest appreciation for your wisdom, guidance, and patience. This has been an amazing ride, and I can't wait for our next book journey together.

I'm forever grateful to the marvelous team at Union Square Kids who believed in me and my story. Laura Schreiber, you are a writer's dream editor. Thank you from the bottom of my heart for your insight, vision, and enthusiasm, and for making this entire process so enjoyable. My huge thanks, to Stefanie Chin, for your clever and brilliant feedback. To Julie Robine and Sija Hong, for the most gorgeous cover I could have imagined. To Jenny Lu and Daniel Denning, for championing this book.

Thank you, Sher Lee, for generously sharing your wisdom and knowledge on publishing. Thank you, Natalia Torres and Kim Fairley, for helping me make the book stronger and tighter. Thank you, everyone in the Ann Arbor Writers Group. It has been such fun to work with all of you.

And finally, thanks to my readers for picking up this book. I hope you enjoy the journey.

About the Author

As a Chinese immigrant, Kate Chenli is a proud US citizen who also cherishes her Chinese heritage. She has an MS in electrical and computer engineering, but has always enjoyed designing complex worlds and characters more than designing complex software. Other than reading and writing, her passion is world travel (five continents down and counting).